THE GIRL
THE CROW
THE WRITER
AND THE FIGHTER

About the Author

George Paterson is a writer, DJ and musician who, as a member of the bands White and DMP, released a number of well-received albums on the Poco Alto Label. His work can be found in a number of independent feature length and short films as well as providing the musical backdrop to the London stage production of the play, 'ISM'.

Since returning to Scotland in 2017, his focus has been split between the spoken word - his popular weekly 'Lost in Music' radio show - and the written, with articles appearing in a number of online publications before finding a home as a regular features writer and reviewer for Into Creative.

In addition, he has written two screenplays and one feature length 'coming of age' story, serialised on intocreative.co.uk, called 'Everybody Wants to Rule the World'.

Acknowledgements

Thank you to Jan Kilmurry and Jessica Hamilton for your keen eyes, to David F Ross, Tom Gillespie, Stuart Cosgrove and Alistair Braidwood for your kind words and support, to John Welsh and Loretta Mulholland at Into for your ceaseless encouragement and to Stephen Cameron for your vision, passion and determination to share this story with the world.

This book is dedicated to Lisa, our attentive
sentinel and ever my partner-in-wonder.

The sun goes down
but it's alright.
Some creatures come alive at night
As night was not designed for sleep...

Chapter 1 - Blood on the Apron

Tap, tap, tap.

The old man knocked the blade against the discoloured porcelain bowl. Stirring the water, he brought the blade back to the left side of his face, going over an already smooth area. An unfiltered cigarette dangled precariously from his fleshy, sud-framed lips. Steam from the piping hot water had condensed the circular mirror hanging from a darkened chain above the sink, rendering it all but obsolete. He didn't wipe it clear. At his age, he knew his face. Weathered and drawn, loose and long. Old but not decrepit. Not like this room.

Tap, tap, tap.

Balanced on the edge of the bowl was a small notebook, its pages held open by a chewed pencil. The last sentence he'd written on the water specked page read, 'Her legs twitched.' His previous attempt - 'There was some movement from her legs.' - had been crudely scored out. His left hand felt its way around his face. A minute clump of bristle on the right side of his neck, just under his jaw and once more, the razor returned to his skin.

Tap, tap.

The old man rinsed the blade, wrapped it in a flannel and placed it in the small, brown leather pouch sat on the ledge by the walk-in shower. He took a hand towel from the small stack, patted dry his long bare head and dabbed the water which had flecked his vest.

He dressed. A pale blue gingham, seersucker shirt with navy corduroy slacks. Not contemporary but still stylish. Not like this room. He turned to the bed. Two ties lay across the mattress. One oxblood red, the other, black with three yellow diagonal stripes. Choosing neither, he placed both into a small leather travel bag and pulled on a light tweed jacket. Though it had served its owner well over the years, the jacket still fit his form perfectly. He reached back into the bathroom, where the sound of the leaky cistern plinked and plonked to its own time signature, an atonal free form, and pulled the toggle at the end of the frayed light cord. From the bedside table, he picked up a pair of brown turtle shell glasses and put them on. His eyes widened, adjusting to his strong but familiar prescription.

The small bag was placed inside a larger, matching travel bag. Tightening its red and blue strap, he fastened the dull brass clip and left the ugly motel room without a backward glance. A room so soiled with the funk of stale smoke and illicit sweat, that no amount of scrubbing or fresh air could ever expunge. The kind of room he once loved. In every stain, a story. A lover in each gouge and a devastated cuckold in every scuff mark. Not now. This meant nothing to him. He could not glean anything from it. And besides, there was not enough time tonight to slide back into old ways, even if his body would allow.

He walked down the corridor, past the triptych of frontier mustangs in varying stages of frolic, into the reception area; an ill-conceived, glass extension which would provide little shelter from the harsh northeastern winter. On a curious evening like this though, in the margin between late spring and early summer, it acted as a hothouse. From behind the paper strewn reception desk, an awkward, wistful looking fellow took the old man's key. His once white shirt had noticeable perspiration marks which seemed to spread from under his lank arms as if he was incapable of preventing his own foulness from consuming him.

Though the sun was about to set, the temperature gauge in the lobby still showed sixty-two in the shade.

The raw-boned receptionist asked the old man if he needed a ride.

"No, I'm fine, thank you," he replied, dusting off the seat of an almost threadbare armchair which backed onto the window.

"There's only two hotels in the whole of Lewiston," the receptionist said, dabbing beads of sweat from his brow.

"You don't say," said the old man, feigning interest.

"Two hotels and Williams from the Ice Truck told me that six hundred people are crammed into ninety-five rooms. Now, I don't know if that's true but if it is…" the receptionist exhaled, impressed by the magnitude of the second-hand statistic.

"And I hear that the Mansion House has been taken over by one of the camps, I don't know which one but there's no room at the inn, so to speak. But that's Lewiston, I guess. I don't know why they don't come here to Mechanic Falls. We have plenty of room and we're only seventeen miles from the venue, as the crow flies. I can keep this room for you…if you'd like."

"Thank you but no."

"So, you'll be leaving Maine tonight, Mr Valentine?"

Mr Valentine was one of the names he'd use when he didn't want questions.

Not wishing to be drawn further, he nodded and looked away. Still, the receptionist persisted. The old man checked the time on the wall clock against that of his watch. He picked up a magazine.

"There's some National Geographic. And a few boxing magazines, if you like the fights. You like the fights? Williams says that this'll make Lewiston the fight capital of the world. Now I'm no fan of Clay but…"

From behind the receptionist's desk, a bright light reflected off the mirror. The old man turned to see a pristine black Lincoln pull up directly in front of the motel. Time to go. As he headed towards the exit, the receptionist, unconcerned with the car, continued to talk.

"And those Nation of Islam fellows? I mean, believe in whichever God you want but I have to draw the line somewhere. That kind of trouble we just don't need at the New Starlit Plains Motel."

The old man smiled.

"Goodbye then."

He walked over to the Lincoln, opened the passenger door and took a seat, his bag tucked between his feet. The car pulled away.

"Nice ride."

"What were you expecting? A station wagon?" replied the driver, a black man in his early thirties, immaculate in a tailored dark suit with a white shirt and matching pocket square. "The motel. Anything I need to know?"

"Nothing whatsoever. It was perfect."

The driver handed the old man a ticket.

"You're about six rows back. Not quite press but still close enough to make contact."

"Just the one?"

"Don't worry. I'll be there. Just not right beside you. We need distance in case of…"

"Of course."

Distance. Of course. They headed east, through the almost deserted centre of town. Aside from two teenagers riding bikes, the main street was empty. The mixture of the old and new, with tree lined, sparsely populated avenues branching deeper into a suburb where not a single blade of grass was out of line. I can see why people buy this, he thought, but it was an American ideal he didn't share.

"Is there anything I should be looking out for? You know, like…"

The younger man detected a sense of nervousness from the old man.

"Don't worry. There shouldn't…there won't be any hiccups."

The old man sighed, his foot tapping at the plate. He was not convinced.

"You might want to look in the glove compartment."

The old man twisted the catch and the compartment door fell open.

Sitting atop some papers was a snub-nosed revolver.

"Will I be needing this?" he asked.

"Call it insurance."

The old man picked up the weapon, gripping it, turning it and feeling its weight on the palm of his hand. He detached the barrel and removed the bullets, placing them in the right pocket of his jacket. The gun he placed in the other.

"If you're stopped and searched," the younger man said, "remember that it is your constitutional right to bear arms against aggressors."

"And if they don't buy it?"

"Blame Malcolm X."

Out of town, they took the almost deserted 121 past Mt. Apatite to the north, now barely visible in the final light of the day. Before long, they crossed over the Androscoggin River into Lewiston itself. Ahead of them, a queue of similarly detailed cars formed.

"It might be best to get off the main track."

Over the bridge, the young man pulled away to the right, parking the Lincoln in the street beside the Basilica.

"It's only a couple of blocks from here but I can get closer, if you'd like?" asked the younger man.

"I can handle a couple of blocks."

The old man opened the car door, wincing as he pulled himself up and out.

They walked slowly down Plender Avenue towards the venue. To the old man, the arena appeared small and unimpressive.

"*This* is St. Dominic's?" he asked.

"No, that burned down a few years ago. It's St. Nicholas' now."

The sign read...

'THE CENTRAL MAINE YOUTH CENTER'

"You wouldn't believe the strings we had to pull..."

"I can imagine," replied the old man.

"Remember the drill. Make contact and get confirmation, however long it takes. You must not leave the area until you get the nod that we're good. Do you understand?"

"I got it," replied the old man, breathing heavily.

The younger man looked at him with genuine concern.

"Are you sure you're up for this?"

"I love the fights," he said defiantly.

At the entrance to the Center's parking lot, between two concession stalls, a noisy demonstration by a group of suited men was taking place. A brigade of police officers with batons drawn, stood close by.

"We will not be intimidated by the forces of evil. For the Prophet Elijah Muhammad has foretold of ..."

"You *will* leave or we shall be compelled to remove you from the vicinity," shouted the Captain through a loud hailer, like an amplified bee in a tin. The body language of the officers lined up behind him suggested that they were keen to follow his orders, each and every one of them straining at the bit for a chance, under the cloak of *legitimacy*, to beat up on some black men.

As the conflict intensified, the old man, detached, observed. To the side of the men was a small collection of women, dressed head to toe in starched, sober garments, steadfast in support of the protestors. Catching his eye was one particular devotee, her flawless, unadorned beauty, proud and unafraid, stopping him cold.

"Keep moving," said the younger man as he ushered him towards the arena. Still, the old man couldn't help but look over his shoulder, fixated on the fervently devout young woman.

Outside turnstile fifteen, the lines that led into the Center split, then slowed to a crawl. A heavy-set police officer, too slovenly to be chosen for head cracking duties, leant against one side of the gate, randomly checking the queuing patrons. The old man presented his ticket and was ushered through to the turnstile itself. He handed it over to the operative who pressed down on the pedal and released the mechanism. Once through, he looked back to see that the younger man had been stopped and searched. The old man reminded himself of the job he had to do. He must not be caught up in any miscarriages of justice, major or minor.

Passing the wood panelled thoroughfare, he checked the remaining portion of his ticket. Down the five-step, narrow staircase to the courtside, he found his spot; Section 104, Row E, Seat 19. The old man scanned the crowd for his colleague to no avail. The final fight on the undercard was approaching its conclusion but most in attendance appeared uninterested.

This should be close enough.

The bell sounded and the lights went up. Gasping for air, cut and bruised, the combatants were brought to the centre of the ring. Their seconds towelled the sweat from their glistening, battered bodies. An epic contest had just taken place but for the crowd, growing by the minute, the efforts of both men seemed insignificant. Dressed entirely in white, a frail, elderly man had begun to mop a hundred tiny pools of blood that during the last hour, exploded from the lacerated brows and pummelled noses of those underappreciated warriors. From above, the white canvas was stained pink.

The old man checked his watch. It was already time.

Another quick survey of the arena proved fruitless. Not that his colleague's whereabouts mattered. None of this did. The old man just needed to know one thing. Nothing else.

The lights dimmed again, and through the arena, there was a swell of something approaching excitement. Everyone, bar the old man, was on their feet. An electric burst of applause rang out. *This* was the main event.

A group of soldiers in their dress uniforms carried the Stars and Stripes into the ring and were joined by some familiar names from the pugilistic past; Willie Pep, James Braddock and Joe Louis. As the old man stood, curiosity piqued, to get a better view, the Challenger arrived, heading towards the centre of the arena. The applause was generous. One well-wisher patted the name on the back of the fighter's white towelling robe but an attempt to engage further ended abruptly as the Challenger's seconds firmly pushed him back into the crowd. None of this affected the fighter. His face was a study in menace. The closer he got to the ring, the more flashbulbs were activated. The back and forth of the applause, the catcalling and the spark and crunch of discarded cubes of glass only added to the intimidating atmosphere. This was not Lewiston, Maine, thought the old man. Here stood ancient Rome, and the untamed circus of the malevolent.

A murmur and everyone turned to look towards the east of the ring. It was the Champion. A decade younger than his opponent, he bounded towards the centre of the hall with the purpose of an upright cheetah, travelling at such speed that his team struggled to follow. He reached the apron of the ring only to find that his access was blocked. But he kept moving, his small contingent of seconds reduced to the role of hapless onlookers. Everyone watched the Champion. Except the old man. He only had eyes for the Challenger. Some sort of sign. He was close enough to see the steam rise from his head. Just then, another thought crossed his mind; this would be the first time that he'd seen the Challenger in his workplace.

It took three men to lift the scales over the ropes and into the ring. Very unusual. The weigh in would normally take place elsewhere, and usually the day prior to the contest. This, he thought, was no ordinary event.

"215 and a quarter to 206!"

"It's going to be a bloodbath," shouted a fellow through his stogie-clenching teeth.

Once the soldiers departed, the scales were removed and the audience was seated. But not for long. An aborted effort at the national anthem was attempted but public address problems would render Robert Goulet even more unlistenable than normal. Despite the difficulties and the impatient crowd, the man from Massachusetts persisted gamely.

"Go back to Canada, ya bum," shouted the Stogieman.

The timekeeper called it. The bell sounded for round one.

And as quickly as it had begun, it was over.

The Champion had barely connected with a hook and a cross but for some reason, the Challenger couldn't - or didn't want to - live with it. He was back on his feet but even the referee, Jersey Joe Walcott, himself a former champion, struggled to comprehend what had just happened.

"Fake!!! Fake!!!!"

Beer bottles, apple cores and hot dogs rained down on the ring as the short-changed spectators showed their displeasure.

The old man pushed his way through the angry crowd. His youthful associate reappeared, assisting him towards the corner of the ring. On the opposite side, as a confused Champion took the plaudits, the defeated Challenger, seated on his stool, looked down at a ring which magnetically drew his gaze towards its rough, stained grip.

"I need to get closer!" the older man shouted over the din. Behind him, the security custodians struggled to keep the angry spectators back.

Leaning against the ring, the young man cupped his hands, creating a makeshift stirrup. The old man quickly climbed onto the apron. Gripping tightly to the thick top rope, he stood, silently urging the fallen Challenger to notice him. He didn't want to call out. Being so close to the cameras, he was already in jeopardy. It was a risk however, he felt compelled to take.

Just then, as chaos enveloped him, the Challenger turned his head and caught a glimpse of a familiar face. Seeing the old man, he snorted. At the moment of this most abject public failure, the slightest trace of a smile appeared on his face. The old man looked back at him, struggling not to reciprocate.

"Is it safe?" he mouthed.

The fighter, reading his lips, nodded slowly.

The old man's eyes closed. A deep sigh of relief emitted from his body.

"See you around Charlie," he whispered.

"See you around, Val."

Tugging at the old man's jacket, the young man spoke.

"We need to go."

He took the old man by the arm and led him up the stairs, past scores of people still unsure as to what they'd witnessed.

As the defeated fighter was led out of the ring, the chorus of boos inside the Central Maine Youth Center reached a crescendo. The old man turned back to see the Challenger, his head shrouded and his once fearsome sixteen inch fists hanging by his side, redundant.

"You're a fucking bum, Liston!" roared a spectator. "Fifty bucks on you and you throw the fight? You no good fucking bum!"

The old man stopped and made a grab for the spectator.

"Shut your goddamn mouth!" he said, "You know nothing."

"I know that he's a fucking bum who has just cost me fifty bucks."

"None of you fucking assholes are fit to lace his gloves."

"Yeah, yeah, yeah. Blow it out your ass, Grandpa."

The old man reached into his pocket but his younger companion's tight grip prevented him from drawing the weapon.

"You've got to let it go," he said, quietly but forcefully. "And we've got to keep moving."

The old man breathed deeply but fury continued to cloud his eyes. He turned his back to the crowd, still throwing bottles and spitting vitriol.

You know nothing.

Chapter 2 - Columbus

How blows the wind, Sir? Onward, onward. Nor'easter. Droplet becomes a circle in the pool. Heaven from hell, the wind howls and away! The circle becomes a wave. And that's where we begin...

"Pull the handle UPWARD, Jerry!"

"Miss Washington, I have unlocked this door the same way, for thirty-two years and counting."

His was a deep, rich voice which displayed a patient authority, one that should be rarely questioned but often was. A grunt then...click.

"There we go. All in the technique."

Before he could reach down to pick up the mail, a rangy, eager young man with thick glasses and a tall, sculpted afro hairstyle beat him to it.

"I've got it, Mr Hector."

"Thank you, Elvin. I'll illuminate."

With a buzz and a crackle, the lights were on and The Columbus Diner in Auburn, Maine opened for business, as it had virtually every day since 1953 when Jerome 'Jerry' Hector, returned from Korea with a stipend for getting in the way of a couple of bullets intended for his CO at the Battle of the Punchbowl. Though still physically imposing, a shattered left kneecap and a fragment of a round nosed shell, lodged close to the brachial artery, meant that the chance of those slugger's forearms smashing baseballs around a diamond for anyone more notable than the Black Bears, was gone forever.

"TV or jukebox, Mr Hector?"

"Surprise me son," replied the owner. Elvin, initially hired as a kitchen porter but now the diner's short order chef and general do-it-all, flicked a switch and slowly, 'Top of the World' by the Carpenters picked up speed and volume. The diner's elderly cashier, Miss Washington, hummed along. With a dish towel to clean her large glasses, she started her work day as she did every morning, with a cigarette, a copy of the National Enquirer and a list of dry asides for any customers who'd dare undertip.

By the time Karen Carpenter had reached the line, 'And tomorrow will be, just the same for you and me', a heavy-set old man with a large and equally slow moving dog entered the diner. He carefully removed a well-worn naval cap to reveal a thick head of dark, synthetic hair, curling up at the back of his completely bald neck.

"Heavy weather, Jack?" asked Jerry.

"Damn squall," he replied. "And damn Sox too, eh?" He removed his wet coat and hung it on the tall stand. The dog, waiting patiently for its master to be seated, took up a position at his feet.

"Damn Sox, Jack. If it wasn't for bad luck, we'd have no luck," he responded. "Coffee?"

Jack grunted. Jerry poured him one anyway.

"Jer, I've seen things that would turn a man's head grey."

As Miss Washington sniggered loudly at the thought of his head, Jerry drew her a look.

"I might have seen a man hang off the side of a Grumman Avenger for close to fifty miles and not let go. And watched Brookline Billy Jenko eat twenty-five cheeseburgers in one sitting but I guess I'll never see the Sox take the series."

"Damn Sox, Jack."

"They've got Boggs, so they've got a chance, Mr Hector," said Elvin, placing a bowl of water beside Jack's tired animal. "A good left hander and hits like a fighter."

"That he does, son."

"So Jerry," asked Jack, following Elvin's lead, "Holmes's left jab or…"

"Spinks' speed?" replied Elvin.

The old man snorted, dismissively.

"I don't see it. A good big one will always beat a good little one."

"Except the little one ain't so little, isn't that right Mr Hector? And forgive me Mr McClean, you're always talking about when Ali beat Liston. No one saw that coming, did they?"

"He's got a point, Jack."

"You like the Heavyweights, Elvin?" asked Jack.

"Middleweights. That's where the real action is, Sir. The Hit Man, Marvelous Marvin, Sugar Ray…"

"Robinson?"

"No, Mr McClean. Sugar Ray Leonard!"

The old man shook his head and waved Elvin away. Jerry took a moment to straighten up a framed photo of the fight, hanging on the wall behind the counter. A floored bear looking up at a righteous young fighter.

"You youngsters know nothing about boxing!" taunted Jack.

"14 and 0," said Elvin, defensively.

"You were a fighter?" chuckled Jack. "You're too tall and skinny. What do you weigh? Like a hundred? A hundred ten?"

"One thirty-five on the money. Lightweight."

Old Jack laughed again.

"Didn't you know that our Elvin here was a very good amateur? Would have made Golden Gloves too," said Jerry.

For thirteen fights, Elvin had no problems. But a detached retina, seconds from the end of that fourteenth bout meant that boxing's loss was The Columbus' gain.

"A detached what?" barked Jack.

"So instead of Sugar Ray Robinson, we have Apple Pie Peterson!" added

Miss Washington.

"Haha. Very funny," said Elvin, sarcastically.

Jack took a sip of his coffee and grimaced, adding a low moan which suggested that his morning joe tasted grittier than normal. Still scowling, he asked, "When is May back?"

Less than a mile away, on a tree lined suburban street, May Morgenstern was having car trouble. Her vehicle had been jumping as much as it was running, when a strong gust blew over a half empty trash can, into the path of a tawny cat, sheltering under a bench. The frightened, weather spooked feline leapt into the street, forcing May's ugly yellow AMC Pacer to swerve, its tyres skidding off a patch of wet leaves and straight into the high kerbstone. The Pacer stopped with a dull thud.

Things may have been different an hour earlier but right now, on this blowy, blustery autumnal morning, there was not another car on the road.

Taking a moment to compose herself, May stepped out to check the damage.

"Not a scratch," she said proudly, overlooking the cracked kerbstone and the latest addition to her car's battered bodywork.

Using her heavy boots, May toed a few of the small bags and bottles back into the trash can before dragging it back to its place, in the alleyway by McGee's Tavern. The terrified tawny, now seeking shelter behind a stack of wooden beer crates, ignored all of May's attempts to coax it out. Given what it had just experienced, the cat seemed understandably reluctant to leave the safety of the alley though it did make a noise which suggested that it accepted her apology. No harm done. Back in the Pacer, May switched on the ignition but her well used, poorly maintained engine decided that it too had had enough excitement for that one day.

"Jesus Christ!" shouted May, more in frustration than as a celestial summons.

A misshapen ear and a twisted foot, both requiring painful, surgical correction, meant that May Morgenstern wasn't predisposed to believing in the kindness of God and his great plan; though at the age of six, she informed her parents that she was moving to a convent to become a nun AND marry Christopher Plummer. By the time she'd read the Count of Monte Cristo at the age of eight, she insisted that she wanted to be a boy and be referred to only by the name Edmond. Therapy was discussed.

Her father had just about convinced May's highly strung mother that this was merely a phase and that it would pass when, at the age of nine, she drew a picture of a horse with an ejaculating phallus. Her mother left the family home soon afterwards and May, wrongly believing that her artwork may have been the cause of the familial split, did not pursue further her interest in equine erotica.

As the kerbstone would attest, May was no Mario Andretti. And if one's inclination was to kindness, she could be described as charmingly ditzy rather than clumsily awkward. Pipe-cleaner thin with shoulders predisposed to sagging gave May Morgenstern the somewhat misleading air of a person who was permanently crestfallen. She wore calf length work boots, her late father's, fitted with her own corrective sole and her hair short, but always over her now fixed right ear. A dreamer, trapped in a world of do'ers, was how one teacher described her, coasting through life, armed only with a quick wit and occasionally, a temper to match.

Maybe there was an element of truth in that. But the thing about May Morgenstern was that while her mouth might run three steps ahead, her customers at The Columbus knew that her heart was most certainly in the right place, and that place was firmly rooted in Auburn, Maine. In fact, she'd only ever left the state three times in her twenty-four years on this planet. The first occurred just before the 'horse incident'. Her father had taken the family to North Carolina to visit an ailing relative. May found the trip, and many of her relations, deeply unpleasant. Worst of all was that damp, cobwebbed basement the guests had to hunker down in for the duration of their stay. She retained a soft spot for her older cousin, Ronald Jnr though. Her only fond memory of North Carolina was listening to records with Ronald Jnr until way past dark. The song 'Ain't Nothing Like The Real Thing' still made May think of him, years on. He wrote a few times but they lost touch when he left and headed west. Her second trip out of Maine was an 'overnight' to Boston for a Randy Vanwarmer concert with her best friend, Connie Barzagli. After the show they were followed by a creepy man and ended up spending the night hiding in South Station Bus Terminal until the early coach took them back to the safety of nearby Lewiston. The third time May had traveled out of state was yesterday.

"There she is!"

May dropped her bag in the doorway and shook the rain from the arms of her wet coat.

"Sorry I'm late."

"Towel please, Elvin," said Jerry, helping May out of her coat.

"So how was it?" asked the young chef.

"Too warm for these boots," she replied.

"Did you get to the Flamingo or the MGM?" asked Elvin. "My folks got hitched right there, on the strip. We'd vacation in Nevada when I was young but I don't remember much about it."

"The MGM's closing down," said Jerry.

"Is that a fact? Well, I'll be..," replied Jack.

"Sorry Elvin," said May, returning to his question. "I didn't have the time. I brought you this, though."

May reached into her bag and took out a branded cap, handing it to the young chef. It read, 'I love Vegas'.

"What do you think folks? Front or back?" asked Elvin, turning the peak of the cap.

"It's very ... you," said Miss Washington with a hint of derision.

After asking Elvin to bring over some coffee, Jerry ushered May to a nearby booth and quietly asked, "How did it go?"

"It went well, I guess. Just a bit sad. To live the life she had and end up alone ... with nothing."

"She had you, didn't she?"

"And The Columbus."

In the six years since she left high school, May had worked at Jerry's diner. She'd gained all the necessary retention requirements to go to teaching college in Portland with Connie but when her father took ill in the August of that year, she decided to forgo her studies, a few night classes aside, to tend to him and remain a waitress at The Columbus.

"Did she leave you anything worthwhile?"

"You seriously think that's why I befriended her?"

"Maybe. Ten percent bigger slice of pie, maybe twenty. And extra cream. Over five years? That's a smart move May. Playing the long game," said Jerry, straight faced but teasing. "If I thought she had money stashed away, I might have considered looking after the old broad myself."

"She did leave me something."

May lifted the largest of her bags onto the seat beside her and picked out a weighty yet ornate box, placing it on the table in front of Jerry.

"Her attorney was present. He gave me this."

"That is quite something," said Jerry, running his fingers along the box's intricate, hand-carved detail.

"He'd traveled from Monterey County to make sure that her wishes were strictly adhered to."

Outside, the wind howled and briefly, the lights dimmed. Jerry sized up the box.

"And there was this letter."

May handed Jerry an opened envelope.

'Dearest May, by the time you read this, I will be as dead as that thing which sits on Jack McClean's head...

The opening line momentarily made Jerry choke on his coffee.

...but don't be despondent and do not grieve. I am in a better place. Then, anything would be an improvement on 'Bide-a-Wee', wouldn't it?? My dear May, I've treasured your friendship over the last few years. You are patient and kind, the type of girl I'd love to have as my own but as

you know, that was never meant to be. I know many from The Columbus thought I was just some doddery old kook with a few marbles missing…'

Jerry nodded and laughed.

'…especially that dog Jerry…'

Jerry stopped laughing.

'…someone who liked to tell tales that were taller than young Elvin's hair but here's the thing, I really can't remember which ones were true and which I embellished for fun. You know how it is. Ha ha joking. There was one story however, that I did not share with you. I could not. Now that I've gone over, I have entrusted my most precious possession to you. This must only be opened by YOU and the contents read in private, and in sequence, by you alone. I cannot over-emphasise this. Follow these instructions to the letter. And, never allow it to fall into the wrong hands. Trust no one…

As Jerry read the letter, May studied his face.

…except Jerry. But no one else. You will know what to do. Since my Clifford passed, I have never known another human being that I felt …

Exhaling slowly, Jerry folded the letter and passed it back. The wind howled and again, the lights dimmed.

"What should I do?"

"Open the box."

"Here?"

"Why not?"

"It's not private," said May.

Jerry looked around the almost deserted diner.

"Not private enough," said May.

"Open the damn box."

"Jerry, it was her explicit wish that she didn't want it to be read by anyone but me. She trusted me."

"Elie trusted me too. It says so in your letter."

"Well, you open it," said May pushing the box towards Jerry.

Jerry ran his hands over the thick leather strap. He'd underestimated not just how important May was to Elie but how important she was to May. Especially since her father's passing.

"No. I can't," said Jerry, pushing the box back May's way. "It's for you and for you alone to open. That's the right thing."

As the wind became more ferocious, the awning over the diner's windows shuddered violently before coming loose, swinging over the window, side to side, like a large, striped windscreen wiper. With a boom, the door to the Diner blew wide open.

"Where's that two-stroke monstrosity of yours?"

"Beside McGee's tavern."

"That explains a lot."

Jerry reached for his raincoat and placed it around May's shoulders.

"Here, young lady. You've had a helluva couple of days. Elvin!" he shouted.

"Mr Hector?"

"I'm calling it."

"Sir?"

"I'm taking young Miss Morgenstern…"

"And my car?"

"And her God-awful car back to her apartment. When I return, get ready to close up for the day. I can't imagine that anyone other than Jack will be dumb enough to brave this weather, even for a slice of our delicious pie. No offence intended, Jack."

The old man's wave suggested that none was taken.

"Yes sir," said Elvin.

"Jerry?" drawled the voice from behind the cash register.

"Yes, Miss Washington, you will be paid for the full day."

"I always said that you're a very kind man," replied the grateful cashier.

"Don't tell the neighborhood."

If one spent time with Jerry Hector, it would be an easy assumption to make that behind the gruff exterior, stood a straightforward, decent man. And if one lived in Auburn, Maine, there would be those who would have real or anecdotal evidence to corroborate the belief that Jerry Hector was indeed a kind man.

But most people didn't know him as well as they thought they did.

Chapter 3 - Cora

'Residents all across the eastern seaboard are bracing themselves for what is expected to be the worst storm to hit the coast in eighty-four years. Here's our man in Long Island, Tom...'

That's enough, thought May switching off her small television. She took a towel from the radiator and wrapped it around her wet, still soapy head. As exciting as it had been to take flight and see, if not experience Las Vegas, May was glad to be back in Auburn. Comfortable. Where the milk is sour and the piles of washing reach to the sky. Good to be home. No work and a night of nothing much in particular from the comfort of her own bed. Music on, coffee percolating. Nothing like a warm cup on a blustery day, ain't that right May?

She missed Elie. They'd only known each other for a few years but the old lady had brought some much-needed colour to her days. As for her nights, sure, she had the occasional date but not many since Connie left for Portland. She was a fully-fledged junior school teacher now. Good for Connie. She'd come back for the holidays, when she could, but the truth was that there weren't too many unattached young bucks of their age left in Auburn and even fewer who frequented The Columbus.

May returned to Elie's bequeath.

Here goes.

She loosened the strap, before placing the box on her bed to open. Released, the leather binding was no longer stiff and taut as it had been while protecting its precious cargo. May slid it off and left it on the floor, spent.

Open the box.

May placed her fingernail under the hooked clasp and with a crisp pop, the box was opened. The smell of cut wood and old paper instantly filled her nostrils. The envelope at the top was not sealed. It contained a handful of monochrome photographs.

First out, a cowboy. Or maybe he just looked like one. Square jawed, Stetson, handsome. There was a name imprinted on the bottom right-hand corner but it was a little obscured. Chas. Langdon? A clue? May turned it over.

'My darling Elie, only three more weeks until I am able to dust off this dirt and return to your loving arms. Stay true for me as I am for you. Your beloved, Clifford.' Photo Likeness made by Chas. Langdon, Artist. Temperance, TX

So *that's* Clifford? What can I say, she thought, the old lady had taste.

Another photo of the same man then one of him with a much younger Elie. May touched the frayed, fading picture of her friend and sighed.

So beautiful.

'Prettiest girl I ever saw.'

In the box, beneath the photographs was a book, bound in thick leather and held shut by a twisted clasp. May opened the front cover and read the following, handwritten inscription...

'Dearest E,

It has been so long since I made it down the coast to see you. I feel a great sense of guilt about that, but I know you'll understand that there are certain physical inhibitors which certainly do not excuse my absence but may mitigate. You have your mother's eyes...

Many years ago, I made a request of you and, given that I feel the cold chill more with each passing year, the time to deliver is

nigh. On certain things, my memory isn't what it once was but with regards this I am crystal clear; our critical moment has arrived.
Stay well my sweet. Wherever the spirits take us...
H.'

Not what she was expecting.

C was for Clifford but H? This was an entirely different kettle of cod.

Who was this H and what was he to her, May thought. Another lover? A brother? No, you don't refer to a sibling as 'my sweet' now, do you? And if she deemed me important enough to be her only confidante during her dotage AND the sole beneficiary of her last will and testament, why didn't she tell me about H? May picked up the handful of letters from Clifford and scoured them for any references to H.

'I was sorry to hear about Henry's fall. I hope that it wasn't too serious. He was something. I know that he didn't care much for me and in those awkward, early days, I perhaps felt a little uncomfortable about your relations with him. I believe he grew to understand that my intentions were honourable. Next time you write him, pass on my regards and tell him that I'll gladly let him bum a smoke from me when he recovers.'

At that moment, a thrash of rain struck May's window. The almighty howl which accompanied it, startled her.

So, H is Henry. But who is Henry? Returning to the book, May pored over the inscription, hoping that perhaps a clue would present itself.

Nothing.

She quickly thumbed through the rest of the book, at least a couple of hundred pages of varying sizes, written in pencil, in blue and black ink, but clearly by the same hand. May returned to the start.

'There was never a grand plan. None of this was intended. Doors opened, I walked through. Gates locked, I climbed over. I guess that this behemothic conundrum we call life comes like one of those waves that rises from the bowels of the Great Pacific, crashing into

the cliffs and coves near my cottage. Sometimes you sense it coming, sometimes you don't. I've found that when the wave comes, it's prudent not to worry about the one certainty; getting wet. Don't argue with me on this. Remember, if it's old, it must be right! Ha! Without wanting to sound like some sub-Kerouac, coffee house beat poet, I guess that the only wisdom I'm qualified to impart is just... ride the wave. Or 'Embrace the moisture'. No, scratch that. Go with the first line.'

May turned the page...

'I first saw her on the corner of Macon and Ralph, outside the yellow brick house where Mrs Ottmaier gave piano lessons, a dime an hour. She was fifteen, I was two years younger. Decades on, I recall her every detail. The emerald-coloured coat, her flame coloured hair tied up beneath a wide brimmed hat, protecting her alabaster skin from the late summer sun. She had a parcel of meat for her father, cut the way he liked it by Unger the butcher. Both men were quite important figures in Bushwick. Most of the neighbourhood, like my own family, was German but the Seawards, your mother's people, were old English, Social Register types. One of her great uncles served as a Senator. They had class.

The same cannot be said of the Militz family who lived nearby. The father was loud and coarse - not MY type of coarse, of course! - and was an unforgiving taskmaster for the engineers and the apprentices who laboured under his tutelage. I wasn't in their direct orbit but was friends with a few boys who ran with their youngest, Casper. An indulged boy, always with spending cash, he tended to attract those who didn't mind prostrating oneself for ready tidbits. He was tall, pasty, heavy set and like his father, had a capacity for vindictive and cruel behaviour. Very different to his neighbour, and the object of my ardour, Cora. She was truly precious. Kind and thoughtful. One day, I shall speak with her father, I thought and ask for her hand. I had an inkling that's what happened but I didn't know exactly why. I was so young, I just wanted to be close to her. To see her was to voyage in the blue and uncharted firmament. My one true love. My dear Elie, there are things I've seen and done in this wretched life but the purest and most Godly truth I've ever known was a smile from the lips of Cora, your virtuous mother. I wished dearly that I could have been there for her and stopped Casper but I wasn't and that regret I'll take to the grave.

The burghers of Bushwick made sure that the Militz family - and their business - bore a terrible price for what happened but as for the boy himself? It was as if he'd snapped a shoelace. A minor inconvenience. After backing him with everything they had, his family was sinking. And in the face of that, he cast them aside and sailed on, surrounded by bootlickers and backers, impressed by his hard shell and seeming invulnerability. He did business with both the Shapiro's and the Amberg brothers but never once spent a night in the Tombs or was dispatched to Sing-Sing. Your mother though was sent upstate to recuperate from the ordeal - and to prepare for your arrival.'

The paper, turned up and dry around the edges, felt fragile, as if it was not long for this realm. May turned the page carefully and read more.

'By the early fall of 1938, I was living in a small but comfortable two-room apartment on the Rue Des Boulanger. A friend, Purcell Griffin, made sure that I needn't worry about the rent. I had an open offer from Anaïs and Hugo but our personal situation was a little more knotty, so, with Griffin's kind patronage, I was able to immerse myself in 'Mon Vie Parisien Inspirant!'

It may surprise you to hear that I've never sought the company of others, especially when I had work to do. I am sociable, yes and in the right surroundings, I can be positively gregarious; but playing the part of a great whale, plunging the depths in order to find a few skinny fish, has never appealed. The poseurs with their notebooks, sitting in salôns, pretending to be tortured, desperate to be noticed.

Pah! As for spending time with other writers, unless they were physically attractive members of the opposite sex, I could not think of a worse pastime. As I said to that old Irish bore Beckett, genius has no peers. Solitude and as close as damn it, a fixed regimen kept me sharp.

Having secure accommodation and cultivating a professional level of discipline allowed me to hone my craft, while the location of the apartment - a healthy walk from my preferred meeting places, the Bistros and Cafés of Montmartre and Clichy - prevented me from out-staying my welcome. If I was lonely for company, and I rarely was, I could always head over to La Sorbonne, a few streets away, blow the dust off some hoary, long forgotten friends and maybe cadge a crust or two. And it was over drinks at Purcell's own residence in Île-De-France that I was introduced to his neighbours, The Mortlocks. Konrad, the husband, was some kind of industrialist, engines for cars or what have you but his wife Xena, to whom I was intensely attracted, was an exotic freebird. Keen to show off his latest Bugatti, Konrad would take off, sometimes for days to the Côte D'Azur or north, to his factory in Alsace, leaving behind his bewitching consort. Not that she longed for company either. Xena hunted companions the way a panhandler closes in on a quarter. There was always a coterie of actors, wrestlers, adventurers, fighting over the physical needs and alien habits that I'd have gladly shared. As I was older than her husband, and not deemed as sophisticated, nor as selective as some of her paramours, I sensed that she looked upon me with a mix of curiosity and pity, which bristled somewhat.

Anyway, following one such night in the company of astrologist, occultist and probable bunco artist, Cedric Al-Lazar, at the Mortlock's Port-Royal address, I found myself lounging by the balcony, spent and slumped, awaiting sleep as the working stiffs began their day. Al-Lazar had long gone, led away into the night by his sycophants but not before he charted the most incredible zodiac for me, to the very day, time and place where I was born. I was 'an angel surrounded by fire', he said. Ridiculous, I exclaimed. Or would've exclaimed had I not been a giddy schoolgirl, consumed by my own narcissism. Can you imagine Blaise Cendrars taking similar guidance from a cheap mystic? He'd have kicked that prick Al-Lazar straight through a fucking window. Apologies again, Elie. That I allowed myself to fall for a cosmic confidence trickster, was bad enough - though I suspected that Anaïs must have tipped him off about my past - uncritical, chichi me was buying straight into all of this nonsense, basking for a moment, in the fiery glow of my own self-importance.

As the day broke, I desperately tried to summon the energy to get up off the lounger, gather my effects and return to my garret. As fun as it had been, I needed to get back to work and cleanse my palate of this bourgeois baloney. Rays of sunshine poured in through the cracks in the drapes and shutters, urging me up and out when, through the ruck of inert bodies sprawled across the room, Xena appeared; jet black hair unfettered, her kohl-masked eyes, crepuscular. Wearing nothing but a loose-fitting peach camisole, she approached me. I stirred to be willingly intoxicated. Follow me, she said. To the Gates of Hell, I thought. She led me by hand through her bedroom into her private bathroom where she began to undress me. As I stood in front of her, the tension from the pit of my guts - and below - became unbearable. I grabbed at her cunt - apologies my dear E, I do get lost in the memory and forget that your view of romantic ardour, while valid, differs from mine. NO! I cannot keep excusing my language. I need you to know everything, therefore everything must be out there, no editing from here on in. I am a spurt of clay from the cock of the Great Creator and as such, this is who I am. There. Enough. I may be coarse, but I am un scoundrel affiné! Anyway, just as things got interesting, she firmly removed my hands from her person. Why are we here? I thought. Get in, she said. I did as I was told and got into the warm bath. She removed my now misted spectacles and placed them beside her on the stool. She looked deep into my eyes for what felt like an eternity before asking, 'Tell me about New York, Henry.'

Where to start? I thought.

'It ain't Port-Royal, sweetheart.'

May picked up her coffee cup and took a sip. It was ice cold.
She turned the page.

'What do you want to know?' I asked.

'Why do you write?'

That question, at this delicate stage of proceedings, was not what I was expecting. Normally, when faced with a poser such as this, I'd consider the following. Who was asking? This was important as the answer given to a crusty academic may be very different from the one I'd offer a prospective bedfellow; and sometimes a standard, 'For me, the written word, is either an attempt to recapture something lost or a design to cast off one's debilitating qualm and have the courage to allow oneself to be dragged along in the slipstream of others impulses' would suffice. That kind of florid babble works more than you'd believe but for the extraordinary Xena, it seemed extraneous.

'A man's gotta eat,' I said.

She nodded sagely, as if I'd imparted the heavier line. She lit a long liquorice-coloured cheroot, took a drag then rocked her head back on her shoulders. Xena's dark eyes closed, her head slowly moving to its own cadence, eliciting deep rhythmic moans.

Where was this leading? I told her that I had an idea that I needed to explore, so if a few drinks and an invitation to watch her meditate was all that was on the table, so to speak, I was leaving. I was too long in the tooth to be strung along in some narcoleptic nonsense like I was one of her other sexual cadavers but she wasn't having any of it. One more drink, she said, snapping out of her reverie. Could I resist? No, is the answer. She walked to the basin and removed a bottle from the cabinet above. 'There's no rush to leave, is there?' she asked, unscrewing the cap and pouring out two shots.

With her back to me, she slowly removed the camisole strap from her left shoulder, then looking over that same shoulder, she removed the other one. The camisole slid down her body, dropping onto the floor, revealing her devastating shape in all its glory. Perhaps, I had been a little hasty. She turned and walked back to me. I was now sat bolt upright. Though the walk took seconds, I've replayed this moment time and again. I wanted it to take an hour, maybe two so that I could memorise every curve, every mark on her perfect frame. There was a gap where her inner thighs met her torso, about the circumference of a

Silver Dollar, through which the light from the hallway shone. I took that as a sign. On either side of her pronounced hip bones, a pair of jet black birds, quite subtly inked onto her skin. Now I'd seen tattooed ladies before, but none like this.

She lowered herself into the tub and placed her legs behind my back, pulling me towards her. I gripped her by the waist and closed my eyes. I could feel her warm breath on my face, the bouquet of the wine she'd consumed filled my nostrils. I was wholly intoxicated. Sanctified. Absolution. Her mouth tenderly touched mine. My stomach tightened in anticipation as her body brushed against me. The distance between us was tantalising but closing. My dry lips and hers welded together. She pulled away from my face, leaving me precariously close to the edge.

'A drink?'

'Maybe afterwards,' I said, knowing that it would be seconds rather than minutes before I was in a position to accept the offer.

She reached over to the stool and picked up a bottle. Different in shape to the previous one. She gently pushed my head back and pried my lips open with her fingers. With her other hand, she took control of me. I was hers unconditionally.

The liquor was sickly sweet. I didn't care for it but at times such as these, you ride the wave.

One shot of liquor turned into two, which seemed to go straight to my head, and before I knew it, I was on the street, woozy and befuddled, being helped into a car that was definitely not a Bugatti. Rue Des Boulangers, I mumbled. Silence. It soon became apparent that we were heading in a different direction. I enquired as to where we were going. One of Xena's boys, a sun kissed, muscular fellow with immaculate hair said, 'You are going to La Santé!'

'The prison?' I asked with a nervous laugh.

'Let's see what you're made of, eh Mr Miller?'

The short drive to La Santé Prison would normally take no more than ten minutes. This felt like ten seconds. Once there, the immaculate boy delicately opened a sachet, no bigger than a pair of postage stamps, tipped it into his flask and gave it a firm shake.

'You thirsty?'

Unsurprisingly trepidatious, I asked what it was but he shook his head and passed it to me. I took a sniff before touching the coffee-coloured substance with my lips. It was cold. I was about to register my objections when I felt something prod into my side, under my ribs, poking out from Immaculate Boy's overcoat. He smiled at me the way I suspect a mongoose would a snake, had it been in possession of a zygomatic bone structure. However, as I am, despite appearances, a true Brooklyn tough, I slugged back on the flask. Immaculate Boy took his hand from his pocket and showed me that the weapon was merely two fingers. He made a shooting sound and laughed at me. Was this a prank? Had I upset Xena or Konrad? Was I being set up? And if so, for what? The door of the car was opened and I was helped out by Immaculate Boy and the driver, a large man of colour, a few years my senior, who looked vaguely familiar. They took me through the courtyard and along the inner wall to an imposing brick rotunda at the centre. A dark wooden hatched medieval looking entrance was unlocked and I was escorted up the spiral staircase.

The solid stone floor had been freshly swabbed. The thick smell of the carbolic in the air brought me back to my early days, sitting on the freshly scrubbed stoops of Driggs Avenue. Immaculate Boy and Large Negro Man led me through a thick glass door and I was sat down on a couch. They left the room. Facing me, the pattern on the door, an unrecognisable astrological hieroglyph, was so ornate, that I couldn't help myself but be drawn into its intricacy. The earlier sense of trepidation and dread was gone. I was entirely comfortable here, at La Santé; the bleak, final destination of assorted French lowlifes. And although, by this time, I hadn't slept for close to thirty-six hours, I was energised. And enraptured by the beauty of this door.

At that moment, I believe that I, a man who had walked on every sidewalk crack and had been sucked into the worst of what that unholy vacuum - Myrtle Avenue - had to offer, was about to impinge upon God Himself. In my crazed fantasy, I was Galileo, the heavenly heretic and celestial pioneer, under arrest, taking a solemn oath. Gripping my genitalia tightly, I vowed to abjure and renounce my wicked ways, without any equivocation, mental reservation, or secret evasion whatsoever, taking the words spoken by me, according to the common and usual meaning of them. So help me God. So help me Door. The Door WAS God. God WAS the Door. It made absolute sense. Even to touch it gave me an inordinate amount of intense pleasure. So much so that I was moved beyond emotion. In the corner of my eye, a dim light went on. Then in the next corner, another. The gloom of the correctional facility and the last lingering traces of ordure was gone and in its place was a warmth that pervaded every pore of my being. The Door opened again and in came Immaculate Boy. He was wearing a shimmering robe. Was he The Divine, I asked myself? In this transcendent intoxication, I reached to touch his garment but it evaporated in my hand. Another corner and another light. Behind me, there was a sky-blue wall of what looked to me, still water. As undisturbed as a freshly pressed sheet and as sheer as gossamer. I could see people through it; Immaculate Boy and Xena. Xena was there. And my mother. My mother was there. I tried to call out to her. Regardless of my feelings towards her - that deeply uncomfortable bond - seeing my mother here, in La Santé, sent me to the floor, sobbing like an abandoned child. But for some unknown reason, I found that I could not communicate. My lips and mouth, weighing heavily as potter's clay, were desert dry.

In my confused state, fear took hold and the remaining strength sapped from my being. The light began to take the form of what I can only describe as ghoulish phantasms, weaving in and out, drawing my energy. Summoning every ounce, I threw myself at the wall of water. Sharp, searing pain soared into my forehead and my hands. A warm liquid ran slowly down into my eyes. It looked like blood but its texture was that of thick latex rubber. As the mercury rose, a host of seraphim came to me, cast off my clothes and soothed me to my rest.

When I awoke, I found that I had been returned to my apartment. The lacerations I received in my dream-like-state were real but all of my wounds were clean and dressed. The psychological effects of such a preternatural experience weighed heavy and I had difficulty piecing together the events at La Santé. I left my accommodation and wandered Montparnasse, unwashed with the scent of those illicit sensations enveloping my damaged body, acting as a sensuous map, a trail as to what had really happened. As there weren't too many in Paris I could trust implicitly, I contacted the one person to whom I wasn't in some form of debt. I met my friend, Joe Do Sappo at his home from home - the Café Bérangère - and over black tea and a bottle of dreadful juniper wine, relayed to him my story.

Joey had lived in these parts for many years, working under the late Antoine Laurencin at the Havas news agency. Before he became a photographer though, he was a drop-out officer of the Quebec City School of Military Instruction, which gave him an ability to flit in and out of even the stickiest scene with the precision of an urban fox. Joe was a sober fellow with strong arms and a light touch. He was also a sport who didn't mind when he caught me waist deep in his paramour - Antoine's widow - after lunch on Easter Sunday. Joe knew Konrad Mortlock in passing but like many of us, Xena held a tighter fascination. I told him of Immaculate Boy and of the Large Negro Man. He knew the latter, identifying him as Papa Koto, long standing off-the-books muscle for M. Bony, the Police Chief of the 14th Arrondissement. The others? He'd ask around.

'Have you spoken about this to anyone else?'

'Not a soul.'

'Henry,' he asked, 'have you heard of Le Corbeau?'

I hadn't.

He looked around, making sure that we were not being overheard. 'Le Corbeau is The Crow. You need a car? The Crow provides. Trouble at work? The Crow will break the strike. You have aspirations? Make sure The Crow gets a taste. You don't be playing games with Le Corbeau.'

'Why?'

Joe pulled me close. 'I've seen this play out before. For whatever reason, someone is in their sights and someone else will take the fall. Make sure it's not you.'

I assured him that I was too long in the tooth to be made anyone's patsy. He looked at me, with his heavy brow pushed down over his eyes.

'I think you should consider leaving town, old friend.'

I returned to my apartment, intrigued and a little perturbed about this Le Corbeau character. What could he possibly want from me? And should I take Joey's advice and get out of Paris? I stripped off, ran a hot bath, and opened the small hopper to let out some steam. The juniper wine, awful though it was, had given me a real thirst. I wrapped a towel around my waist and searched for the cleanest glass I could find.

On my bedside table I found one, right beside an envelope which was addressed to me but was not there the last I'd looked. I broke the seal and opened it.

The handwritten card read...

'22 Rue Delambre, Apartment 2. At 9pm. Come alone. X'

I took my glass and from the cupboard in the hall, plucked the bottle of Scotch I had been saving 'til the end of my latest book. With one hand on the card, I put the cork between my teeth and popped it out. Fuck the book, I thought. Three fingers straight and I slid into the tub. The sting of my fresh wounds passed momentarily. I was rarely home at this time of the day so I took succour in the honest warmth of the bathe. The afternoon sun cut through the clouds and the steam onto the off-white tiles, setting the floating particles of pollen and dust to dance. I caught sight of something on the mirror, a mark, perhaps? I twisted my head to the left so that I could see more clearly. I picked up my glasses, wiped them with a dry face cloth and looked again at the vanity. There, as a rare ray of autumnal light broke through the dimpled glass, I saw it. Crudely drawn but it was indeed the unmistakable outline of a bird.'

Without looking, May reached for her cold coffee and without taking her eyes from the page, took another long gulp.

'I told no-one where I was headed that evening. It was best, I reckoned, not to drag my closest Parisienne acquaintances deeper in than they needed to be. Concern for my own general wellbeing was not nearly as great, largely due to the possibility of a carnal conclusion that I would nary ignore.

I wrapped a scarf around my neck and pulled my Fedora down as I took a circuitous route around the streets of Montparnasse. Was I being followed? I couldn't tell for sure but my senses told me that it was prudent to be circumspect. I arrived at No. 22 Rue Delambre at precisely 8.52pm. After a final scan of my surroundings, I looked at the list of buzzers for the apartments, to the right of the heavy oak carriage doors. Every apartment had a name beside the number. Apartment 6 was Devanne. Rêmy occupied 4 while 8 was D'Abruzzi. There was no name beside the button for apartment

2. After a cursory look around, I pushed the button and I waited.

I was about to ring again when I heard the electric mechanism click and the door sprung open a fraction. I pushed it and stepped into the dimly lit passageway, closing the door firmly so that anyone who may have followed would now be behind a four-inch thick barrier of heavy wood. There was little light to illuminate the way so I proceeded slowly, and with caution. Through the dank passage into the courtyard, there shone an orange light to my right, one floor up. I took the staircase with the prospect of De Maupassant's thought... 'the best part of love is walking up the stairs' only partially assuaging my lingering unease.

Standing in the gloom, I knocked on the door of Apartment 2. Not so loud that the neighbours would be disturbed but enough to be heard by the, hopefully scantily clad, inhabitant. There was no immediate answer so I gripped the handle and gave it a twist. It opened. Again, I looked to see if I was being watched but still, nothing was untoward. I gave the door a push and I was in. Closing the door behind me, I walked down the tiled hallway, my shoes tapping out a warning to anyone I may surprise. I undid my scarf and removed my hat as I continued down the long passage, toward the orange light. In the lounge, I could see the silhouette of someone, sitting facing the balcony. The bay window was open and the net curtains blew in time with my footsteps. Xena? I called out quietly. There was no answer. I could see a shadow lounging in the wide armchair. The left arm of the inhabitant, draped over the side of the chair with its hand almost touching the glass positioned on the floor. As I got closer, I could hear the faint sound of a drip. By the time I was within touching distance, I could see that the person in the chair was not Xena nor any woman for that matter but a man. The net curtains blew over again, the light from the street glistening against the top of his head. I heard that drip again. My eyes followed where the sound came from. It was blood. Running from a gaping divot on this man's head, down his arm and into the glass. My heart was beating so loudly that I didn't hear what came next.

Darkness.

I have no idea how long I was out for. My skull hurt and my glasses were gone. I motioned to my head, to check the damage but my wrists were tightly bound, behind my back. I heard a man say the words 'Capitaine, il est reveille'. He is awake. Trying to remain calm, my eyes began to adjust to the dim light. The pain from my head was dull and continual. Another figure approached me. I could not determine who he was but the other men, three or four of them, demurred in his presence.

'Batarde malade,' he said, which means, I believe, 'sick bastard' in French. A statement I couldn't argue with, I thought but what has that to do with why I'm being held? He repeated the curse, louder and this time accompanied by the back of his hand across my mouth. I could taste the leather of his glove and the blood from my split lip which certainly distracted me from the pain of my earlier head trauma.

'Enough!' I exclaimed. 'What the hell is going on?'

'Monsieur Miller,' said the Capitaine, 'You have spent enough time in Paris to know how we operate. We tolerate ... vous les Americins ... you Americans. Even the low rent pornographers like yourself bring a certain colour to the place. We like that.'

Thank you, I think.

Bringing his face close to mine, he tapped the side of my face with his finger. 'We are missing something no?' Another officer handed him an object. He brought it to my face and naturally, I winced.

'Your spectacles, Monsieur.'

A flicker of recognition shot through my damaged brain. With his slicked back hair and his neatly pruned pencil moustache, he could have been...maybe a friend or a lover of Xena? In my fearful state, I simply couldn't process the information my damaged brain was receiving.

'*What we don't like is when your New York disputes spill into our territory, namely my arrondissement.*'

'*I don't understand what you're getting at.*'

Le Capitaine sighed. '*Enough of this charade. Tell me what you know about Le Corbeau.*'

'*Le Corbeau? You mean The Crow?*'

'*Exactement.*'

'*I know nothing.*'

His leather glove smashed into my face for a second, more painful time. In addition to my lip popping like bubblegum, one of my teeth dislodged.

'*Monsieur Miller, I would advise you to consider what you say next, very carefully.*'

'*In case you get really angry?*' *I spat!* '*Goddammit, I KNOW NOTHING!*'

'*You know La Santé Prison, don't you?*'

What's he getting at? Was he there last night?

'*That's where we take murderers.*'

Murder?

'*Why did you kill him?*'

I was lost for words. '*I... I... I've done nothing,*' *I said.*

The Capitaine motioned to his men and they picked me up. My legs were as weak as those of a newborn calf.

'*You broke into this apartment.*'

'*I was invited.*'

'*By whom?*'

'*I don't know exactly.*'

'*There was a struggle...*'

The wounds on my face were still conspicuously fresh.

'*Then you took this couteau...*' *said Bony, snapping his fingers, searching for the correct terminology. 'Eh, a couperet, a cleaver ...'*

'No...'

'And you buried it in the head of poor Monsieur Militz.'

'Militz?'

In the moonlight, I stood before the lifeless body of a man. His skin was pale, his mouth agog but his eyes...those eyes were unmistakable.

At that moment, dearest Elie, an all too real manifestation of a long standing, deeply held animus was ominously writ large.

That I, Henry Miller, may have murdered the bastard who sired you, Casper Militz.'

Chapter 4 - The Unlikely Capitaine

'The officers cuffed my hands tightly behind my back and took me by the arms down into the cobbled courtyard. A handful of locals had congregated at the heavy wooden door, keen to see what business the Sûreté had on their street. For some reason, the Capitaine threw a blanket over my head as he led me out. In trying to perhaps protect me, he'd unwittingly turned the scene into a drama. Cloaked, I couldn't see what was happening but I sensed the mood of the public was not with the figure under cover. En route to the car, I was struck again, at least three times, by whom, I do not know. I've taken that trip downtown in many places and on a number of occasions but, I can tell you this with the utmost sincerity; I have never felt as worried as I was that evening. Legions of possibilities raced through my mind. Every step that I'd taken in Paris, as far back as I could recall, I walked again. Every salôn entered, every drink imbibed, every whore and showgirl toasted, every fist I saw swung in my direction. And Militz? I'd stored that grievance in a mental cabinet marked 'unfinished business' but his gruesome demise was not of my making. 'Les joueurs locaux' would have offered long odds at these two particular Bushwick men being in the same area of the same city at precisely the same time. Nothing about this made sense. Nothing.

They removed the blanket from my head for the short drive to the holding tank. That's something I noticed about Paris; one is never too far from a jail. Upon arrival, my hands were uncuffed and I was placed in a dank cell with a hard wooden bench. The blanket that had earlier covered me was thrown in as my only comfort. No fresh carbolic here. This spartan, piss sodden chamber was, for a corral, uncommonly grim. As grim as my future appeared to be. I slid down onto the bench and stared directly into the bright of the buzzing electric light above. I couldn't rest. My heart seemed as if it was attempting a jailbreak through my chest and my tenderised lower jaw felt as if it had been prised from its pair by a crowbar. Thoughts ricocheted around my exhausted brain like pinballs filled with tiny explosive charges. A grave mistake had clearly been made and soon they'd be along to rectify it, I told myself. Any minute now. Those moments of calm rationality though, were punctuated by wave upon wave of panic and fear.

I thought of my family, back in New York. My browbeaten father. And my mother. Our deeply unsatisfactory relationship is a discussion perhaps for another time. She belittled my father and thought I was unworthy of her concern. Did I see her at La Santé? I could've sworn I did. I tried to return to that curious experience but events since had overtaken them. I closed my eyes and attempted to transport myself back home. In this, my moment of hopelessness, I wanted nothing more than to be seated at their feet, warm and safe again. I closed my eyes. I closed my eyes. The waves kept coming.

****

How long was I asleep? I had no idea. Exhaustion had taken its toll. The old wristwatch I wore must have been damaged in the earlier scuffle but the shafts of daylight which broke through the small, barred window high to my left told me that the dawn had already passed. I could hear the faint sound of light rain and the Parisienne public going about their business, and for a moment, I'd forgotten where I was. The Mortlock's grand balcony in Port-Royal may have been a stone's throw away but it may as well have been on another planet and boy, didn't I know it. Again, I thought of that Militz bastard. Throughout my youth, I'd fantasised about my role in facilitating his departure from the Garden of Human Delights, and though I admit my desire for vengeance had dimmed over the decades, I can't say I was desolate to see his bloody, lifeless husk draped over that chair. But the list of unanswered questions continued to grow...

Why was he in Paris? Why was he killed? Who killed him? Why am I being framed?

I dug into my coat pocket and found a single partially smoked cigarette. I reached down, struck a match off the stone floor and lit what I hoped wouldn't be my final drag.

Tap, Tap, Tap.

I rubbed my eyes.

Tap, tap, tap.

What was that? Too heavy and defined to be a rodent, even for these parts. The sound seemed to be coming from above my bunk. At the corner of the room, high and indented, was a ventilation brick; a standard slab but with a few holes formed, allowing air to flow from one cell to another.

Tap, tap, tap.

I put on my glasses, stood on the bunk and stretched as high as my battered frame would allow.

Tap, tap, tap

'Hello?' I asked. No answer.

Tap, tap, tap.

I tapped back.

From the top left ventilation hole, I could see it. A thin sliver of tightly rolled paper, no longer nor thicker than a lollipop stick, ever so slightly, protruding.

The tapping continued and the paper moved to within touching *distance. I took it down, sat on the edge of my bunk and opened it.*

Crudely written, it read;

'We are coming to get you.'

In my fragile state, my first reaction to this message was naturally one of alarm. They're going to get me? What are they going to do? And who are they?

At that moment, I could hear footsteps heading towards my cell. I swallowed hard and looked around the spartan room for something...anything I could perhaps fashion into a weapon to aid my defence. I kicked hard at my bunk in an attempt to dislodge a plank or two but the combination of superior French workmanship and my diminished physical capacity meant that nothing budged.

The sound of the keys going into the lock. The turning of the lock. And of my stomach. I steeled myself in anticipation.

Then...nothing.

I waited until my heart rate had decelerated before walking over to the cell door. I placed my ear close to the sliding metal hatch and listened. The tapping behind me had stopped. As there was no handle on the inside of the cell, I squeezed my fingers through the bars on my side of the metal hatch and with enough pressure, I was able to slide it over about an inch. Enough for me to look out of the cell. No one was there. I listened. Nothing. My heart began to race again. I placed my hand around the hatch bars and pulled for all I was worth. The cell door cracked open, slightly but noisily. Breathlessly, I hid behind the door, lest I alert the guards, too scared to brave another attempt. But this might be my one chance because, as the note intimated, they were coming for me. I peered out again. Nothing. I have no idea what the hell the guards were meant to be doing instead of guarding, but I made the decision to take the chance. If anyone stopped me, I'd wing it. I'm undercover...no, a lawyer attending an American client. Yes, that's dumb enough to work. I pulled the cell door enough to pass through. Straight ahead, around fifteen feet, was another cell. I looked left down the corridor which curved out of view, then to the right which dead-ended after the neighbouring cell. As curious as I was about the note, it made little sense to extend my period of captivity by introducing myself to my fellow inmate with an offer of constructive criticism. I headed left.

Within five or six strides, I turned to see my cell disappear from view. Keep going.

A staircase.

I knew from the small window in my cell that I was at least one floor up so I took the vinyl floored stairwell down, slowly but two steps at a time, ever careful not to make the kind of sound that would certainly alert the one conscientious guard in the poste de police. At the bottom, there was a long, wide corridor heading back into what looked like the main building. Silently, I stuck my head around the wall. In the near distance, I could hear the sharp clink of bottles and a number of men talking. From the aroma, my aching stomach instinctively knew that it was the garrison's mess; though I would have eaten a plague-ridden dray horse at this point, I thought it wise not to proceed in that direction. Under the stairwell, the corridor narrowed towards a door. On each side of the corridor, there were around twenty pegs and hanging from each was the heavy coat and hat of an officer. My eyes darted left and right. Nothing. Right, let's go.

I removed my glasses, put the first kepi I could find on my head and placed the dark blue tunic with the silver braiding over my own jacket. I put my hands into the deep pockets and felt cold steel. There was footwear available but I didn't want to spend another second in this Godforsaken hole. Out I went.

'Capitaine!' shouted a very young cadet sprinting through the door behind me, out into the rain. I nodded, made a vague salute and continued.

'Pardon!' he shouted.

51

I ignored him, hoping that my rank may prevent him from pushing further.

'Pardon!' Louder this time. My heart was racing as fast as my legs. I put my hand on the service revolver in my right pocket. In my forty odd years on this planet, I'd never fired a weapon in anger.

As he caught up with me, I cocked the hammer. Whatever happens, I wasn't for returning.

'Capitaine, vous avez laissé tomber ceci!'

A leather glove had fallen from the pocket of the heavy tunic and this kind soul was returning it to me.

'Merci,' I said, thanking him with a rap on his shoulder.

I uncocked the pistol in my pocket, and as I walked out of the compound into the damp Parisienne morning, I thought only of that young cadet's mother; of the pride in her rosy cheeked son's achievements and the devastation she would've felt had he pushed and I reacted. All of my, thus far, meagre achievements would count for nothing, particularly in the haunted eyes of a woman who would curse the day I was shat into existence. I had long considered that the life I'd chosen had in a way indemnified me against conventional morality but this episode shook that credo. For a number of profound reasons, relief washed over me.

That sense of solace didn't last long though for across the street, by the open back door of a very familiar car, stood Papa Koto and Immaculate Boy. But for a brief stare at an even more familiar stockinged leg, I most certainly would have gone unnoticed. But stop I did; and see me they did.

At this stage, I remained unsure as to what their plans for me were but my gut instructed me that it may be wiser to consider my options from a safer distance. Pivoting, I set off in the opposite direction. Looking around, I saw Papa Koto assume control of the car while Immaculate Boy took to the street on my tail. Hoping to shake them quickly, I took a sharp left down Rue Clothilde, then a right onto Thouin. Given how physically impressive he was, I have no doubt

Immaculate Boy could've caught and apprehended me with relative ease but given that the car hadn't quite managed to keep up with our pace, a scuffle with this particular uniformed officer of the law would draw undue attention to us both. By now, Papa Koto had locked on to my movement and the car drew perilously close. Evasive action necessary or capture was a certainty.

I deftly skipped over a low hanging chain suspended between two bollards and took a right turn. A bicycle, leant against a wall outside a butcher's shop, was going to aid my escape. Naturally, as a newly appointed police capitaine, I didn't seek permission. Pedalling furiously, I went east down Rue Rollin. Any preconceived idea they may have had about a simple snatch job evaporated like the morning rain on the now sun kissed pavements as Immaculate Boy, keeping an Olympian pace, sprinted behind me. As locals, it was their Paris but this 'interlope Americain' had become familiar with the labyrinthian streets and alleys of their town. The car had found its way onto Rollin and it passed Immaculate Boy as the street narrowed. Its engine roared as they closed to within forty feet. Thirty feet. Twenty.

Papa Koto obviously didn't read the signs. He only saw the wrought iron railings, which lead down the stone steps to the Rue Monge when his car smashed through them. Was Xena in the smouldering wreck? I glanced back but through the smoke and steam, all I could see was the mangled steel with wheels still spinning, hanging precariously over the edge. Concerned locals swarmed around the vehicle but I wasn't about to offer assistance. Immaculate Boy stopped, briefly, to assess the damage. The driver, Papa Koto, was both in and out of the car at the same time. I bounced the bike down the steps as Immaculate Boy continued after me. I took a sharp left down Rue Monge, pedalling with all I had when my front wheel clipped something. In an instant, my legs sprung up behind me, swinging over my head. And as I kept my grip tight, the bike followed suit. My landing however, wasn't as hard as I'd anticipated. A well-worn drayman's cushion had broken my fall. From my prone, inverted position, I could see Immaculate Boy come towards me. He slowed to savour my capture, as a fox would a cornered cockerel. I was almost within his grasp when a dull thud from behind his head turned him into an involuntary gymnast. A wise fellow once said, 'Happy the man whose thoughts, like larks, take wing'. Now, I don't know exactly what Immaculate Boy was thinking as he 'took wing', spectacularly somersaulting over my grounded body and down an open hatch into the cellar of the Salôn Audmar, but as he hit quite a bit of wood, metal and glass on his way to the bottom, I'm certain that he thought that the partially perforated Papa Koto had gotten off lightly.

At this point, I would've happily called time on this morning's entertainment and settled for a hard-fought tie but as I was to find out, the final bell was not even close. I was helped from the ground by two burly men. They said nothing but I thanked them in French. With one hand under each of my armpits, despite my protestations, they launched me onto the back of their wagon. I landed heavily as they locked the vehicle's back gate. A heavy canvas sheet dropped down and the wagon pulled out. I sat in the darkness for a moment wondering what further trials lay in store. Blind, the smell of wine and rattle of the beer crates invaded my senses and the monumental pang of thirst that I'd forgotten I had, heightened my desire. I dug deep into the Officer's coat and placed my hand on the weapon once more. Just in case.

Flash! My eyes, nay, my brain was blasted by a bolt of incandescence, instantaneously shooting through my frontal lobes, into my medulla oblongata, down my spine and filling my boots with terror as if poked by the furious finger of Zeus himself.

'What the …?'

And again! Flash! I rubbed my fists into my eye sockets to alleviate the searing shock of the violent bursts of light. The area returned to darkness but my scorched eyes struggled to adjust.

'Cigarette?' came a voice from the opposite end of the vehicle. 'I'd prefer a beer,' I said. A match was struck and momentarily, I saw

two figures. 'Why not have both?' came back the voice. I walked to the back end of the wagon, mindful not to lose my footing, using their lit cigarettes as my guide. Under my feet, I could feel the crack of discarded camera flashes. Two men, one intense and whippet thin, like a lightweight awaiting a command for his seconds to leave, the other, three times his size, the build of a carnival wrestler with a slicked mop of dark, wavy hair, sat on a mound of grain sacks. The larger man took a newly lit, unfiltered cigarette from his mouth and passed it to me, smiling. The smaller fellow cracked open a bottle and handed it to me. He spoke first and in English.

'Do you know why you are here, Mr Miller?'

'You know my name?' I asked, anxiously.

'Of course!' said the large man. 'Henry Miller, Tropic of Cancer.'

The smaller man interjected, 'Le roi de la crasse'.

I knew what he meant; the king of smut.

'Please excuse him, he prefers the classics to the more...'

'Outrè contemporary pieces?' I offered.

'Exactly!' he grinned.

I turned to the smaller man. 'Not a fan?' I asked sarcastically. His hostile gaze remained fixed upon me, with a look suggesting that it would be unwise to take another swing.

I commended the larger man on his excellent English. 'Merci,' he replied. In French, obviously. 'Where did you pick it up?'

'Here and there,' answered the smaller man, sucking the life from his cigarette. The truck slowly came to a stop. 'Again Mr Miller. Do you know why you're here?'

'If it's to do with Militiz, I can assure you that it was nothing to do with me. I'm no killer.'

'Every man is a potential killer.'

'Not me. I'll take an oath on any book you care to offer, I found him like that. Dead.'

'Oh, we know,' said the larger man.

If they knew it wasn't me, did they...

'So, who killed him?' I asked before I had the chance to process what I'd meant to say. 'I'm not for a second implying that you did it,' I added, sounding exactly as if it was. 'It wasn't you, was it?' I asked as again my mouth independently took sole charge of my thought process. *Shut the hell up Henry!* The men tightly flanked me as the back of the truck opened to brilliant sunshine. They each took an arm and spoke.

'Are you hungry, Mr Miller?' asked the larger man.

The smaller man, gripping my arm tightly, spoke too.

'We need to talk about Le Corbeau'.

Chapter 5 - Gates of Steel

May woke with a jolt. The display on the clock beside her bed, underneath the worn-out snooze button, was flashing boldly. After taking a moment for her eyesight to adjust, May reached for her glasses, hurriedly pulled herself out of bed and shuffled through the lounge to the small kitchen. The clock on the microwave was also flashing. Power outage. In the bathroom, May opened the tall cupboard. Under a stack of multi coloured towels, May found her late father's wristwatch. The storm of the century might not be able to keep her awake but the quiet ticking of his timepiece always could. It was 6.30am. There was time, but not much. Opening the curtains to this greyest of Maine mornings merely confirmed that yesterday's inclement weather had not as yet abated and that short of a miracle break in the skies above, she'd be expected at The Columbus shortly. Even so, she turned her TV on, more out of habit rather than a desire for daybreak entertainment. May had few vices, but a quality set on which to watch reruns of Cheers and Columbo, she considered a necessary indulgence.

'And coming up, we're talking Pete Rose, Bruce Springsteen and is the President right to sanction South Africa?'

'Yes he is,' said May, turning down the sound on the cartoon channel she'd just switched to. For a moment, she was lost in the silent, animated mayhem.

'Jerry, hi. Is the diner opening today? Looks quite rough out there at the moment but ... it's your call, obviously. Call me back when you get this. Bye.'

May replaced the receiver and took a striped bowl from the cupboard. Filling it with brightly coloured cereal, she looked inside her fridge.

'Damn.'

Being out of state for the last few days meant that her supplies were at a minimum, something that rarely happened when she still had a roommate. Dana Gift was her name. A red headed girl from upstate in Brunswick. She'd worked as an au pair for the Senator and his family until that arrangement went predictably awry. A few years her senior, Dana in her heels was as tall as May but much more shapely. In an attempt to smooth over their 'misunderstanding', the Senator found Dana employment at the Auburn airport as an 'executive assistant' which meant she was an attendant on call for small, private commercial flights. On a short hop to Austin, she met a realtor and never came back. She called May to explain that when true love called, one had to go, no questions asked. Though she left behind a VCR and a copy of 'Funny Girl', Dana's explanation never sat well with May. The notion of 'true love' was one she considered absurd; though she'd watched enough Sam and Diane to hope for something similar, at her 'Cheers', the only retired 'sportsmen' she encountered were the middle-aged proprietor and a short order chef with defective eyesight.

One young fellow though had made a dent in her impenetrable barrier. His name was Dennis and he worked at Phillips Record Store on Main. A physically unremarkable sort, of medium height and build, Dennis had dark, wiry hair and a bit of an Elliot Gould hangdog look about him but he was quietly confident and well mannered. When May showed an interest in taking philosophy classes at the Town College, Dennis was very encouraging. They dated briefly before he took an offer to become assistant manager of Tower Records in Portland. On the occasions when she wasn't mid-air, Dana had a series of 'gentlemen callers' but May didn't mind being shunted out of the bedroom and onto the couch. Mostly she'd put on her Walkman and take a walk down by the river, listening to one of the seventeen mix tapes that Dennis had compiled for her; one for every human emotion, he said. Number Eight was her favourite. Dennis knew what she liked but now, as with Connie and Dana, her father and Elie, he was all gone. May stayed in Auburn and at times, she wondered why.

Dana said that once she'd settled in Austin, she'd send a cheque to cover her side of the bills but she never did. Last May heard, she was running a shoe shop in a mall in one of the Carolinas. Since then, their small but adequate first floor flat, above Mrs Krupa's 'Artyfacts' shop, at the junction of Court and High St, was her sole sanctuary from the glamour of McGee's Tavern and that gilded palace of sin that was The Columbus Diner. May had a propensity for the dramatic.

She returned to her bedroom, stood her pillows up against the headboard and sat back. On the ledge behind her bed was a shoebox. May opened it and took out a cassette. Mix Tape Number Four, it said. With her headphones on, that noisy storm could keep on blowing for all she cared. Picking at the bowl of milk-free cereal, May re-opened Elie's book.

I'll try Jerry again, she thought. Right after 'Gates of Steel' by Devo.

Chapter 6 - The Brothers Castagne

"*I was escorted into a dimly lit salôn and placed in a booth near the back, away from the windows. The restaurant was empty, which wouldn't be unusual given the time of day, but in any case, the shutters were pulled down and the door was locked behind us. My captors sat, the large man taking up almost the full side opposite with the smaller man next to me, seated on the edge of the booth, still sizing me up. Two men, presumably the driver and the smiter of Immaculate Boy, took the small table near the door.*

'Nice place,' I said, looking around, full of bravado.

'This?' said the larger man. 'We like it. Let me tell you a story, Mr Miller. For generations, our people like many who settled here were originally land workers, or farmers from the Dordogne, Auvergne and Occitanie regions but the harsh harvests of the 1840's and the petit bourgeois rebellion forced them out of business. With everything laid bare, our family, along with many of their compatriots, moved north to Paris. Settling in the Faubourg Saint-Antoine area, they managed over the course of a few years, to build a small business specialising in fresh fruit and vegetables. And the Paris of today is quite different from what they had to deal with; cholera, tuberculosis and the rest. Did you know that one in two infants born in the area would be dead by the end of the year?'

'I did not,' I replied.

'These were tough times but our family were honest, honorable and hard-working people and soon one stall became two, then five. Soon, there wasn't a single passageway that didn't have a stall belonging to us. When the Emperor chose Haussmann to modernise the city, he was told to spare no expense. And while our city is now the envy of the modern world, it came at a very human cost for many families and businesses, including ours. Licences issued by the city council meant that all works would be under their control and if a city clerk didn't like you, you didn't get the permit. Which is how our grandfather lost everything.'

'That's rough,' I said.

'Our father though, instilled in us the need to use the Emperor as an example. Who gave him the right to judge? God? No, he was as much of a criminal as the boy who steals the apple from the cart. Actually, he is worse. The boy steals because he is hungry and only takes what he needs. He is caught and is severely punished. The Emperor takes everything, faces no sanction as he operates above laws he himself presides over. Now, he, and his state, have you on your knees demanding you pay him respect.' The large man shook his head. 'They do not subscribe to the principles of fairness. Why would they? So, everything we lost, we took back. We are not greedy men, Mr Miller. There is work with us for anyone who wants to earn a crust and we are loyal to the last with those who stand with us. You are a learned man, yes?'

I gave a half-hearted nod.

'Was it not Lawrence who said that being alive constitutes an aristocracy which there is no getting beyond. He who is most alive, intrinsically, is king? Is that not so?'

The larger man leant back in his seat and smiled.

'We, Mr Miller, are the most alive. The state beneath the state. We are the true Emperors of Paris.'

I couldn't help but agree.

'What do you know about The Crow?' the small man interjected with a fierceness which suggested that the history lesson was over.

'I don't know what you're talking about,' I replied with more than a hint of honesty. I slid my hand into the deep pocket of my stolen police coat. The gun...where was the gun?

'Is this what you're looking for?' asked the larger man as he slapped the officer's revolver onto the table. For the first time, his light demeanour darkened and my fear that this ordeal may not be at its conclusion resurfaced. 'Don't worry,' said the smaller man, taking the weapon and dropping the contents into an empty ashtray. 'If we'd wanted you killed, we could've done it in your cell or at the Rue Monge,' he said matter-of-factly.

'We could've done it in the truck,' said the large man. 'We could have poisoned your cigarette.'

'Or my beer?' I offered, joining in.

'Exactement!'

The message was clear, if they could take a heavy revolver from my pocket without me noticing, they could've stopped all of this before we sat in our booth.

With a smile, the larger man said, 'We could've killed you at Rue Delambre?'

'And made it look like a struggle with Militz.'

'Did you kill Militz? Because if you did...' I said, 'I have no problem with it.'

'We want to know what you know about The Crow', asked the smaller man again.

'I've heard the name from friends but...'

'Which friends?' the larger man asked.

I was very reluctant to drop Joe Do Sappo into this mess so I adroitly changed the subject.

'I've not eaten since yesterday. Could I trouble you for some bread?'

'Of course. Where are my manners?' said the larger man, raising one bulbous digit. One of the men stationed at the door rose immediately and headed into the kitchen.

'My name is Benoit Castagne and this is my brother, Etienne.'

The smaller man gave a curt nod. He seemed nervy compared to his more serene sibling. I was on the verge of making a humorous comment on their lack of physical similarity but as I'd seen how well they'd deployed violence as a tactic, I thought it expedient to keep my counsel.

'Henry ... may I call you Henry?' asked Benoit.

'Sure,' I said, in no position to insist on formalities.

'Henry, you have no reason to fear us. Maybe you are in a great deal of danger at the moment but ... from us? No.' he said convincingly, shaking his head and his heavy finger in conjunction.

'We are your friends,' said Etienne Castagne, much less so. 'But make no mistake Mr Miller, a wrong move now may be your last.'

'I'm sure that you have a host of questions but right now, let us eat.' One of the Castagne goons reached over from behind the booth, startling me and started taking off my police coat. 'It's OK Henry,' said Benoit in a reassuring way. Did I trust him? Not particularly. Did I have a choice?

The waiter brought us a tray of food which I devoured almost as soon as the first plate hit the table. The Castange brothers sat in silence, Benoit picked at his dish as I tore through stuffed pigeon breast with sausage, a generous dollop of moutard and a hint of fennel. I recall every minute detail of that meal, from the white wine based jus which I mopped up with a couple of slices of newly baked bread, still warm, to the succulent freshly picked petit pois and Etienne Castagne's steely stare as he watched, with one hand in his coat, ever ready. If this was to be my final culinary experience on this plane, a condemned man's last supper as it were, then it should be as magnificent as this. I sat back and let rip a belch for the ages.

'There we go!' said Benoit as if his horse had just crossed the line first at Longchamp. The waiter brought a tray of Armagnac. And not the cheap stuff either. This was the most potent digestif I'd ever downed. If they are going to kill me, I thought, they are at least sending me off in style.

Etienne spoke.

'It is abundantly clear that you have no idea about The Crow.'

'That's what I was saying,' I poured another Armagnac.

Benoit pushed his glass towards mine. I gave him a decent measure. 'We need to ask a favour of you, Henry.'

'You name it. Do you want me to write something? A restaurant review, perhaps?' I suggested, frivolously. Etienne Castagne's face suggested that my offer wasn't what they had in mind. My heart sank a few leagues further.

'No,' said Benoit. 'We need you to leave Paris tonight.'

'Tonight? No, I can't...I have...'

I verbally staggered around looking for a reason, any reason to politely turn their request down. 'It's out of the question.'

'It's not. And you must,' replied Etienne, firmly.

'Why?' I asked.

'For two reasons. Firstly, the gendarmarie are looking for you in connection with the murder of Casper Militz.'

'I said that I had nothing to do with that.'

'Again, we know. You need to be as far from Paris as you can so that we can clear up this mess.'

'Where am I going?' I asked. 'Versailles? There is a park that I

know, about 20 km south of the city, south west of Melun that I am familiar with. I know people I could lay low with for a day or two and then...'

Benoit interrupted, 'You're going to New York.'

'What? I don't understand.'

'There is a train that leaves Gare De Lyon in just under an hour,' added Etienne. 'You will take that train to Marseille where you will be met by one of our trusted associates.' I asked who. 'It doesn't matter. He knows who you are. Once you disembark, he will take you to the port where a ship is bound for New York. The Athenia will depart at 11 o'clock.'

'You said there were two reasons.'

'The second reason is more complex. We don't need to go into the details at this point as we are in the middle of a delicate situation but we need you to deliver safely a package which has come into our possession.'

If you need a delivery boy, call Wells Fargo, I thought.

'What's the package and why me?' I asked, losing patience with the riddles.

The Castagne brothers looked at each other. Benoit's eyes widened but Etienne shrugged. Those gestures said more than they'd intended. Their level of trust in me was not as complete as they claimed. Etienne turned his back on me.

'The world is changing, Henry. We take for granted certain freedom. Movement, freedom to believe what you wish or not at all,' said Benoit, solemnly.

I nodded in broad agreement.

'And something you, Mr Miller should be particularly keen on retaining; the freedom to express some of one's more vulgar thoughts in print.'

You're damn right Etienne, I thought.

'You must realise that many, and not just our neighbours to the east, are readying themselves for another war. Do you believe in God, Mr Miller?'

'I'm not particularly religious,' I said.

'I do not look for God in religion any more than I look for meaning in art. No, Mr Miller, this is more a question of faith. Are you a believer?'

'I believe that I'd be considered more of a sinner.'

'Then you are the perfect man for this job,' replied Benoit. 'War is coming. For us, that is bad for business. The last conflict and the depression which followed had a huge impact on our country. There was hardly a family in France who did not feel the weight of that burden. But for certain people, certain groups, it's an opportunity not just to pick the carcass clean but to burn everything to the ground. We are simple men. As I said, we want little more than to keep our beak wet and if we can assist others, we will. As your own Mr Lincoln once said, 'We are not enemies, but friends. We must not be enemies. Though passion may have strained, it must not break our bonds of affection. The mystic chords of memory will swell when again touched, by the better angels of our nature.'"

I was about to remind them of Honest Abe's fate but I thought better of it.

'With all due respect, you need me to act as a go-between?'

'Mr Miller, please don't take offence at this but we wouldn't require your mediocre talents to referee a local squabble. Your myopic view of this is childishly naïve.'

'None taken,' I replied. 'So, what if Herr Hitler is a little less Chaplin and a little more Stalin? What's that got to do with the price of butter? Why is this package so important and why must I return to the employ of Western Union?'

'You enjoy living?' asked Etienne.

The blunt simplicity of that question staggered me. Of course I *do.* 'It sure beats the alternatives,' I replied. I know my flippancy irritated the lean Castagne brother but I didn't give a hoot. He then said something that stopped me, for want of a better word, dead.

'We know all about your excursion to La Santé but which of the alternatives to living did you favour?'

'Excuse me?' I asked as I considered the implications. From the limited time I'd spent with the Castagne Brothers, it was apparent how connected they were but was he returning my cockiness or was this something else?

Benoit spoke again, steering the conversation back to more familiar ground. 'Time is a factor, Henry. You must leave immediately.'

'What about my belongings? My papers, my writings?' I asked, not unreasonably. 'If I am to leave Paris immediately, I will need to speak with my friends. To tell them that I'm leaving.' I thought of Anaïs. She was rarely far from my thoughts.

'Out of the question,' replied Etienne, forcefully.

'But I have friends, people who will be looking for me,' I argued.

'Like whom? A couple of pipe smoking whores and a handful of salôn owners who'll only recall you as a wastrel who never paid his tab?'

I felt the anger rise in my face only to be met by the humiliating realisation that if I did lash out, my futile gesture would likely result in another unwanted physical beating. I scowled at him, with impotent contempt.

'Regardless, I still need to go to my apartment to collect my belongings, my papers, my work. I need to bathe and change.'

Etienne stood up and reached over behind the booth. He lifted up a worn, military kit bag and dropped it where he'd just been sitting. 'I hope you don't mind but we took the liberty of preparing this for you,' said Benoit.

I unzipped the bag and rifled through its contents. My clothes, scraps of writing, notebooks.

'And my personal effects?' I asked.

Benoit passed me a holdall. Brown leather, with a red and blue fastening strap. I depressed its brass catch and opened it to find my documents, an envelope and a small package, wrapped in cotton and bound by twine. I removed it from the holdall.

'This is not mine,' I said, passing it over the table to Benoit. He pushed it back towards me.

'As we mentioned earlier Henry, we need your assistance in a certain matter,' he said.

I felt my way around the item, flat but ridged and the width of both of my palms, placed side by side.

'What is it?' I enquired.

'This is what you must deliver,' he replied. 'It is of the utmost importance that you do not let it out of your sight from the moment you leave here today until you safely deposit it with our associate in New York. You go to sleep? It's under your pillow. You take a piss? Keep one hand free. Do I make myself clear?'

'Crystal,' I replied, still curious.

'We have made provision for your safe travel as well as some remuneration for any unforeseen expenses you may accrue.'

I opened the envelope. There was at least one thousand dollars inside.

'We have mutual friends, and they have assured us that you are precisely the man that we need for this job'.

It must have been Anaïs, I thought. But why? Whatever her opinion of me, Etienne doesn't appear convinced. I need to speak with her, to clarify. Of all people, she would understand. Above everything, she would be truthful.

'Time is a factor, so collect your things,' said Benoit.

Swiftly sinking the remainder of my third glass of Armagnac, I reminded the Castagne brothers of my current personal hygiene issue. 'Excuse me, but given that I smell like a pickled mountain *goat, I am in no condition to spend the afternoon cooped up on a train, in close proximity to an assemblage of polite, unwitting passengers. I would be thrown off before we got to Dijon.' My desire for disinfection brought the ever-temperate Etienne to the boil once again.*

'You can wash in Marseille harbour with the other drunks, for all I care. Get up.' Etienne forcibly lifted me from my seat.

'Please!' I petitioned Benoit, still seated. Consulting his watch, he gestured to Etienne to unhand me.

'We have a little time, Henry.'

I thanked him. He got up and led me down a narrow corridor with a door at the end. 'This is where our staff change,' he said.

I opened the door and turned on the light. Chef's whites and a collection of discarded aprons were in one corner beside a small square table and two chairs. Upon the table was an ashtray which hadn't been emptied for days.

'You can wash in there,' said Benoit pointing to an anti chamber. ' It isn't The George V but you will be able to clean yourself and change.' I offered my hand to Benoit. In the midst of this subterfuge and chaos, his small gesture of kindness affected me. He smiled and shook my hand. 'But be quick. Time is against us.'

I filled the sink with steaming hot water and stripped naked. Although the conditions weren't ideal, it was infinitely preferable to spending another moment in my prison soiled apparel. At least on the train, I will be clean and safe, able to sleep and maybe dine. Even though my mind was as full as my belly, my thoughts turned towards my next meal. I'm sure that the Brothers Castagne wouldn't begrudge me a few dollars on some fine chow and perhaps a bottle of wine from the dining car during my passage.

I discarded the thin cotton dish towel that I'd been using as a flannel and picked up a handful of thicker ones to dry my now clean frame. I opened the large kitbag and removed a fresh shirt, a pullover, a jacket and a pair of trousers. Oh and clean undergarments. One never knows who one might meet on a train, I thought as I hurriedly dressed. Then I saw it. Affixed to my right, a few feet from the door, a black wall-mounted telephone. I looked at my watch. Benoit, or worse, Etienne, would be back to fetch me at any moment. But Anaïs...she will be concerned, unable to concentrate until I let her know that I am safe. Throwing caution to the wind, I removed the ear piece from the receiver. No tone. I clicked on it again and again. Still nothing. Of course, I realised. It was a pay phone, the blight of the modern café. No one wanted to talk in person anymore, but I digress. Needing a coin, I searched my pockets. For the first time since I arrived in Paris, I was genuinely flush but at this moment, I'd willingly exchange one of these crisp $20 notes for a 20c piece. My old jacket. There were usually a few coins and buttons in the pockets. I grabbed the jacket from under the heavy coat on the chair and as I did, I heard the sweetest sound; that of a small coin hitting the ceramic floor tile and spinning under the table. I got down on my knees and searched. The lack of light made finding it an issue but with the use of a match from the book that I'd taken from the table earlier, I found it.

As the door was closed but not locked, I put my ear to it, listening carefully for impending intruders. I could hear voices but thankfully, they were distant. At this time, only the wealthy or the prominent had a telephone in their home. My friend and patron, Purcell Griffin didn't feel the need for one but Hugo and Anaïs did. I inserted the 20c piece and called the only telephone number that, until this moment, I'd memorised. 52042.

In the years that followed, I've come to realise that there are few sounds in life more desperate and aching than that of the never ending telephonic loop. The flower which blooms at the sound of hello, finds its stem snapping as the rings travel past the fourth, the fifth...

At any moment, the door will open and some strong armed gallic goon will start me on my long journey from the Gare De Lyon *to a place which increasingly does not feel like home. I returned the earpiece to the receiver, bereft. At that moment, I realised that Anaïs' number wasn't the only one I knew. 46773...or was it 774? I tried the latter but the number was dead. And I might be too if I didn't get a move on. I dialled the former and to my relief and surprise, the phone rang. I leant over to the door to check on potential incomings when the call was answered with a perky...*

'Bonjour. Café Bérangère!'

'Bonjour! Puis-je parler avec Monsieur Joe Do Sappo, s'il vous plaît!'

'Qui?' the voice asked.

'Joe Do Sappo, le grand Canadien?'

'Joe Do Canadien?' asked the voice again. I could feel my hackles rise. The last remaining sands of the hourglass dropped onto the pile.

'Rapide Lisette! S'il vous plaît!' I urged.

The voice recognised mine.

'Henry Miller, is that you? You have some nerve calling here. I waited one, no two hours for you at the Gaumont. And it rained. It was humiliating. I never want to see you again!'

I liked Lisette, I really did. She would have made a fine third wife, if I was that way inclined. Petite but hardy with a cute turned up nose, pert breasts and a smile that... I'm rambling again. I could not recall this broken appointment with her but as my social diary at this time was as liquid as my lunches, there may have been some credence to her claim.

'Lisette!' I pleaded. 'I must speak with Joe. It is a matter of some urgency. I implore you sweet Lisette. Fetch him now.'

'Why should I do anything you ask?'

'I'll make it up to you when I return.'

'Where are you going?'

I covered the receiver and let out a silent scream of frustration.

'Mon chere, things have been a little strange over the last few days. Events have overtaken me in a way that I could not have predicted. I need to leave town today or a terrible injustice will befall me.'

'Henry,' she said, 'I just don't believe you anymore'. Delivered with an honesty that cut me like a hundred Hank Armstrong jabs but when your stock-in-trade is the moulding of a fable, it can be difficult, even for me, to know where the truth ends and the fabrication begins.

'Lisette, I was going to surprise you but here goes. If I don't speak with Joe immediately, I will miss my connection and if I miss my connection, I will lose the chance to speak with the publisher who was going to give me the advance which will enable me to rent a cottage on the Cote D'Azur where we shall spend the winter months together, tightly braided until spring.'

I could hear her sigh down the wire and for a moment, I allowed myself to rest on the soft bed of the warm lie I'd just spun.

'Okay,' she said and left me hanging. Maybe there was something in domesticity. For a man approaching fifty, having no need to chase one's tail, with a sweet angel at home, a loyal and faithful presence to return to, someone to piece you together when you're being torn into pieces by patrons, lovers… and critics. Maybe one lover, just to make sure that one didn't go as stale as three day old bread. I may need a divorce first…

'Henry?' boomed a voice down the line.

'Joey!'

'Where are you? I've been worried about you.'

'Really?'

'Word round here says that you were involved with The Crow and things got a little ugly.'

'That would be an understatement.'

'Henry, did you kill the American?'

'Sweet Mercy, Joe! How long have you known me?' I replied in anger.

'Long enough to know that you're as dangerous as a housecat.'

'Exactly. It's nonsensical.'

'You are aware though, that people are looking for you. At your flat, in the cafés and salôns. Word is spreading. You are a wanted man.'

'I know and that's why I need you to contact Anaïs and tell her that I had nothing to do with that murder. I'll explain it all when it blows over.'

'I've got a friend over in Nanterre who owes me a favour. Maybe you could lay low there until...'

'I'm leaving Paris tonight. This afternoon. Actually, immediately.'

'What? Where?'

'I don't have much time Joe, my train leaves soon. They're coming for me. Stay well my friend.'

I'd just put the phone down on the receiver when the door swung open and that sly bastard Etienne Castagne stood in front of me, flanked by his goons. I don't know what the word for 'henchmen' is in French but they were tres intimidant.

'Just need to straighten myself up,' I said.

'You're fine as you are,' he replied, clutching me by the shoulder. His men took me and my bag back through the Café, to the front door.

Benoit approached, towering over me like a dormant volcano. 'Here...' he said, handing me the parcel. His large, olive skinned paws enveloping both the package and my hands. He held tightly on to both.

'Take very good care of this, Henry. Be our 'better angel.' Many lives depend upon it.'

The seriousness of his demeanour - and the overall situation - warranted no further words. I was getting a free pass out of a jam, one not of my making but a perilous predicament all the same. I shook his hand and following a cursory, final look around Paris, they hustled me into a pristine car and so began my journey back to New York City.'

Chapter 7 - Tweed

'We arrived at the Gare De Lyon with less than ten minutes until departure. Safer to have less time, commented Etienne who sat closer than was comfortable, all the way from the café to the station. I knew he didn't trust me, which was reasonable as I didn't exactly trust me either.

'Go to the Kiosk by Platform Six and ask for yesterday's Tages-Anzeiger.'

'Tages what?' I asked

'It's a Swiss newspaper.'

'Why on earth would I want a Swiss newspaper? From yesterday?' I asked, knowing the answer but wishing to further irritate the lesser Castagne. He sighed with a growl.

'You ask too many questions,' he said.

'Do I?' I goaded.

'In case it's escaped your attention, we are in France. Everyone asks for French newspapers.'

'Why not an English one? Or the New York Times? Yes, that would keep me out of trouble for an hour or two,' I said, mocking him, unwisely. I realised I'd pushed him too far when he grabbed my lapel and snarled menacingly in my face at a distance so close, I could almost taste which brand of toothpaste he didn't use.

'No one asks for a Swiss newspaper,' he pointed out.

I was going to say, 'Not even the Swiss?' but thought better of it.

'Inside, you will find fresh papers, a ticket for a first class compartment and a key for a room at the Hotel Dacroix, situated on La Canebiere. When you arrive in Marseille, you must go immediately to the Hotel and await confirmation. Once everything has been cleared, you will be taken to the port at dusk where you will board the boat back to New York City. Do not engage with anyone in the station nor fraternise with the other passengers. If you are stopped by the Gendarme or encounter any unforeseen peril, we have placed an associate on board who will come to your aid.'

Etienne opened the door of the car. For the first time, his look was one, not of disdain but of concern. He spoke softly.

'We are relying on you. Please follow your instructions and do not draw unwanted attention to yourself.' He took my hand. Though not in the same ballpark as his hulking brother, his grip was no less firm. 'Take this'.

Into my palm, he pressed a one Franc coin.

'For luck?' I asked.

'For the newspaper,' he replied.

I laughed for the first time in days.

'Bon voyage, Henry,' he said with convincing sincerity. I gave him a nod and a tip of the hat that suggested that I had this.

I got out of the car, slung my bag over my shoulder, turned up my collar against the rain and crossed the street, joining the assemblage headed towards the station. It was still mid afternoon so the area wasn't as congested as it would be in a few hours. I could've blended in far easier at five than at three, for instance but my flight factor was at play. The current downturn in the conditions was helping though. I removed my rain speckled glasses and pulled the brim of my hat down over my eyes. Every moment I remained in the city increased the chances of me being apprehended by the police, or worse still, *The Crow*. I still had no idea who or what the hell The Crow was but if it spooked people like Joe Do Sappo and forced the Castagnes into evasive action, that was sufficient for me to consider my options elsewhere.

I held the heavy station door open for a young family to pass through which gave me time to scope the area into which I was heading. A couple of station workers, tourists and ladies with small dogs, heading my way. To my left, the train listings. The clock showed four minutes to three. My damaged watch agreed. There wasn't much time. The kiosk by Platform Six had a number of people standing around it. A few children looking at the colorful magazines, parents in conversation. Behind the counter, an elderly man was arranging books into piles.

I greeted him but he either didn't hear me. Or chose not.

'Bonjour Monsieur!' I said, loudly.

He turned and looked at me over his pince-nez.

'Bonjour.'

'Tages-Anzeiger?' I asked.

He replied in English. 'Today's?'

I replied to him in English.

'No. Yesterday's.'

He nodded and reached under the counter. Handing over a bulky newspaper, bound with a thick rubber band.

'Anything else, Monsieur?' he asked, looking up at the station clock.

'Ten packs of Gitanes.'

'Monsieur?'

'No, you're right. Make it twelve.' If I was going from the station in Marseille, directly to the hotel and then on to the boat, I wanted to make sure that I had the basics for the voyage. I handed the elderly kiosk attendant a crisp 20F note and told him to keep the change. Stuffing the cigarettes into my bag, I stepped back and searched the *board for Track Nine. One minute. I hot-footed it to the platform, weaving in and out of plodding Parisiennes, waving my newspaper at the ticket inspector who stood guard at the gate. He urged me on. The whistle blew and as the flag was being waved, I arrived at the train. A portly fellow had almost pulled his door shut before spying me and reopening it before it caught the lock mechanism. Bonne chance en effet!*

'Rapide, Monsieur!' roared the station guard, almost shoving me through the door of the last carriage. He gave out two short blasts of his whistle and the train pulled out.

'Merci beaucoup,' I said, leaning against the glass panel of the door, to catch my breath.

I removed the binding from the newspaper and retrieved my ticket. I'd look over my documents later, maybe from the comfort of the dining car. Coach C, compartment 12 was where I was heading, down the long, narrow corridors filled with children playing and travellers clinging on to their last glimpses of Paris.

As the train passed through Bercy and on to Vincennes, the rich baritone of the train commandant proclaimed, 'Attention, mesdames et messieurs, la voiture-restaurant est maintenant ouverte.' The light dimmed and the more famished passengers started drifting from passageways. I took a moment to make a mental snapshot of those familiar buildings, not just of the avenues and boulevards, but the aesthetic blight of those cold factories in the near distance, belching smoke from their hellish furnaces and the inky, arterial tracks from the yards which ran alongside us. I wondered not just when but if we'd ever be entwined again.

The allocated compartment was perfectly adequate. Clean and private. With any luck, I'd have it to myself for the entire journey. Opening the newspaper fully on the seat opposite, I found a flat leather purse which contained my new (false) documents. My name was given as Harry Valentine, which was rather insightful. Surely the Castagne's did not know that my given name was Henry Valentine Miller? Maybe they did... anyway, the hastily arranged photograph in the back of their truck didn't do me any favours but that was a minor quibble. The parcel now safe, I tucked the documents into my jacket and placed the hotel key deep in my trouser pocket. I lifted the bag onto the rack above my head and wearily, pulled my hat over my face with a chasmal yawn. A quick forty winks would see me right. That twilight time between the waking world and the slumberous is normally my most fertile ground, an allotment on which I can nurture my most lucid, honest and on occasion, creatively profound seeds; but whether it was this curious situation, a sense of lingering unease or just sheer fatigue, my mind raced like Konrad Mortlock's 3L Delahaye.

****

I'd reached Wink #12 before my solace was interrupted by an unwanted agent. Or agents, to be more precise. I peered through the gap between my hat and my sleep starved eyes and saw three people at the door of a compartment I'd hoped would be mine alone. Subtle, they were not. The dominant male of the group, dressed in a very refined brown three piece with thinning hair over a balloon shaped head, pomade slicked beyond natural and sporting a 'Ronald Colman' moustache, stood in the doorway, blocking his party's access to my sacred space. Clutching a handful of ticket stubs, he spoke in an accent that, while not native to me, still sounded familiar. Growing up in Brooklyn, many of my non-German neighbours were from the eastern reaches of the Danube. Not Polish, possibly Hungarian was my initial thought as my ears, disobeying the instinct for rest, trawled the frequencies for clues.

I turned to the side, facing the window, pretending to be asleep. I grunted my disapproval at their presence, hoping that they'd take the hint and find alternative accommodation. Undaunted, they crashed into my compartment, and my life for the near future. As they put their bags on the racks beside mine, the train shunted across a set of points, causing the carriage to jerk violently. This *motion helped bring the one female of the pack down on top of me, finally putting paid to any hope of relaxation.*

'Pardon!' she exclaimed while using my prone body to steady herself. The mortified madame was helped off me by the 'Oily Ronald Colman' and their much younger companion, a mediocre looking lad in his early 20's with a short, military approved haircut, but not before she had a good feel around. Not my type normally, I thought but it's already been a very unusual few days. Let's ride the wave again.

'Je suis très désolé, monsieur!' offered Oily Ronald who, for some reason, also was very handsy.

'C'est bien,' I responded, firmly swatting away their unnecessary attention. 'It's fine.'

'Ah!' exclaimed Oily Ronald. 'English?' he asked, his eyes widening.

'No, I'm American.'

'Clark Gable! Errol Flynn!' he said, waving an imaginary sword as if possessed by the spirit of Captain Blood himself. His companions smiled on, but as this was way beyond where I was willing to take this au courant exchange, I didn't feel the need to prolong it by pointing out that the latter was Tasmanian, not American.

Oily Ronald took the seat by the door with his glamorous but hefty companion to his side, opposite me. The younger chap sat to my left, scratching and fidgeting. Oily Ronald leant forward and stared at me with, what your Clifford might have described as a 'shit eating grin', willing me to converse. I gave a polite nod and pulled down the brim of my hat. That should have been that but...

'Ocksi! Maradj veszteg!' said the ringleader, confirming my suspicions. Definitely Hungarian. With a bit of Austro-German thrown in.

The knees of the fidget knocked into mine, more than once. I let go a deeper growl of disapproval but after an all too brief silence, the twitching and bumping started again. I pointed my hat back up, which brought the party's conversation to an abrupt halt. The pair opposite 'ate shit' again.

'I am sorry,' said Oily Ronald, in halting English, unapologetically beaming for all his worth. 'We are not meaning to be disturbing your time.'

'It's fine,' I said, hoping again that this would be the end of the matter.

'Tibor Babits,' he said, offering his hand. Reluctantly, I shook it. His grip was strong. And despite his princely attire, the dry callouses showed that he'd clearly spent years working with his hands.

'And my wife, Eisabet.'

She offered up her gloved hand in a way that she expected it kissed. I raised my hat and shook her fingers. She tightened her thumb around my hand, gripping me longer than was comfortable.

'And this is our Ocksi,' he said, gesturing towards the fidget who bore not even the remotest resemblance to the pair. 'Ocksi,' he said, superfluously.

Tibor, Eisabet and Ocksi. Three Hungarian stooges who were so conspicuously suspicious that I couldn't help but chuckle to myself. Was this a test?

'Are you going to Marseille?' asked Oily Ronald, or Tibor as he professed to be.

'With any luck,' I replied.

'I hear that it's wonderful at this time of year, yes?'

'I've never been so I wouldn't know,' I replied, coldly.

'The carnations…will be almost blue,' he said, oddly as if he wanted to elicit a password in response, which I realised I didn't have.

The Castagne's did say that one of their representatives would show themselves if I was in imminent danger. Was I in trouble already? Perhaps Tibor my contact? In any case, his random statement firmly shook the complacency from me.

'Yes...carnations,' I muttered. 'So, what takes you to the south?'

Tibor looked at Ocksi and his 'wife' then at me.

'We are cruising.'

'That's good,' I said, turning the tables on them. 'To where?'

I'd started to suspect that this was some form of crude set up as soon as this disparate party entered my compartment. OK, I was hemmed in but I reassured myself that I'd been in tighter spots in the last 48 hours and still managed to wriggle free. They weren't police. If they were, they'd have arrested me as soon as they saw me. They could be testing me on behalf of the Castagne's. That seemed needless but I needed to wring out every possible clue before I worked out how the hell I was going to extricate myself from this latest peril.

'Eh...' Tibor hesitated. Ocksi interjected.

'We're travelling from Marseille to Sainte Maxime, a few days in Nice then on to San Remo and Genova,' he said in almost flawless English.

'Business or pleasure?' I asked, continuing my role as inquisitor.

'A bit of both,' said the boy.

'What's your line of work?'

'All of these questions!' said Tibor, steering the conversation back in a direction he was more comfortable with.

'Ink,' volunteered Ocksi. 'We manufacture ink'.

Solid ground for me, I thought, so I pressed him a little further.

'Absolutely fascinating...Ocksi, isn't it?'

Something from my childhood sprung to mind. Hungarians referred to one another as Ocksi. It meant pal, or buddy.

'And you are, Mr...?' turning it back to me.

'Valentine,' I replied.

'Mr Valentine!' exclaimed Tibor. 'Please you must join us.' He removed a hip flask from his jacket. Just before he took a swig, he said something I didn't understand before offering it to me. Nice try, I thought but if I fell for that again, I'd be the clown.

'Thanks but no,' I said.

'But Mr Valentine, you must! Today is the feast day of St. Gabor the Uneven. He fought a legendary battle against the terrible Wolf of Pécs. Some say that the creature was the reincarnated soul of Mehmet the Conqueror, others say it was the devil himself. The beast followed the blessed Gabor for a week before trapping him in the woods by the shores of Lake Molmvölgy. A hellish battle raged on for two days and though exhausted, the heroic Gabor triumphed. He lost a leg but the wolf lost two! So you see, we must toast his holy name.'

'Then, I'll raise my hat to him,' I said.

Tibor could see that I wasn't for budging. 'I am, though, very interested in your ink,' I lied, though I was interested to find out if the little I knew could trump these 'experts'.

'Mr Valentine, we wouldn't want to disappoint a man of such culture with our boring interests'.

Try me, I thought.

'If you'd be so kind, Ocksi, I'd love to hear all about it, the compounds you use, the whole debate over US Standard ink versus the German Urkundentinte formula. Which do you prefer?'

Ocski looked at Tibor, valiantly holding onto his idiotic gawp.

'An ink enthusiast? What are the odds?' said Ocksi

Yeah, what are the odds, Buddy. Had I pushed too far? My smart ass overreach may have dragged me back into another avoidable situation.

'Forgive me,' I said, backing down. 'You good people are on vacation and I'm sure that the minutiae of your inner workings must be the furthest from your mind.'

'No, it's fine. I'm just surprised to happen across a fellow inkist. And yes, we use an Iron Gall mix at our factory in Debrecen though we do cater for other tastes. For instance, without becoming too *technical, our German customers prefer 27g of tannic acid per litre with an iron content of around 4 to 5g while those further north in Denmark, Norway and Sweden are comfortable with a degree of sediment which gives the colour a more bluish hue once it has settled. As for transportation…' He sighed. 'That's a completely different matter.'*

He clearly knew more than I did. My mouth became dry and beads of sweat ran down the back of my shirt.

'Are you perchance, a writer?' Ocksi asked.

'Me? A writer?' I laughed at the thought, probably too loudly. Thinking quickly, I said, 'No, I'm a tailor,' finally following in my father's footsteps. My fellow travellers looked at my workaday duds, unconvinced. Time to put into practice what I'd learned at old Heinrich's feet.

'Don't let appearances deceive you. This is a two-piece suit, slacks pleated, 2 inch cuffs, made by Holmes of London, practical and perfectly comfortable for touring.'

Five out of ten for effort, minus a point for the blatantly obvious literary reference. Understandably, they're not buying. I turn my attention to Tibor.

'Now what do we have here?' I said, reaching over towards Bibits Sr. 'May I?' I felt the lapel of his brown jacket. Tweed, for certain. But Harris or Donegal, I ask. I shush him before he can answer. Clutching at the front of the jacket, I open it slightly, primarily to check for weaponry. Buying a bit of time, I give his sleeves a good hard tug and ask him to turn around so that I can inspect his collar. We both stand. A minute strap of leather flashing under his waistcoat suggests to me that he may be concealing a holster above his shirt.

I return to my seat, convinced on both counts.

'Tweed three-piece, woven and dyed on Harris, finished on the Isle of Lewis.'

'Remarkable!' exclaimed Tibor.

'Quite,' added Oscski. 'And tailored by?'

'One of two shops, both in Edinburgh. Herbert Ross on George Street or...'

I paused for effect.

'James Macintosh and Sons on Rose Street.'

A stunned Tibor applauded heartily.

'How could you possibly know that?' asked Ocksi, suspiciously.

'What can I say but, I know my tweed,' I replied, failing to add that while I do have some basic knowledge in this field, I caught a glimpse of the tailor's label while doing my robust material checks.

'What about Ocksi's suit?' asked Tibor, excitedly.

I looked for a second then I picked up the Tages-Anzeiger.

'That's easy,' I said.

'Double breasted 2-piece, Glenurquhart plaid, also Scottish in construction. This one was made by Simpson of Piccadilly and fitted in Paris, yesterday. No, this morning. I have one just like it.'

Tibor laughed like a drain and passed Ocksi the hipflask.

'You do know your tweed,' he said, taking a cigarette case from his pocket. He opened it. It was empty.

'And look at that! Now I'm out of whisky and cigarettes,' he said to his wife. 'I told you we should have picked some up at the kiosk.'

Interesting that he should mention the kiosk, I thought.

'Shall we take a trip to the dining car to...replenish the stock?'

Much as the prospect of some soft food and hard liquor appealed, I was sure that I wasn't being let off the hook while so much was still at stake.

'Thanks but I'm good,' I said, making my play.

Ocksi immediately stood up, straightening his creases and buttoning up his jacket. Eisabet yawned. She said something to her husband in Hungarian which I couldn't comprehend but she clearly wasn't for moving. And if she was staying here, with all I had to protect, *then so was I. He looked at me as she was talking, still smiling. This was either part of his grand scheme or he was legitimately suffering from some form of medical ailment. Chronic cretinism, perhaps. I don't know.*

Ocski left and Tibor followed suit, stopping only to say 'Have fun' with that stupid expression, one that I still recall decades later, all over his bulbous face.

Then there were two. Eisabet finally removed her coat revealing her thick set but voluptuous figure. She smiled at me and I smiled back. For someone as young and as desirable as Xena to be attracted to a middle-aged man with my supporting actor looks was welcome but strange. Sure, I was no Ronald Colman but in fairness, neither was her betrothed. Eisabet was precisely the kind of woman I'd expect to come on to me but as I had a thousand bucks and some sort of priceless artefact on my person, not to mention the proximity of her tooled up husband, I thought it best not to engage in any japery at this stage. And anyway, a grand of the folding stuff would get me any number of clean whores of a decent vintage in Marseille.

But Eisabet kept smiling. Not the imbecilic beam of her husband. A definite 'come on' smile. She spent the next few minutes rearranging her personal effects and her clothing in an attempt to ensnare me. Nothing doing, I maintained. Even her tiny hat, which was held on by the longest pin I'd ever seen, was removed.

As I only had mild interest in Swiss German business news and the one name I recognised, that of Friedrich Glauser, was in an article which made no sense to me, I admitted defeat in my attempts to read the Tages-Anzeiger. I folded it up and placed it on the table. My attention needed to be diverted into something constructive. My notebook, which was in my bag in the rack above her head, was going to prove a formidable challenge. Quick as you can, Henry, I thought. I stood in front of Madame Tibor as we approached one of the several tunnels the train had to pass through in order to reach the town of Lyon. Entering the tunnel, the compartment went completely dark. At the same time as I grabbed my bag, she grabbed mine. All of it. I pulled back but this game broad held tight.

I can't recall which sound I emitted at this stage, probably a howl for help but nothing was forthcoming. I looked towards the door as the train ventured back into the light. She had undone at least two of my buttons before I managed to force myself backwards, landing on my seat with a bounce.

In an instant, she was beside me, lapping at the side of my face, trying to get her meaty hands into my trousers. Her stockinged legs were like shanks of ham, tightly strung with diamonds of flesh squeezing out of every bind and her chosen scent, Eau de Dead Orchid, was frankly, off-putting. She was all over me like an insanely frisky hound, but gentle Elie, man will be man. I confess that I couldn't help but become aroused. Firstly, by close intimate friction and secondly, with the imminent and probable danger of being caught. If Tibor returned to the compartment right now, he'd either pistol whip me or his bulbous head would pop like a child's balloon. Either way, this couldn't end well. Madame Tibor hitched up her skirt and straddled me, wrenching out the head of my member from its cotton bondage.

She brought her entire weight down upon me and let out a primal moan. A couple of strong thrusts and I was spent. She kept going, determined to draw every last piece of me, like the mephitic Magyar succubus she was.

When her breathing slowed to the rate of mine, she disembarked and straightened herself out. She took her seat again, opposite me, beside the door. If Tibor and Ocski returned now, they'd not suspect a thing. Apart from the pool of post-coital drool which I'd just noticed was deposited on my lap.

'Damn,' I said, trying to mop up the evidence before Eisabet's party arrived back, stocked with booze and cigarettes.

Eisabet leant over to me, handkerchief in hand in an attempt to assist the evidence removal. I batted her away. That was how we got into this mess in the first place.

She returned to her previous position and opened her purse. She took out a vanity mirror and reapplied her ruby red lipstick. Looking at me, it was clear that she'd left a trace of the lipstick on the side of my face. She turned her vanity towards me and it looked as if I'd been mauled by a panther. I instinctively reached out to rub it off but as my hands weren't exactly pristine, I just made matters worse. 'I'll take that handkerchief now,' I said.

There was a knock on the compartment door.

'Billets, s'il vous plaît!'

As the conductor entered the compartment, I quickly grabbed one of the complimentary blankets and placed it over my soiled groin. I handed him my ticket and he scribbled something on it before handing it back to me.

'Madame? S'il vous plaît?'

She stood up and reached into the attaché case beside mine. Taking the tickets, she turned and gave them to the conductor who, upon inspecting them, hit her with a lightning-fast right to the jaw, knocking her out cold. I instinctively jumped to my feet only to be met by the long, thin barrel of a Luger, pointed straight at my head, stopping me in my tracks.

'Sit down Mr Miller,' said the assailant in perfect English. I did as I was told, still in shock at the speed of the brutal attack. Eisabet was sprawled on the seat opposite, completely motionless, her slack jaw open. A stream of blood mixing with the lipstick, created a violent tributary in the corner of her mouth. The hollow cheeked conductor sat her up and turned her floppy head to lean against the outer window.

I thought about making a run for the door but I couldn't move. Fear had once again paralysed me.

'Play dead,' he said.

'Excuse me?' The conductor removed his hat and gripping tightly to my lapels, pulled me close.

'If you want to survive this, I need you to keep perfectly still,' he said, his flat, boxer's nose pressed against mine.

'What's happening? And who are you?' I asked.

'Not important right now, Mr Miller. Just tell me that the package is safe.'

He was Castagne's man. Thank heavens! I immediately nodded in relief.

'Good,' he said, peering out of the doorway.

'The other two are in the dining car, they should be back soon,' I said.

'Then we don't have much time,' he replied, tightly screwing a muffler onto his weapon.

'Surely not...you don't have to kill them?' I spluttered, naively.

'Would you rather it was you?' he asked.

The answer, though unpleasant, was obvious.

'Maybe we can just knock them out, keep them bound up until we get to Marseille?'

'I'll be able to keep a lid on this until Lyon, possibly Avignon at best but we are going to have to reroute.'

'What about my passage to New York? Benoit and Etienne arranged for me to be onboard the Athenia at eleven.'

'Don't worry, you'll make it,' he said cocking the gun, 'I'll make sure of it'.

I could hear Tibor's irritating voice approach our compartment. For a second, I felt genuinely sorry for him. Sure, he was planning to kill me, steal the money and the Castagne's precious package but I'd only taken an instant dislike to him based on the shape of his head. And, in his final role, I had just made him a cuckold, though I'm certain that Madame Eisabet has visited the rodeo on previous occasions. The man I described, accurately though unfairly, as Oily Ronald was blissfully ignorant of this heavy-lidded ticket checker and his draconian methodology.

'Leave this to me and don't say a word,' said the conductor with a seriousness that brooked no argument.

The compartment door opened and in walked Tibor.

'Cigarettes for everyone!' he said as Ocksi followed him into the compartment. The conductor had picked up my newspaper and had started fanning the still unconscious Eisabet. I squeezed down into the corner of my seat, close to the window.

'What has happened?' asked a concerned Tibor.

'Your wife felt light-headed and collapsed. We helped her back to her seat but she is quite unresponsive. Perhaps your voice can revive her,' said the conductor.

Tibor gently tapped his wife's cheek, imploring her to awaken. An anxious Ocksi looked on.

'She has been suffering from headaches recently,' he said. 'That's one of the reasons we were in Paris.'

Tibor looked at his hands and turned to me, slowly. On his fingers, there was blood. His wife's blood. Confusion took over.

'What did you do?'

Lying for all I was worth, I put my hands up and shook my head. That's when the first shot hit him. Right into the temple. A spray of Tibor's blood splattered onto the window. His head thumped against the arm rest with an even more nauseating crack.

There was a yelp of alarm. It may have been Ocksi but it could've been from me. As chaos engulfed us, I couldn't tell. I was now party to an uncomfortable level of brutality and I reacted badly. I turned to Ocksi who looked at me, wide mouthed and frozen in shock. The conductor grabbed his tie, pulled him in and fired two shots into his chest. The flash from the close range discharge burned into his beautiful, brand new suit. The conductor dropped him back onto the seat beside me as the last gasps of life spurted from him. Then, pulling the sleeve of his heavy coat over his hand, he patted out the small flame on Ocksi's chest. A deep circle of blood spread from the charred caverns in the fabric, turning his latterly lithe torso into a terrible burgundy canvas.

I looked on in horror as instantaneous, violent death surrounded me.

'A little help please?' asked the conductor sarcastically, bent over the body of Tibor.

I got down on my knees and lifted his head; now, if anything, even more absurdly bloated. The trauma from the gunshot must have severed some of his interocular wiring as his eyes were looking in unnaturally different directions. I hadn't noticed their colour before. They were a beautiful shade of pale green. The things one remembers...

We hoisted Tibor on to my seat, opposite his wife, and leant each of them against the window. The conductor took another blanket from the rack above and fashioned a makeshift pillow for the lifeless husband, wrapping his head in such a manner that it looked as if he was in a temporary slumber rather than an eternal one. Moving on to the stifled Ocksi, the blood which he'd vomited up from his wounds was now dripping from his mouth.

'Another blanket,' barked the conductor. 'The darker one'. I did as he ordered. Once Ocski's mouth had been wiped, the conductor packed the crevice in his chest with the lighter blanket before covering him, loosely with the darker one.

'We need to make this compartment look as if nothing untoward has happened. Three sleeping travellers, minding their own business. That will buy us enough time to make our escape,' he said, checking his watch.

Pointing the Luger directly at my head, he said, 'We have about 15 minutes before we get to Lyon, get your belongings. Nothing left in this carriage should show that we were ever here.'

He spun the gun around and handed it to me. 'In case you have a

91

visitor before I get back.'

Very reassuring. I'd seen enough death over the last few days to suspect that this instrument may be more of a hindrance than a help.

Once I'd wiped the remaining flecks of blood from the carriage window - the short, dark curtains did help - I removed my bags from the rack, placing them on the seat. The envelope with the expense money was still tucked into the back of my waistband. I pulled up my jumper and undid the lower buttons of my shirt. And there it was, pressed tightly against my stomach; the Castagne's treasured package. At this point in proceedings, I was uncertain as to whether I was being pursued for the murder of Casper Militiz, for breaking out of captivity or for the enigmatic package entrusted to me by Benoit and Etienne? All I knew was that if I ever got away from this, I'd be as content as a demobbed grenadier with a bag of commandeered swag. Still, curiosity took a grip. I'm a person of considerable trust. Benoit himself told me that, in not so many words. What harm could it possibly do to have a little peek at something so sought after? I placed the package on the seat beside Ocksi's now inert frame and undid the knotted, crimson twine. Gently, I peeled back the layers of protection and there it was. It was some kind of plate, formed from rock or something. It looked antiquated, lightweight but strong. Certainly sturdy enough to endure an intense pounding from a galloping Hungarian mare. Perhaps it was a dish? Or a clock without hands. Around its edges were ornate, colored symbols, a dozen of them, delicately carved and crafted. And unlike anything I'd previously seen.

Though I was in the dark as to the significance of the Castagne's chattel, my curiosity for now was slaked. I carefully wrapped the object, binding it again and placing it back under my shirt and pullover. As for hidden treasures, I thought, didn't Tibor have a leather holster under his waistcoat? I looked at his pallid head, eyelids closed by the conductor and surmised that there was no harm in confirming my suspicion that Tibor had been packing a persuader. I opened his coat and carefully started to pat him down. I was aware that in a recently deceased person, pockets of air would still be in his exanimate cadaver, waiting to escape but his first, involuntary death moan sure scared the bejesus out of me. Not wanting to move the body, I used my hands to feel the way from his collar, down the satin back of his waistcoat to his side and a conspicuous bulge. Ha! The snoop in me. I reached in and fished out not a gun, but a wallet. Thick, leather and laden with money. Surely the ink business couldn't be this good, I thought. I opened it and there, inside was a picture of Tibor as a younger man, maybe twenty years younger, looking quite the handsome chap. Beside him, a very attractive brunette, smiling. Was it? I think it was Eisabet. Of all that had occurred from that moment to this ... the complexity was dumbfounding. What was it that turned them from being just another sweet looking couple into these blemished agents of misfortune? Blackmail, political pressure? I couldn't put my finger on it. Tibor's head slid forward. The blood from his fatal head wound had been partially stemmed by one of the blankets but a red droplet slalomed from his eyelid to the edge of his nose. As I bent down to the floor to pick up Eisabet's handkerchief, a ghastly moan chilled my blood. Then another. The sound though...

A sob, then a howl. And a realisation, on my part, that in the brief spell of butchery that left Tibor and Ocksi slain, the fate of Eisabet had inexplicably slipped my mind.

The first puncture felt like a punch to my back with a bee sting at the end of the shot. If a bee had human sized fists. Consider! Sharply through my jacket and shirt and straight into my left shoulder. The second and third strikes slashed into the nape of my neck.

The force of the blows from the justifiably vengeful Mrs Tibor laid me flat out. I didn't have the chance to react as she continued to stab me another four or five times in the back. Though I didn't see the instrument, I could tell that it wasn't a knife that she used. Probably that hat pin. Or a knitting needle. Another puncture and I'd be beyond repair.

Lying prone and ready to join Ocski and Tibor in the celestial waiting room, I saw the door slide open and again, I heard that high pitched whiz and a great weight was lifted from me. Eisabet dropped to the floor at my side, her mercilessly disfigured face and mine almost touching. I turned my gaze away not wishing to have the sight of her left eye socket, now a scorched cavern, as my final memory. On the wood slatted flooring, among the discarded cigarette stems and dirt, I was drawn to the tiny pools of blood that lay within the ridges. Red, as rich as fondant, shimmering in time with the movement of the carriage. Even though my glasses were within reach, I could not move. A fly, the tiniest little creature feasting on our misfortune in this collective pool of congealed cruor. I wondered whether it knew or cared about the harbinger of its hematic feast. I heard voices, muffled. The conductor and one other.

'Where is it?'

'He said it was safe but...it's not in his bag.'

'What about the other bags? Find it.'

I tried to speak, to tell them that I had it, the package, and that it was still safe but I hadn't the strength. I was too weak to do anything other than watch that damned fly, dart around the floor, oblivious to this all too human farce, as content as a kid at the funfair, with pockets filled with quarters. Walking Kosciuszko Street, without a care. Being treated to a pretzel the size of a catcher's mitt and a mouthwatering pickle from Fisks on Pitkin, bought by my father, beaming with pride that he'd just taken fifty bucks from a Pole in a two-handed game of Hasenpfeffer. I thought of Cora, your mother. In every window, I longed to see her. That face, framed as a portrait, to be displayed in the finest galleries on Park Avenue. La Gioconda of Brooklyn, the golden Madonna of the East River...

I can recall the train slowing down and being lifted off by at least two men, into a car. I was placed face down, on the back seat and they cut open my jacket and shirt.

The conductor spoke to another man, in French this time. He told him quite forcefully that it was not permissible to allow me to die. The man said that he would try his best.

And that's all one can do. I had no beef with him.

'That's not good enough,' he said. 'He dies, you die.'

I thought of smoked herring, of sauerkraut. The windows open, the smell of the rotewurst and its skin, crackling on the grill, a rabbit pie constructed by tight lipped matrons for their brutish, hungry menfolk. I can pay now. I have money. The odor of the alehouses and almshouses in the shadow of the Bridge, a sweat infused cornucopia of hope and misery. An innocent redolence. The light from the street moved around the floor of the car, soothing and mesmeric. Urging me to continue. The meaning beyond. This elemental, unyielding desire to return to New York made me ache. I'm sorry for ever leaving you. I want to return. I will return. I will build a bridge to you, Cora, wire strung, caissons firm and bound for eternity. I should have never left.'

Chapter 8 - Prometheus, Fried.

'Drink,' he said.

My eyes, bonded shut with the warm gum of thick sleep, could not respond to him but my hands did. With a palate as dry as the Gobi Desert, I desperately reached out in the direction of the gruff voice and with both hands, grasped the cool cup. The water was fresh and it hit my stomach like pebbles. My internal compass had been stamped on, leaving me helpless. As the warm day turned to cold night, I broiled in my bunk, feverish and drifting. Anaïs once said that I was often absent from the present. Never more true than at this moment. My thoughts undulating wildly between the worlds of the sentient and the mindless; my brain processing unfathomable theories and the queerest notions about dogs, architecture and all the principles of statehood that I'd never before pondered. And all at breakneck speed. During lulls in this altered state, I was able to rest my mind enough to deduce, from the rocking motion, that I was aboard a vessel of sorts. The East Coast beckoned, I presumed. I hadn't eaten for, perhaps a couple of days; my empty belly felt as if my throat had been sliced open. Worse still, I hadn't written a single word and that hunger was just as keen. All that will change once we disembark, I thought and I will be done with the Castagne's burdensome package forever.

'Drink,' he said again. I pushed away the cup and tried to talk but

my throat was even more tightly closed than the white stockinged legs of the primmest, most abstinent bible school teacher. Dear Elie, I know you may laugh but then, even at my most incapacitated, carnality was never far from my incorrigible loins.

A small pair of rough, calloused hands cradled my neck and shoulders, helping me sit up. I'd seen newborn kittens with more strength. Again, I took the cup, sipping rather than gulping down the water offered to me.

'You have to eat,' he said, his accent heavy and guttural. He placed some bread, soft and doughy, into my weak hands, and raised it up to my mouth; a foreign but necessary communion. I slowly chewed the bread as if it was a fistful of pork rind. 'Bones are good for dogs, not for men,' he said, leaving me a tin cup. I forced my eyes open in order to cast a look at my gruff benefactor, now standing in the doorway. He looked miniscule. The dog beside him, remarkably silent until now, was colossal by comparison. This was too much to take in. I closed my eyes again and drifted off once more into the land of Gods and monsters. If I manage to get away with it this time, survive this violent pandemonium and put it firmly behind me, then perhaps there was another way for me to live.

Too long have I eked out a pittance, endured the life of the artist as animal, scavenging for food, drink and attention, whoring myself out for francs to the periodicals while those condescending assholes in their oak lined suites have the nerve to sanction my writings? No, fuck them. It may or may not have been during one of these hallucinatory moments that I came to the conclusion that if I was going to be fucked by life, then I may as well be fucked by religion. I recalled Militz and his gang of scumbags heading into churches. While the parishioners had their eyes on the almighty, they had theirs firmly on the collection plates, though in my sly gambit, I won't need to steal like a street criminal. So, I shall publicly renounce my works, prostrate myself at their feet and beg forgiveness for my ghastly indecency. Once I have shown the requisite contrition, I will be free to enter the houses of the holy, bathe in the sacred waters and become the most recalcitrant radical they could imagine, subordinate, only to the Creator. When it suits, of course. An artist needs an audience. And a support network. When it comes to fawning gullible cretins, they don't come much bigger. This wily stratagem, I thought, shall be my wickedly enduring masterpiece. The Castagne's had the right idea. One is only held back by the limits of one's imagination. Once I deliver their package, I will take what is mine and my torture will be over. I shall be Prometheus, unbound.

The package. My hands immediately reached down towards my lower stomach. Nothing. My eyes opened and I pulled myself upright. The pain I had in my back matched the sinking feeling in the pit of my gut. I threw my legs over the side of the bunk and tried to stand. But my Paris to Marseille exertions proved too much and, light headedly, I sank back into the blood stained, sweat dampened sheets. From what I could see, the room, to my ailing eyes, as incandescent as a billion candles lighting a circle of suns, was a basic cabin. Unburnished timber floors, painted girders and a porthole the size of a dinner plate. Beside the bunk, an upturned wooden crate acting as a makeshift table, upon which sat my glasses. I picked them up, licked my fingers and cleaned the tiny specks of blood and matter that clouded the lenses. Once donned, I could see the colourful straps belonging to the leather bag, given to me by the brothers, beside a heap of my torn, stained clothing and a length of thin rope.

In my diminished capacity, I offered no danger to others and if I was facing an imminent threat, well, I was in no position to repel any attack.

I called out as strongly as I could, barely carrying above the gentle chuntering of the engine below. Another attempt to stand, my weak calves strained under my weight but did not buckle. At the door, the dog reappeared. Though my memory of this encounter may be vague due to my enfeebled condition, I swear on all of the stars in the cosmos that this German Shepherd had the head the size of a mighty lion.

'What are you doing?' it asked, in an accent which wasn't immediately familiar.

'I need to speak with the little man,' I said.

'There is a chamber pot by your bed,' remarked the lion headed dog.

'No, the little man. The man who was here.'

'Ah, you want Sevak!'

He barked three times and the little man arrived, wiping oil from his hands with a rag.

'What are you doing?' he asked, more blunt than the lion headed dog.

'The package…where is my package?' I asked.

'That's long gone,' he said. 'The Englishman took it.'

Good, I thought. It's safe. 'Did he leave a note for me, instructions, anything? '

The little man - Sevak - turned to the lion headed dog with a confused look.

'You need to rest some more,' said Sevak.

'I don't need to rest, I just want to know what the hell is going on,' I replied with as much anger as I could muster.

With his cold wet nose prodding at my bare legs, the lion headed dog gently pushed me back towards the bunk. He looked at me with his handsome deep brown eyes.

'Please, you need some more rest, Mr Miller,' it said. Maybe the lion headed dog was right.

****

Some hours later, I woke to the distinctive smell of fish being fried and the shimmer of light bouncing from the porthole, swaying across the walls and the ceiling to the tempo of a slow waltz. Sunrise or sunset, I had no idea. I stood unaided, and assessed the condition of my decimated clothing. The normally bracing Atlantic wasn't as cold as I was expecting so a clean vest and drawers would do for the moment. As some sage wrote, a middle aged man in his underwear carries little threat. I followed the sound of the sizzling, though in truth, it was my stomach that led the way.

I headed for the light at the end of a corridor so narrow that two stringbeans couldn't pass simultaneously. By the doorway, I stepped over the dog, who looked up at me, mid feast with a satisfied nod, and into the galley. Sevak confidently tossed the charred pieces of fish which were cooking in his blackened pan, the crackle which accompanied each of his snapping wrist movements beckoning me closer.

'Sit,' he said, without turning to acknowledge me.

For a brief moment, I didn't know whether he was barking out a command towards me or his remarkable canine companion.

'You must be hungry.'

Yes, I was but the delights of being press-ganged then fattened up by a second forceful pair in quick succession was starting to wear as thin as my most loyal undergarments.

Sevak tilted his pan and the deliciously seared white flesh of the fish dribbled onto the plate. I picked up the one item of cutlery that was close - an ornate soup spoon - and started shovelling it into my mouth. I found, as with the Castagne's more lugubrious station, that the hunger I'd built up through adrenaline and fear, had been sated, in quite splendid fashion.

A glistening rim of grease around Sevak's pursed lips suggested that he'd already partaken.

'Freshly caught,' he said as I scraped around the tin plate for flecks I'd missed the first time around. 'Drink?'

'Why not?' I replied.

Sevak opened the cupboard over the stove and placed one bottle of beer, another of Coca-Cola and a bottle of Pernod onto the table. He cracked open the beer and chugged it back. Pernod it is then, I thought.

'So, how long will it take us to get there?' I asked, following him over the now dormant dog and down the corridor.

'We should reach our destination in a couple of hours,' he replied, which surprised me somewhat given that the North Atlantic was perfectly clement and the sky, nowhere near as dappled and foreboding as I'd expected. On this day, deep in the fall, it was the most perfect, eye splitting crystalline shade of azure.

Maybe it was my fragile physical fettle, fatigue or the glimpses of that spectacular sky, I don't know, but breathing in that sweet sub-boreal breeze, reminded me that I couldn't stop thinking about America. It was alive, with an infinite number of possibilities and permutations. It was alive and so was I. Alive and like the Castagne brothers, I was King and ready to go home. To New York and to my family; my wives and fancies, my guileless sister, poor innocent Lauretta, Uncle George and sweet Melia for whom everything became too much. Heinrich, my witless father and the manipulative matriarch, Louise, my mother. They may not be ideal but they were mine. As Tolstoy said, 'Happy families are all alike; every unhappy family is unhappy in their own way.'

'If you look closely...' said the diminutive Sevak, standing on a step by a large curved window, pointing, 'you can see land. Just there, on the horizon.'

I tightened my gaze, squinting against the sun. 'That can't be Nova Scotia on the right. It's too flat. Rhode Island perhaps?'

Sevak looked at me and said, 'No, that's Corfu.'

Chapter 9 - The Beautiful Guilt

"Nothing much. Just finishing my laundry," said May, kicking at a large pile of clothes on the floor.

"So, what was in the box?"

"The box?"

"Yes, the box. Elie's box."

"Oh that?"

"Yeah. Find anything interesting in it?"

"Not really. Just some pictures and papers," she lied. May didn't like telling lies and especially not to Jerry. She swiftly changed the subject.

"So we're back in business?"

"We're taking the boards and the bags away tonight so once final checks are done, yep. All systems go."

"Opening as normal tomorrow?"

"God willing. It'll be wet but it'll be manageable. Come in at twelve and do the back shift. Hold on…"

May cradled the phone between her shoulder and her chin as she continued to read the journal that Elie left. She could've done with another day to finish the book but at this pace, it might be done tonight.

"Elvin says that he and a few of his buddies are going to McGee's to watch the Sox, if you want to join them."

"Who are we playing?"

"Orioles. Third game."

"Are you going?"

"Hmmm...I've got a few drop offs but I should be finished in time to catch the last couple of innings."

"Ok, tell him that I might pop over."

"He says, don't forget, it's Wing Wednesday."

The Sox AND Wing Wednesday? Might be forced to put the book down for an hour for a big bowl of those honey glazed, Maine marvels, she thought.

"Tell him to save me a seat."

May picked up her bookmark, a laminated green ticket stub, which bore the legend, 'The Heathen Shrubs Plus Support, Downstairs at Malvolio's - $5 in advance, $7 on the door', amateurishly typeset in black, and placed it in between the pages of the journal. Another keepsake from her dalliance with Dennis. Deciding against changing out of her red plaid, and very comfortable, pajamas, May grabbed a pullover from the soiled pile and her late father's trapper's hat from the cupboard. I'll shower before I go to McGee's, she thought, straightening the corrective insole in her boot. Picking up a blue tin, May sprayed a cloud of deodorant in the general vicinity of her body. It's not that May was unhygienic. Quite the opposite, in fact. The story woven in Elie's bequest had her hooked and was reeling her in. She'd moved on from the sci-fi of her youth, past the pulp detective novels favoured by her father to the wry humour of a John Irving and the sassiness of Dorothy Parker but this collection was different. Filled with secrets, intrigue and characters who might only be one stage removed from someone she actually knew, it felt even more personal than the works of Maine's most beloved writer, a fellow who lived less than an hour away in Lovell.

Wrapped up warm, May skipped between static traffic, across the road to the Court Convenience store. Fresh bread, milk and eggs, enough to keep her going until the weekend shop. A tin of Campbell's soup and a couple of Three Musketeers as a treat. That should do it. May took precisely $5.65 out of her purse and paid the cashier. The Auburn Municipal Library was a couple of blocks away. There was time.

The Municipal, or the Mooney as Elvin called it, was far less busy during the last hour of the working day. Studious kids looking for answers in an environment more peaceful than a cramped flat could offer, lifelong bookworms seeking hidden treasures and the lonely old souls keeping warm while finding new friends among the well-worn pages of the potboilers, tended to be the only ones scouring its shelves at this late hour. May visited the Mooney often, mainly for a Stephen King fix and the occasional biography but she rarely interacted with the staff, particularly the doyenne of the atheneum, Mrs Holloway. Short, serious and perfectly coiffured, the ever stern looking Rose Holloway had been the chief librarian at the Auburn Municipal Library for more than thirty years and tended to view her domain from the desk, like a single-minded sentinel. She rarely raised her voice but when she did, you knew about it. She was acquainted with May's parents, but not intimately. An occasional customer at The Columbus, always a black coffee and a half slice of pecan pie, Mrs Holloway had been frosty towards May since she was a kid. Their personal Cold War started because of an incident one April afternoon.

A party of school kids, one of whom was May, became a bit too boisterous and was asked to leave. A book that was on Mrs Holloway's desk at the time, 'The Love Machine' by Jacqueline Susann, vanished but as she remembered May leaning on the edge of her desk, she was the one who took the blame. A call was placed to her father and over dinner, he sat her down and asked her what she knew. She never kept secrets from him but on this one occasion, she didn't reveal the whole truth. Though he didn't say, this was one of the few times that she disappointed him. Not because she may have taken the book, he didn't believe that of his daughter, but because she couldn't bring herself to talk to him about it. And, years later, it still hurt. Connie Barzagli was the one who stole it, slipping it under her sweater, and she'd only taken it because she'd overheard her mother talk about how gratuitous the sex in the book was, arousing some curiousity among the pre-pubescent girls at school. Connie brought it to the playground near the woods and over a shared bottle of Dr Pepper and a cigarette, sneakily removed from the sleeping Mr Barzagli's coat, she and May scoured the mildly salacious text for pointers.

Connie was fearless at times. May often wished that she'd possessed some of her unflinching nerve. She'd never have stolen a thing, never mind a copy of a 'pornographic book' from right under the nose of old Holloway. She was too cautious but Connie would and Connie did. Their high school yearbook named Connie as the 'Most Likely to Marry a Millionaire'. May? 'Most Likely to Get Injured at Work.' To her folks, Connie, the youngest of five and the Barzagli's only girl, was a blessing from God but to many, she was a little indulged.

May pushed open the heavy doors of the Mooney and stood in the hallway, shaking off the excess rain from her hat and coat. Milton the security guard, if one could call him that, was himself long retired when he took the less than onerous task of protecting the Mooney's collection of well-thumbed paperbacks and thick encyclopedias. Almost bent double, his guardsman's cap was held on by a thin strip of fabric, fastened under his chin. Due to his poor posture, Milton looked sideways when he had to address someone. May had known him all of her life.

"Whadd'ya in for, May?"

"Fifteen to life, Milton," replied May, delivered like a Borscht Belt warm up act, with a finger snapping wink. The elderly guard coughed with chesty laughter and waved her in. Habit took her along the right-hand passage, circumnavigating her away from Mrs Holloway's realm at the central desk. Biographies, straight ahead and left, fiction to the right.

May placed her shopping bag on the vinyl padded reading chair situated under one of the section's five large lead-lined windows. As special as the red bricked public building looked from the corner of Spring Street, the inside of the Mooney was even more remarkable. Built in the early years of the 20th century with a Carnegie grant, the library had recently been placed on the National Register of Historic Places. It was somewhere that all Auburn residents were rightly proud of, even if they didn't spend much time inside of it. May did though. Music had usurped books in her artistic strata but while she rarely left the confines of her hometown, through the printed word, she'd travelled far and wide.

May scoured the fiction section. Mailer, Makepeace, The Holy Sinner by Thomas Mann, a reminder of college days, Cormac McCarthy, the historic romances of Judith McNaught, Elie liked those. Ah! The Tomorrow People by Judith Merrill. May stopped her search and removed the hard-backed copy of the book. The bright colours of the cover betrayed the novel's age; written during those early, heady days of the space race, when the possibility of reaching the moon was more attainable than a trip to Paris might've been. She opened the jacket and checked the library's date stamps. Two slips, one glued down over the other. May gently peeled back the more recent and less stamped slip to reveal a much fuller one underneath. From 1968, presumably when the book came into the library's possession, right up to and beyond the three weeks in September 1973 when she'd first read it, the book was consistently borrowed. Yep. That there would've been me, she thought. May searched again for the time she revisited it, late 1980 it would've been. By this time, Ms Merrill would've been lucky to see her work taken out twice a year. Loved it in the seventies, less so in the eighties, she digressed. Nicholas Meyer, Arthur Miller but not…

"Are you looking for something in particular, Miss Morgenstern?"

The unmistakable clipped tones of Mrs Holloway cut through the absolute silence.

"Jesus!" boomed May with fright.

"I'm afraid you won't find Him there. Theology is by the second arch to your left."

"Yes, I know … I'm sorry," said May, off guard. "I was just looking for something."

"If it's not there, and it hasn't been stolen…" said the librarian, pausing for effect, "then it may have been borrowed because Miss Morgenstern, that's what one does when one wishes to read something from the Auburn Municipal Library."

"Of course," said May.

"Follow me," said Mrs Holloway, already walking.

May grabbed her shopping, her jacket and hat and did as she was ordered.

At the reference card file near her station, Mrs Holloway stopped. She opened up the drawer which bore the letter 'M' and stood perfectly still, for May to catch up. "I'd like to say that I was very sorry to hear about Miss Elie. She was a decent citizen and a good friend of the library."

"Thank you, she.."

"Which author are you looking for?" interrupted Mrs Holloway, the détente over.

"I'm looking for Henry Miller," said May, quietly.

Mrs Holloway stopped straightening the reference cards, firmly closing the drawer.

"We do not carry any books by Henry Miller. If one were inclined to read that kind of work, I would suggest any number of specialist book retailers in Portland which would be able to help one with an enquiry of that sort. Good day Miss Morgenstern."

"What about Anaïs Nin? Do you have any of her work? Or what's his name? Yes, Blade Cenatars?" asked May, reluctant to take no for an answer.

"Cendrars. Blaise Cendrars. No, we do not, nor do we have any Anaïs Nin," replied Mrs Holloway, firmly.

"Oh, I see," said May, slightly chastened.

"Tell me Miss Morgenstern. Why, after years of reading celebrity hagiographies, science fiction and the occasional horror, have you suddenly developed an interest in the more licentious and the lascivious? Wasn't Jacqueline Susann enough for you?"

Mrs Holloway had a long memory and clearly, still held a grudge.

"I didn't take that book. I told you that then and I'm telling you again now. I. Didn't. Take it!" said May with a rarely seen display of ferocity.

"Then who did?" hissed back Mrs Holloway.

"Does it matter?"

"Of course it matters!" barked the librarian, losing her cool.

The few remaining patrons looked towards the pair.

Slowly but firmly, with her finger pointed forcibly toward the rattled Mrs Holloway, May repeated her statement. "I did not take that book."

Her face flushed with rage, May stormed towards the exit.

"Miss Morgenstern?"

May stopped, her teeth gritted, primed for one final round with the library's cantankerous curator. The colour which had momentarily filled Mrs Holloway's cheeks with a rare burst of life had faded, returning her wan pallor to a more recognisable powder grey.

"Please, come with me."

May followed Mrs Holloway upstairs, through the young adult and children's sections. Since the refurbishment, she'd rarely been in this part of the library.

"Jeremy, the cart," she said, her clipped tone directed towards the trainee in charge of this unpopulated section. One small admonishment and the junior librarian instantly closed his book, quickly got to his feet and restarted his overdue rounds.

"Without order, nothing is possible," remarked Mrs Holloway.

"Though, out of chaos comes…" started May.

"Half a semester reading community college philosophy text does not an expert on Hegel make, Miss Morgenstern," jabbed Mrs Holloway. She stopped walking. "That was uncalled for," she said. "Forgive me."

"Forget it," replied a stung but intrigued May. Until the last few minutes, she'd never experienced anything other than outright hostility from Mrs Holloway. At the chief librarian's door, she looked directly at May, as if sizing her up one final time.

She opened her cardigan and lifted up the bottom of her pullover, revealing the hint of a silken slip and a round metallic retractable key ring, fixed to the waistband of her skirt.

"I was fortunate enough to spend some time with her back then," she said, unlocking the door to her inner sanctum.

Who? May thought. Elie? She never let on.

"Though when I say that I spent time with her, I'm afraid that's perhaps stretching the truth. We both had business at the time with Havilane Publishing on Christopher St, in the Village, though in very different capacities but I was fortunate enough to be in her company on a handful of thrillingly stimulating occasions."

She's definitely not talking about Elie, thought May. Gentle, sweet, kind? Certainly. Absolutely. Thrillingly stimulating? Hmm...

Mrs Holloway removed her glasses, placing them on her neatly arranged desk, behind which stood a locked, glass fronted bookcase. Taking another, smaller key from a thin drawer in the centre of her desk, she unlocked the case.

"I'd have very much liked to have spent, what you young people refer to as, *quality time* with her. She was a remarkable force."

Reaching up, Mrs Holloway removed a dark, hard-backed volume of work from the full top shelf.

Handing it to May, she said, "Please be careful with it. It is very precious. To me."

May looked at the spine; in embossed silver it read, 'Diaries - volume one'.

"Is this a first edition?"

"No, it's considerably rarer than that. A personal print. Hand pressed and unexpurgated."

May opened the cover and read the inscription.

'This bud awaits the touch of the sun, ready to bloom. Burst into life. Anaïs x'

May's heart raced.

"Is this really...?"

With a playful, mischievous smile, Mrs Holloway nodded.

"She had the most amazing scent. Not instantly detectable though. One would have to get very close in order to breathe it, and her, in." Mrs Holloway reached over the book and inhaled deeply.

"Mitsouko, with jasmine and honeysuckle. Just as she wanted."

May took a little sniff herself. The subtle notes of the fragrance filled the space between them, splashing colour onto the picture her imagination had painted.

"The word Mitsouko means mystery in Japanese," said Mrs Holloway, eyes closed but seeing everything as she bathed in the aroma.

Very appropriate, thought May. She watched as the librarian took the writer's advice, the layers peeled back, to reveal the essence of a woman, unfettered by convention.

"Intoxicating, isn't it? I keep a small atomiser handy for moments such as these. I never tire of it."

There was a lightness about Mrs Holloway's display of unbridled femininity which May never dreamed she possessed.

"So tell me Miss Morgenstern, what do you know about Anaïs and her amour fou?"

May looked perplexed. She'd studied basic French in high school but not the intricacies of its spoken form.

"Her amour fou...her dangerous obsession."

Henry Miller, of course.

"I learned of him through Elie."

"I never met the man. He gave a talk at Vassar about twenty years ago, before they dropped the standards and became a co-ed," said Mrs Holloway, finishing off the sentence with a large droplet of disdain.

"He was quite old then but from what I heard, he still had that spark. I do wish that I could have heard him speak. On a personal level, I did think that some of his prose was rambling and more vulgar than it needed to be but who am I to judge the great Henry Miller? He was the golden sun for whom Anaïs first bloomed. While he had his flaws, and frankly who doesn't, the respect she had for him as an artist and a literary force was unbending. And that, Miss Morgenstern, is good enough for me."

"Were you aware that Elie knew him?"

"Yes. It's hard to imagine two more contrasting people. She said that towards the end of his life, he'd resumed correspondence with her again. I intimated to her that I would be in her debt if she'd permit me the honour of reading some more of his words. She said that when it was appropriate, she would bring them here, to my office, and allow me to cast an eye over them. But she never did," whispered Mrs Holloway, dolefully. "And once she passed, I was hoping that she may have bequeathed something of that nature to us but alas, no."

May wondered whether to tell Mrs Holloway what Elie had entrusted to her. Ordinarily, she was the kind of person who would give you her last but on this occasion, May felt no guilt in keeping Miller's illuminating reflections all to herself. For the time being anyway.

"You said that Elie was a good friend to the library."

"She was indeed."

Mrs Holloway carefully closed the Diary and placed it back in the cabinet. On the shelf below, she removed a book with a gaudy dust jacket. On the front, was a luridly painted woman by a window, in tears with a man standing behind her in the doorway. The kind one would find in the type of pulp romance novels that Elie adored. This one was titled, 'The Beautiful Guilt', by an author whose name she didn't recognise.

"Elie was one of the few people who knew about my passion for this period. She gave me this, and a few others which I've placed in safe keeping. Now the cover? You have to understand Miss Morgenstern, that until recently, in many parts of this very country, one could be arrested for being in possession of such an item. So I took measures to protect the library and myself against the ignominious prospect of action taken."

Puzzled, Elie removed the sleeve, opened the front cover and there, within the handwritten inscription, the truth behind 'A Beautiful Guilt' was revealed.

"It's him!" she exclaimed. "This was written by Henry Miller himself! I recognise his style."

"Yes!" replied Mrs Holloway, excitedly before stopping. The librarian's manner had changed, from giddy to precise and composed. "Miss Morgenstern," she said, coolly. "That does raise a curious question. How would someone barely acquainted with Henry Miller immediately know what his handwriting looked like?"

Busted, May thought. Maybe Mrs Holloway did know about Elie's literary treasure trove and was just reeling her in? If so, well played Rose.

"Elie did leave me a few things."

"Including items from the pen of Henry Miller? That would explain how you could immediately recognise his trademark scrawl," said Mrs Holloway, locked onto a different scent.

May thought about spinning some nonsense about reading some of his handwritten letters in a book but that wouldn't have fooled anyone, particularly one very experienced and fastidious librarian.

"I only returned from Vegas yesterday and I've not had time to go through it all as yet."

"How was Nevada?" asked Mrs Holloway, changing the subject. "I've not been there in years. A fascinating place."

"I didn't get time to see much."

"And you returned home yesterday?"

"Yes. I arrived yesterday morning, just after the storm broke."

"Terrible, wasn't it?"

"Yes it was."

"Kept me up all night, it did."

"I slept through most of it, thankfully."

"I'm up on Williams so I was mercifully unaffected but some of my staff took a bit of battering. How about you?"

"No, I'm good. Apart from the rain lashing the windows, my place was pretty much untouched."

"That surprises me," said Mrs Holloway. "I was sure that quite a few houses down on Grove suffered some damage. That's where you are, right?"

"No, I moved from Grove a few years ago. I'm only across the road at the corner of…" May paused. She'd already said too much.

Mrs Holloway took a seat at her desk and clicked at her keyboard. The crackle of dust from the back of the computer monitor and the faint smell of electrical burning instantly made May more nervous. Mrs Holloway, glasses now back on, punched up May's details.

"Morgenstern...Mary. There we are. It says here that you're still in McKenzie. As we're here, why don't we update the file with your new address?"

"Maybe next time? How about tomorrow?" May looked at the space on her wrist where her late father's wristwatch rarely was. She picked up her bags and opened the office door. "Got to go. Right now. Tomorrow is good for me, Mrs Holloway."

"It'll only take a second...Miss Morgenstern..." pleaded the librarian, in vain.

"It's May. Just May," she shouted back along the short corridor.

Mrs Holloway returned to her seat and removed her glasses.

"Rose," she said, quietly to herself. The librarian made one more minute adjustment to the already orderly papers on her desk. Tilting her head slightly backwards, she savoured the last traces of the book's mysterious scent.

"And it's *Miss* Holloway."

May made it back across the road and into her apartment in no time at all. She stepped straight out of her heavy boots, dropped her shoulders and slipped out of her wet coat, throwing her hat in the general direction of the radiator. That was close, she thought. The old bloodhound of the Mooney, after years of the hunt, had almost caught up with her but see that May Morgenstern? She's no fool. Her close shave with Auburn's most formidable municipal employee had left her wondering, though. Did she give too much away? She did mention what Elie had left her; idiotically letting her know that she recognised Henry Miller's handwriting. May kicked herself for that but it did satisfy the doubt in her mind that what she had in her possession was the real thing. That was for certain. What wasn't clear though was exactly how far Miss Holloway would go to get her boney mitts on the journal. Just need to keep away from her until I can figure out what to do with all of this information, she thought. And I need to find out more about Henry Miller.

Seated on her bed, journal in hand, May prepared to re-enter the writer's wild world when the bell from the telephone made her jump. No way. She couldn't have gotten my number already, she thought. However, old Holloway does work for the government and it wouldn't be hard to find me. Not too many Morgensterns in this part of town. I'll just ignore it. She removed a Three Musketeers bar from her shopping bag, tearing at the wrapper with her teeth. Keep ignoring it, May. When they realise you're not home, she told herself, it'll soon stop.

But it didn't. And with each ring, May became more anxious. By the twelfth ring, she'd reached breaking point.

"Damn it!" she yelled down the phone. "What the hell do you want with me?"

"Where are you?" shouted the voice, straining against the background noise.

"Elvin?"

"May, where are you?"

"I'm at home. Obviously," she said.

"McGee's is jam packed and it's already the bottom of the third. I've kept a place and I've ordered a bucket of wings for you, with the barbeque dip that you like."

"Thanks Elvin, that's very kind of you but I'm…"

"But nothing May Morgenstern. If you're not here in ten minutes, I cannot promise that your saved seat or those piping hot, glazed wings will still be here. That's all I'm saying girl."

From the sound of things, May could tell that Elvin had already sunk a few drinks, which made her laugh as he was a lightweight in more than one sense of the word. Might be an ideal night to get out of the house. May closed the journal and placed it in the one place no intruder would dream of looking; beneath her growing pile of unwashed laundry.

"Elvin, tell me. What do you know about Henry Miller? The writer."

"He's the guy who was married to Marilyn Monroe, right?"

Chapter 10 - Durango

May couldn't sleep. The display on her clock radio wasn't flashing but its harsh red digits reminded her that it was gone twenty past three in the morning. She tended to stay awake late, especially when she didn't have to do the morning shift. Usually around 2am and she'd start drifting off. Not this time. Even 'Mellow Moods', Dennis' Mix Tape #15, which featured a host of coincidentally tragic artists, like Chris Bell, Dennis Wilson and Donny Hathaway, the kind which would normally take an edge off, had played out. If she had to repeat it, she thought, then it had failed in its purpose.

Something was bothering her. It wasn't the narrow defeat in the ball game. Sure, it killed the buzz in the bar a little but everyone knew that the Sox were going nowhere fast this year. Even Jerry didn't show up, that's how bad things were. No, she could feel it in her gut. Something was amiss. Unanswered questions waiting until sleep was about to take hold before prodding her awake again. If truth be told, that second bucket of wings didn't help but she wasn't going to bail on poor Elvin who took the loss so badly that he had an unprecedented fourth beer. Sober, he wouldn't be seen dead in May's car but drunk, he had fewer qualms. Her Pacer had just enough gas to get Elvin up the hill to his folks' place before doing an about turn and cruising back down on fumes. A $10 wage advance tomorrow should keep her beloved but hideous car on the road for another week. And if that offends all of the auto enthusiasts in Auburn, well that's just the way it was. And like Ol' Man River - also on

Mix Tape #15 - that ol' Pacer will just keep rolling along. And now it's 03.26. Each second that passes is an escapee, she thought.

Right, I need seven hours sleep. That means that I can still crash by 4am, wake at 11am with enough time to get a much needed wash before getting to The Columbus. Half an hour. Might be able to stretch it to the full hour and have a quicker wash in the morning, reasoned May.

Decision made.

She turned on the bedside lamp and once her tired eyes had adjusted to the light, May rummaged underneath the mountain of sleeves, hoods and trouser legs building up under her window and found Elie's book. This is what she'd really wanted to do instead of agreeing to accompany some other human beings out into the social world, if McGees Tavern qualified as such. That's what Henry Miller would have done had he been here. He would have gone out and grabbed Auburn by the lapels and either fought it or fucked it. And that was why, at 03.30am, May was sitting up in bed, reading glasses on with pillows propped up behind her.

One hour, maximum; she lied to herself. May was starting to feel comfortable with the chicanery.

****

'Corfu? Why aren't we going to New York?' I asked him.

'Corfu is pretty.'

'So is New York!' I countered.

'But New York is cold.'

'Yes? So?'

'And New York is wet, no?'

'And your point is?'

'Corfu is good. We have fish and we refuel there.'

'And then to New York?'

'In this?' Sevak laughed. 'It'll still be there. Don't worry.'

We continued in this vein for a couple of minutes before I realised that there was no convincing him. He was right about New York though. It would still be there. We'd be lucky to get as far as Madeira in this boat before the cold grey grip of the Atlantic claimed us. New York would have to wait. We were bound for Corfu and that was that. I left Sevak and his sleeping companion and headed out into the baking sunshine. Using what little strength I had, I clambered onto an empty, wood slatted box on the port side of the stern and cast my eye west, in a futile attempt to see home. Sevak's meagre haul, strewn across the deck, may fetch enough to feed and water the pair of them for the best part of a week but I had loftier plans. Maybe God was listening after all. On a wooden throne of ineptitude I sat, the gentle sway of the sea, the cool breeze and the soft putt-putt of the boat's turbine were elemental reminders of exactly how insignificant and powerless I was. I closed my eyes and ran my fingers across the coarse-grained wood, thinking of Manhattan and Central Park, the Linden lined pathways which swirl like iced flourishes, the Red Maple bursting into life with scarlet defiance as its cycle draws to a close. And the russet sodden flooring of the Paris to Marseille train. Maybe, I thought, slipping back into slumber, it was time to forswear self pity.

Sevak woke me, before I burnt to a crisp.

'Drink,' he said and I obliged.

Sevak pulled at the neck of my vest, edging me forward checking my wounds. Though still tender, one could tell that they - and I - had improved.

'You're very lucky,' he said, pointing a knife at me.

'Tell me about it,' I replied. 'But thank you.' I was grateful for his actions in preserving my life.

'You survive. That's enough,' said Sevak, bluntly.

I quoted De Montaigne, 'Death, they say, acquits us of all obligations. No?'

Sevak shrugged. 'Que sais-je?' he replied, whittling at a small block of wood. What do I know?

'So, where are you taking me?'

'Corfu,' he replied.

'And the plan of action?' I asked.

Sevak's brow lowered as he gave me a confused look.

'There is no plan. We go to the harbour, we get off and continue with being alive.'

'That's it?'

'That's it,' he replied firmly. Now I was the one who looked confused.

'How long have you worked for the Castagnes? Is this normal?'

'I don't know anything about Castagnes.'

'You know, the Castagnes. From Paris. Working with the man who brought me here.'

'The Englishman?'

'Yes!' I said.

'I don't like him.'

Understandable, I thought but why?

'I'm fixing my nets when he arrives in the harbour with you. I think he is a tourist pushing his father in a chair. He pulls a gun on me and takes over my boat. I help him lift you onto the deck. You are cold and stiff. I think you are already dead. He forces me to leave Marseille immediately, in the dark with no lights. I know my way in and out of the harbour but at night with no lights, this is difficult. I have had a gun in my face before and I don't like it. Once we get onto the high water, I turn the lights on. He wants me to go faster - twelve knots - but the Durango can only make eight. With a good wind behind us, I tell him, we can be in Sanremo by the morning. That's not good, he tells me but que sais-je? You know? He is very angry. Everyone is nervous. Except you. You are dead. But then you move. He grabs you and slaps you. You respond but not well so he orders me to wrap you in blankets. I tell him that

we have no blankets and he hits me with the butt of his gun. Here.'

He shows me the back of his head. His dark, wiry hair is matted with blood.

'And your dog?' I ask. That huge creature would surely have something to say about this.

'I keep him locked in the brig.'

'Big mistake.'

Sevak shrugged his shoulders.

'There has been enough blood shed on this boat.'

'What about the package?' I ask, swiftly changing the subject.

'We were about four hours into the voyage,' said Sevak. 'He was tired but I was waiting until he fell asleep before making a move. Then you coughed and woke him. He called me in to check on you while he stood over us with his gun. I didn't want to be struck again so I stayed back. Your eyes opened and you mumbled something about Paris. He raised your head up and asked you where you'd left the package. On the train? Back at the station? Where? You smiled at him and told him that it was safe. That's when you started to unbutton your trousers. I was confused. The Englishman was too but you were delirious and close to death. I thought, what harm could it do for him to have one final grip at it.'

At the moment of my passing, one last libidinous hurrah. Clearly, I had no recollection of this but I have to admit that I was proud to find that in my terminal moments that I would return to say a heartfelt goodbye to my most loyal companion.

'That's when you pulled it out. The Englishman was very pleased. Especially when he saw that it was still in one piece,' said Sevak, not quite capturing the nuance of the language.

'He asked me how long it would be before we made Genova. I told him that at this speed, we'd be there just after midday. This news displeased him. What about Sanremo, he asked? We should be there just after daybreak. Good, he said. There's a cove just past the town

of Bordighera in a place called Madonna Della Ruota. That's where we'll stop. The fishermen of the area will be out so we should go unnoticed. But your passenger? He asked me where I was heading. I told him that I'd intended going down to Tropea and Tonicello as there were plentiful schools of bream and bluefin in those cool Calabrian waters. He made a mental calculation and offered me three hundred francs to take you with me.

Maybe he did work for the Castagne brothers, I thought.

'I told him that you needed medical attention as soon as possible or you will certainly be dead by the afternoon.'

'And what did he say?' I asked.

'He stuffed the money into my hands telling me that now that the package was safe, your services were no longer required.'

That didn't make sense, I thought.

'Once I was in deep enough waters, I was to bind and weigh down your body before I deposited you in the sea. Dead or alive, it didn't matter, he said.'

'The sneaky limey fuck...'

Sevak continued, 'We made good time and we arrived at the cove just before ten in the morning. As he left, his gun reminded me that he expected our 'deal' to be sealed. He looked at the name on the stern of the boat and nodded, telling me that if you should suddenly appear somewhere, he'd know where to find me. For three hundred francs, I said that was fair.

'Life is cheap,' I said. Sevak nodded in agreement.

'The Englishman left the boat and we continued east along the Ligurian coast. I purposefully suggested this area as I knew that on foot, it would take him a couple of hours to reach Sanremo. And even if he had an accomplice waiting somewhere in the region, it would take them quite a while to locate him. That bought me enough time to contact a medic I know in Imperia. He owed me a favour but given the circumstances, he was reluctant to get involved.'

'How did you convince him to help?' I asked.

'It's remarkable how much leverage you can get with Hippocrates, three hundred francs and a large dog,' he replied with a devilish chuckle. The hitherto unseen levity suited him.

'Appreciating that time was a factor and making sure that we weren't a sitting target for the Englishman, the doctor worked on you, using various medicines and poultices, all the way to Genova. He was the one who saved your life.'

No Sevak, I thought, you did.

For reasons best known to himself, Sevak insisted that we coast on the waters outside of Corfu until dusk. He'd certainly earned not only my gratitude but my trust. Over some more fried fish and the rest of his booze supply, I learned that most of Sevak's people were driven from Yerevan by the Turks. Passage through Georgia proved equally brutal. His own family's escape was halted when they were captured, separated by age and gender. The menfolk were placed in work camps until the Ottomans decided exactly how to execute them. The women and children weren't as fortunate. Placed on boats and barges, thousands of them were taken out into the middle of the Black Sea where, locked beneath the deck, they were powerless to stop their captors capsizing the vessels. I'm sure that Sevak's reluctance to tie a stone around my neck and hurl me into the clear blue had as much to do with his fundamentally unblemished humanity as it did the fate which befell his mother and three sisters, all of whom he recalled tenderly, and in loving detail. A long way from land, Sevak's grief, as unique as his fingerprint, was everywhere, framed by surroundings initially not of his choosing. Of the years he spent listening to the water, picking up the threads, the voices of those he held dear - live, those spirits told him. Of the land he left behind, generations of his people, rootless and persecuted - live, they said.

He asked me about my life and the circumstances which brought me to be lying face down on a fishing boat on the Mediterranean, gasping for life. Perhaps the spirits of my own had implored me to continue, just a little while longer. I asked him to guess what I *did. Sevak took out a small drawstring pouch and filled the pipe he'd been whittling with tobacco. He considered a while before concluding that due to my violently distressed condition that I was either a crooked accountant or a bookie! I laughed so hard that I felt my wounds strain. I might resemble a burst pin cushion but I was in fact, a writer. His turn to laugh! Ha!*

Sevak told me that his father was a well-travelled and learned man. He'd hoped that his two sons would either follow him into law or become men of medicine. His younger brother Rami had chosen the latter. Pity Rami wasn't here earlier, I said. Might have saved you three hundred francs! He is here, Sevak said. All of my family are. As the sun rises, they are the wind which carries The Durango and as it sets, they are the stars which light my way, protecting me as I dream.

'Do you miss your home?' I asked.

'Wherever I feel the cool breeze, I know that I am home.'

I could not argue with that. The amorous chaos of the 14th Arrondissement and the oppressive oppidan of my borough couldn't be further from where I was, if not literally, then certainly figuratively. At this very moment in time, I too was home. The murder, threats and subterfuge, Benoit, Etienne and Le Corbeau? No, I felt as safe and secure as I'd done in recent memory. The pressing issues I had - contacting Anaïs, as undoubtedly she would have been beside herself, and my friends in Paris to let them know that I was fine - were a dim and distant second to getting into Corfu at this stage. A soft bed and, with apologies to Sevak, a meal that I could enjoy without getting my fingers greasy, were imperative. I headed back inside to check on the state of my clothing. The unblemished items I was wearing when the train pulled out of Gare De Lyon had been obliterated by crude gashes and blood-stained perforations. The other pieces of clothing that the Castagne associates took from my apartment were suitable for less temperate climes than the Greek Islands. I decided that I would partake in a much needed cigarette or ten and count out exactly how much money remained in the envelope before I planned my next move.

'Sevak!' I shouted from the cabin. He was already at the door.

'You won't find anything there,' he said, taking a long suck from his pipe. 'The Englishman also took your cigarettes and your money.'

'The sneaky limey fuck!'

Chapter 11 - Marseille Soap

'A bright light shone from the silhouetted hilltop overlooking the coast. Darkness had enveloped this part of the island. The Durango had coasted for the last hour of daylight and now sat a mile or so off a small tree lined islet. Embedded within its dense thickets, stood a small white chapel.

Sevak hadn't told me what his business here was but as we were intending to disembark under cover of night, I presumed that he wasn't selling dictionaries. He started the engine and on the lowest of gears, with the lights covered, we headed for the islet.

'This is Pontikonisi,' he said as the dark atoll filled our view.

'It translates as Mouse Island but the locals call it 'The Isle of the Dead'. As I didn't want my mood darkened, I thought it best not to press him for the reason. Sevak switched the engine off and momentum carried the Durango towards the jetty. He veered hard right, expertly turning the boat into the tightest of spots.

'Tie the ropes,' he said, throwing me the heavy cable. While I did what I could, he skipped off at the stern, secured his cable and reboarded the Durango before I had the chance to complete a basic hitch. The large dog leapt from the boat and onto the jetty, scouring the area for danger.

'What now?' I asked, hoping he would say 'Remain in your underwear and return to the cabin for the duration.'

'Just stay close,' he said, ominously. I followed Sevak, semi-naked (me, not him), down the jetty, through the overgrown shrubs which led to the whitewashed chapel. The moon's bright glow offered the only escape from the night's black pitch.

'We'll do the trade off and we'll go back to the Durango,' he said.

In the distance, I heard the sound of a boat approaching. Smaller than Sevak's, the high-pitched frequency of its tiny engine whirring against the gentle waves.

'It's him,' said Sevak, tapping out his pipe and putting it back into his shirt pocket. 'Don't get too close,' he said, worryingly. The small boat pulled up beside the Durango.

'You'll need this,' said Sevak, handing me a knife, around six inches long, serrated edge with the handle heavily taped. 'For when you go into the hold.'

Through the gloom came a man. A good ten years younger than both Sevak and I and in far better shape. Though my hands shook, I held the knife tight. Just in case.

'Wolfgar!' he snapped. There was a rumble and a growl as Sevak's canine companion took off at pace towards him. Sevak was unmoved, except for the slight trace of a grin.

The dog leapt up on its hind legs and onto the man, whose arms wrapped around its mighty dome, his hands grabbing at its fur. They tussled for a moment...

'Good boy!' cried the man as the dog repeatedly licked his face. 'Good...boy!'

The young man approached Sevak and they embraced.

'Did you get what I asked for?'

'And more!' replied Sevak. 'Take a look.'

The young man and the very contented dog boarded the boat, heading for the hold.

'Who's your friend?' he asked, casting a critical eye on my unkempt and undressed self.

'This is…' Sevak paused. He knew my name but wanted to give me the option of protecting my identity.

'Henry', I said. 'Henry Miller.'

'Like the writer?' he asked.

Sevak looked at me and nodded.

'Yes, like the writer.'

'Welcome to Corfu, Henry!' he said as I sliced the cable which secured Sevak's stash.

Lord Anthony Grier, youngest brother of the 4th Duke of Westmore, was his titled name. Tony, as he was known to all and sundry became my host, my patron and a trusted confidante. Warm, generous and very funny, Tony was also a world class bullshitter. I'd always thought that Americans were the greatest liars in the world, especially those old Brooklyn Jews but this fellow was on a different level.

He told me that he won the Marathon at the '24 Olympics but was stripped of his title because he spent twelve of the twenty-six mile course in his cream coloured Rolls-Royce Twenty. He would've gotten away with his ruse had he not stopped, still dressed in his running gear, for some baked John Dory at Le Poisson. He told everyone who'd listen that he was the love of Nijinsky's life and once, he was seduced by Isidora Duncan but didn't enjoy it. He claimed to be the world's greatest filmmaker and that in the Philippines, he was once anointed a god. He understood at least two hundred of the native American dialects but had a lifelong aversion to using the word 'No'. Tony also insisted that he'd invented a cure for the clap by taking two parts Polish vodka and one part Marseille soap then mixing the paste into the purines extracted from French mushrooms, which explained why he was so happy to see Sevak return from that part of the Med. While much of that was fanciful (especially the cure for the clap, trust me), he did make films and he was from a family of middle ranking English aristos who, after failing to marry him off to some distant cousin in an attempt to cure him of his *affliction - a condition I hasten to add, which is publicly proscribed but privately practiced - sent him to the Dark Continent with an elderly equerry and a generous allowance. An outbreak of typhoid in the Côte d'Ivoire claimed his valet, but an indomitable spirit, as well as a trunk full of that continent's booty, kept him afloat until he reached Tunis. And that is where he first encountered Sevak but that part of the story can wait.*

While the cogs of war were being greased on the mainland, the wary sought shelter wherever they could. As days turned into weeks and weeks into months, I gratefully spent the next year and a half in the secluded comfort of a small but perfectly homely quarter of Tony's grand maison.

Furnished with the freshest of food, endless sunshine and an Underwood typewriter, snatched from the estate of the late Robert E. Howard, my afternoons were spent writing, my evenings mingling with properly vetted locals and my mornings swimming then recuperating in Tony's well stocked library, where shark fucking, proto-surrealists like Le Comte de Lautrèamont spooned into the more conventionally decadent works of Lawrence and Huysmans. And I wrote. And I wrote. Reams of the stuff. Sevak sailed and scoured while Wolfgar kept watch, Tony headed into the towns with his Paillard Bolex camera but I stayed and I wrote. The Gothic grind of Brooklyn and the troubles that I encountered in Paris and Marseille were fertiliser for the bountiful harvest that Corfu bestowed upon me. Everything about this wondrous place broadened my horizons. The scales had fallen from my foul, amoral, miserablist eyes. And in between daily solipsistic arguments about existence, wine and Ginger Rogers, my host provided a solution to the one issue that had been bothering me since I left France. I would start to write letters to Anaïs, to Joe Do Sappo, Lisette and to my family in New York to let them know that I was fine and well. On his travels around the Mediterannean, Sevak would disembark in random towns and post them for me. Upon arrival, the postmark would show Genova or Toulon, even La Spezia but never Corfu.

Nowhere close. No one needed to know what I didn't want them to. That's why the whole arriving 'under the cover of darkness' hooey appealed to him. Discretion was the key.

I even composed a letter to Benoit Castagne, explaining precisely what had happened from the moment I left Gare De Lyon. It took me a while to build up the courage to send that one but eventually I did, giving it to Tony to mail on one of his regular trips to his financiers in Switzerland. I figured that with France about to fall, he'd have bigger problems to deal with than me mislaying an heirloom.

By the summer of 1940 though, my Hellenic hiatus was about to run its course. As Italian forces were chipping through Albanian defences across the bay, Tony's protracted return from Switzerland had put him in a foul mood. Like most of us, he had his battles with his 'ennemis psychologiques' which sometimes took days for him to shake. His highs were colossal but his lows were crippling. For simple folk, like myself, a combination of food, function and fornication could be trusted to even out one's keel. And surprisingly, given the hand that he'd been dealt, Sevak was never bound to his melancholy. He took it on, embraced it and subdued it. The tranquillity he found at sea played its part. Tony arrived in Corfu around midday on the Friday. I'd been lounging beside the pool, drying off after a swim, re-reading the final draft of the book I'd just completed. France was now under occupation and central Europe was about to be torn asunder for the second time in a generation, but for us blinkered artistic sorts, there was an imperviousness to the dangers lurking beyond our narrow purview. I wouldn't say all was well in the world but at this moment, as a new American, blithely detached from the internecine beefs of the old world powers, this was pretty much biscuits and gravy time for me.

That night, Tony had company. This wasn't unusual. He was a gregarious man with a range of interests which made him a sought-after presence on the island. Politics however, left him as cold as the cubes in his raki. Coming from the kind of background he had, he'd intimated that there was something of a necessary evil about the politicians that he'd hitherto had dealings with. To me, they all looked alike. White men, grey skin, black hearts. He told me that he'd been intimate with two members of the Greek cabinet. I took from his tone that this wasn't his regular name-dropping horseshit. They'd told him, separately, that he must prepare to evacuate the area. Anyway, this particular evening, one of these sticky fingered, freeloading cunts - Lambraskis, I think - was pontificating about morality. I think that he'd recently read a book and wanted to share with anyone who'd listen, his new-found knowledge. The ones who weren't bored into blasting their own skulls starward, had started to shuffle off into the sanctuary of the cool, peaceful night. Still the dimwit Lambraskis persisted. Duty, virtue and a modest obligation to the common good was paramount, he said, carefully overlooking that he'd arrived in a pristine Daimler Double-Six.

I don't know exactly what trite generalisation triggered my ire but I'll admit that I may have had a few more shots than normal by this point in proceedings. Seemingly, I told him to shut up and started to deconstruct, deride and ridicule everything that he'd communicated; if he said black, I said white and I could prove it. I mocked his accent, his nostrils and even his hair style; the irony of a bald man having a go at someone with hair? Ridiculous I know but my first barb got a big laugh so I kept on shooting. I picked on his shoes, his moustache and his decision to side with Kant over Aristotle. I was on a roll. Tony caught the end of my act and expertly drew the event to a close. I left the ring, crowned the island's undisputed champion and Lambraskis skulked off, no doubt crying onto his driver's shoulder.

I had a late breakfast the following morning. A couple of aspirin, some fresh fruit, toast and coffee was all my sensitive constitution could handle. I thought about a quick dip to jolt the system back to life but as my head felt much heavier than usual, I was fearful that my swollen cranial mass may carry out its threat and finally sink me. Tony arrived and I greeted him as I normally would.

'Henry, we must talk,' he said, cutting me dead.

'Sure. About what?' I replied.

'Last night.'

'I know, I know...' I said, in a partially contrite way.

'You insulted one of my guests.'

'Who? The politician?' I spat. 'He was being a pious prick!'

'Regardless. He was a guest of mine, at my home and you made him very uncomfortable.'

'Ok, I apologise.'

'Not only that but the Minister is a person of considerable influence.'

'Aha! That's what bothered you?'

Tony had watched me get into fierce arguments with a whole host of people since I'd come to stay. Some bested me but generally, I held my own. Until now, none of it had amounted to as much as a two storey anthill.

'Yes. It did bother me.'

'You...fucking toffs. You will always look out for one another,' I said. This was particularly unfair as, in reality, I was more of a leech than Tony ever was.

'The Minister will be a very important figure, should the Italians arrive on the Island. I cannot risk alienating him.'

'If this island is invaded, neither Lambraskis nor any partisan resistance will give a rat's ass for you or your fancy things. This place will be looted and turned over faster than you can say The Sacred Band of Thebes. Trust me on that.'

Tony turned his back on me. He ran his fingers across the top of the glass drinks cabinet, an ornamental feature I'd grown very close to.

'I would like you to leave,' he said. 'Today.'

'Fine,' I replied, masking my surprise and hurt as well as any scolded seven year old.

'I will arrange your safe passage,' he said.

And with that, he was gone. Step over the line with these sorts and boom! You're out. The speed with which I was removed from Tony's inner coterie staggered me. Within the hour, with the few belongings I possessed, I was aboard the Durango. Rarely did Sevak take his modest fishing boat past 'The Isle of the Dead' and never during daylight but on this occasion, Tony must have insisted.

Standing at the stern, I took one long and final look at Pontikonisi, Vlacherna Monastery, the blue domed, white houses jutting from the craggy hills around Kanoni and at Tony's house, hoping that this would be one of his practical jokes, a wheeze which we'd laugh about into the night over French cigarettes and Italian wine. But it wasn't to be. I moved upfront, alongside Wolfgar, the breeze blowing through his massive mane while Sevak plotted our course.

A couple of days of travelling; Corfu to Siracuse, then over some unexpectedly rough seas to North Africa, the Durango again earned her corn. Once we'd moored - at a private residence on the northern side of the Cap Carthage - Sevak walked me over to the rather splendid looking Hotel El Kacem. As I'd left Corfu with only the clothes on my sun-tanned back and little in the way of cash, Sevak intimated that the accommodation had been taken care of. Indeed, when we arrived in reception, he was greeted as if this wasn't the first time he'd been here. I was given a key and a small boy dressed as though he was a miniature concert pianist, took my bag to my room. Sevak gave him a coin for his troubles and he seemed happy with that. On the journey out of Corfu, we hadn't spoken much. I sensed that I'd disappointed him by wasting this opportunity Tony had given me, these blissful eighteen months, in order to flex my intellectual muscles. While most of that was true, I did long to be tested again. To feel the stab of hunger in my gut and the pressure to deliver those goods, even for a buck a page. To feel alive again. The paradox of the matter was that without Sevak's selfless and timely handling of my condition, I would've long been a fleshy feast for the fish. I'd apologise to him but Sevak was never comfortable with those kinds of gestures. And anyway, he lived by his own conventions, his own code.

'A man named Chadli will take you to the town of Bizerte this evening. The ship you will take, a British merchant cruiser called the 'MS Duncan', will sail to Lisbon under a Spanish false flag. Once it docks, it will remain there for a day but you must remain on board. The ship will then sail, as part of a protected convoy, to Chesapeake Bay in your home country. From there, it's up to you.'

He stood and offered his small, calloused hand.

'Don't think harshly of Tony. It is easy to say 'come' but difficult to say 'go',' he said.

I wanted to tell him that I was sorry for upsetting Tony. And I wanted to say thank you to him, for everything. The moment caught me. I couldn't speak. I just gripped this little man's hand for as long as I could.

'May fortune remain by your side, Henry,' he said with an honest smile. Just before he walked out of the door, he turned and said, 'I took the liberty of putting something in your bag. For the journey. You never know who you might meet.' And with that, he was gone.

The ride to Bizerte and the convoy to Lisbon were uneventful so I won't bore you with the details but the voyage from the Portuguese capital was fraught with danger with reports of clusters of U-boats seemingly on the hunt for vessels sympathetic to the Allied cause. The Marseille soap and mushrooms that Sevak cheekily placed in my bags didn't alleviate the tension but the bottles of Polish vodka sure did. As Europe disappeared from sight and the bracing Atlantic air bit, for the first time in a considerable while, I needed a heavier jacket. Expertly stitched back together by Tony's seamstress, one would never imagine that it was the same coat which was cut to ribbons two years earlier. I fastened the buttons and turned up the collar against the wind. I hadn't the foggiest idea what was in store for me, on the voyage or back in the States. The Captain of the cruiser had a trunk full of charts which mapped every possible permutation and manoeuvre, should she find herself under attack from one of the German Wolfpacks but as the Captain of my ship, the master of my own course, I had no such plans. The cosmos and my soul alone would guide my hand. Wherever they took me, I'd go. On the page and off. East, West, High, Low. Where didn't matter.

The time spent on Corfu had brought out in me a realisation that my failures had as much relevance to my craft and this life experience of mine as my few successes had. What had once been a trial, now flowed like a tributary. And when it didn't, instead of force, I simply put it aside and lived, accepting that what may seem hard to comprehend now, will at some undetermined stage, present its significance. Perfectly imperfect, riding the crest, sinking in the swells. That could come in useful. I need to write that down, I thought, searching for my notebook; a beautiful leather bound hard-backed volume given to me by Tony the previous Christmas. This book, he thought, was robust enough to suffer extreme manhandling and would keep safe the half-finished notions and steams of inconclusive doggerel that graduated from the innumerable scraps that were eternally filling my pockets. Around two hundred pages thick, I'd already scribbled on three quarters of it. I peered into my bag, looking for the red ribbon bookmark which acted as the tail on this magnificently jumbled behemoth. I sat on the edge of my bunk and opened the notebook.

An envelope, very pale lilac with the initial H, stylishly penned, dropped from the book and onto the floor.

I picked it up, broke through the lightly glued seal and removed the contents. Folded inside the letter were five $100 bills. This is what he wrote:

'Dearest H,

I do hope that this letter finds you well. It was never my intention for our association to end in the manner in which it did but I will endeavour to provide you with an acceptable explanation for the seemingly abrupt action which I took.

From the moment you arrived on the island, honesty and discretion were the foundations on which we built our friendship. What took place at the Villa was of no one's concern but ours. H, these old rooms have been positively refreshed with the laughter that your keen wit brought and your perceptive take on cultural, art, political matters, not to mention your incisive grasp of the affairs of the heart, have illuminated many a previously darkened pathway. It is, therefore, with genuine remorse and contrition that I have to inform you of an indelicate slip on my part which set the cogs turning on your hasty eviction.

During my recent trip to Switzerland, I happened to be at an event in the company of my cousin Laurentz. Like me, certain lifestyle choices he has made have placed him at odds with his family and despite his title, he was advised to relocate by the newly appointed Gauleiter of the Weser-Ems region to prevent any embarrassment befalling his family. In the small hours, most of the guests had retired for the night but a handful of us sat in our host's library, talking revolution and partaking in Cognac and Cubans. The usual haute bourgeois bullshit. Talk had swung from the minutiae of war, to the influx of emigrè whores into Zurich and the dilution of quality therein. The hours fell away as one 'expert' opinion after another was debated or debunked. The occasional remark aside, I kept my thoughts to myself. I did not know many of my fellow revellers but as a relative of Laurentz, I presumed I was in safe company. It certainly didn't stop me from imbibing enough Cognac to float our tiny acquaintance's fishing boat.

When the subject matter changed to literature, I opened up. More so when the topic branched off into American literature. Hemingway and Faulkner. Faulkner and Hemingway, on and on and on it went. I couldn't hold my tongue any longer. Henry Miller I cried! Silence. These ingrates, philistines had no idea. He is only the most inventive and imaginative writer of prose in the English language today, I claimed. And that was not the drink talking. I mean that, Henry. An artist out of the ordinary who shines a light into the darkest corners. This is a writer who has chronicled the sexual underbelly of Paris during 'les années folies' more accurately than any other.

Miller? asked Laurentz, labouring under the effects even more than I. Rambling titillation, he said. A manual for unimaginative house husbands and nothing more.'

You don't know Miller, I rebuffed.

Tropic of something, he replied. Diseased trash.

I was outraged. Wait until you read what he is writing at this minute! said, robustly defending your honour.

He's writing now? asked another voice in the room; a sallow skinned fellow who like myself had been relatively silent during the conviviality.

Yes, it is a marvel, I said.

When should we expect to read this...marvel? he asked. Miller is not the most prolific writer.

That is true, I replied but he is very disciplined. Every morning, after a swim, he locks himself away and we don't see him until late in the afternoon.

Miller is staying on the island? With you? Asked Laurentz, enviously.

All eyes in the room were trained on me. I hesitated, knowing that my vanity had raced ahead of my prudence. I'd broken our covenant. The sallow man stood. He was tall and familiar but not overly so. He pressed me. Henry Miller is a guest of yours? How marvellously fortuitous, he said. I have an associate who is terribly keen on his workings. Perhaps we could arrange a mutually beneficial time for a meeting between them? The heavy doors opened and a waiter arrived with more drinks, the conversation mercifully diverted. However, the tall sallow man persisted. He approached and spoke quietly. Sir Anthony, he said, I would consider it a personal favour if you could permit my acquaintance the honour of visiting you and your esteemed guest.

No, I don't think that it would be practicable, I replied hastily. Come now, he pushed. From what I hear, you can be a very persuasive chap, am I not right?

Henry, I've fended off enough overtures in my time to know that this was no quid pro quo. He asked me to carefully consider his proposition, reminding me that his offer would be 'mutually beneficial'. Some other time, perhaps? I said. Corfu, isn't it? He asked, walking back towards the party. Pittacus, he said. Excuse me? Tell me, was it Pittacus... or one of the other sages of ancient Greece who said, 'Know the right time'? That was unambiguous.

I left at first light, and calling in all manner of debts, I bartered my way back to Corfu on the morning of that fateful date. Unbeknownst to you, I hastily organised an event that night, knowing that if you were true to form, you'd over-do it with the booze and as soon as that tedious little worm got on his soap box, you would bite and I would have a ready-made excuse to exile you. And the reason why? If I told you the truth, you'd become all self-righteous and insist on staying to fight it out. But Henry, you and I know that you're not that man. I feel that I have gotten to know you very well during your stay. I am loathe to become mawkish and sentimental but I have come to consider you not as a brother - familial bonds are often forced rather than forged, don't you think? - but as a Quixotic cousin tilting at windmills - and windbags - all his days. A fighter you aren't Henry but a champion you most certainly are. Knowing you as I do, I'll wager that the physical pleasures of North Africa and Lisbon will tire your old bones out and that you'll not reach for that notebook until you're safely out in the Atlantic, heading home. As for poor Sevak, I couldn't tell him for the same reasons that I couldn't tell you. This was my mistake, my slip. And I alone will deal with it. Sevak's people have a saying: 'Part with your head but not with your secret.'

If only I could undo this mess but alas, I cannot. Hoist sail, Henry, and hoist it high while the wind is fair. One day, I hope that you can find it in your heart to forgive a friend.

T.'

I kept that letter closer than any other piece of correspondence I've ever received, from Anaïs, from June, anyone.

A choppy month or so later, I was home free and finishing off a breakfast of ham and eggs at the diner at the north end of Baltimore's Penn Station. The familiar rattle of crockery, wise cracks from the one, tired waitress and the smell of onions frying on the grill was surprisingly reassuring. As I had another hour to kill before taking the Pullman carriage on the final leg of my drawn-out return to New York, I bought the lunchtime edition of the local newspaper.

As I'd been starved of good old American news for the last few years, I pored over the sports section first. The Dodgers were doing fine, tucked in behind the Reds for the pennant. Reading names such as Joe Medwick and Cookie Lavagetto filled my soul the way Blaise and Fodor might have done a few years earlier. Dem good ol' bums! I said to myself. As a young man, I snuck into Ebbets Field when it opened, for the first game against the Yankees. Thirty thousand people, shoulder to shoulder. The land they built it on, by Bedford and Sullivan, used to be one big field of swill. Pigtown, they called it. I was never a huge fan of baseball but I'd say that I flirted with its angular structure and its communal goal. Similar to another youthful passion; socialism. One never knows, I thought. I might very well reacquaint myself with both. Not much about the boxing though, other than speculation as to who was next on Joe Louis' list of hopeless challengers so, onto the Arts.

I'd been so long away that I didn't recognise the names of any of the writers being reviewed. Back to the start. I skimmed over the first few pages and found myself in the Europe section. I was thousands of miles from harm's way, I reminded myself. So why did I have a knot in my stomach? A short piece on page 10 caught my eye; no more than a couple of paragraphs, about a recently signed pact between

Axis powers, in which each of the antagonists would recognise and respect their partners' interests. The piece, penned anonymously by one of its London bureau writers, mentioned the breaches in the Albanian border and that Greece was about to fall under the spell of Mussolini. The final, perfunctory paragraph read as follows:

'A squadron from the Royal Airforce, led by Air Commander Sir Patrick Grier, has been dispatched to assist the Greek defence forces. For Grier, second son of the Duke of Westmore, the exercise comes days after news of the death of his youngest brother, the documentary filmmaker Sir Anthony Grier who was among those killed during exchanges with an invading sub-unit of the Italian 9th Army on the island of Corfu.'

'You look like someone who could do with a slice of pie, Sir. Tell me if I'm wrong?' asked the wisecracking waitress, not hanging around for the answer. 'We've got Pecan, Blueberry...'

'Thanks, but no.'

'Your loss,' she said with her chipped-tooth smile, refilling the mug I'd been nursing. As the skies opened, the rain, its rhythm irregular, battered onto the corrugated roof of the diner, I thought of Sevak and of Tony and his parting words; hoist sails while the wind is fair. I slid my fingers through the handle and gripped tightly, the heat of the freshly brewed joe searing into the palm of my hands. It came in waves.

Chapter 12 - Twenty Bucks

"Caesar salad, French fries and a Pepsi. That's all I wanted, Jerry. It's not as if I asked for the Waldorf salad, horseradish potatoes and a diet Tab?" said Jim Howard, a thirty year Columbus regular.

Jerry Hector's face was turning the colour of ripened rhubarb.

"May!" he hollered.

"Don't be mad at May. She looks so tired. I think you're pushing her too hard," said Jim.

"Damn it. Elvin! Where is she?"

Without turning, the short order chef shrugged and continued flipping burgers and boiling greens. He didn't say a word and he didn't turn around because although he would cover for May, like her he drew the line at lying to the face of the fellow who gave him his first and only job.

"Miss Washington, have you seen her?"

Without raising her eyes from the enthralling story in her beloved National Enquirer, the cashier sighed and removed the cigarette from her mouth.

"Jerry, you know that I'm not one for telling tales out of school," she drawled, "but if you'd like to find an answer to your current staff related conundrum, I suggest that you check the payphone by the toilets."

Down the corridor, the Columbus' errant waitress was adding to the well scored wall.

"And what time do you close...hello? Hiii?"

The line went dead. May turned to see Jerry with his finger, pressed down on the prongs.

"Pick a number between one and ten."

"I'm sorry Jerry. I just needed to make a very quick call."

"And the phone at the cashier's desk isn't good enough?"

"I didn't want Miss Washington listening in. She always does."

"Pick a number between one and ten, May."

"Is this a trick?"

"No trick. Pick a number."

"OK, four."

"Good call May. You have four seconds to get your ass back into the diner and fetch Jim his Caesar salad or you're fired!" yelled Jerry.

As May scurried back into the diner, Jerry Hector looked at what she had been scribbling on the wall. Maybe it's time for a lick of paint, he thought.

May reappeared.

"Jerry? One more thing. I need a favour."

"Three! Two!..," he bellowed.

Back in the dining area, May fixed her apron and straightened the paper cap perched precariously on her head.

"Caesar salad, French fries and a Pepsi, table five. And make it quick!" said Elvin.

May took the tray and weaved through the patrons.

"Sorry Mr Howard. We were fresh out of Caesar's there so I just had to go out and fetch some more."

The old man shook his head.

"I came, I ordered, I waited," he quipped.

"Very good, Mr Howard. That's one free Pepsi refill for you."

The bell rang again. "Order up, table three!"

A steaming plate of steak and eggs with a side of fries for the large man with a shock of red hair and moustache to match, seated around most of table three.

"Some more coffee, Mick?" she asked. The large man cast her a look, grunting in the affirmative before returning to the sports column. "Damn Sox, eh Mick?" There was a simultaneous grunt and nod from Mick. "All or nothing now against the Indians, eh?" With the precision of a surgeon, he sliced off an inch thick wedge of steak, dipped it into his egg yolk and grunted again. "I mean, if we can't get a couple of wins against those Cleveland bums, we may as well just pack up and go home," said May, giving his coffee spoon a clean. The man grunted again. "Imagine moving Franco from shortstop to second base. Even worse is benching Bernazard. That's criminal, Mick. Criminal." Mick speared at his plate three times in succession, capturing eight French fries. Dabbing them in the browny, bisque-hued crater that was, until moments ago, a perfectly fried steak and egg, Mick fit the entire forkful into his mouth with not one droplet touching his moustache. He continued to chomp and grunt purposefully.

"Always good talking with you, Mick," said May, spotting Jerry with his coat on heading for the door.

"Where are you off to?" she said, darting into his path.

"Samson's. We need paint," he replied, curtly.

"Jerry, about that favour we talked about earlier."

Jerry sighed and rolled his eyes.

"Contrary to what you and everyone else here thinks, I do not run a charity out of The Columbus. Get back to work."

"Charity? You didn't mind when I worked twenty-six days straight in July? Or those times I stepped in, at short notice on my days off? Or when Elvin was in hospital? Or when Miss Washington had to go to Denver?"

"You got paid, right?"

"Yes I did but ask yourself, Jerry Hector, is that why I'm here? The money? I'd kindly remind you that there's half a dozen places within walking distance where I'd get at least fifty bucks a week more. Is this what you want Jerry? Really Jerry? Really. I'll do it."

May stood in front of the proprietor and pulled her most serious face. Jerry stifled a chuckle. No matter how infuriating she was, he couldn't stay mad at her for long. And she did have a point. Erratic, yes. Flighty, sure. Reliable? He trusted her more than just about anyone else. They'd always been close, even more so since her father passed. He didn't have kids of his own but he had been married. Establishing and operating the diner cost Jerry his first wife. An even briefer second attempt ended about fifteen years ago but he seemed fine with that. Keeping May and more latterly, Elvin on the right path more than scratched that parental itch.

"I'm gonna make you a deal," she said, buttoning up his raincoat and fixing his scarf.

Jerry shook his head. "Hear me out first," insisted May.

"I'll do the twelve to five shift tomorrow and you don't have to pay me double time."

"OK, what's the catch?" asked a suspicious Jerry.

"I need to leave early. And I need a twenty buck advance on that extra shift."

Jerry laughed and gently moved May out of the way.

"You're lucky that I've got a great sense of humour."

May repositioned herself in front of him.

"Please. I have to get to Portland today. Now. Before the stores close. There's something I need to get."

"Something you can't get in Auburn? Or Lewiston?"

"No, I checked. It has to be Portland."

Jerry grimaced. "It's Dennis, isn't it? May, you told me that you were over that…"

"No. Honestly, it's not," she replied, earnestly.

"So who's going to cover the rest of today's shift?"

"Elvin said he'd double up," she lied. "Isn't that right Elvin?"

Behind Jerry's back, Elvin shook his head, silently mouthing obscenities May's way.

Jerry sighed. "Twelve to five and you'll be here, ready and serving at twelve?" he asked.

"I'll be here at eleven thirty, how's about that?"

"Twelve's fine. Miss Washington?"

The cashier sighed dramatically and replied. "Yeah?"

"Twenty for May," he said, walking out the door. The cashier looked at May with familiar disdain. Elvin summoned May over.

"What are you playing at? Do you want to get us both fired?" he asked, annoyed rather than angry.

"Hand me my coat. I'm off to Portland."

Elvin placed his hand on her arm.

"Tell me it's not Dennis."

"Please..."

"May, going over old ground is never good. That's what you've always told me. Move on. When a ship has sailed, it has sailed, you know?" said Elvin, taking May's still damp coat from the peg behind the counter.

"Elvin, trust me. It's not Dennis."

"Then who is it?"

"I'm sworn to secrecy but here's a clue. He shares the same name as your Uncle in New Jersey," she whispered playfully.

May grabbed her coat and the twenty dollar bill Miss Washington was holding up, freshly removed from her till under duress.

"Hoist sail while the wind is fair, Miss Washington!"

"Yeah, yeah," replied the unimpressed cashier as May left the restaurant at pace. In the last booth by the window, a diner who had just finished eating, stood up and walked over to the cashier.

"What was it today, Rose? Fillet mignon and a black beer?"

The customer stared back, unimpressed with the cashier's snarky attempt at humour. "Half a slice of pecan pie and a single, lukewarm black coffee. No refills offered nor requested."

Miss Holloway gazed beyond the cashier, through the tilted blinds, her head darting like a little hen. May was already halfway down Main Street before she'd had a chance to remove her standard $2.25, minus the usual 10% tip.

"Where's young Miss Morgenstern off to in such a hurry?" she asked.

"What am I? The Oracle?"

The librarian opened her handbag and removed a dollar. She slid it towards Miss Washington. The cashier looked at the lone note, contemptuously. The librarian stared at the cashier. Miss Holloway took out another single dollar and placed it on top of the first note. Still, Miss Washington remained motionless.

A third dollar was removed from Miss Holloway's handbag. The cashier swept all three notes into her midriff with the seasoned speed of a Vegas dealer.

"She's off to Portland to meet with some fella named Henry."

****

Since Dennis took the Tower Records job and left Auburn, May was reluctant to consider Portland as anything more than another place crossed off her own personal map. She'd been places, not many but a few, and uniformly, they'd been a disappointment. Auburn never was. The familiarity of home, of the small town she'd been born in, grown up in and very rarely left. It had everything she needed. Except for Dennis. Though she thought about him often - and had almost worn out his magnetic ninety minute analogue love letters - he'd still left. Therefore, she no longer needed him. However, Portland had one thing, Dennis aside, that Auburn lacked and for that she needed to club together more than the few bucks she normally carried.

Her savings account, standing at a reasonable $716.87, was inaccessible due to it being a Saturday afternoon. She didn't own a credit card and for a few slices of pie at The Columbus, Mrs Krupa kept the rent affordable. Between pay days, Jerry acted as an unofficial cash machine when she needed a new tyre or a record she'd heard. May wasn't frugal but she wasn't a spendthrift either.

Dumping her bag by the dresser near the door, May headed straight for the tip jar, in the cupboard beside the catering sized drum of out of date coffee that the diner was disposing of. Her savings fund tended to be augmented by these gratuities but on this occasion, the seventeen bucks and change had another less lofty purpose.

The journey south from Auburn to Portland normally took just under an hour, even less at this time on a Saturday afternoon. No point in taking the car, she thought. One hundred mile round trip in the Pacer would be tempting fate. Just short of forty dollars should be enough for a ride to Portland, get what was needed, maybe have a sandwich for the trip home, especially if she utilised her expired student card for a discounted bus ticket. After a quick freshen up, May filled her old college satchel with a banana, the final Three Musketeers bar, a pack of tissues and Elie's book. She toyed with the idea of taking some basic cosmetics, just in case. No. Take me as I am, she thought, closing the door. On second thoughts...

At the Transit Stop, a handful of waiting passengers sheltered under the canopy of the adjacent thrift shop. Three minutes, if it's on time, she thought. She reached deep down into the pockets of her coat and took out a quarter. The call box outside the shop was unoccupied. She dialled a number from memory.

"Tower Records, Portland. Lacey speaking. How can I help you?"

"Dennis Hudson please," she replied.

"I think he's up on our classics and VHS floor. If you hold the line, I'll transfer you."

At the corner of Hollander Street, the silver single decker bus eased out and slowly turned left towards the waiting passengers.

May put the phone down. She didn't need to speak to him. She wasn't going to spring herself on him. In his place of work. No. He was there, that's all.

May took her place in the queue, her right thumb over the date at the bottom of her student I.D. card.

"Portland, same day return. Student," she said.

The driver looked at the picture, then at May. Then at the picture again. He raised an eyebrow and that was about that. It was Saturday afternoon. He'd worked this route for years and was in no mood for anything remotely confrontational.

"Four fifty," he said.

"It used to be three seventy-five," said May. "When did it go up?"

"In April," replied the driver. "But you'd know that, being a student and all..."

May handed over a five dollar bill and said, "Keep the change."

She took a seat three rows directly behind the driver and took out Elie's book.

"Miss," said a voice. "Miss!"

"Yes?"

"This is yours," The man handed over a 50c piece. "He asked me to tell you that he don't take tips. He ain't no waitress."

A week ago, May would've sunk down in her seat, mortified. Not today. Nor would she spend the next hour listening to The Temptations, REM or Tom Waits, glancing enviously into the passing lives of those she'd see, living their best days, buffing their pristine cars on their power blasted driveways, painting their fences the whitest of white, in every town from Auburn to Lisbon, from Freeport to Falmouth, where Connie now lived, down the 295 coastal route to Portland. Not today. Henry Miller had her complete and undivided attention.

Chapter 13 - The Bookplate

Every Saturday, from late spring until early winter, Portland's Deering Oaks Park hosted a Farmers' Market. When she was younger, May's father would drive them down for some hockey and freshly cooked sausage. He liked Portland. They'd spend hours with the weekend editions, figuring out the jumbo cryptic crossword. The summer she turned sixteen, not long after they received word that her mother had passed, May's father borrowed a camper van. His intention was to drive down through the old colonial towns of the eastern seaboard, New Hampshire, Massachusetts, Connecticut and Rhode Island. As it turned out, apart from a single outing to Cape Elizabeth, they didn't go further than Portland. Her father's aversion to far flung adventure was something which didn't skip a generation. He told her that Portland was *the* town with the most men named 'Bob' in the entire country. She didn't believe it, even though it was the truth.

The bus stopped by the park before continuing downtown. May got off one stop early, by the park's entrance, for old times' sake. When Dennis left Auburn, he rented a place down by the wharf. A New York style loft apartment, for Maine prices. Dennis liked a bargain. He'd left her a forwarding address - 5 Danbert Place, Apt. 6/A - which she'd memorised, in case she ever visited. She never did, figuring that old lovers, like overdue bills, were things best left behind.

The Farmers' Market - a mix of dressed cuts, bottled pickles and fresh dairy produce, wrapped in a quintessential yet cutesy old world charm -

was exactly how she recalled it. The tempting aroma of the freshly grilled würst though wasn't going to distract her from the primary purpose of her trip; a store called The Bookplate.

At the west entrance of the two-levelled building, in between the sports and health sections, an elderly man held open the door for May. The fresh perfume of a thousand brand new books usurped the best of what The Schwitzer Family Butchers and their famous twenty two varieties of meat had to offer. Fiction or biography? When she placed the call from the diner earlier, she hadn't asked the clerk to put the books aside, chiefly as she hadn't gained the requisite permission - and funds - from her employer. She figured, correctly, that there'd more likely be a queue around the block for the latest Sidney Sheldon than there would be for old volumes sat for decades on some dusty shelf.

As she had in the Mooney, May followed the letters; from Mailer, to Makepeace and Mann.

Miller, Arthur took up the full bottom section, so May looked to the next level and there he was, up and almost out of harm's way; Miller, Henry.

There was almost a full shelf dedicated to his work. Thick compendiums, thin novellas. Although quite tall, even this was out of May's reach.

"Do you require some assistance, Miss?" asked a politely spoken voice. It belonged to a neatly dressed, middle aged man whose name badge said, 'I'm Kenneth and I'm here to help'.

"Please," she replied. "I just can't reach the top shelf."

"And unless you're Kareem Abdul Jabar, my dear, you never will," said Kenneth, snapping open his portable steps. "Stack 'em high, that's what they want. I'm five six and I'm nowhere near the top. You must be close to six foot tall."

"Five ten and a half," replied May.

"Exactly. One day, as God is my witness, someone will overreach for a Garrison Keillor and bang! They'll take out a full display of Harold Robbins. I've told them time and again but what do I know? I've only worked here for twenty years," he said, ascending his steps. "What are you after, my dear?"

"I'd like to see Henry Miller," replied May looking up.

"You and a hundred dead broads," he replied in a voice more akin to a movie gangster than a bookseller. "Are we ready?" he asked.

May nodded in anticipation.

"We've got The Tropics, Cancer and Capricorn," he said, blowing dust from the booktops before tossing them down to May.

"Then we have 'Sexus', 'Plexus' AND 'Nexus'..."

May juggled the books into a manageable pile.

"Hmm..." he paused. "What about 'Quiet Days In Clichy'? Usually a big favourite with you 'young bohemian' types."

Yeah, I can see how popular they are, she thought, waving through the stoor.

"Keep 'em coming!" May replied, enjoying the repartee with Kenneth far more than she did with old Holloway at the Mooney. "Mind the cobwebs," he said, launching the thin novella May's way.

"Oh!" exclaimed Kenneth, stopping for a second. "I have not read this for years!" he said, gently shaking the dust from the jacket of a hardback volume.

"This is 'The Colossus of Maroussi'!" he declared, descending. "Most new readers of Miller tend to go with his more, shall we say, salacious books but this one, is arguably his finest. Many reckon that this is as honest and close to a 'self-portrait' as the author ever committed to paper."

If only you knew, thought May, clutching tight her bag. She pored over the description on the book's jacket.

"Written while he was in Greece, just before the War," said Kenneth.

"That's the one. I'll take it," replied May in an instant.

Kenneth checked the inner cover. "This one is priced at...$23.95! Goodness me!" he said with a sharp intake of breath. "There may be a paperback version up there. Let me go back and check."

"No, it's fine," said May, without a thought for the cost.

"If you don't mind me saying Miss, you don't look much like a typical Miller reader."

"There's a type?" asked May.

"I'd split them into three categories. First, you have your unhappily married, middle aged former literature students, curious about the life they wanted to lead but were too afraid to commit to the disappointment of poverty."

May snorted.

"Second, you have the scholars and critics. Looking for answers while chipping away at his reputation."

"And finally?"

"Last but not least you have the plain old, depraved perverts."

May laughed again. "Hold on a minute. Didn't you say that you were a Miller reader?"

"I prefer Wodehouse and Waugh but I will admit that I find myself delving into the old rascal's work from time to time."

"So, into which category do you fit?"

Kenneth thought for a moment.

"A pinch of two and a double scoop of three," he replied, ringing up the bill. "That'll be $23.95, please!"

May opened her purse and took out the twenty from the diner. The balance she made up in coins. Kenneth placed the book into a brown, branded paper bag with stiff twine handles.

"Do you mind if I have a look at the others before you lead them back up Dust Mountain?" she asked.

"There's a reading seat over by 'Gardening and Horticulture'. I'll put this aside for you for now. Take all the time you need, my dear," he replied. "Until six that is. That's when we pull the plug on this dive and head on out into the downtown lights."

Kenneth closed his eyes and began to recite.

"In the meantime, we should read to give our souls a chance to luxuriate," he said with a flourish. "That's Henry Miller. If only Monument Way was the Place De Clichy…"

"You've been most helpful, Kenneth. By the way, I'm May," she said.

"How perfect! And Henry will be right here, behind the desk," he replied, patting the bag containing her newly purchased hardback.

May took the well-used bucket seat beside a display of books about Winter Gardens. She tucked her satchel, and Elie's book, under her feet for safekeeping.

Where to begin? The old analogue clock with the elongated numbers read 3.44pm which gave her a good two hours to skim, scan and flip through twenty odd years of Miller's work. Two hours. Twenty years. That's probably long enough, she thought. Within minutes, she'd read enough to conclude that the author of 'Black Spring' and the writer of the letters to Elie were indeed one and the same. She moved onto 'Quiet Days…' which quickly confirmed that belief. May stopped searching for clues and fixed on a paragraph about the narrator's Montmartre. The aroma of sexual arousal and lust infused every letter. His words, his phrases were immediate, threatening, and alive. The more May delved into his world, the more profound the sensation she felt. Whether the setting was Paris or Portland, May had begun to realise that the straps which secure even the most tightly bound cases can loosen, revealing hitherto unacknowledged truths. These passages were far more candid than anything Connie Barzagli would dare steal from the Mooney and as May read, the deeper into her own desires those verses penetrated.

"Attention shoppers. The Bookplate will be closing in 10 minutes," came the announcement.

May looked at the clock in disbelief. The hours had flown by, the display of books beside her, untouched. Portland locals clearly hadn't been taken in by the allure of a neat wintertide foliage.

At the cash register, a different clerk was on the till; young, blonde and attractive though heavily made up with a hairstyle more suited to a woman twice her age. May approached the desk with the pile of books she'd been reading. She placed them neatly in a pile and waited for the clerk to finish her calculation.

"I'll be with you momentarily," she said cheerily, humming an indecipherable tune while slowly punching numbers on her calculator.

"And there we are. I'll just ring these up for you?"

"No, they're for Kenneth. I was just browsing."

The clerk sighed, grabbing the books from May. "Now I'll have to put them all back. Thank you Miss. Thank you so much for visiting our store. Do come again."

"What's with the attitude?" May replied.

"This is not a library."

"I am quite aware of that, thanks," May replied bluntly. "I bought a book here earlier and Kenneth said he'd leave it aside in the bag. Behind the counter."

"Of course you did."

"Seriously lady. What gives?"

"Do you have your receipt?"

"No. He must have left it in the bag," May spotted it, beside a pile of books behind the clerk.

"That's it there. Look!"

The bag stood alone.

"It's got my name on it. See?"

Though Kenneth had written her name, in bold, on the bag, the clerk wasn't convinced.

"Do you have any identification on you?"

Jesus! May thought. She went into her purse and took out her student identification.

"This says Morgenstern," said the clerk. "Not May."

May snatched it back, "Give that here."

She'd never noticed that it didn't have her first name on it.

"And it's expired," said the clerk smugly.

"Have a look inside the bag. The receipt will be there," said May, becoming exasperated at the clerk's antipathy.

The clerk stared at May. She wasn't going to check the bag.

May placed her hands on the desk and leant over.

"Give me the bag. You. Stupid. Insipid. Fucking. Cunt," she said calmly.

The shocked clerk took a step back. She put her finger on the intercom button and said, "Security to till number five, security till five, urgent."

"What's wrong with you?" May raged. She stretched over the desk, making a grab for the handles of the bag. In a panic, the clerk grabbed May's arms and the bag. May's feet were off the ground as the clerk pulled her over the desk and onto the floor.

"This is mine!" she growled.

"Security!" shouted the now hysterical clerk. An elderly couple looked on, quite excited by the melee.

At that moment, a tall, uniformed man arrived. He stepped in between the two warring women, prising the bag clear.

"Miss... Miss!" he yelled at May, his plastic nightstick urging her to remain at a distance. "You need to calm down. What is the problem here, Casey?"

"She's trying to steal one of our books, Bob!"

"Steal it? I bought it, you fucking dolt."

If May was aghast at her own language, she didn't let it show. "If you rubbed a couple of those brain cells together and took a look inside the bag, you'll see that it's Henry Miller, 'The Colossus of Maroussi' with a receipt for $23.95 to prove that I paid for it. It even has my name written on the bag."

"Miss ... Miss ... I need you to remain calm. Please. Can you do that for me?" asked the security guard.

May took a deep breath.

"I am perfectly calm, thank you," she replied.

"OK Miss, Thank you. Now, do you have any identification on you?"

May roared in frustration. The small group of shoppers in the vicinity had turned into a throng. "Look in the fucking bag, you moron!" she said.

"You need to calm down or we're going to have to take you downtown," said the security guard, sternly

"Oh Robert, do shut up. This IS downtown. And please, lower that little stick of yours," said Kenneth, returning, just as war was threatening to break out on the peninsula between 'Ben Gavin's 101 Evergreen Favourites' and 'Grow Your Own Poinsettia'. The security guard meekly obliged.

"Miss Richards, please tell me that you're not alienating our customers again?"

The clerk looked at the floor, sheepishly.

"Eyes up here please," said Kenneth.

"She was trying to steal some books."

"Bullshit!" snarled May, still flushed with anger.

"And the evidence you have of her obvious criminality is precisely where?" asked Kenneth, patiently.

"She tried to snatch that bag."

"This bag?"

"Yes."

"The one with her name written on it?"

"She was very rude to me," said the clerk, starting to tear up.

"If I was in her shoes, I'd be a darned sight more than rude, Miss Richards. I'd be demanding the most severe action. The most severe."

Kenneth looked at May and winked. May shook her head. "It's ok. Just a misunderstanding."

"Very well. Lessons will be learned from this. Won't they Miss Richards? Off you go now. We'll do some more work on your customer skills on Monday."

"Mr Kenneth Sir?" asked Bob the security guard, checking the bag.

"This receipt here only covers one book," he said, holding up the hardback. "It doesn't cover this one."

The security guard removed a second book from the bag.

"Hadn't you heard? We're running a special. Buy a Henry Miller, get one Anaïs Nin absolutely free."

May looked at Kenneth who remained calm and unaffected by the guard's discovery.

"But Sir?" the guard replied, confused.

"Robert, your job title is 'Store Detective' is it not?"

The guard nodded.

"Perhaps we should be concerning ourselves with the word Store rather than the word Detective now, shouldn't we? Don't you have your final rounds to make? We wouldn't want to sully your first week's employ with a black mark, now would we?"

"No Sir. I'm on my way," he replied, head bowed, his authority reduced. Kenneth handed the bag to May and rolled his eyes. "I'm sorry for that. The customer is always a suspect with those two."

Kenneth escorted May out.

As the store lights dimmed, he lit up a cigarette and took a long drag.

"May I?" asked May, breathing in the menthol aroma. She had only smoked one cigarette in her entire life; with Connie Barzagli, of course. May had never cared much for the taste of tobacco but at this moment, post conflict, she was curious.

"Sure!" replied Kenneth. He took his pack of Virginia Slims from his pocket and offered one to May. Awkwardly, she held the cigarette as Kenneth lit it. "Inhale!" he exhorted. May did as he said and spluttered. "Here, let me do it for you." Kenneth put the second cigarette into his mouth and again, flicked open his lighter. He took a long drag and handed it to May. "You can't read Henry Miller without a cigarette. I think that's actually law in France. And if you're going to read Miller - and smoke - you really need to be reading Anaïs Nin. Twenty pages of this will explain more about their condition than every text otherwise written."

May took the book in her hands. The dust cover was glossy but stark white, with the title and author's name in an unremarkable font.

"It may look nondescript but trust me, it isn't."

May tentatively held the long menthol stem, attempting a couple of short puffs. "That's it," said Kenneth. "You're getting it now. But a word of warning. Once you start, it can be a hard habit to break. Same goes for the cigarettes."

****

As the stores of Portland closed, the bars and restaurants of downtown came to life. A hundred different neon crackles, urging you to come in and take a load off, tempting you to spend some of your hard earned. Even the billposters, between the boutiques and bakeries, seemed to imply that one's existence might be incomplete if one wasn't immediately planning a trip to a European café to join its sophisticated model for a coffee. Her teeth, her life. So perfect.

May checked her purse. She had just over seven dollars left. Just enough to purchase something to cleanse the taste of mentholated tobacco from her palate. Nothing fancy. Two bucks on a Big Mac, fries and a Coke for the coach journey back to Auburn would still leave her five bucks for something a bit more potent. Recalling Miller's time in Corfu, May realised that she'd never tasted ouzo, nor had she sampled raki but she figured that she'd probably need to order food in a Taverna for that experience and seven dollars just wouldn't cut it. Ouzo would have to wait. Small steps May. A beer or two, somewhere not too busy, with a TV showing the Sox on in the background would have to do. Why didn't bookstores open late into the night, she thought, not unreasonably. If the bookshop was still open, she would've stayed, curled up at a reading station, until departure time. She could take an earlier bus but the thought of being somewhere other than Auburn on a Saturday evening was surprisingly thrilling, even if it was only Madden's Beer Hall, a dimly lit, run-of-the-mill bar at the junction of Middle and Franklin. She ordered a bottle of Canadian beer at the bar and took a seat in a booth close to the small stage where a young band had just finished their soundcheck. She'd be long gone by show time, she thought.

Above an ornately framed print of an Irish Wolfhound, there was just enough light emanating from the green glass fitting on the wall for May to delve into Volume One of the Diaries of Anaïs Nin without attracting the unwanted attention of any of the bar's few patrons.

May pulled on her bottle. The freshness had long since departed and only lukewarm suds remained. She'd been nursing it for a full hour, enrapt in the book gifted to her by Kenneth. I'll get another one in a minute, she thought. May looked up. She hadn't noticed but the bar was busier now. There's no way the waitress will see me from here. Leaving her newly acquired literature face down and her satchel hidden at the foot of the table, she made the short walk to the bar, intermittently turning to make sure that her space wasn't taken. Behind the bar's collection of non-vintage booze, May could see her spot from the large mirror which bore the debatable legend 'Madden's - Finest Beers and Spirits since 1948'. Above that was a clock which indicated that she still had an hour and change before the Auburn bus left. One more beer and a few more pages.

"Can I buy you one?" said a voice.

"No, I'm good," replied May, tilting her head slightly.

"No hard feelings, Miss?"

May turned to see Bob, the security guard from the bookstore standing beside her. Out of uniform, he quite looked different.

"I didn't recognise you without your little stick," teased May.

"I know," he replied, scratching his head, deflecting the shame. "I am sorry about that."

"Don't worry about it," replied May, struggling to catch the attention of the staff.

"Excuse me!" shouted Bob, his voice cutting through. The barmaid appeared.

"What can I get you?"

"Two more Molsons."

"You got it," replied the barmaid, cracking the bottle tops into a little bucket under the bar.

"Well, thanks for the beer ... Bob," said May, edging back towards the refuge of her booth.

"Mind if I join you?"

"I'm actually in the middle of a…"

"A book. Yeah, I know. I saw you. Just one beer. That's all. As soon as the stretch is over, I'll be out of your hair, promise."

May had forgotten about the baseball game.

"What's the score?" she asked instinctively, before instantly regretting it.

"The Sox lost again, three to two."

"Damn," said May. "So who'ya watching now?"

"Blue Jays and Yankees. If Toronto wins, they take the pennant. So, you Sox too?"

May nodded. Bob, took this as an invitation and slid into the seat opposite. May moved her books from the table, placing them at her side.

"Bob Valley," he said, offering his hand.

"May," she replied, brusquely.

"I ain't seen you in the store before."

"I'm not from Portland."

"Where are you from?"

May reluctantly replied.

"Auburn? Never heard of it. Me? I'm from Southie," said Bob, asking and answering his own question. "I don't get to go to Fenway much these days. Too far to travel, especially with the job and all. But I do miss it. There's nowhere like it."

"So why are you here, in Portland?" asked May, impatiently.

"Well May, that is a long story," replied Bob, stretching back and smiling.

"I'll bet. Listen, Bob, it's been great catching up with you again, it really has, but I've got to get back."

"To Auburn? Tonight? You'll never make it in time."

"How would you know? You've never heard of it."

May reached for her coat.

"Please," asked Bob gently, putting his hand over her wrist. "One more beer. After that, I won't bother you again, I promise." As he removed his hand from her person, his voice broke. "It's been a rough couple of weeks."

May sighed, and glancing at the clock, she realised that she was going to hear Bob's story, whether she wanted to or not.

"Ok. One more."

One more she said. That's all. Just to be polite. However, by the time the band were introduced to the now crowded tavern, Bob and May had cracked open enough Molson and Canadian Club to toast the entire Blue Jay roster. Though not normally a heavy drinker, May's tolerance to alcohol was impressive. More so than Bob's. For the last hour, in between cheers at the abrupt end to the Yankee season, May had listened to Bob spouting forth on the benefits of maintaining one's power tools, the futility of electric cars and why Phil Collins would be nuts to leave Genesis. Her instant appraisal of Bob was that he was a bit dull but generally harmless. His non-ironic love of terrible music and his thrift store Kurt Russell look, weren't anathema to May.

"Did you choose to live here because of all the other 'Bobs' or was there another reason?"

"What other Bobs?" he replied with a vacant look. He'd clearly never checked the record books.

"Never mind," she said, draining the remainder of her bottle. "So what brought you to Portland? I mean, the wharf is pretty enough but…"

"I came here when my wife…"

Bob's eyes began to fill up. He swallowed heavily.

"She's gone."

May instinctively placed her hand over his. Her innocent question hadn't been intended to elicit such a reaction. A knot of anxiety formed in her stomach. If she could have left right then, she would've.

"It's ok," he said. Bob rubbed his eye socket with the balls of his hand. "She's in a better place."

May didn't know what to say and how to react. The thought of unloading one's heartache onto a complete stranger just didn't register.

"I loved her so much but I didn't tell her often enough. The worst thing about it is that I still see her every now and again," said Bob choking on his words.

"Like, in your dreams?"

"No," he said "When I pick my boy up."

"Hold on a minute," said May, taking her hand back. "You see her when you pick your boy up?"

"Yeah. He's thirteen. I get visitation rights every other weekend."

"But you said, 'She's in a better place'?"

"A New Haven condo is far better than any of the shitholes I made her live in. I'll say this for that Ivy League cunt she's shacked up with, he's got better taste in real estate than he has in pussy, pardon my French."

May struck Bob on the arm.

"Hey! What the fuck's that for? I said 'Pardon My French', didn't I?"

May struck him again. The penny dropped with Bob.

"Oh. You thought I meant..."

May pulled a face, mocking Bob.

"Duh! Did she leave you because you were a dumb shit?" chortled May

"Kick a man when he's down, why don't you?" replied Bob, a smile returning to his tear sodden face.

May grabbed her coat and bag. "It's been fun, Bob, but I've really got to go."

As she stood up, Bob said, "Can I at least walk you to your bus?"

The band, already on a winner with the crowd, called out for requests. Among the plethora of bar room classics offered up, someone shouted 'Play 'Power of Love' man!' A cheer went up as if the Sox had just won the pennant. May liked the movie but not as much as Elvin did. He'd seen it three times the first week it came out. Initially, she hadn't minded the theme song but its ubiquitous presence on TV, radio and every jukebox since its summer release had started to test her patience. Familiarity was fine, May thought, but only on her terms.

"Only if we go this minute," she said, slaloming through the tightly packed throng. Bob followed, his head nodding along to the song's familiar opening riff.

A chilly haar from the nearby wharf had settled over the town. Outside the warm confines of the bar, May thought that the now muffled noise made the band sound more interesting. Less Huey Lewis, more Sonic Youth. As May buttoned up against the cold, Bob helped her straighten out her collar.

"So, you came all the way to Portland for a book?"

"Yeah," replied May.

"Hope it was worth it."

Me too, she thought.

"They sure got a lot of books in that shop."

"It's a bookshop, you dolt," replied May, relishing her role as Bob's tormentor-in-chief.

"Yeah, I know," replied Bob, self-consciously. "Takes a lot of guarding."

"I'm sure it does," said May, sarcastically. It may have been the effects of the drink mixing with the cool night air but May was enjoying Bob's awkward yet sweet attempts at conversation.

"I was wondering..."

"Yes?"

"Was there anything else in the store that you had your eye on? You know, the kind of thing you can't get back in Auburn? If there was, I could put it aside for you. If you'd like."

Is he talking books? May thought. Bob fortified and emboldened, offered May his arm.

"I'm good," said May, her hands remaining warm, nestled in her pockets.

Familiarity, but only on her own terms. As they reached the corner of Congress and State, May stopped.

"I'll be fine from here. I don't want to be taking you out of your way."

"Nonsense," he replied. "Besides, what else would I be doing on a Saturday night? Sitting in some bar, listening to Huey Lewis songs?"

"There is that," replied May.

"And thinking about Laurie," said Bob, sliding back towards melancholy. "She was the reason I came here. Her uncle was head of the local teamsters and I thought he might give me a break, you know, start me up, driving one of his trucks. That way, I could make enough money to win her back. He said he'd see what he could do but he never answered my calls, the two faced douchebag. Laurie must have talked to him. I wasn't a bad husband..."

As Bob's moan continued, May's attention was drawn to a couple walking towards her. The girl was as tall as she, with long red hair. Her arm, and that of her partner were tightly entwined. Whatever he was saying to her was working. They looked as blissful as Bob and her were mismatched. May reckoned that he wasn't divulging his woes as Bob was to her. As they came to within a few feet of where Bob was unburdening, the lines between the familiar and overfamiliar blurred, becoming as smudged as May's eyeliner. She wanted to turn away but couldn't. The girl caught her eye, smiling as she passed this stranger with the odd hat and long coat. Her partner, his face buried deep into her lustrous red hair didn't even notice the woman for whom he'd once declared his love in the form of seventeen mixtapes.

As they passed into the Portland night and Bob continued on his breathless voyage of self-pity, May's emotions swirled like the long reeds on the banks of the bay.

"Bob ... Bob ... stop."

"Ok."

"How close is your place?"

Bob, surprised by the question, looked around.

"About ten minutes, maybe twelve from here. Why?"

May looked him in the eye.

"This is what you're going to do. You're going to shut up about your wife."

Bob nodded.

"You're going to buy me a seven dollar bottle of wine."

'Sure…"

"Then you're going to take me back to your place and fuck me."

****

"What can I say? I'm in the mood for some Camille Saint-Saëns."

A small puff of smoke rose from behind a high-backed chair. A near empty wine glass was carefully placed onto the cork coaster. Beside it, an ashtray with two thin menthol stubs was about to receive a third.

"Well?"

"Yes, she took it," he said.

"Poor girl. She has no idea what she's getting herself into," said the voice at the other end of the phone. "So, what now?"

"We wait."

Chapter 14 - Killer on the Road

The dew from the immaculately tended greens seeped through the canvas upper of the rubber soled basketball shoes that he favoured for his early morning runs. From under his sweat-soaked white cotton tee, his huge chest pumped like an engine. In the trees, bordering his route, the sound of the Steller's Jay seemed to mimic his strained gasps for air. Can't stop. He'd heard that Robert Johnson had once claimed that there were 'Hellhounds on his Trail'. Got off easy, he thought. The ghosts which pursued him were relentless. He must go on. No one was around at six in the morning. The course wouldn't open for another hour. Hard yards, soft fairways. Better for his knees. Take the shots, said Moe Cohen. You're ruining my fucking greens. A needle into my joints? I'd rather tie my robe with a rattlesnake. What are we gonna do about you, they laughed. He didn't. He'd seen it a hundred times. Better to keep running. Of all the places, Vegas was where he'd stopped. St. Francis County, Arkansas. Sand Slough, to be precise, is where he started to run. Picked up the pace and onto St. Louis soon after. Not now. Two more holes. Do not look back. For a man of thirty-eight years, his breathing was laboured. Some ventured that he was older than thirty-eight. Truth? He didn't know and to be honest, he didn't give a fuck.

One hole. Push.

Need to get in shape. That last fight, he didn't enjoy. Big tough white boy from Jersey. In front of his own people too. Still cut him up real bad though. That's not what they wanted. In front of his own people. Seventy stitches, give or take. Now they know you're still serious. Need to get in shape. No more bleeders. No more trips. No Sweden. The Garden or Vegas. That's it.

Done.

The sound of his now bare feet slapping on the resin coated path alerted the waiting groundskeeper who folded his newspaper and handed him a fresh white towel. He removed the tied shoes from around his thick neck and buried his head deep into the dense pile of the cotton, his breathing still heavy but steady.

"There's someone over by your car, Champ," said the groundskeeper.

Dabbing the last traces of sweat from his head, the Champ handed back the towel.

"Same time Saturday?"

The Champ didn't respond as he walked over to his black sedan, heat rising from his head in the cool air of daybreak. A neatly dressed man crouched by the whitewall tyre on the driver's side.

"That is one fine automobile. Brand new Fleetwood. Tell me. Is this the seven or the seven point seven?"

The Champ didn't acknowledge him. He popped the trunk of the car and dropped in his running shoes.

The neat man continued, "I'd say that, as you banged your last Fleetwood up, this one's the seven point seven. Does that extra point seven make it faster? Because anything over seventy on the Strip and you'd be running into blue lights before you hit Henderson. Unless, that is, you took it down to Phoenix or Tucson. You'd be able to really open it up there. Maybe drive through the desert on the 15? I tell you what, a brother could really get lost out there. You know what I'm saying, Champ?"

As the Champ gripped the car door handle, the neatly dressed man placed the palm of his hand on the window above.

"I read this thing about Vegas in the National Geographic. Killing time in some motel somewhere. Anyway, did you know that people have been doing deals, right here, for over one thousand years? Right here. I kid you not. The Paiute, the Navajo and the Shoshane people used this very land to stop, rest some, trade a little then move on. They always moved on. Me, I can't stand Vegas at the best of times but at New Years? I'll be following their lead. They know something that us latecomers to the party haven't quite grasped. And that is, when exactly to get the fuck out of town. Sure, Ma and Pa Kettle come here by the busload with their fifty bucks for chips and twice that again for that watered down piss they pass off as Scotch but welcoming in 1971 with Tom fucking Jones at the International? I don't need that and neither do you. Me? I was thinking that I might take a drive up to 'Frisco with my wife. Ten years married today. Can you believe that? Maybe you should get out of town too. I hear Northern California is where it's at. Look up some old friends, y'know?"

The Champ's shoulders straightened and the bones in his massive, clenched fists, normally hidden under eight ounce gloves, cracked with tension. The safety was off. Toe to toe, heavyweight versus middleweight, this was a mismatch, but the slighter man did not take a backwards step. The Champ himself hadn't willingly taken one of those since his father whipped his young frame into a bloody mess back in Arkansas. Yards away, as the Golf Club prepared to open for the day, the groundskeeper lifted the drop bolt, wheeling back the grand iron gate. The clang of metal barrier into its side fixing chimed like the peeling of a bell. The Champ's eyes narrowed, his teeth grinding in his jaw. His oft neglected body had just received its orders. Taut and primed. The smaller man could not ignore this message. He stepped back, turned and leaned on the car.

"Chuck fucking Wepner, man. You know I can't help you with that mess, Champ. But I've left something for you. Usual place. Just in case," he said quietly, conciliatory.

The neatly dressed man put on his shades and moved away from the car. The Champ opened the door, climbed in and drove off, with one eye on his rear-view mirror.

Anywhere but Vegas.

****

White boy rock, easy listening, nursery rhymes with that bubblegum beat. No matter the preset, nothing pleased the Champ. Even on WJSX, home of his favoured down and dirty, backwoods rhythm and blues, they were playing The 5th Dimension. 'No more falsehoods or derisions, golden living dreams of visions, mystic crystal revelation and the mind's true liberation'.

Aquarian fantasy aside, the Champ didn't dream much. When he did, he rarely remembered the details. A few nights ago however, he'd had one which he found harder to let go. Sealed in a small, cold room which was filling up with water, he didn't panic as it rose around his waist. He was content. From the top of the room, an old friend reached down, offering him an escape. The Champ stood on a stool to reach him and as their hands met, he pulled his friend down and into the water with him. As his friend thrashed around, desperate for life, the Champ held him under the water. As it reached his own nostrils, the Champ woke, the sweat dripping and his heart pumping as hard as it did after his morning run.

He'd been living in an area east of the Strip, known as Paradise for a couple of years now. Walking distance to the International, the Nevada climate and its lack of accountability were pivotal reasons the Champ set his family up here. Sun, broads and opportunities. Few understood the Champ's predilections better than Geraldine, his wife of thirteen years and she accepted that her 'big man' needed to stretch his limbs from time to time. She'd returned to St. Louis for Christmas and wasn't expected back to their Ottawa Drive home until after the New Year. The figures who controlled his career had promised him another crack at the title in the spring but first he had to take care of the Canadian, Chuvalo. The money was in Vancouver but they'd rather stage another event at the International, that way they'd all get a taste. That worked for the Champ. The decision was pending, they said. Leaving Vegas now would confuse matters.

The Sahara-Nevada Country Club backed onto the street where the Champ lived. While he preferred to do his running on the courses not on his doorstep, he wasn't averse to the occasional round here with his celebrity neighbours. Shecky Greene didn't judge him and neither did his hero, Joe Louis. They didn't want a piece of him the way others did. They were content enough to shank a few balls into the long grass and shoot the breeze.

The Champ pulled his Fleetwood into the car park, took his kitbag from the trunk and headed straight for the modernistic, pastel coloured stucco clubhouse. He'd often stop here for an early morning bite after a night on the tables.

"Good Morning, Sir. The usual?"

The Champ nodded as he headed for the locker room. As no one had completed a round by this time, the showers tended to be empty. The Champ didn't care either way. He'd spent most of his adult life in either gyms or County but as with his training runs, he found peace in the quiet.

After his wash, he took a seat, not his usual booth but at the table in the corner. Within seconds, a youthful waiter had delivered his regular breakfast; scrambled eggs and Canadian bacon, freshly squeezed fruit juice, a short stack of pancakes with maple syrup and black coffee.

"Beautiful day out there today."

The Champ stared out of the window.

"Any plans for New Years, Champ?" he persisted.

He shook his head. "What about you?" he asked.

"Taking my girl to the Strip to watch the display, then maybe afterwards, we'll go to the Cobra."

The Champ peeled off two ten dollar notes and passed them to the waiter.

"Well, you have a good time."

"Thank you, Mr Liston," he replied. "Can I get you anything else?"

"Bring me the phone, kid," the Champ replied.

The waiter returned with a sky-blue phone which he connected via a long cable to a socket situated under the station of the Maitre D'.

"Ready to go, Sir."

The Champ nodded. He picked up the receiver and called a local number.

"Yeah?" answered the groggy sounding voice.

"I'll be over before lunch."

"Sure thing."

The Champ picked up two lumps of sugar and dropped them into his coffee. He stirred slowly and looked out of the window, down the 18th green. The sun shone on Paradise. Peace reigned here.

From his back pocket, he took out his wallet. A faded picture of his wife sat behind the clear insert, his drivers permit behind it. He removed a number of business cards from one of the wallet's pockets. Between Vasquez's Body Shop and one from the deputy Attorney General of Nevada, there was a cream-coloured card with a plain black border. It read;

JEFFERSON STREET GALLERY, MONTEREY CA.
Fine arts and original books.
Open Tuesday to Saturday
(408) 624-1887

On the back of the card was a telephone number which didn't correspond with the digits on the front.

The Champ dialled the number. After a few rings, a woman's voice answered.

"Hello?"

"Hi. Is Val there?"

"No, I'm afraid he's in Europe at the moment. He won't be back until late next month."

"I see."

"Are you calling from the publishers because I already told someone in your office just before Christmas that because of his fall, he wouldn't be able to type for at least three months."

"No, it's Charlie, just an old friend."

"Oh Charlie! How wonderful! You know he often talks of you."

"That's nice to hear."

"Would you like me to pass your number on to him?"

"No, it's good. Maybe I'll take a drive up to see him when he returns."

"I know that he would like that very much, Charlie."

"You take care."

The Champ hung up. On the lawn outside the window, a mutation of thrushes darted around a discarded crust. Too heavy for one bird alone to carry, each thrush took it in turn to peck at the bread. Often, in his own garden, the Champ would relax with a drink, and allow himself to be mesmerised by the music of their light trilling. He admired their tenacity and speed far more than the brute force of the larger birds who invariably want to muscle in on the happy scene. In their moment of gaiety, they couldn't see what was coming but the Champ could. He knew exactly how this was going to play out.

Looking up, he spotted a familiar face at the bar. Taking fifty dollars from his money clip, he called over the youthful waiter.

"You still got a set of clubs in your locker, kid?" he said, placing the money into the waiter's hand.

"Sure do, Mr Liston."

"Good. I want you to take every club out of the bag, except the driver, the putter and the seven iron. Then meet me on the First. You got that?"

'Whatever you say, Mr Liston," replied the young waiter, confused.

"Now go tell The Fox that I'll be the one taking his money today."

The Fox was Jackie Shilling, a gag writer for hire back in the golden age of Hollywood. Tired of fixing different versions of the same New York melodramas, Jackie moved west after receiving an offer to work on a Bob Hope film that was meant for someone else. He became so popular, polishing dialogue and bumping up the laughter count, that the studio kept him on contract for twenty years. Off set, it didn't hurt that he could charm a smile from a stuffed snake. Jackie loved Vegas but he was the kind of gambler they hated. Nowhere near high roller level, Jackie went in and got out when he won what he intended to. Once the Strip blossomed and the casinos expanded, a new breed of comics hit town. The smarter ones adapted their LA acts, with some expert tweaking from the silver haired, gravelly voiced Fox. And if they wanted to find him, they didn't have to look far. Early morning tee off, Sahara-Nevada Golf Club, he'd be found standing at the bar, five foot three, one hundred and twenty pounds wet, pants pulled halfway up his chest, smoking a cigar, supping a soda and looking for someone, other than Patti, his very non-showbiz wife of years, to spend the next few hours with.

"Put 'em up, ya bum!" said the Fox, lifting his thin, sun-spotted arms into a fighting pose. At full stretch, the Fox's right barely reached the Champ's jaw.

"Champ," he whispered. "Did you know that one of the members here is a fairy? Seriously."

The Champ had heard this one before but as a willing stooge, he played along.

"No! Who?"

The Fox turned his cheek to the Champ, "Give me a kiss and I'll tell you!"

"How you doing, Jack?"

"Hey, I've got a bone to pick with you," he said as they walked towards the first tee.

"Fire away."

"I'm still sore about losing money on that Wepner fight."

"What do you mean? I won, didn't I?"

"But everyone had money on you going down. In the sixth. Ten large. Jeez. I had to sell the wife and her mother to that bastard bookie."

The Champ waited.

"Champ, you couldn't lend me the other nine thousand, nine hundred and ninety bucks?"

Even though he knew the punchline was coming, the Champ still laughed. As someone who operated at the zenith of his profession, the Champ always admired the fact that, though he was perhaps past his peak, the Fox never let his standards drop. His timing and delivery were razor sharp, even if the gags weren't as fresh as they'd once been. To the unobservant, here was an old timer, marking out time, living on past glories and sure, thought the Champ, playing with the Fox certainly felt light and easy. But it was an illusion. The science of thought was just as important as the science of movement. Not a single word was wasted. To the Champ, working the fast, economic, instinctual combinations with a partner locked onto his own rhythm was something that had been missing from his life for quite a while.

"You'll get your chance to win some of it back this morning, I promise."

At the first tee, the waiter handed over his depleted golf bag. Despite it now weighing as much as one of Jack's cigars, the Champ placed it in a trolley.

"Conserving your energy? Smart guy."

"You up for the full eighteen?" asked the Champ.

"What else am I gonna do? Go home and make love to the maid? I'll save that for when Patti's asleep."

"A hundred bucks a hole?"

"Funnily enough, that's what she charges."

That one the Champ wasn't expecting. He snorted with laughter which tickled the Fox.

"You have a lovely smile, Sonny."

"I'm still not giving you a kiss."

"I'm being serious. Has anyone ever told you that before? Apart from Geraldine?"

Someone did, he thought. Years ago.

"I know your game. You're just trying to put me off my swing," said the Champ, launching his ball, straight and true, two hundred yards down the fairway. Large puffs of smoke exhaled from either side of the Fox's cigar.

"Fifty bucks a hole, you say?"

The course's first hole veered to the right after about three hundred yards. It would take a professional around four to five shots to complete the hole. The Champ might've been able to strike a ball with menace but an inconsistent short game tended to bump up his score. He'd often score an eight on a par four and dependent on who he was playing, he might mark it a six. With the Fox, a level of respect they had for one another meant that the Champ played it straight. The Fox couldn't propel the ball with similar ferocity but as with much in his life, he knew all the sweet spots, especially on a course so familiar, it might well have been his back lawn.

"So Champ," asked the Fox. "What's next on the agenda?"

The Champ shrugged. "I don't know exactly. Chuvalo, then maybe Quarry or Bonavena. I'm easy."

"Surely there must come a time, if you don't mind me saying, where a man tires of getting punched on the nose and decides to move on to pastures new? You're still a young man. Surely you've got a plan for what's coming next?"

No one had asked that of the Champ in years. Since his arms expanded and his youthful frame exploded into a two hundred pound mass of blunt force and malevolence, he wore the accoutrement which best fit. He chose to lace up those gloves and hit hard. This singular, intimidating persona was all he had. Like it or not, he figured that there was more to be had from being America's favourite 'bogeyman' than there was breaking his back, like the hard but unschooled men he grew up alongside in Arkansas. Professional sport and working the fields weren't the only choices he had though. His 'educational' stint at Missouri State Penitentiary taught him that if harnessed properly, his aggression could pay a handy dividend. And in Vegas, as there was in St. Louis, there was always work with those who do their deals in the sun but deliver their invoices from the shadows.

"I got a few things in mind."

"That's good to hear," replied The Fox. "A man needs a broad...range of interests." He couldn't help himself.

An awful nine at the par four second meant that the Champ was already $200 in the hole to The Fox by the time they reached their next test; uphill and over the creek at the short third. The Fox, by dint of winning the last hole, teed off first. His ball sailed high over the creek into the clear blue Nevada sky, before curling left and landing in the sand trap just short of the green.

"Wrong decision, old man. If you played your nine iron, you'd have made the green. Even with those old saggy, pipe cleaner arms of yours," teased the Champ, dispatching his tee shot to within thirty feet of the hole.

The Fox shrugged his shoulders. "Maybe that's part of my plan..."

"To nail it in the bunker? Good plan," laughed the Champ.

"Good plan, bad plan, we won't know what's the right decision and what's the wrong one until we stop, mark it and it's over. Until then, you gotta make the best of it. That's something I learned years ago. You know what I mean?"

"Maybe trade in that driver for a bucket and spade," continued the Champ, thoroughly enjoying his moment.

"Yeah, whatever. As I once said to Jimmy Cagney, 'You crack the heads, I'll crack the jokes'," replied the Fox.

"You knew Cagney?"

"Sure. Edward G and Bogie. Gable too."

"I heard Gable was a mean sonofabitch."

"Yeah, he had that reputation but I liked him a lot. Treated me well. He'd seen this Bill Powell comedy that I'd worked on and because he liked it, he got the studio to hire me to write for his wife, Carole Lombard. She was doing the whole War Bonds thing at the time. Anyway, she was going to be in LA for a couple of days and the studio got all three of us together, to kick around a few ideas. We hit it off instantly. Gable left on the Friday but she insisted that I headed out to Indiana with her, her mother and Gable's press agent for another couple of days, working en route. Why not?

On the way back, we took one of those Douglas Sleeper planes back to California but we had to make a short stop in Vegas to refuel. Lombard and her Mother stayed aboard the plane, getting some shut eye. I liked a drink or five back then so I told them that I had to see a man about a White Horse. They sent one of the War Bond GI's with me to make sure that I'd be back in time for the next leg of the flight. We found a diner a couple of miles away, out near the Hoover Dam and we had a few. He'd taken a bullet, during basic training of all things, and for some reason was still fucking sore about it. And to make things worse, he couldn't understand why I, in the apparent prime of my life, wasn't part of this great war drive. I told him that I was more than happy to take on those Jew hating cocksuckers but I was disqualified. He said that he didn't buy it and I told him I couldn't give a fuck whether he did or not. Anyway, after another five or so drinks, he keeps on at me so I say, 'Right motherfucker, we're doing the Act of Manliness. Right here, right now."

"Act of Manliness? What the hell is that?"

"Wartime fitness test to see if you're physically up for the challenge of going into combat. We went out into the parking lot and round for round, I matched him. By the end, I'd beaten his score in every discipline; sit ups, push ups, you name it, I whupped him. So as you'd imagine, I'm busting his balls about it which clearly didn't help with his self-esteem. He then says that I only beat him because he's infirm, you know, because of getting shot. That's when I play my ace. You got shot? Big deal, I say. You lost to a 120lb man with one fucking leg."

"One leg?"

The Fox tapped his club against his right leg.

"I had blood poisoning as a child so they amputated below the knee when I was six years old."

"You gotta be kidding?"

"That's what he said so I rolled up my trouser leg and took it off. Here you go, I said, tossing it to him. One wooden leg, with stocking and shoe still attached. He held it in his hand for a moment, looking at it in total disbelief. Then he started to howl with laughter. What's so funny, I asked. And I thought I had it bad, he said. I've just been beaten by a one legged Jew, he roared, the tears rolling down his face. I didn't have the heart to tell them that I was Polish Catholic so I joined him, the ridiculousness of our mutual situation bobbing on the half bottle of Scotch we'd destroyed. Then, just as I think we're starting to connect, he tosses my leg into the bushes, and says, 'Get out of this one, you goldbricking cunt.' He climbed back into his jeep and drove off, back to the base, leaving me to hobble around in the twilight, looking for my missing limb. Stranded, legless, in more ways than one and if I don't make that flight, Lombard could whistle out of the window and have her pick of writers. I was royally screwed."

"What did you do?"

"I got down on all fours. Well, all threes actually. And I started to feel around for my leg. The waitress at the diner came out and helped me. She'd poured my drinks but to that point, I can't say that she'd made any impact on me at all. I'd started to panic but she was kind and thoughtful, which calmed me down immediately. She went back into the diner, came back with a flashlight and soon we located my leg, sticking out of a scrub. I thanked her and gave her a run down of what had transpired. 'Carole Lombard?' she said. 'Wow! I love her.' Come with me. I strapped my leg on and went back into the diner with her. 'Jack,' she said, 'can I borrow your pick up?'

Jack tossed her the keys and that girl put her foot down hard. We made the base in twenty minutes flat, just in time to see Lombard's refueled Douglas Sleeper take off. That was at 7.10pm."

"Damn."

The Champ and the Fox stood atop the green at the raised third. The Fox reached up on his toes.

"Do you see that range over there? That is Potosi Mountain."

The Champ removed his sunglasses and peered into the middle distance.

"The large ridge to the right is called the Double Back Peak. At 7.12pm, that same Douglas Sleeper crashed into it, killing everyone on board."

"Of course," said the Champ, remembering, "she died."

"She died, her mother died, the publicist. They all fucking died."

"The GI?" asked the Champ.

The Fox nodded. "Get out of that one, eh? And that's the point I'm making. Grand plans are all well and good but all you need is for one plane to crash into the mountain, and the right decision becomes the wrong one. Once you've got eighteen or nineteen, you don't ask the dealer to hit you, do you?"

"I guess not," replied the Champ.

"And if that prick GI hadn't thrown my leg away, I'd never have met the woman who changed my life."

"The waitress was Patti, right?"

"No, I took the waitress to the cinema the following night to watch Dorothy Lamour and Eddie Bracken in 'The Man Who Couldn't Leave'. I'd written it so I was anxious to know what she thought of my work. She fucking hated it. The girl seated to my right didn't. She laughed like a drain and better still, she didn't smell of fried onions. That was Patti. Plans, Champ. Plans. When you get knocked down in the dirt, start looking for quarters. As I said, you gotta make the best of things. Right, here we go. Fourth hole. Downhill, par five. The great leveller. Get your Benjamin's out, Sonny."

The Champ considered The Fox's words as he drove a shot straight down the fairway.

"All the power in the world won't save you, my friend."

He was talking golf but the greater significance of The Fox's words chilled Sonny's blood.

From the fairway, the Champ could see the pin. Two more straight shots would put him on the green. The Fox, lagging behind a few yards, gave the Champ a nod to play his second. He took aim and fired his ball into the trees, a hundred yards to the right, near the running brook.

"Haha! I told you!" roared the Fox. Plans, thought the Champ. He pulled his trolley off the fairway and beyond the rough. Removing the seven iron and a towel, the Champ propped the trolley up against one of the large trees which delineated the course.

"It's further down," shouted the Fox, to no avail. The Champ was already deep into the wooded area, exactly where he wanted to be. Beyond the second row of trees, there grew a thicket of hawthorn. The Champ used the borrowed golf club to hold back enough of the thicket to edge his way through. A couple of heavy swings could clear the way but as the Champ might need this again, he didn't want a path forming. To the Victorians, the hawthorn represented hope but the Champ had no opinion on that. He did though recognise the importance of the foliage in acting as cover for an old, almost rotten tree stump he'd once hit with a wayward ball. Looking around to see if the Fox, or anyone else had followed him, the Champ haunched down and inserted the seven iron into the stump, giving any resting creature a sharp warning that this was his stump, not theirs. Satisfied that there were no rattlers inside, he placed the towel down on the ground, lay on his back and using his hands pulled his head and shoulders into the hollow base of the trunk. The Champ reached up into the darkness, feeling his way. A quiet rustle and the cold touch of damp, plastic sheeting. He brought the item down onto his chest, his legs now bent and pulling him out of the stump. The Champ stood and brushed himself down. Shaking particles of earth from the towel, he wiped the dirt, moss and bark from his hands. He picked up the item and carefully peeled back the tape which had secured it within its protective coating. To be safe, the Champ again scanned the area for prying eyes before opening the package.

From the fairway, an impatient golfer from the following group approached the Fox, who had been puffing on his cigar, patiently waiting for his playing partner to return from the woods.

"What's the hold up?"

The Fox, aware that the Champ's attempt to find his ball was taking longer than expected, played it down.

"Do you hear that?"

"Do I hear what?"

"That."

The impatient golfer took off his shades. "I don't hear nothing."

The Fox knew all the local wiseguys and more importantly, they knew him. He was also familiar with most of the businessmen who patronised The Sahara-Nevada but this testy fellow was an unknown quantity. Given his accent and his apparel, the Fox reckoned that he was either one of the many car salesmen who had headed west in their white walled wagons, hungry for a slice of the town's fuel injected gold rush or he was one of the new generation of tough guys, respecters of nothing and no one, eager to offer the old guard the back of a hand or a trunk. Either way, it made him think twice about correcting his use of the double negative. However, he wasn't too long in the tooth to be averse to a bit of chain yanking.

"If you listen carefully, you'll hear the sound of a grateful mother whitetail being reunited with her little one after it got tangled up in the fence by the bushes. My colleague was just freeing it up."

The impatient golfer removed his shades, unconcerned by the kind rescue mission.

"Well, you tell your colleague that if he don't move his ass, there will be two more creatures that need assistance, you understand?"

"Why don't you tell him yourself?" replied The Fox, unperturbed as the Champ stepped out of the woods.

"We got a problem Jack?" bellowed the Champ, striding protectively towards his playing partner.

"Is that…?" stuttered the impatient golfer, realising who the target of his ire was.

"Not at all," replied Jack. "Young fellow here was just admiring my back swing, weren't you?"

"Yeah…nice back swing," he said meekly as the muscular frame of the Champ blocked out the sun.

"You want to play-through?" he growled.

"No...we're fine. Take your time. Nice to meet you, Mr Liston," replied the golfer, his accent now less pronounced. The Champ grunted as the mollified golfer returned to his party.

The Fox noticed a leaf and some earth on the back of the Champ's sleeve. Normally, no one would dare attempt to brush the Champ's clothes while he was wearing them but The Fox did.

"I see you were in the dirt. Did you find a quarter?"

The Champ smiled and dropped his ball at his feet. "I'll take a drop on that."

"Sure you will," replied the Fox.

As the morning drew to a close, the Fox and the Champ headed off the green at the eighteenth and walked the two hundred yards back to the clubhouse. The Fox was so far ahead in terms of holes that the Champ stopped counting. He had already handed over the bulk of what was in his money clip but compared to what he'd retrieved from the stump, it was chicken feed.

"You ever been to the Catskills?"

"Yeah," said The Champ. "I used to train up in Fallsburg. Why do you ask?"

"I've got a little place in Greene County. A small cabin in the woods near a town called Windham. It's not much but it has a couple of bedrooms and enough mod cons to stop you blowing your brains out with boredom. Ain't been up there for a while but Patti's nephew spends his weekends hunting there. If you ever feel the need to get out of the way for a while, you know, if your plans change, it's yours for as long as you need."

The Champ knew what the Fox meant and he appreciated it. They shook hands.

"And when Geraldine gets back, we'll have you over and..." he whispered, "I'll tell you what Errol Flynn did to my leg!"

See you around Jack.

The Champ walked to the side of the clubhouse and behind a white washed half wall, out of public sight, he reached into the spartan golf bag and removed the item. He untucked his shirt, opened his belt buckle and slid it into his waistband. He'd just pulled his shirt over his belt when the young waiter appeared.

"How was your round Mr Liston?"

"I got Foxed," replied the Champ, passing back the borrowed golf bag.

"For what it's worth Champ, you're not the first to lose to Mr Shilling."

The Champ removed his money clip from his pocket and ruefully pressed the remaining notes into the palm of the grateful young waiter.

"I'll get him next time," he said, walking over towards the car park.

"Have a great New Year when it comes, Mr Liston," said the waiter. Raising his hand in acknowledgement, the Champ continued towards his Fleetwood, stopping at the car door. When he was sure that he wasn't being watched, the Champ cautiously touched the door handles, then the trunk. It wasn't locked but that wasn't unusual. A cursory look. Nothing concerning, he thought, firmly clicking it shut. He dropped to one knee and pulled loose his lace. Tying a shoestring is something anyone would do. This gave him a chance, not only to remove the item from his waistband but to take a glance under the car. Again, nothing obvious. On the balance of probabilities, he suspected, it wouldn't be here. Not now. Too messy. But still...

The Champ placed the item on the passenger seat and slowly pushed the key into the ignition. He took a deep breath and made a sharp clockwise turn. The engine started. It's coming but not right now. Putting it into gear, his Fleetwood bumped out of the golf club and onto the main road. A few streets away, he made a sudden right turn onto Caravelle and pulled over. In his rear-view mirror, he watched for the Cherry coloured Lincoln, the one which left the Golf club right after him. But it drove on, past his street. Just being careful, he thought. Everything is possible. Only one outcome is probable.

He got out of the car, climbed into the back and pushed forward the front passenger seat. Around the trim of the red leather seat, was a length of thin off-white piping. The Champ explored his way around the trim until one section felt slightly different to the rest. He gave it a slight tug and it came away from the seat. He used his index and middle fingers to prise open the light stitching of this section of the upholstery, just enough to fit a hand. Beneath, there were four stud poppers, spread out. He put his fingers in between those and the section released with a collection of clicks. On a standard Fleetwood, that wouldn't happen but this was no typical car.

He reached into the passenger seat, picked up the item and into this hidden compartment, the item fit perfectly. Snapping the studs closed, the Champ pulled tight the threads that held the red leather seat together and reattached the off white trim to the edge. To the world and his dog, his 1970 Fleetwood looked as if it had come straight from the dealer. Only the Champ and his connection knew about the compartment, hidden deep inside the red leather upholstery. He returned to the driver's side and sped off west, towards Winterwood.

Back at the golf club, the young waiter returned the clubs to his locker, along with the money he was given that morning and locked the door. He headed out and towards the Maitre D's station, where his boss was on the phone.

"Al, I'm going to take five," he mouthed quietly. The Maitre D' placed his hand over the receiver and said, "Rickles foursome here in thirty minutes. Make sure you're back to greet them."

The young waiter gestured that he understood.

He took off his pale blue waiters jacket and unclipped his bow tie, and hung them on a peg in the kitchen. The staff door opened and he walked out into the midday sunshine. Putting on his shades, he took a cigarette from his pack and boarded his scooter. Skipping between cars headed along Desert Inn Drive, the young waiter pulled into the lot behind Gilly's Bought and Sold. The occupants of a black Oldsmobile were waiting.

"Whaddya know?"

"He left the club around five minutes ago." The waiter handed over a small tin.

The occupant of the car opened the tin. Inside, on a bed of putty, was the imprint of a key.

"2058 Ottowa."

"Was he alone?"

"He was."

An envelope was passed from the window to the young waiter. He quickly folded the envelope, tucking it into his pocket as the Oldsmobile pulled away.

Chapter 15 - Seven Dollar Bottle of Wine

May had only slept with two men before tonight. An art history major at college was the first. That was brief and painful. She met Dennis later that year. He was the man she'd been most physically familiar with but even with him, at their most intimate, she had never lain by him, by the light of a clear moon, watching his stripped form recuperate. As cold droplets of sobriety stirred May from her post coital slumber, the thought of Dennis lying somewhere nearby, with his new love by his side, was like a scream at the end of a nightmare. But Dennis belonged to another and May's green and tender heart was as drained as that seven dollar bottle of wine on the floor; a beverage which lasted longer than each of their lustful grapples.

From where she lay, she couldn't clearly make out the time on Bob's wristwatch; it looked like just after four a.m. The now bitter taste of the fermented grape countered the sweet sting of sex as she watched her latest lover sleep. The uncertainty of what she felt was overridden by those phantom pulses between her legs making her want him inside her again. May caressed his exposed lower stomach. It was far firmer, and smoother, than she'd thought it would be. May hoped that this sensual action might awaken him but Bob was out cold. Her hand moved to his penis which, she was happy to learn, worked off of a different circuit. She clasped it gently, then tightly squeezed. Still, Bob remained flat on his back, motionless but for his semi erect member. As May attempted to straddle him, Bob's hands gripped onto her hips, pulling her down upon him.

****

"Sorry for waking you, Mrs Peterson."

May sat by the window overlooking the wharf. The bell in the church tower had just struck eight and her shift at the Diner was due to start at midday. Last night, it felt good to let herself go. No books, no music, nothing but physical pleasure. To hell with the consequences, she'd thought. Only now it was morning and there were no buses between Portland and Auburn on a Sunday. Wild, passionate May had skipped town, leaving the careful, cautious version alone with a naked stranger, four hours from being fired.

"Sweet Jesus, May. What do you want?" said Elvin, still half asleep.

"I need you to come get me. Immediately."

"Where are you?" asked Elvin.

"Portland."

"Portland!" exclaimed Elvin. Aware that his parents might be listening, Elvin reduced the tone of his voice to a whisper.

"Are you out of your mind? What the hell are you still doing in Portland?"

"Pick me up from Congress Square and we're even. I promise."

"Drive me to my fight and we have a deal."

"Your folks would kill you if they knew you were even thinking of fighting again and they'd kill me for helping you."

"Take it or leave it. That's the deal," replied Elvin, playing his hand.

As reluctant as she was, May was in no position to turn down Elvin's offer. She didn't care much for the fights and thought Elvin foolish for attempting to restart his career in secret but if she didn't show for her shift after promising Jerry she'd be there AND borrowing twenty bucks, she reckoned that there would be one more figure on the unemployment line come Monday morning.

"I don't have a car."

185

"What about your Mum's?"

"She needs it for church."

"Your Dad still has that vintage car, doesn't he?"

"May, you clearly don't remember him threatening to whup my ass if I even dared take the cover off?"

Mr Peterson, Elvin's father, was now wheelchair bound but both Elvin and May knew that he was still a man not to be messed with.

"I could always borrow Jerry's…"

May interrupted Elvin's proposal. "No! Keep Jerry out of this. Go to my apartment, Mrs Reynolds on the second floor will buzz you in. My door key is under her plant pot. The keys to my Pacer will be somewhere, either on the counter or on top of the TV. And Elvin, you may have to put a little gas into it…"

"You owe me big time, May!" said Elvin, exasperated.

"You didn't mind when I drove your drunk ass home a few days ago, did you?"

There was silence on Elvin's end of the phone.

"OK," said Elvin. "Congress Square?"

"As soon as possible."

May quietly placed the phone back on the receiver and gathered her clothes, still strewn across the sleeping Bob's room. Unwilling to risk waking him again, May decided against showering. She stared long and hard at herself in Bob's bathroom mirror. Who had she become? A couple of days ago, going back to a man's flat on a drunken whim, was behaviour she'd have found shocking. But that was before she'd accepted an invitation into the world of Henry Miller. A dick grabbing, carnal comet burning through the ether, on a collision course with the benign Planet Dennis. Dennis with his new love. The very thought. That breezy slut. Why should they have all the fun, May thought. Her encounter with Bob may have been the antithesis of what, until recently, she'd have considered romantic but it was real. And in the night, she took control of her own body and used it for her own pleasure. Any unease she may have felt at the interaction was gone. May had sacrificed caution for experience and the decision left her empowered. Maybe this is how sex should feel, she thought. She took a flannel and ran it under the hot tap. The dark lines of kohl, smudged into the crevices at the edges of her eyes made her look exotic. She liked that. Her mouth was red, her chin raw from a night of deep kissing. A fresh sensation. The wet face cloth pushed her curls, still damp with sweat, back from her forehead. Again, she looked at herself in the mirror, vaguely reminiscent of the *naif* who landed in Portland with an invalid bus ticket, a few hours earlier. Once she'd washed her face, May turned to the strongest odour. The scent of the night lingered on her body. She wasn't ready to give that up just yet.

Shaking out her clothes, May dressed quickly. She picked up her heavy boots and walked to the door. She'd toyed with the idea of leaving Bob a note.

A 'See you around. Mx' or a 'Here's my number. If you're ever in Auburn, call me' just wouldn't suffice.

She thought, 'What would Henry Miller do?'

Bye Bob, thanks for the sex.

May carefully depressed the latch and after catching one last look at her still sleeping lover, she closed the door and left for Congress Square.

****

The Sunday shift at The Columbus was pretty uneventful, as it turned out. Hardly worth opening as most of the regulars stayed at home rather than brave the recurrence of the storms that battered the Eastern seaboard earlier in the week. That suited May fine. She'd scored points earlier with Miss Washington by letting her leave in time to catch the rerun of Jeopardy. Jerry came in just before closing and commented on May's appearance.

He asked her if she'd changed her hair or her make up. He wasn't sure but he did know that something about her was different. Elvin, brought up to speed with events during a testy drive back to Auburn earlier, kept his nose out of it. When the lights went out and the doors closed on that Sunday evening, all May wanted to do was to get home, sate her hunger with a large slice of home-made lasagne, drink her body weight in iced tea then bathe her exhausted body. Normally, the radio or a mix tape would provide the ambient texture to a Sunday soak but this time, Dick Clark and Dennis found themselves relegated behind thoughts of a security guard and the words of a long dead writer.

Chapter 16 - The Big Sur and The Great Payoff

"'My return to New York City was not as triumphant as I'd hoped it would be. I don't know exactly what I'd expected. I mean a ticker tape parade up 5th Avenue was unlikely for a barely conquering hero such as I, even with my latest book being rightly lauded as my best work to date. My father died two hours before I arrived in Brooklyn.

By the time I'd settled, I found that a number of my Parisienne compadres had also relocated to Manhattan. I wasn't surprised to find that Anaïs and Hugo had escaped Port-Royal and set up shop on the Upper West Side. She and I met for a congenial enough afternoon in the Café at Saks on Broadway, lightly dusting over the prints of our past. Hugo wasn't there which, affable chap though he was, was a blessing. I could never understand his willingness to allow such a beautiful butterfly to slip the net as frequently as he did. She told me that I looked older than she'd expected which stung a little but she qualified it with some ancient anecdote about the fatal vanity of man. I asked her if she'd received my correspondence from Corfu but her answer was as vague as only she could deliver. From the moment we embraced, I could tell that she'd agreed to the meeting in order to draw a line under the chapter marked Henry and Anaïs. For sure, I may have unlocked some potent forces previously dormant in this gamine housewife, and I was not averse to seeing if our chemical attraction still stood but she was now free. The heat we shared will always smoulder but right here, in New York, our famous passion was just another burned out star, lost in time, floating in the firmament. She handed me a parcel containing some of the letters I had composed to her during those intoxicating, early days we spent together. She'd wanted to return them to me rather than destroy them - that thought saddened me more than any enforced parting we endured - and she made me promise not to write about her anymore. Though my èlan vital was incurably cracked by her request, I reluctantly acceded to her wishes.

Following the harsh winter of 1941, I beat the rush and offered an unconditional surrender of my own, taking the decision to head west to more temperate climes. Before I left, I spent some time connecting with the remaining members of my family, which was a surprisingly comforting experience. I remained frustrated with my father for not holding on until I returned and felt tremendous remorse for feeling so. Maybe my mother's intuition regarding him was worth revisiting. She was not as ill as I'd been warned, but she remained a challenge. We parted on amicable, if not affectionate terms.

However, a particularly sobering encounter with my, one time, spouse and muse, in the East Village made me start to consider things from Anaïs' perspective. I hoped that I hadn't repulsed her the way that seeing June had affected me. Her once impressive looks had gone but ageing in poverty will rot even the most elegant of beauties. It mattered not one bit to me that her jacket was stained and frayed and her shoes were scuffed beyond the epidermis. What shocked me most was how mentally frail and feeble she'd become. I couldn't help but feel a wave of guilt. This barely breathing shadow of a woman, a once exquisite figure who had us all hanging on every word, a beguiling sorceress who'd lure a family man beyond the stage of abandonment, a soul whose spark I'd admired and desired, now sickened me. There was nothing at this stage I could do to right the misdeeds that had befallen her, nor was there any point in a brutal bout of self-immolation. We all have choices to make. I emptied my pockets and gave her everything I had. She smiled through addled tears and held my hand tightly, as if that twenty-six dollars and change was heaven enough. Though thoughts of her and our shared experiences would dominate my creative output in the coming years, I watched her careen like a nebulous wisp, drifting in and out of sight. I said goodbye to the present, physical June on Bleeker St. This was not an au revoir.

As you know, the war years were unsparingly merciless. Offers arrived from Hollywood but not what I'd hoped for. A hundred bucks here, two hundred there. Nowhere near enough. I was introduced to Lepska. She was much younger than me but whip smart. She liked to tease too. But you remember that, don't you? When you came up to visit with your cowboy fellow, Lepska made him pronounce 'Bryn Mawr' over and over. Before we'd been introduced, a friend of a friend told me that he had read her some passages from one of my pieces which had moved her deeply. Henry Miller, conqueror of youthful hearts! Ha! Did you know that she quit Yale to move to California with me? Might surprise you to hear that my insecure heart was not disinclined to making demands that didn't necessarily benefit mi amorata.

She was a good wife and an excellent mother but one can only cage a bird so long without being cruel. Anyway, she stayed in New York, settling her affairs, while I spent much of the $500 advance I'd secured against 'Colossus...' on a ten-year-old Buick sedan. I took the strapped leather bag for clothing and filled a suitcase with books; Hansun, Whitman and Lá-Bas by Huysmans, to lighten the mood. The Buick took me south to Bowling Green, Virginia, where I encountered, of all people, Salvador Dali. Awful man. Nothing more to be added. From there, it was Jackson, Mississippi then west, searching for an oasis amidst the apathy and the filth. With the exception of New Orleans - a spirited, free willed, rambunctious town that you heard and tasted before you saw - I found that many of my homeland's urban sprawls lacked the spices and flavours *to which I had grown accustomed. The realisation that this was not a place conducive to the furtherment of those with an artistic disposition was a profound disappointment.*

The further into the south west I went though, the more I understood that while America lacked the cultural heritage of Europe and the stunning centres of worship from the East, it made up for it with natural beauty. Forget those fifty story monuments to the worst of human excess and consider the Arizona vista. My belief in God was never firm but standing on the approach to Death Valley as the blood red sun disappeared behind the rocks, I felt humbled in the presence of something greater. By the time I reached the noise and dirt of Los Angeles though, all bets were again off.

At the start of 1953, Lepska had taken about all she could take and finally left, along with the children. For the first time, I was alone at Partington Ridge. Mrs Miller moved back East to Long Island, but not before instigating long overdue divorce proceedings. I wasn't going to challenge it. I made tentative provisions to send money to them when I could. The peace and tranquility that I found in Big Sur had been transformative. Thoughts of heading out on the road again couldn't have been further from my mind when, out of the blue, I received the most curious correspondence. Postmarked St. Louis, and addressed simply to 'Mr Henry Miller, Northern California', the official looking letter was delivered, as was all my mail, by the most determined US Mailman I'd ever encountered; Ernie Suplee. For the last decade or so, he travailed this unforgiving route, armed only with a shoulder sack and a dusty wind cheater. He'd occasionally stop in for a coffee and some of my wife's home baked scones. During one of our increasingly frequent arguments, Lepska blurted out that they were lovers. The revelation was designed to hurt me. Perhaps she wanted me to fight for her, I don't know. Behind those heavy lids, hidden under his frayed cap, his tortured gait and the weariest of demeanours, I fashioned stoic, unspectacular Ernie as a mythic herald, tied to his fate, perpetually circumventing the globe dispensing messages from the Godhead. I needed a break from thinking. Come in Ernie. Take a load off. No home cooked treats today but there's a pot brewing if you want one. Nope, she's gone East. Kids too. Long Island. I'd give you her new address but you work for the US Mail so, go figure...

Anyway, over a pot of coffee, I opened this letter typed on a blank sheet of heavy writing stock, with no masthead. It read:

'Dear Mr Miller,

It has come to our attention that you are currently without a fixed publisher. We have noted that while many here in the United States may be unfamiliar with your writing, in Europe, sales of your work have been steady and consistent for a number of years.

We at Clarion are very fond of your work and would like to propose to you an offer to become your sole agent. As such, we would like to formally offer to publish any completed works from a mutually agreeable date and in return, we will pay you an advance against future receipts recouped and a guaranteed royalty; our current rate of 47c per paperback, 82c per hardback. In addition, through reciprocal agreements we have in place, we will collect and transfer to you all outstanding monies owed you from international territories.

If this meets your broad agreement, please telephone or wire your response to the number listed at the top of the page. We have also taken the liberty to enclose an open ended, first class Pullman ticket to our offices in St. Louis so that we may discuss the matter in more detail.

Kindest regards,

J.H. Moreau

Clarion Publishing'

'How's about that for a serendipitous occurrence, Ernie?' I said, slapping the letter in joyous validation.

'Does that mean you're leaving Partington Ridge?' he asked, fearing that if I said yes, his route would be irrevocably changed.

'Not necessarily.'

Relieved, Ernie agreed to stop by every couple of days, as standard, to make sure that the place wasn't taken over by racoons, snakes or worse. As a way of thanks, I said that I'd attempt to source some scones from St. Louis. I made no promises.

I'd travelled through Missouri the year before I moved to California. My first tentative steps away from American urbanity were spent with the unlikely figure of Abe Rattner, the artist, as my travelling companion. He did most of the driving before calling time on the tour. I'd intended to hold a mirror up to my country's head. And if that failed, I'd try a gun. No weapons were needed in St. Louis. This was going to be 'The Great Payoff', a position from where I could pay off my debts, and my wives, with money left over to concentrate fully on that neglected facet of my life, the reason for getting out of bed in the morning; my work. And my children, of course.

Ernie took a couple of hours off from his route and drove me down the coast to Los Angeles where I caught the train to St. Louis and impending financial independence. I'd have flown if they'd offered and been there in a few hours but travelling by Pullman, with my own sleeping berth, was a more than acceptable substitute. I read, scribbled a few notes but it wasn't until the train was crossing into Arizona that I felt the weight of the last decade slide from me like raw chicken from a plate. The high-end fare served in the dining car was deliciously impressive and its well-stocked bar kept me engaged until the sun rose from behind the craggy hills on that cool Colorado morning. A couple of my fellow hardy barflys attempted to rouse me into mischief making but I had neither the energy nor the inclination to indulge them. I needed to sleep. Changed days, huh? I did sneak a bottle of Canadian Club from the bar while the stewards changed over. For the remainder of the near two day journey, I drank, wrote and slept, in roughly equal measures.

With my central compass bent out of shape, we berthed at the imposing Union Station, on schedule and just after breakfast, which I skipped. After a moment to admire the architecture, I hailed a cab and asked the driver to take me to Clarion Publishing. He growled that he'd never heard of it so I showed him the company address; 14 Park Avenue, Lafayette Square. Twenty minutes later, and despite crossing Chouteau Avenue four times, we were there. I handed the driver five bucks. I was too bushed to argue.

I opened the black iron gate, climbed the well-tended stoop to the main door and rang the bell. Within seconds, an exotic looking young woman wearing an elaborate, colourful headdress answered.

'Mr Miller,' she said, recognising me instantly. 'What an honour it is to have you here. Please, do come in.'

She led me into a sitting room, with two couches facing one another. The room was spartan except for two vividly colourful canvases, which hung from the walls. Yellows, greens and browns mainly. Modern art by numbers, I thought to myself but a damned sight more interesting than the cracked corn gold and magnolia that I'd been used to. Shimmering morning sunshine flooded into the room, sharpening all the edges so I took the liberty of taking the couch which backed onto the tall windows.

'Mr Moreau will be with you presently. Can I get you something to drink?'

I was about to ask for a quart of vodka when she directed the offer towards an impressive selection of teas.

'Surprise me,' I said.

As I stood by the window, awaiting a cup of Earl Grey or a lapsang souchong, the sun's brilliant rays reminded my tired bones that normal folk sleep at night, not guzzle booze with argumentative transients on trains. This was Clarion Publishing; serious people, not a gang of fly-by-night wiseguys. I made a mental resolution to start acting like a serious professional from tomorrow.

'Mr Miller! Welcome to Clarion!'

Bounding into the room, offering his hand, J.H. Moreau was tall and slim with a slight accent and the look of a thirty-five-year-old Don Ameche.

'I trust that your trip was acceptable?' he asked.

'It was just the ticket,' I replied. 'Lovely place you've got here.'

'We like it.'

The exotic young woman returned with a tray which she placed on the small table between the couches. The perfume of the infusion was as subtle and tempting as Moreau's assistant, it has to be said. Since Lepska had departed, it had been, without being crass, a long season without rain. She poured the tea into two long, clear ornately handled glasses.

'Will that be all, Sir?'

Moreau smiled and nodded.

To business.

'I have to say, Mr Moreau, that I was pleasantly surprised to receive your offer. You know, I have to admit that correspondence like yours doesn't fall into one's lap that often, especially working in a field considered obscene by some.'

Moreau joined me by the window.

'You're more than welcome, Mr Miller. We at Clarion prefer the word 'niche'. Men with your unique overview should be sought out and listened to. Writers of your calibre, even more so.'

I couldn't agree more, I thought. Finally, a straight-talking publisher. And one who gets me. I'll sign this deal on the back of a napkin, if I have to.

'Mr Miller, Clarion could've placed our American office where the majority of this nation's writers are based, in New York or in Los Angeles, but we decided not to. We too would like to consider ourselves 'niche'. St. Louis works for us for a number of reasons. For instance, our current location is, of course, Lafayette Park, named *after Gilbert du Motier, the Marquis of Lafayette.'*

'Le Héros des Deux Mondes? Of course.'

'Exactly. Lafayette remains revered both here and in France, a revolutionary symbol of what great nations, and great peoples can achieve when they work together for a common goal.'

'Mr Moreau, I couldn't agree more,' I said, sipping the pale tea like a sophisticate.

'Now, to the reason you're here,' he said, sitting on the sofa. 'You received our proposal and from what I gather, it meets with your approval?'

'Where do I sign?' I asked, eagerly.

'Mr Miller, our proposal, comes with one caveat.'

'Sure. What is it?'

'Section 8, point A. The terms of proposal will only come into effect following the satisfactory conclusion of the accord the client entered into with our partners. Once this has been finalised, the block will be removed and the contract can be signed off by all parties as binding.'

What accord? Which partners?

Moreau sat back and removed his spectacles.

'Mr Miller, a few years ago, you entered into a binding agreement with our partners and as of today, that agreement has neither been completed nor have you made any provision to renegotiate the terms.'

'I don't understand.'

'Our partners entrusted you with an item that had significant value.'

The penny dropped, as did my stomach.

'Simply put, you will be required to finish what you started.'

'That was years ago.'

'Doesn't matter. You made a deal.'

'No, a deal was forced upon me. And I was almost killed.'

'You were well compensated.'

'A thousand bucks? I managed to spend about twenty before I was left for dead. No, that deal is off.'

'If that is the case, Mr Miller, then so is ours.'

'Can't we just remove the clause?'

'Without that insertion, I'm afraid there can be no deal.'

'Fine. I'm going back to California.'

'I was worried that you'd say that. Mr Miller, if I may be blunt, you were once the prime suspect in a murder investigation, were you not? The death of a certain Mr Militz?'

'I didn't kill him.'

'That's as may be but I need to make you aware of some new and potentially incriminating evidence which could prejudice your claims of innocence.'

'Really? Like what?'

'I've been told that the murder weapon is about to be found by the Parisienne authorities.'

'So? As I said, I didn't do it.'

'From intelligence gathered, it seems that your fingerprints are all over the handle.'

'That's impossible. How...?'

'Quite easily. Your mark is on at least three items in this room alone. The door handle, the glass...'

'You're saying that they'd copy my fingerprints and put them on the handle of the weapon?'

'That would be tricky but it would be a more straightforward exercise to remove the handle of the cleaver, and replace it with another handle, of a blade perhaps, but one that your hands had been familiar with.'

'What makes you think that you'd find one?'

'That's the easy part. Your mailman has already provided us with a number of samples. They're on their way to France as we speak.'

'Ernie? He's...'

'... been a partner of ours for years.'

'He always delivered. And on time too. I should've known. Damn.'

'Apparently, it helps with his fitness. Correspondence aside, he's been keeping harm away from you for most of the last decade.'

'I'm finding this very hard to process.'

'Mr Miller, our partners have invested a great deal of time and effort in keeping you from the clutches of those who would do great harm to you and countless others like you.'

'Why now?'

'Some new information has come to light regarding the whereabouts of the item that was lost.'

'Stolen,' I said, firmly.

'Our partners accept that you weren't party to the disappearance and that you suffered great hardship as a result of its loss.'

'What's so special about the plate anyway?'

'You looked at it?'

'I snuck a peek.'

'You saw it? How did it look?'

'It looked like a badly painted plate. What's so special about it?'

'You are an educated man, Mr Miller but I'm afraid that the importance of the item is greater than either of us could possibly fathom.'

'Try me,' I said.

'Any questions you may have should be directly towards our partners.'

A plate's a plate, unless it's a dish, I thought but this was an impasse that needed resolution, and quickly so that I could begin this *chapter of my career as a well-paid, rebellious iconoclast. So what now? Once 'our partners' took one look at me they'd realise that I was now too old to fuck my way out of trouble, and clearly too weak to fight. I took another sip of the bitter infusion Sufiah had brought. It tasted like cat piss but when you're in a bind, doesn't everything?*

Chapter 17 - Mr Brick Wall

'So, for the first time in decades, I was on my way back to Paris. And not by boat either. Before I could submit my terms and demands, I was led into a car and escorted, by Moreau's assistant, a dozen blocks or so to the McAdam Hotel. Heading undoubtedly into the jaws of the unknown, I asked if she'd take pity on a frightened old man and spend the afternoon in my company but she delivered a firm but sweet rebuff to my advances.

'You must try to be brave Mr Miller,' she said as would a junior school teacher to a child with a skinned knee. God may love a trier but I guess The Prophet remains unconvinced.

I checked in under an assumed name and was given explicit instructions not to leave my room until I was taken to the airport in the morning. This time, I wouldn't be making the long trip alone. Fearing that I may be a target, or a flight risk, they assigned their most hardy guy, a former Marine, to be my chaperone. He was due to arrive at the hotel late in the evening to run over our trip itinerary. Until then, I was to stay put. Bored, I took a long, whisky induced nap, then a bath and a shave. The room allocated to me had no reading material but it did have a television set. I called reception for refreshments and over a serviceable club sandwich and a lukewarm soda, I watched the Lucille Ball show, which I'll admit was intermittently amusing followed by 'Life is Worth Living' *with a priest named Fulton J. Sheen; a corny - and misleading - visual homily which reminded me why I despised religion so. A few minutes of this bilge persuaded me that Ms Ball's screwball story was more believable than the Archbishop's and was therefore a more fitting subject matter to be pumped into the docile gaze of the willingly pliant American viewing public.*

Pulling the plug on the valve powered pacifier, I began to compose a letter to my children. Without giving too much away, I told them that I was going to Europe to attend to some urgent business affairs, which in a way, was true, and that if all went well, we'd be able to spend more time together. The details of my trip, the plate, the Castagnes and the murder of Casper Militz, I felt were best omitted, to protect them as much as me.

Once my parental duties were completed, I began to write another letter, this time to Anaïs. I hadn't seen her in quite a while but even during my marriage to Lepska, she remained an inescapable fixture in my thoughts. Two pages of desperately yearning, flighty prose later and it was filed, alongside the empty soda bottle, in the waste paper bin. Retreading the same old territory was boring the pants off of me. Retreading my actual steps though made me nervous. And, if truth be told, excited. It had been a long time since the blood pumped as it did that night. All I had to do was climb into bed and get some shut eye and in the morning, I'd be going back to my spiritual home. I tried, I really did. But by ten o'clock, I'd been tossing and turning for a full hour. I needed to stretch my legs. Not long, just a little walk. And if there was a bar open, I'd have a quick night cap. Take the edge off. Nothing major.

I pulled on my slacks, jacket over my shoulders and threw my cap on then opened the door. At the end of the corridor, near the elevator, a heavy-set fellow in a tailored black suit rose from his seat and asked if everything was alright. I told him that I was just going downstairs to the bar. He told me that he'd bring anything I wanted to my room. I got it. I was being baby sat. I understood why. I'm fine, I said, closing the door. I walked over to the window, pulled back the drapes and unscrewed the locking clip. In their desire to keep me quiet, they'd checked me into a room at the side of the hotel, which meant that there was a fire escape within easy reach. I went back to the door and looked through the peephole. The heavy-set man was back in position, seated at the end of the corridor. I fed the bolt through the latch, pulled it as quietly as I could and propped the chair from the desk, under the door handle as a secondary measure. Belt and braces. I returned to the window, pushed the white sash up and shuffled from the ledge onto the fire escape. The light downpour earlier made the leap more precarious than an old man should take but this was not the first time I'd snuck out of a hotel window at night. The last six feet from the ladder to the ground was harder on the ankles than I'd anticipated. Nevertheless, I was a free man in St. Louis, if only for a couple of hours.

The Midtown Hotel was the first non-tavern that I found which had any sign of life. I sat at the bar, sank a few drinks and listened to the pianist go through his half assed Lawrence Welk routine. It could've been the booze, or a trench of sentimentality carved into the pit of my gut but I was hours away from being back in a situation where destiny was no longer in my own hands. Maybe it was ever thus? All I knew was that, tonight, I wanted to live a little dangerously and on my terms, before the risk became real.

The barman - Rick or Steve, maybe Bill, I can't remember - asked if I was in town on business. I played along. Yep, I said. You're not a resident at The Midtown, are you? Nope, I'm a fugitive on the lam, I said. Got you. Is there anything I can help you with, he asked, to make your stay in St. Louis more pleasurable? I wouldn't say no to a card school and an exotic companion, limber enough to help me back onto a hotel's fire escape. I slipped him a twenty which, from the look on his face, was the correct amount.

He made a call and told me to go to room 327. A few high rollers were playing and according to Rick Steve Bill, the occupants of that room didn't mind if an old out-of-towner sat in for a few hands. As my feet were still tender from my daring fire escape leap,

I took the elevator to the third floor and knocked on the door of 327. It was opened, but only halfway, by a chunky fellow with a cigarette hanging from his lip. He looked me up and down and once he determined that my threat level was close to nil, with a nod, he invited me into the smoky suite where around a green baize covered table, sat four similarly cagey looking men. Had I not partaken of Speyside's finest distilled grain, I might have been more concerned. But I had and I wasn't.

'Evening gentlemen. What's the game?' I asked. They thought I was some travelling donk; a fish with cash to burn but they were wrong. I'd played once or twice.

'Big O,' said the heavy man with the hair as black as a bottle of blue ink. A five card drop instead of two. 'You can buy short for a hundred bucks,' he said, meaning I could enter into the game for a lesser fee as it had already started. I had around another hundred tucked into my belt.

'Whaddya want? Two Hundred?' asked Inky who was perspiring more than was healthy.

'Sure thing,' I replied. 'Deal me in.'

For the next couple of hours, I went from being the wet fish in their eyes to a shark. Long hands, short, for every three we played, I won two. And the ones I didn't win, I folded early, which began to infuriate Tommy, Vito and Johnny who cursed me with the kind of fruity Italian expletives I hadn't heard since I was chased around Corona as a kid. Around 1am, and aware that my presence would be required at the McAdam shortly, I made my excuses and cashed out. I was over twelve hundred bucks up, more than four times my best ever return. I've thought about this night a number of times over the years, for reasons I'll shortly elucidate, but I believe that I played, no, performed in a state of grace, due to my complete lack of fear.

Normally, I'd be as sweaty as Inky or as itchy under the lights as Tony and Vito appeared to be. In my surreal condition, I stored *away the worry of the trip, the Castagne's, the return of the Militz case and lived in the moment. I would've explained this to my card playing confederates but I feared that this disclosure may push at least one or two of them over the edge. They didn't look as if they were used to losing so painfully. I stuffed my pockets, while taking time to leave a crisp $50 bill for the table, and bid my fellow gamblers a hearty 'ciao'.*

'Where are you staying, pal?'

'Not too far from here,' I replied, unwilling to disclose the location.

'You wanna ride?'

'No I'm good, fellas. Thanks.'

'A lotta bad guys around out there. You gotta take care of that money or some big spook will knock you round the head for it.'

'Thanks for your concern, guys. I'll be fine.'

'Jus' sayin''

'Ci vediamo,' growled Inky, which in Italian meant, see you again. I sincerely hoped not but I was starting to suspect the opposite. As I stood in the hallway, waiting for the elevator and regretting my earlier hubris, a sharp sense of unease took grip. The stairs would be quicker. I took the flights, three steps at a time, disregarding my previously pained pins. The bar was deserted except for Rick Steve Bill. He'd just put the phone down and something told me that he wasn't wishing his Aunt Myrtle a happy birthday. His earlier cordial demeanour had been replaced by the look of a man who had just found out that he'd royally fucked up. I decided against a night cap.

The streets of Midtown St. Louis after midnight were, as you'd imagine, not exactly bumper to bumper with cabs so I had to shift and fast. Maybe the blessed Father Sheen had the right idea; life was worth living. If I could only get back to The McAdam. I pulled down my hat and turned up my collar. I had to make myself as unseen as possible and as the power of invisibility had not yet been bestowed upon me, I was up against it. The ornate street lighting blossomed like a mighty night flower, illuminating all around it, within a twenty yard circumference. Between those bursts, there was murk and darkness. I moved as quickly as I could from shadow to shadow, diving into closed shop doorways. Markey's Flowers, Pender's Big and Tall. I may not remember Rick Steve Bill's name but strangely, I do recall the stores which offered me temporary sanctuary.

I made my way past a now closed tavern which I'd seen earlier. I was close to The McAdam. Maybe a couple of hundred yards. From behind, I heard the growling revs of a car. There was nowhere for me to go to evade being seen so I kept on walking. As it got closer, its low beam added to the night illuminations and the dim moonglow. I couldn't avoid it so I ducked down an alley, around a hundred yards in length with a clear opening at the other end. The car that was behind me sped up, driving past the alley before taking a sharp left. I'd bought myself some time, maybe enough to get back to my hotel. I waited a few seconds then looking backwards, I moved to double back onto the main street. That's when I walked into a wall, one constructed from flesh and sinew. A finger jabbed into my breastplate and my internal organs shrunk, bracing themselves for impact.

'What's the rush old man?' came the voice, deep and not at all comforting.

I must have muttered something which gave away the terror I'd instantly been dropped into.

'You got a smoke?'

'Yeah, yeah. Sure,' I stammered as his eyes, unblinking, locked on to mine. He was young and tall, yes, but he was physically more imposing than any man I'd ever seen. I handed him a cigarette.

'You know what?' I said, I'm trying to give them up. 'Here. Take the pack.'

He took the pack from me and again without blinking, he asked, 'What you hiding in there?'

At this stage, I was thinking to hell with the money.

'Look, I didn't mean to step on anyone's toes tonight. I just wanted a couple of drinks and a friendly game.'

The man mountain looked confused.

'So, you had a good night?'

'Kinda...'

I had money stuffed into my trousers and jacket pockets. I pulled out a handful and shoved it his way. Must have been around three hundred bucks.

He received his unexpected windfall with a puzzled look. Behind him, a dark sedan crawled slowly. The driver leaned out of the window, tapped on the panel of his door and shouted,

'Finish it up, man. We gotta go.'

My body tensed, preparing for the worst but inexplicably, he didn't strike me. He spoke, his voice softer and less menacing than it had been a few seconds earlier.

'You know, you shouldn't be out here at this time of night, old man. There's a lot of people who will look to take advantage, do you know what I mean?'

The 'advantage' that he seemed willing to take was much less than the money that I'd won in the game. Which got me thinking. Who was he working for?

Given his ethnicity, it was unlikely to have been Tommy, Vito and Inky. From his expression, I came to the conclusion that he was a low-level hoodlum, happy enough with the easy score. And using me as a punchbag, while sending out a message, didn't appear to be in his plan. So, I made him an offer.

'I'm staying at The McAdam. If you can get me there, in one piece, I'll double what I just gave you.'

As he thought it over, another car, this one driven by Inky, cut across the road and mounted the sidewalk. Out stepped Johnny, Vito and Tommy.

'Beat it spook. You. Get in the fucking car,' said Tommy, like he meant it. The thing is Elie, back then, guys like Tommy could say what they wanted and Mr Brick Wall, impressive though he was, just had to suck it up. Especially when his accomplice put his foot to the floor, leaving Mr Brick Wall to work out the finer details with the Sore Loser Gang alone.

'Fellas. C'mon. Surely we can talk about this like reasonable men,' I said, attempting to put a lid on the boiling pot.

'What did you call me?' said Mr Brick Wall defiantly, his fists tightening into fleshy rocks of rage.

'I said get lost, nigger,' said Tommy, clearly not used to being spoken back to.

Although as tall as Mr Brick Wall, Tommy was much more slender. The pistol he removed from his waistband though, evened up the contest. He pressed it under Mr Brick Wall's chin. While my head was asking me why I always seem to find myself in these avoidable situations, my heart was charging around my ribcage like a Souza playing marching band. And all the while, Mr Brick Wall didn't as much as blink.

'You some sort of tough guy?'

'You wanna find out?'

Tommy turned to us and laughed.

'Who have we got here, Joe fucking Louis?'

Tommy swung the butt of his gun towards the head of Mr Brick Wall but instead of making contact, in one rapid movement Mr Brick Wall blocked his attempt and hit him with a one-two so hard, Tommy was out cold before his face hit the damp Missouri stone with a sickening crackle. After a two second pause for disbelief, all hell broke loose. Vito whacked me on the top of my head, dropping me to the ground. I looked up and through my dazed vision, saw that both Johnny and Inky were swinging wildly at Mr Brick Wall, who appeared to have no trouble swatting them away as if they were arthritic flies.

'Don't move,' said Vito, pressing the barrel of his gun to the head of Mr Brick Wall who slowly raised his arms in a reluctant surrender. Johnny and Inky caught their breath. Once straightened out, the two of them hit the forcibly subdued Mr Brick Wall with a couple of punk shots. As Vito prepared to play judge, jury and executioner, a shot pierced the night time air, ripping a bloody hole out of the top of his left shoulder.

'The next shot goes eight inches lower,' said a man holding a pistol, while helping me to my feet. 'Stay exactly where you are and nobody else will get hurt, you understand?'

Johnny and Inky stood alongside Mr Brick Wall with their hands raised. Vito moaned in pain.

He gripped my arm tightly and said sotto voce, 'You were told to not leave your room.'

Aha! The Marines have arrived to save the day! Semper Fidelis indeed. From the Halls of Montezuma to the Shores of St. Louis? It almost scanned. I told him that I just needed to stretch my legs. You know how it is? From the look on his face, he didn't. Worse than that, he didn't see the prone Tommy starting to stir. But Mr Brick Wall did.

He shouted a warning just as Tommy fired a couple of rounds our way. They whistled past me but one caught the Marine on the inside of his right arm. Its impact spun him around, landing him hard on his knee. Vito, still slumped against a wall, lunged for his gun but couldn't reach it. Inky leant down to pick it up but Mr Brick Wall, like an angry six foot mule, planted the heel of his shoe into his rib cage, sending him tumbling. Tommy fired another shot, this time towards Mr Brick Wall but missed him and clipped Johnny, sending him to the floor too. I picked up the Marine's pistol and aimed it in the general direction of the Sore Loser Gang but before I could fire off a single shot, the Marine was back on his feet. He grabbed the gun from me and with his left hand, discharged the remainder of his clip into the skulls of Vito, Tommy, Inky and Johnny. He turned his pistol towards Mr Brick Wall.

'No,' I waved in front of him. 'He's with me.' The Marine depressed the catch on his pistol and staggered. I tried to hold onto him but he was half my age and twice my weight.

'Don't just stand there! Give me a hand,' I yelled.

'The keys are in my pocket. Red sedan, over there,' he said, clutching his arm tightly. His car was close enough to drag him towards but Mr Brick Wall threw the Marine's good left arm over his shoulder and picked him up, by himself and carried him over to the car. I opened the door and the Marine slid onto the back seat.

'Get in., he said, taking the tie from around his neck.

'I don't know about that,' said Mr Brick Wall.

As he pulled the tie around his arm, the Marine asked, 'Do you hear that?'

A distant police siren was getting louder by the second.

'They'll be here in fifteen, twenty seconds. You can run but if they catch you, all of this gets pinned on your ass. You know that's the truth.'

As Mr Brick Wall considered his diminishing options, I started the engine.

'And it's straight to the chair. Unless the mob gets to you first,' he said, before turning to me. 'Pull this tight.'

I did and he groaned in pain. Although still lucid, the Marine was shedding a considerable amount of blood which meant that he was in danger of losing consciousness. We didn't have long.

'Now or never,' I said.

Mr Brick Wall put any concerns he may have had to one side and climbed in the back. I took off before he'd even closed the door.

'Not too fast,' barked the Marine. 'Don't draw unnecessary attention to the vehicle.' From the sound of the sirens, the police must have been increasingly close.

'What if they pull me over?'

'Don't act suspicious. But if the situation gets out of hand, in the glove box, there are another two semi automatic pistols.'

The car went quiet.

'And you,' he said to Mr Brick Wall, 'keep your head down. An old white man driving a young black man? In this town? That would fall into the category of suspicious.'

The Marine groaned again, and muttered, 'Three blocks down and take a right. You should see the sign...' He was fading. By the time the authorities had reached the slain parties, we had already sailed by Tucker, Market and Jefferson and were now at the McAdam.

A doorman in a long grey coat stepped into the night to greet me as I ran towards the entrance.

'We need a medic,' I said. He peered towards the car, recognising the Marine before running back into the hotel. Mr Brick Wall remained in the car, trying to prevent him from slipping under again. Within seconds, a battalion of people appeared - all types, from porters, to men in morning suits - and carried him through the deserted reception area, into a nearby conference room. While this was going on, Mr Brick Wall and myself caught our collective breath in the grand and now untended bar. I reached over the counter and poured a couple of drinks. We found the two most comfortable, high backed chairs and settled down.

'You think he'll make it?' I asked, my senses still racing.

'As long as the bullet didn't hit the artery,' he replied with certainty. 'I've seen that kind of wound before.'

He was too young to have served in the War.

'Can I ask you something?'

'Sure,' said Mr Brick Wall, savouring the cold beer.

'In the alley. You had your chance. You could've been gone, with a very tidy score but you didn't.'

'What if I was just taking a leak?' he asked. 'What's your point?'

'Would it be fair to call you a robber?'

211

Mr Brick Wall shrugged. 'Call me what you want.'

I continued, 'Then my point is this. The primary consideration of a robber is to get as much as he can while disabling any impediment to his escape, am I not correct?'

'On that, you would be correct,' he replied.

'So why not beat the crap out of me and get out of there?'

Mr Brick Wall loosened his tie, sunk the remainder of his beer and leant forward. He wiped the suds from his mouth and simply said, 'I know what I am.'

Not who, I hasten to add. What. Because of his hulking frame and his fast hands, he was a useful cog in whatever machinery needed a part. For a young man - he must have only been in his early twenties at this point - this power could feel an unnatural burden. While most fellows of his age were setting up home with their sweethearts, Mr Brick Wall was in and out of State and County on various charges, usually related to his 'skill set'. He'd only been out for just over a week but found that the industrial captains of St. Louis weren't in a rush to accept his penance. They had ten good men for every job they needed filled. Ten good, family men. Clean, affable, responsible. Not sullen, not violent.

But before he could put more meat on that particular bone, Moreau arrived with his exotic assistant in tow. In marked contrast to our earlier acquaintance, he was unbuttoned and agitated, fearful perhaps but annoyed certainly, that his part in this pinpoint plan had been set ablaze by the unconscionable actions of others. To be specific...

'Stay in your room. That was all you had to do. Just stay in a very comfortable hotel room, enjoy the television, the room service. Anything you wanted, it was yours.'

I wanted to shoot a glance at his alluring assistant but my head was bowed in remorse. I could see though, that she was barefoot and her perfectly shaped toenails were painted a deep bottle green.

'Are you even listening to what I have to say?' raged Moreau, his tone shaking me out of my languorous moondream. I stood, chided like a schoolboy who'd deliberately smothered his homework in marrow and fed it to a ravenous mutt.

'Is there anything you would like to add at this juncture? Some mitigating circumstance that forced you out of your room, presumably down a fire escape and off into the night to have a gunfight with half of the St. Louis mob? Well?' he ranted, losing any semblance of control he may have had. The head of Clarion Publishing had become so hysterical I felt that I had to bring the conversation back to more pressing matters.

'So, Paris is off?'

Moreau's earlier cool demeanour was long gone. His nostrils flared, his teeth bared and his eyes widened. If I'd been a gambler, I'd have put every penny I won tonight on him having a seizure within the minute.

'No, Paris is not off. You're going and thanks to your stupid stunt tonight, you'll have to look out for yourself.'

'Suits me fine,' I replied, which wasn't what Moreau wanted or expected to hear.

'You have no idea what lies in wait for you?'

He was right. I didn't.

Moreau laughed.

'When they find out that your actions may have cost the life of one of our most promising operatives, The Crow won't be the only one queueing up to kill you.'

Moreau pressed his face up against mine. 'And if they need anyone to pull that trigger, I'll gladly oblige.'

'You'll have to go through me first,' said Mr Brick Wall, standing up.

'Who the fuck is this guy?' asked Moreau, rhetorically. 'Get him out of here.'

While my contretemp with Moreau was boiling over, Mr Brick Wall had been quietly sitting, observing. This was not his place, nor was it his fight but by speaking out, he'd upped his stake. The big fellow from outside my hotel room, walked over to Mr Brick Wall. He already looked vexed. I imagined that he was about to forfeit his bonus for failing to keep me locked down. 'You heard the man. Get the hell out of here.'

Mr Brick Wall didn't move. The big fellow looked over to Moreau who gave the sharpest of nods. In a split second, Moreau's man let fly with a straight left aimed at the centre of Mr Brick Wall's face. He leant away, with lightning quick reflexes, and the left overshot the target. Before the big fellow had a chance to respond, Mr Brick Wall slammed a double into his rib cage. Moreau's man had not anticipated the heavy shots. As he struggled to stay upright, gasping for breath, Mr Brick Wall delivered the coup de grâce; a piledriver left into the side of the big fellow's jaw. A blow which connected with such maleficent accuracy, it not only separated his jaw bone from its fixed position but laid the big fellow out cold. And like the fight in the alley, the reaction to this impromptu dust up was just as chaotic. The porters and bar staff who'd carried the Marine into the hotel had all been packing - as was Moreau - and were now pointing their weapons towards Mr Brick Wall who was starting to think that he'd have been better off taking his chances on the street.

'Can we please lower our weapons?' demanded Moreau's assistant, firmly. The voice of reason. Her words had a calming effect on her boss who instructed the staff to do likewise. The porters tucked away their guns, lifted the still prone big fellow onto the top of an unused Bain Marie and pulled him into the hotel's newly designated sick bay.

'So, what now?' I asked.

'We proceed as planned. You will travel to Paris alone...'

'Mr Moreau, our French partners will insist that Mr Miller is chaperoned,' interrupted Moreau's assistant. 'On that they were crystal clear.'

'Sufiah,' said Moreau, 'within the last hour, both our number one and number two choices have been disabled. I have no option but to accompany him myself.'

'Out of the question,' she replied instantly. 'With the greatest of respect, you do not have the physicality required for such a task. And besides, your presence is required here.'

As Moreau and Sufiah conferred, I could see that Mr Brick Wall was even more baffled than I. At least I'd had some experience of this madness.

'What the hell is going on?' he asked, 'Are these guys Feds?'

'No,' I said, 'They're publishers.'

I wasn't being glib or facetious but his taciturn expression suggested that he thought that I was. He didn't ask another question and I felt it unnecessary to offer any further explanation at that time. It was too complicated.

Moreau and Sufiah finished their conflab and returned to where we were seated.

Moreau spoke first. 'That was an impressive display, Mr...?'

Mr Brick Wall looked at me for affirmation. I shrugged.

'Liston,' he said, guardedly.

'What is your line of work, if you don't mind me asking?' enquired Moreau.

'I'm between appointments at the moment,' he said.

'Would you be willing to consider working for us?'

'I know nothing about books.'

'You'd make one hell of an encyclopedia salesman,' I said, my attempt at humour missing the board altogether.

'No, Mr Liston. We have a sufficiently staffed Literary Division. What we were thinking is that we could use someone with your talents in some of our other departments.'

'I'm listening,' he replied, curious.

The offer Moreau and Sufiah made to Mr Brick Wall Liston was detailed and generous. Take the place of the Marine, get me into and out of Paris without drawing the attention of the authorities - and parties with malicious intent - and he'd receive $200 per week for the duration, with all expenses and costs taken care of by Clarion. In addition, they would agree to furnish Mr Liston with a cast iron alibi for the Sore Loser Gang slayings as well as a guarantee to act in his interests, should he require additional help upon our safe return to these shores.

As Sufiah handed me my paperwork, a photographer stood me in front of the hotel's red velvet drapes.

'Glasses off, please,' he said, screwing the flash bulb tightly in.

I obliged, the room illuminated and once again my corneas sizzled.

Once my eyes had readjusted, I put my glasses back on and took a look at the documents.

Again, I was Harry Valentine, hardly incognito and certainly not original. I was also now a July baby, and three years younger than I actually was.

The photographer moved Mr Liston into position and repeated the process.

'Will you be travelling under an alias too?' I asked.

'He'll be travelling on the Marine's papers,' she said.

'We've not been properly introduced. Henry Miller.'

He offered me his giant mitt. Mine felt miniscule by comparison.

'Though, according to these, I'll be travelling as Harry Valentine.'

'Charles Liston. Most folk call me Sonny,' said Mr Brick Wall, checking his documents.

'But it seems that I'm now called Jerome Hector.'

Chapter 18 - Overflow

It can't be. It just can't, thought May as she read the page again and again. It must be another Jerome Hector. That's it. Can't be our Jerry. My Jerry.

Pull yourself together, May. Let's go through the facts.

Marine? Check. Wounded? Yes, but in Korea not in Missouri. The same arm though. He doesn't speak about it much, if at all. And you don't get a shattered kneecap from falling to the ground, do you?

May's examination of the scant but pointed evidence had unravelled before she'd had the chance to piece together a more palatable construct. The idea that this man she'd known since childhood, might be a cold-blooded killer was too absurd for words.

May dialled Jerry's number then quickly hung up. What am I going to say, she thought. Hi Jer, sorry for calling you at home. See the game last night? That was something, wasn't it. Jerry, while you're on, can you explain why an aged writer and the heavyweight champion of the world helped you escape from the scene of a multiple homicide? May fell face first onto her bed and roared into her pillow. She read the pages again. It had the same outcome. Jerome Hector, in cahoots with Sonny Liston and Henry Miller, was a hired killer. May went to the kitchen and turned the coffee pot on. There was enough for a cup. Just needed heating up. She emptied the contents of her ring-stained mug into the sink and opened up the sugar jar. Taking the least dirty spoon from the sink, she scooped out a heaped measure. That's when she noticed how much her hands were shaking. May looked at the spoon. Refined granules tumbling over the edge, the heaped spoonful now level.

She picked up the phone and called the only person other than Jerry who she could confide in.

"Mrs Peterson, it's May. Sorry to bother you but may I speak with Elvin, please?"

"Oh, he went out. Said something about running an errand for Jerry. I don't know. I imagine you might find him later at the diner. Is everything alright, May?"

"I might try him there. Thanks."

May's conversations with Elvin's mother tended to last longer than this abridged version.

The coffee suitably warm, May poured, stirred and returned to those crucial last three pages. She read slowly, examining each word of the letter in the hope that she'd taken a wrong turn or had misunderstood exactly what the author of the letter was relaying but however much she looked, it returned her to the same, inalienable conclusion.

Over the last stewed drops of the pot, May pondered whether to chance calling the diner or not. If she was in luck, she'd get Elvin. If she wasn't…

"Miss Washington, hi."

"Hi yourself. What do you want? Another advance? More time off?"

"Is Elvin there? Can I speak with him, please?"

"That would be a no. And refer to my first answer as your second question is redundant. As you'll be, young lady, if you don't show up on time tomorrow. Jerry's not happy, let me tell you."

Getting on Jerry's wrong side had just taken on a different meaning.

"Don't you worry, I'll be there."

"Oh, before you go. There was a delivery for you."

"For me? Really? What is it?"

"How should I know? It wasn't for me."

"OK, I'll get it tomorrow."

"You'll get it today. It needed a signature, so I gave him your address.

You're welcome," said Miss Washington, ending the call abruptly.

One unscheduled delivery aside, May had nothing planned for the day but the explosive revelations of those last few pages had put paid to that. The Mooney had an extensive archive section, probably the best in the whole of Maine. Council records, minutes of business, with periodicals and newspapers, local and state, going back to the turn of the century, captured for posterity on microfiche. May didn't need to go that far. 1953 would suffice. But first, to quieten the noise of the hundred questions simultaneously bouncing around her head, her daily soak. Return a semblance of equilibrium to matters and restore her heart rate to something approaching normality, she thought. Logic would win the day. Run the bath, take possession of the delivery, leave the mountain of used clothes with Mrs Kaplan at the laundromat then get digging, Colombo style.

May liked to bathe. Reading a book, listening to music, drinking some wine. Sometimes, simultaneously. May enjoyed the refreshing and meditative qualities of a hot tub, filled to the brim. When Dennis was a feature in May's life, he'd regularly arrive with the latest 'must hear' albums and occasionally, a pouch of weed that he'd scored from his friends at the Diavolo Club. While he claimed that the pungent plant greatly enhanced both the listening and the lovemaking experiences, May remained unconvinced. Once, after a weekend of Rush and middling sex, Dennis left a half-smoked reefer on the ledge in the bathroom. May found it and decided to partake, alone. She ran a bath, lit up the joint and drifted off to the strains of 'Inspiration Information' by Shuggie Otis. She woke up three hours later, as wrinkled as a pale prune with the block's super banging on the door, telling her that she left her tap running. It cost her two hundred and seventeen dollars to pay for the damage to Mrs Krupa's shop below - most of which she'd borrowed from Jerry - and while she kept the Shuggie Otis record, she never touched pot again. The water blasted out, spitting and sputtering from the old-fashioned taps, into the even older tin bath. May didn't hear the phone ring and neither did she hear the message Elvin had left after the tone.

The bath was about a quarter full when the outside door buzzed; cutting through the bathroom cacophony like a two second chainsaw rev. May went to the intercom.

"Delivery, Morgenstern."

She pressed the door release mechanism and quickly returned to check the bath; now a third full.

As her doorbell rang, May tied her robe together and answered the door.

"Did you miss me?" said Bob, the security guard, smiling. "These are for you," he said, thrusting a bunch of flowers into May's hands. As shocked as she'd been about that paragraph in Elie's book, it was nothing compared with the 'right here, right now' reality of Bob's impromptu appearance. Despite her reticence, she'd enjoyed loosening the self-imposed binds of suppression, allowing herself, fleetingly, to get lost in the intimacy, the frisson, the friction. But she'd presumed that their fling was nothing more than that; a casual, fleeting moment. From Bob's demeanour, she could see that he thought otherwise. He wrapped his arm around her waist and pulled her in, kissing her on the lips. He tasted different, she thought.

"What brings you here, Bob?" May asked, breaking the clinch and refastening her robe.

"I was in the neighbourhood, so I thought I'd drop by and say hello."

"You were in Auburn?"

"Yeah," said Bob, "Sometimes my work takes me here."

May scanned the conversation they'd had in the Portland bar. He said he had no idea where Auburn was. Bob was either lying to her then or he was lying to her now. As he sat on the edge of her couch and stretched out, May walked over to the kitchen area.

"Bob, now's not a good time. I've got to go to work."

"But the nice cashier lady said that today was your day off?" he said, removing his jacket.

May's head was spinning. She needed a diversion. She needed to think.

"Making a fresh pot," she said, her back turned to him. "How do you take it?"

"What say we forget the coffee and continue what we started at the weekend?" he said, patting the couch.

"Today's not a good day, Bob," May said, her mind racing. "Women's troubles, you know?" A line that May used to good effect on Dennis.

"Well, I don't mind if you don't," he said, walking over to the kitchen counter. May took a step backwards.

"What are you reading?" said Bob, picking up Elie's book. May wanted to grab it from Bob but she fought the urge to react.

"Just some letters, nothing much," she said, playing down the book's significance.

Bob looked straight at her. He knows, she thought. He knows. Bob opened a page and started to read. May had to think fast. She unfastened the cord on her gown, opening it suggestively and revealing just enough, she thought, to divert Bob's attention away from the book. It didn't work.

"This wasn't the book you were reading at the bar."

"Yes, it was."

Bob chuckled, closing the book and placing it carefully on the counter.

"Bob?"

"Yes, May?"

"How did you know where I lived?"

"As I said, the cashier told me," he said, moving closer.

"But how did you know where I worked?"

"Ah May," he said, pushing back a loose curl. "You look so pretty. So natural. It's a damn shame."

At that moment, May's doorbell rang, cutting through the silence.

Bob placed one hand behind May's head and pulled her close. "You expecting anyone?" he asked, in a whisper. May, almost frozen with fear, shook her head.

A shrill voice called out her name.

"Miss Morgenstern! Miss Morgenstern! You've left your water on. It's dripping through my light fittings!"

May reacted quickly. "If I don't respond, she'll call the super and he'll use his key to get in."

Bob considered the options.

"Tell her you've got it."

May took a breath and shouted, "Sorry Mrs Krupa. I'll take care of it."

Bob held May tight and stared deep into her eyes. May's arms were pinned to her side. Her heart was beating as fast as she breathed. He smiled but this was no tender moment. They were lovers no more. May was in no doubt as to his intent.

"So, take care of it," he whispered gruffly, relaxing his grip. May pulled her shoulders together and shuffled from his side. The coffee percolator, not yet filled, was within reach. May took the chance. Grabbing the pot by the handle, she swung it, lid first towards Bob's head with all the force she could muster, sending him crashing sideways into the breakfast bar and onto the floor. May stepped back in shock over the prone, dazed Bob. She dropped the percolator and made a run for the door but Bob's hand reached out, grabbing at her ankle, tripping her. Falling to the floor, May cracked her head against the waste receptacle by the door. Within seconds, her chance to escape was gone. Bob rose to his feet and steadied himself against the counter. Reaching up, he touched the side of his face which bore the brunt of the impact. From where the sharp edge of the spout sliced his eyebrow, blood poured. His cheekbone was now puffed and swollen. Picking up Elie's book, Bob placed the blood-stained journal on top of his jacket.

"I should've taken this from you on Saturday. Saved myself a whole lot of trouble," he snarled, dragging the disorientated May to her feet and towards the bathroom.

She raised her hands to shield her head, her breath becoming shallow.

Bob propped May up on the toilet seat, leaning her bruised head against the tiled wall by the window. The water continuing to pour into the bath was cascading over the sides, onto the floor. Bob turned off the taps, stopping the flow before yanking the plug from the hole. May's drain gargled and croaked as water slowly disappeared from the bath. Once the bath was two thirds full, Bob put the plug back in. He turned to the semi-conscious May, now muttering incoherently. Pulling the cord from her gown, he tied it around her hands, then straight up and around her neck. Tight enough to hold her in place but not so tight as to leave a mark. He lifted her over his shoulder and dropped her into the bath. May slid under the water without a sound.

Failure. Failure. Birth death. Birth death. Birthdeath. Nothing. Slip sliding away. Mother. Soon enough. Mother, father, dog. I don't know. Night time is the right time. The wrong time. I cannot cry. I'm fearful of night time. The sound of silence being squeezed. Pressure. Nothing to compare. It's coming soon, I know that much. Squeezed, coming now. Wheels of Steel, Tower of Power. Broken Glass, Broken English. The boy looked at Johnny. I looked at Patti Smith. I want to put my hand inside her white shirt, opened low. Cupping her heartbeat. Horses. Horses. The way I held Connie when she slept. Now she don't call.

May's doorbell rang again. Bob got to his feet and took a towel from behind the door. He was drying his hands when the doorbell sounded once more.

"It's all under control, Mrs Krupa. Thank you," he shouted.

For a third time, the doorbell rang. Bob went to his jacket and from its inner pocket, he removed a semi-automatic handgun. He looked through the spy hole on the door. The corridor was dark but he could see a figure with his back to the door.

"Open up, Miss Morgenstern. Landlord," said the voice, now banging on the door.

Bob cocked his weapon.

"I'm a friend of May's," said Bob through the closed door. "This isn't a good time right now. Maybe later this afternoon."

"Scheduled visit. Open up."

"Sure. Give me a moment, will you?"

Bob removed the clip from his weapon, checked it then slammed it back into place.

"Be with you in one minute," he said, unlocking the door.

Bob opened the door a crack and peered out

"Listen buddy, you're a businessman. May's feeling a bit under the weather at the moment. How's about I give you twenty bucks and you come back here in an hour, maybe two? Once she's caught up with her beauty sleep, you know?"

"What happened to your eye?" asked the voice behind the door.

Vespertine. Crepuscular. Rolling around my mouth. Like your tongue. Coddled. Cradled. Cover your face. Hide your face. Hide. Nothing matters. Just this. Nocturnal. Blue.

Bob handed over a twenty dollar bill.

"Two hours?"

"Two hours," repeated Bob, closing the door. But as it was about to make the catch, the door flew open, cracking Bob on the damaged side of his head. He reeled backwards, slipping into May's vanity unit, the soles of his shoes wet from the water overspill, contributing to his fall.

"May!" shouted the intruder. "Elvin, check the bedroom."

Looking around the room, Jerry Hector hadn't noticed Bob springing back to his feet. He slammed a punch into Jerry's side, the force of the blow almost cracking a rib. Jerry grimaced as his first sharp breath confirmed the damage.

On the hall table stood a novelty wine bottle lamp, cast in an ugly ceramic glaze. Jerry grabbed it and crashed it against the side of Bob's head, sending him staggering back. Elvin returned to deliver a combination, stopping him briefly but the effect of the chef's pinpoint punches on the much heavier man was not a lasting one. Bob swung for Elvin, his forearm catching him on the side of the head, knocking him over May's couch. In an attempt to bring an end to this unforeseen intervention, Bob dropped to his knees and scoured the floor for his weapon.

As he did, Jerry took as deep a breath as his ribs could muster and summoned enough strength to kick Bob hard and in the side. In the damaged rib department, they were now level but Bob, much younger, rallied quicker. Two straight jabs sent the injured Jerry stumbling back towards the main door. Bob reached over the kitchen counter and grabbed May's bread knife. He swung it at Jerry. The first swipe missed but the second connected, slicing him a fraction above his jawline. Jerry let out a roar before charging his attacker.

As both men hit the floor, Jerry moaned again as the kitchen knife was thrust into his hip. Bob pulled the blade out, lifting it towards Jerry's blood-soaked neck. Gripping Bob's hands, Jerry halted his attempt to bring their battle to an end. With every pained breath, Jerry, wounded and weakened, clung on to life. Bob too was damaged but he knew that he had time, and thirty years, on his side. Hold the knife in place and the older man would soon succumb. Not a matter of if but when. As the knife inched closer to his throat, Jerry fought, each strain sapping him of energy, determined not to concede as much as the width of a thin dime.

Suddenly, a thud and Bob's grip was not as firm as it had been. With his eyes rolling in his head and his teeth grinding, Bob groaned and fell to the side. Jerry pulled himself up to see the dislodged leg of May's coffee table embedded into Bob's temple, like a thick wooden horn, held in place by a pair of three-inch screws.

Thanks to Elvin, this unscheduled bout was now over.

"You alright, Mr Hector?"

"May. Where's May?"

Acetate, indigo. Blue, blue, cold blue. Cod blue.

Elvin ran from the kitchen, calling May's name. In the hall, the overspill spread. A semi-circle of water provided him with a telling clue.

"Jesus!"

Elvin pulled May out of the bathtub, her moon tanned skin even more pale than normal.

"No…" he exhorted, upset and panicking. "Mr Hector! I need your help here."

Elvin untied the cord around May's hands and neck. He took off his jacket, and wrapped it around her cold, wet body.

"Turn her head to the side, quickly," said Jerry, leaning against the bathroom door, unsteady on his feet, with blood running down his jaw, dripping onto the already sodden floor. Elvin acted fast. From May's now blue lips, a trickle of water poured out.

"Is she breathing?"

Elvin placed his ear close to May's mouth. He shook his head.

"Hold her nose, then four strong breaths into her mouth."

"She's not breathing, Jerry," cried Elvin, emotion clouding his eyes.

"Do it!"

Pinching the bridge of May's nose, Elvin exhaled into May's mouth.

"Nothing's happening."

"Do it again, Elvin."

May lay on the wet floor, motionless.

"I think she's gone," muttered Elvin, shattered.

Jerry placed his hand over his eyes. He couldn't bear to look. The girl he'd known all of her life. He dropped to the floor, joining Elvin crouched over May's still body.

"I'm sorry May," Jerry said, "I wish you hadn't gotten involved in this."

"Her hand...Jerry, her hand."

May's hand spasmed. Not much. Just a couple of jolts.

"Again!"

As he placed his mouth over May's, there was a splutter. Then another. A mouthful of bathwater and bile sprayed over Elvin and onto the wall. May's chest heaved as Jerry and Elvin lifted her shoulders. Elvin grabbed a couple of towels and wrapped them around May's shivering legs. Jerry breathed a sigh of relief and leant back into the wall. Looking up, he grabbed one of May's hand towels from the rack above, folded it in half then again before carefully administering it to the wound on his side.

"Hey. Those are my best towels," said May, weak and groggy.

"Don't worry. It'll come out in the wash," said Jerry to May.

"You know what? Keep it," she replied as Elvin, unusually emotional, held her tight.

"You need one too?" she asked Elvin.

"No, I'm fine," he said. "Not a scratch."

"Here," she replied. "Dry your eyes. Don't want you dripping all over me."

Recalling what had happened, May tensed up.

"It's OK," said Elvin. "He won't be bothering you anymore."

May sighed, at first staccato then long and hard, the air escaping from her lungs like a punctured ball. As she held onto Elvin, she looked over at Jerry. He knew what was coming.

"Jerome Hector," she said, "We need to talk."

"Before that, I think we need to call 911," said Elvin, concerned that his boss's condition was about to deteriorate.

"Don't worry about me, guys," said May sarcastically. "I'm just fine. No problems at all."

Elvin reached for May's phone.

"Call the library," said Jerry, quietly.

"This is no time to be renewing your overdue books," said May, returning quickly to her old, snarky self.

Jerry shook his head in frustration.

"Elvin, listen to me," said Jerry, firm and calm. "Call the Municipal Library. The number is 31291. Speak to Miss Holloway."

"Rose Holloway? From the Mooney? You gotta be kidding me," said May.

Jerry was serious.

"Quickly. Rose knows what to do."

Chapter 19 - The Horizon's Verge

"Not a problem at all, May. I've made up the guest room for you. There are fresh towels in the cupboard in the corner of the bathroom. You stay as long as you want," said Mrs Peterson, in her late forties and still an elegant, attractive woman.

"The landlord said that they'll replace the whole boiler in one go, which is good, so hopefully we can get rid of her in a few days," said Elvin.

"Watch your manners, Elvin," said Mrs Peterson. "Can I get you some ice for that bump?"

"No, thank you Mrs Peterson," said May, pulling away from her touch. "I really appreciate you putting me up but I don't want to be too much of an imposition," said May.

"Nonsense. You stay as long as you need to," replied Mrs Peterson. "I'm just relieved that you weren't too badly hurt. And besides, it'll be good to have another girl around the place. Lighten the mood a bit, you know?" she said, looking at her husband, wheelchair bound but still a formidable presence. He looked up from his newspaper to cast her a stern look.

"Don't you be giving me no eyes," said Mrs Peterson. "It's a long way down that hill with your brakes off."

Mr Peterson appreciated his loyal wife's attempt at humour, though he'd never show it. Once fit and handsome, now he was withered and diminished. Three years he'd been in the chair. Three years at home, his body wasting away. Elvin didn't like to talk about his father's illness and

May didn't want to ask. The gruff confidence he'd once had was now penned in around the perimeter of the Peterson family home.

Elvin closed the door, listening to the sound of his mother's heels on the hardwood floors, gradually disappearing out of earshot.

"You ok?"

May nodded. She wasn't but she was going to be. She felt safe here. More so than back at the apartment where Bob's body still lay. Elvin may not have had a scratch but he displayed a bruise on his head that looked as though he had half an egg under his skin. The cap May brought him back from Vegas kept it out of sight. The Peterson's didn't need to know what had happened earlier.

"There's a phone here if you need to call me at the diner," said Elvin.

"Surely you're not going to work now? After what happened?"

"Mr Hector needs me. I'll just say that he needed to go out of town. On business."

"If you're going to work, so am I," said May reaching for her coat.

"Like hell you are," replied Elvin, firmly. "You are not leaving this room until I get back, you hear me?"

May sat on the edge of the bed.

"Can I ask, what made you come to my apartment?"

"Jerry said that you might be needing some help."

"Did he...you know...take care of things?"

Elvin swiftly changed the subject.

"You don't need to be worrying about that right now, May."

"But he is going to pull through?"

"You know him better than anyone, I guess. What do you think?"

May lifted her bag onto the bed and took out the few clothes that she'd managed to grab before she stepped over the impaled body of Bob.

"Maybe I don't know him as well as I thought I did," replied May.

"Get some rest," said Elvin, punching her gently on the arm.

When the door closed, May unzipped the front sleeve of her bag and removed Elie's book. Its stained cover was still wet to the touch. She wasn't sure if the blood belonged to Bob or to her. May carried it from the shaded bedroom into the light filled en-suite and ran some lukewarm water. Taking a handful of tissues, she dabbed the dappled leather cover before flushing away any incriminating evidence. May took a second to remind herself that she was the victim, not the aggressor. That was all Bob, if indeed that was his name. She had no inclination that their latest encounter would prove so final. The recollection of the most harrowing morning of her life was as fresh as the blood she'd wiped from the book.

She looked up, catching sight of herself in the cabinet mirror above the sink. Eyes sunken, skin grey, hair matted. The face which stared back was one she hardly recognised. She wanted answers. The questions she had about Jerry's murky past had been superseded by a host of others. For instance, who the hell was Bob and why did he come for her with such murderous intent? And how did Jerry and Elvin know that she was in danger? Also, why was Jerry so keen to contact, of all people, that miserable old shrew from the library, Rose Holloway, rather than the authorities? The answers would have to wait. She returned to the edge of the bed and removed her socks and sweatpants. The Peterson's guest bed was clean and soft, the sheets washed with a lemony scent. May leant back and relaxed. Her body, sore and stiff, reminded her that Elvin was right; she needed to rest.

Just a few more pages, she thought to herself.

****

'Young Mr Liston and I left the hotel before sunrise. I had a single bag, packed with enough clothing to see me through a couple of days on a Pullman car, not a flight to Europe. My travelling companion didn't even possess that. Moreau wasn't around to bid us adieu but as dutiful as she was beautiful, the radiant Miss Sufiah was. A welcome out of hours stop at one of the town's gentleman's outfitters and Sonny Boy was kitted out, good to go. Sufiah asked if we needed to make any last minute phone calls before we embarked. Neither of us had anyone we felt needed to know. It was just us two, waiting to board a plane that, I thought, resembled a massive chrome dildo. With wings. Whether it was the recent sexual drought I'd endured, or a bout of nervousness about being stuck in the aforementioned phallic bird for twenty-two hours, from St. Louis to New York, refueling at some place called Gander before flying on to France, via Ireland, or the knot-in-the-stomach sense of trepidation I was feeling about returning to Paris, with all of its delights and all of its problems, I didn't know. But I was tired. Sonny wasn't. The initial thrill of having a wallet full of legitimately earned corn and a wardrobe to match was beginning to wear off.

"You okay?" I asked of him. His lips pursed and oddly, he looked far more fearful than he did when facing down the Sore Loser Gang in the downtown alleyways.

'I've never done this before,' he confided.

'It'll be fine. Just make sure no harm comes to me and you'll get your money,' I said.

'That's not what I meant,' he replied, quietly and out of general earshot. 'I ain't flown before.'

'You've got nothing to worry about,' I said lightly, putting his mind at rest. 'We go up, have a few drinks, a light meal, a little sleep and before you know it, it's the Champs-Élysées, Montmartre and the Moulin fucking Rouge!'

'Okay,' he said, his breathing decelerating to an acceptable non-fighting rate.

'Listen, there's really nothing to it.'

'So, you fly a lot?'

I took a long drag of my cigarette and told him straight.

'Nope. This will be my first time too.'

Thankfully Sufiah arrived back to inform us that the pilot was *ready and that we could board the shiny flying wang.*

'You'll be met when you land in Paris. We're not expecting any deviations from the schedule but stay together and remain alert. Good luck gentlemen and I await your safe and successful return.'

Sonny and I boarded the flight, along with a handful of other travellers, mainly businessmen, who did seem curious as to why this old kraut should be travelling with a young negro. Pretty hard for this odd couple to travel incognito. We needed a back story. Sonny, still nervous, agreed. The pretty hostess furnished us with some hard liquor and we sat back and worked on our narrative. We could be agents, suggested Sonny. Heading into the unknown, taking care of some bad guys. Not bad, I said, omitting to tell him that it was probably a little too close to the truth for comfort. A boxer and writer? Some people have no imagination, he replied. By the time we had settled on our script; a nite club owner and his financier, scoping out premises in France for a new jazz club, we were high over Missouri, heading north to New York and our first stop.

As Sonny paced the Idlewild tarmac below me, like a tiger awaiting the crack of the ringmaster's bullwhip, I looked west from the window, past the low rises of Cypress Hills and the billowing ferns of Highland Park to Ridgewood. Decatur Street. Perhaps four, maybe five miles away. Without my father's presence, it held little appeal. Lepska took the kids to visit her a few years ago. I stayed in Big Sur. I had work to do. I'd been in New York a few times since I left for good but never to Decatur Street. If we get through this, then maybe...

The fifteen hundred mile leg of the tour from Idlewild to the northwestern corner of Newfoundland was scheduled to take around five hours. As on edge as my travelling companion was, I didn't have any problems with the art of flight. The journey itself was nondescript though the take off and landing experience felt like being a child at Coney Island. No, my brain was in Europe, computing every possible Parisienne eventuality, factoring in permutations, most of which resulted in violence against my person.

A small but potent supply of a strain you might know today as Mandrax, sent to me by a thoughtful correspondent who was known to dabble in pharmaceuticals, would allow me to be enveloped in a blanket of deep blue for fifteen to twenty hours. Waiting on the other side would be Paris or death. I was ready for either.

I drained what I could from my bladder before returning to my seat. With a final nod to my hometown, I ate a soft, dry bread roll and swallowed the tiny white time capsule, washing it down with a small measure of vodka. Sonny returned and took his seat. The hostess asked if he'd like a snack or a drink. Large brandy and a beer, I heard him say. Together? asked the hostess. Yeah, he said, getting back to his feet for yet another rest room visit. Removing my eye mask, I could tell that this long haul may prove problematic. The hostess returned with his refreshments but while he was squeezing out his own final droplets, I thought I'd do him a favour by sharing my supply of not quite prescribed medication. Now, young Mr Liston was a much larger fellow than I. If a single tablet was enough for me, then perhaps two would quell his personal sense of turbulence? Just to be on the safe side, I made it three.

Before Sonny had returned to his seat, I was gone. Back to Coney Island, only this time I was with Lisette from the Café Bèrangère, between two worlds, twixt night and morn, life hovering like Byron's star. Holding hands, we zig zagged along the bleached decks and it mattered not that she wouldn't let me kiss her. That would come. I bought her a balloon, a pink one, from Jimmy Kramer's Uncle Fritz who'd somehow given up his delicatessen to bring a little joy to the kids of Brighton Beach. I unbuttoned my collar, loosened my tie and felt a cool refreshing breeze on my neck, a mistral blowing in from the Bight. Oh no, cried Lisette as that same gust lifted the balloon from her hand, carrying it off, left and right, down the boardwalk. Lisette gave chase. I'll wait for you right here, I shouted and watched her disappear out of sight. I removed my cap and mopped my brow with my pocket square. Ahead of me, beyond the boardwalk railings, stood the stalls and bunco booths. She will find me there, I thought.

The first attraction was the House of Mirrors, its warped, elongated panels, reminding me of the dread I felt as a child, the nightmares I had of my father being miniaturized, my mother chasing him around the kitchen with a knife, as though he was a rodent. I knew I had to move on. 'Wilson's Seven Amazing Wonders' said the next billboard. I kept moving. Sundaes and knickerbockers. Pennants, rattles and soda. Sarsaparilla. I took a seat and stuck my hand into the glass bowl of cold taffy coloured gelato and brought it to my mouth. It tasted of soup. Fish soup. A boy laughed. He looked familiar. Cruel features. I raised my hand to strike him but I could not administer the blow. His laughs turned to taunts but try as I might, my hand wouldn't budge. Tears of frustration formed in my eyes as the boy, having bested me, disappeared into the crowd. My hand dropped and smashed into the glass bowl, shattering it into pieces. My hand was bleeding but I felt no pain. Let me help you, said a familiar voice. It was Sufiah and as she wrapped linen around my wounds, she cradled me as if I were her child. You are safe here, she whispered. I stayed perfectly still, frightened that if I moved, she would release me and leave. I wanted to remain in her protective embrace for all times but the sun was starting to set.

On the beach, the water lapping around my bare feet, I had to leave. Sufiah was gone. I walked behind a man wearing a white shirt. His trousers rolled up to his knees as he stepped lightly in and out of the foam. He ran his hands through his hair, thick and wild, silhouetted against the fading light. He turned to me and smiled. He said my name. He knew who I was and asked me to join him but as fast as I could walk, I was unable to catch him before he too disappeared beyond the boardwalk. I put my hand down and felt the warm dense mane of a large dog, walking by my side. The dog looked at me and said, 'This is as far as we go today, Mr Miller.'

****

'Are they breathing?'

'I can't tell.'

'Better inform the captain.'

The voices were clear. I'd been listening for about five minutes. My problem was that I simply couldn't move. Perhaps taking a full tablet had been a bit too cavalier on my part. My body could cope with the half dose but double the amount meant double the effect. I'd been expecting the 'chemical cosh'. Poor Sonny hadn't. Much as I knew he could take a shot, his fighter's instincts took over at those moments. He had no idea that his Courvoisier would have the kick of a furious mule. I needed to alert the flight crew of the fact that we remained of this realm.

'He's not dead!' said one of the hostesses, a pretty blonde I hadn't noticed earlier. I may not have been dead but I sure was stiff, in more ways than one.

'Are you okay, Mr Valentine?' she asked with real concern. I shifted to the side, so that she couldn't see how okay I really was.

'Yes, I'm fine,' I said, casting my eye down the empty aisle. 'Where are we?'

'Le Bourget,' she said, my suspicions confirmed. 'We landed in Paris fifteen minutes ago. You and your companion slept all the way from Newfoundland.'

'Well, it's a credit to you and your crew for such a smooth flight,' I offered.

'Smooth flight? Mr Valentine, that must have been some sleep you had as we encountered the worst turbulence over the Atlantic that I've ever experienced with TWA. We were up, down, side to side. It was as though we were on an extremely uncomfortable funfair ride.'

'Just like Coney Island,' I said.

'Worse!' she exclaimed.

I was actually quite put out that I'd missed all the fun. Still, trying to rouse the great grizzly from his sleep might make a tumultuous substitute.

By the time that The Castagne's driver had helped him off the airplane and into the car, Sonny was awake but confused. 'Are we in Paris?' he slurred repeatedly, still 'hungover' from the mickey.

As the city circular turned onto the boulevards and petit rue, one thing struck me, aside from how much busier my former home had become. Fifteen years since I'd been in Paris and for fifteen years, I'd dreamt of my return the way I'd once felt about going back to New York. Yet like that long voyage back from Europe, the overriding sensation was one of disappointment. Yes, the buildings remained, with the same torn billposters, the smell of the once familiar Gauloise and Gitanes, instantly evocative. But this was not 1938. That world was gone. And where were the people with whom I shared mon vie Parisienne? Anaïs and Hugo were maintaining a pretence of normality in Manhattan. I hadn't heard from Joe Do Sappo since the day I left for Marseille. Was he still alive? My old patron, Purcell Griffin wasn't. I received word a few years ago that he succumbed to some dreadful illness. And though we still had liaisons in my odd narco fantasies, there was no au revoir for Lisette from the Bèrangère. I imagine that she finally tired of waiting outside the Gaumont and settled for a consolation prize from the collection of aimless rakes and barflies who followed in my less than auspicious trail.

The driver took us to Saint-Germain-des-Prés, to the Boulevard Raspail and the once regal Hotel Lutetia, a place which had witnessed Josephine Baker dance, Picasso sketch and drifted off while Joyce wrote a few pages of that indecipherable garbage with which he made his name. The war may have left the Lutetia looking more pockmarked and scarred than in its heyday but this was no Clichy slophouse. We were checked in, under our assumed names, and placed in adjoining rooms on the fifth floor. As the fellow entrusted with my safe passage remained sluggish, the driver left a number to call if anything unexpected happened. He advised us to stay in our rooms until he returned to collect us in the morning for our Castagne rendezvous.

'Get some shut eye,' he barked in an accent which suggested that he'd picked up English from watching Edward G. Robinson films. We won't, I thought as I closed the door on him. I set my wristwatch to Paris time and as it was technically twenty-four hours since my last refreshment, the bottle of Chivas, so kindly left by the housekeep, was cracked and a generous measure was poured. I sat by the open window and took it all in. Paris. Maybe I'd been a little harsh in my assessment...

Soon, young Mr Liston was awake and as thirsty as I was. We freshened up and headed out into the mild evening. I took the role of tour guide, showing my young companion some of the salons and cafés that I remembered. I may have embellished some of the details but that, I'd say, is a storyteller's prerogative.

'How long were you here?' he asked as we walked north on Les Invalides towards the Seine.

'Seven or eight years,' I replied. The kind of time that tends to form a man.

'Before today, I've never been anywhere further than Chicago, and that was for one night,' he said.

'For a fight?' I asked. He nodded. I later learned that he'd beaten the Olympic champion in that Windy City contest but as I was to discover, Sonny tended to underplay his achievements and his abilities.

We stood on the Pont Alexandre III in silence, taking in the view. A tonic for my tired eyes but for Sonny, I could tell that his experience was going to be more profound.

'Ain't that something?' he asked, rhetorically. It sure was.

'When I was in the joint...,' he paused a moment, but it was fine. Until he could fully trust me, he felt that he needed those 'personal checkpoints'.

'When I was in Missouri, I hadn't been in State before, so things were tough. That's how State is. I kept myself to myself and didn't join up with any team, I figured that if I stayed solitary, I'd have a better chance of getting out of there without any complications, you know?'

I nodded again, not wanting to stem his flow. Up to this point, it was the most he had spoken.

He continued. 'There was a fellow by the name of Myers. Worked at the library, had done for most of his term. Wheeled a little trolley around the floors, Charles Dickens, Mark Twain. I had no real interest but he did no harm. Now, Myers was a...,' Sonny searched for a polite term, 'a gentleman. A gentle man. He'd often talk about all of the places he'd visited, to the short to mid termers, like me. Not the murderers, the institutionalised, it was too much for them and they'd get angry but if you could count the end of your time, a few minutes with Myers gave you something to dream about. The world was a small place when Myers talked. But of all the places he spoke of, none of them could compare to Paris. I didn't hang around much, you know. What a man does, especially when life is tough, is up to that man and him alone but I'd sit by the window and look through them big books, with the colourful maps and the pictures of Siam, Italy and Africa in them and listen in to what Myers was talking about, from a distance. He always said that when he made parole, he'd ride the rails, St. Louis to Lexington. He had family there. He'd get enough there to see him as far as Norfolk and from there, he'd board any ship that would take him to Europe. He'd peel potatoes, scrub fucking decks, whatever it took, you know? Determined. To get to Paris, France, find a soft bed and follow the sound of that gypsy guitar.'

Sonny looked out over the Seine, a young man at peace with his past and the entire world at the end of his wrists. He shook his head and smiled. He'd come a long way in two days.

'If only Myers could see you now, eh?' I said, unaware that a housebreaker called Knucks had taken exception to Myers' ways and *stabbed him in the neck with a dislodged piece of tiling.*

'Let's go and find us some of that gypsy guitar.'

The following morning, we were up early. A light breakfast for me and half a dozen eggs for Sonny before French Edward G. arrived to pick us up. A short drive later and I was back on familiar ground; the Rue Gabrielle, in Montmartre. The driver took us as far as he could. The rest of the way was by foot, up the steep steps towards the side of the Sacré-Coeur. Sonny had a job to do - protect me - but for him, every street we walked was a new adventure. I kept a lookout for the both of us. Near the top of the steps, stood a small establishment, the Café Chappe. Seated at the only table outside was a fellow smoking a foul smelling cheroot. He stirred his coffee very slowly.

'Go right in,' he said without looking up. 'He'll be with you shortly.'

Even though the people we were meeting were 'friends', Sonny suggested we took the table at the far end of the L-shaped café, the furthest away from the bar. It had a small off-shoot to the right and nothing behind it but a large mirror and a clear view of the front door, the kitchen and the bar. Just in case. If they'd wanted me dead though, that could've been taken care of at any time in the last fifteen years. With that in mind, I was remarkably sanguine about reacquainting the Castagnes.

The café had two visible members of staff. Behind the bar, a tall and attractive but quite young waitress with the most remarkable almond shaped eyes poured a pale beer for the fellow scribbling notes at the counter. The other was a portly fellow with a shiny head who, without prompting, brought us over some coffee and a small bottle of pungent liquer. He used the towel over his shoulder to clean a pair of shot glasses he kept in the pocket of his waistcoat. If the idiosyncrasies of Café Society were confusing to Sonny, he didn't show it. A game of poker with young Mr Liston might prove interesting.

'What do they look like?' he asked.

'The Castagnes brothers?' I replied. 'I've only met them once,' I said.

'That's once more than me,' said Sonny, looking for something, a head's up. He wanted to be prepared.

'Think Laurel and Hardy,' I said, 'but with more firepower.'

I poured some of the liquor into my small glass and raised the bottle Sonny's way but he wanted to keep a clear head. At least there would be one of us taking this seriously. I slugged back my shot and quickly poured another for good measure.

At that moment, from the kitchen appeared Benoit Castagne, followed by a younger, well-dressed man carrying a small case. I was quite taken aback by how much weight Castagne seemed to have shed in the years since our brief but memorable meet.

I stood to greet him and Sonny followed suit but with a shake of his head and a wave of his kerchief, he made it clear that the ceremony was superfluous. We sat and he took a moment to size me up. Maybe the years had been as unkind to me as they'd been to him? I hadn't given it too much thought, if I'm being honest. He brought his kerchief back to his brow, now dappled with beads of sweat.

'Henry,' he said, gently. 'It is good to see you. I'm sorry that we couldn't offer La Belle Daphne today but this is a much safer place for us to speak.'

Castagne chose well. The Café Chappe was dark, humid and almost airless but as it was lodged into the hill that housed one of Paris' most sacred architectural treasures, it was close to impenetrable. But it wasn't the location that had me scratching my head.

'Your brother Etienne,' I asked, 'Will he be joining us?'

The café staff glanced at each other and from their reaction, I knew that he wouldn't. Benoit's big eyes said more than his simple reply of 'No' did. Realising I'd moved out of the comfort 'arrondissement', I changed the subject back to business.

'So Benoit,' I said, 'how can an old man be of assistance to you?'

'Tell me, Henry. What do you know of al-Eizaraya?'

My blank expression answered his question.

'Al-Eizaraya, or Bethany, is a town in what is now known as Palestine. It lies close to Jerusalem,' said Benoit.

'It's where Jesus brought Lazarus back from the dead,' added Sonny. Before I could remind him that he was being hired for his muscle not for his theological chops, he said 'I remember Bethany from Gospel studies.'

Benoit nodded. 'Indeed. But what the Gospels wouldn't have told you was that Lazarus' sisters, Mary and Martha, grateful for Our Lord's intervention, crafted a vessel from clay in his honour. In John's Gospel, both he and Lazarus bore witness as the receptacle was blessed by Christ himself.'

Benoit leant in close and lowered his voice.

'Weeks later, when Jesus returned to the town, a woman of flawed character offered to bathe his tired feet and dry them with her hair. This action caused consternation within the ranks of the gathered, even more so when our Lord invited her to dine. He insisted that this fallen soul should be treated as they would a family member and that she use the plate that Martha and Mary had made for him. From then, it became known as the Sinner's Plate.'

Benoit motioned and his assistant handed him the case he'd been looking after. Castagne laid it on the table and carefully opened it, removing the contents. Peeling back the layers of material, Benoit spoke, 'I asked you many years ago if you were a believer?'

'And I'm still willing to be convinced,' I told him.

'Some things you just have to take on faith,' he said.

'Is that…?' I asked. Benoit grinned.

'The Sinner's Plate,' he said, triumphantly.

'Tell me,' he asked, 'how well do you know your Gospels?'

'Sure. Matthew, Mark, Luke and John,' I said, looking to Sonny for some biblical back up but other than a concentrated look of *intrigued silence, he offered nothing.*

'But did you know that there was a second Gospel of Mark, a secret Gospel?' asked Benoit. He looked over his shoulder and the young waitress brought a fresh bottle of liquor. She looked at Sonny and across her long, full lips, there was the trace of a smile. She poured measures for Benoit and I.

'Merci Delphine,' said Castagne. Sonny, staring back at this emerald eyed vision of loveliness, decided that now was as good a time as any to join us.

'Within the text of Mark's secret Gospel lay more, pertinent information about the Sinner's Plate.'

'May I?' I asked. 'I'll be careful with it.' Benoit didn't need to know that I'd once stashed this sacred relic near my own holiest of holies.

'Sure,' he said, lifting it gently over to our side of the table. Sonny leaned in to take a closer look. We both tried, and failed, to pronounce the inscription, written in an ancient text I wasn't familiar with.

'I don't understand what this says,' I said.

'It translates as 'No one is lost who yearns for salvation' and they are words that we live by. For the best part of two thousand years, it was guarded by the keepers of Mar Saba Monastery, until the uprising of 1866. Insurgents, funded by imperialists, sacked the monastery taking whatever artefacts they could. The Sinner's Plate was one such item but without that Secret Gospel, few understood its importance. The plate swapped hands on a number of occasions, finally ending up in the collection of an unwitting dealer in your town of New York City. And it may still have been there today, a nondescript antiquity in a glass display case in a rich man's trophy room had there not been an emergence of a transcript from that Secret Gospel. That changed everything. Once the Secret Gospel became common knowledge, the significance of the Sinner's Plate made it the most desirable collectible. To the true believer, only the Ark of the Covenant and the Holy Grail itself come close. It became

a free for all. Men were killed just for knowing about its existence. Governments around the world worked with the Holy Roman Church to locate it but as ever, it was left to people like us, the state beneath, to do the dirty work. Using our contacts, we managed to locate it. Securing it, though, that would be another matter.'

'But you did.'

'Yes but it came at a cost that we seem to still be paying.'

'Where does that leave us today?' I asked.

'I asked you if you were a believer and at this moment, all I can ask is for you to entrust me with your faith. The monastery at Mar Saba is still in a disputed territory so we need to keep it safe until the time is right.'

'To return it to its rightful place?'

'Exactement.'

'Is that why you gave it to me to take to New York?' I asked.

'In a way, yes,' replied Benoit, curiously.

'I don't understand,' I said.

'The plate you were given was a replica. Identical in every feature.'

'Wait a minute. You're telling me that I was nearly killed for a fucking fake?'

'I'm sorry Henry. But it was a risk we had to take,' said Benoit.

'Well thank you for that,' I replied sarcastically.

'...to establish the identities and key personnel of Le Corbeau.'

'Oh yes, The Crow. Whatever happened with that?' I sniped.

'The Crow, as we knew it back then, is no more.'

'Oh, that is peachy,' I said, the sarcasm dripping like molasses. I poured another glass of the strong liquor and downed it in one. I could hear Sonny sigh beside me but at this point, I'd enough anger festering to take him on too. 'Can I ask a question?'

'Of course,' said Benoit.

"Why am I here? You already have the plate so why do you still need me?'

'As I said, The Crow as we knew it then is finished. The war tore a hole through their operation and we've been picking off loose threads ever since but its Command eludes us still. And this is where you come in.'

'Oh really?' I said, less than impressed.

'You are the only one who can verify the identity of the man who left you for dead in the Mediteranean.'

My old shipmate Sevak would most likely recognise him but even in the unlikely event that he was still alive, dragging him back into this mess wasn't an option.

I took another drink. If I was going in, I wanted to be forearmed but just as I thought I had a handle on the situation, Castagne dropped another charge. He motioned to his assistant who walked over to the alcove by the pillar to our left and reached into a display cabinet. He returned to the table and placed another plate beside the relic. To my untrained eyes, and to Sonny's, they were identical. Every detail. The same. I lifted both and I couldn't determine which was heavier and which was lighter. Not that this would've indicated anything. I was confused. I didn't understand. When I stated that I didn't know which plate was real, Benoit smirked like he was a schoolboy playing a trick on a parent.

'Exactly,' he said. 'I cannot risk you taking the relic for real. All you need to do is go to the agreed spot, draw him out and confirm his identity.'

'What if things turn ugly?' asked Sonny.

'It won't turn ugly as long as Henry gives him the plate. That is all he wants. The drop is in public so the last thing he'll do is create a scene. If he gets the plate, he wins. One positive identification, Henry...' Castagne slowly wiped his hands together, 'and a great service you will have performed.'

'I'll be there with you,' said Sonny.

Both Castagne and his assistant shook their heads.

'Out of the question,' said Castagne. 'He must make the drop alone.'

He picked up the original plate and handed it to me. His man carefully lifted the genuine item and returned it to its place beside a faded soccer club pennant and a dusty ceremonial beaker. Just then, a well heeled man entered the café alone and took a seat facing the bar.

Castagne said that he had other business to attend to and wished me bon chance.

His assistant took his seat and mapped out the where and the when of the meet.

After a rather brusque pep talk, he too joined Castagne and his business acquaintance. As I stood, Sonny gripped my arm.

'I don't like it,' he said. 'Nothing about this makes sense.' He couldn't understand why he wasn't being permitted to accompany me but I understood Castagne's position; The Crow might be weakened but they'd still be watching.

'I'll be fine,' I said, for my own benefit as much as for his.

I took the fake plate and ventured down the steps and onto the streets of Paris, alone.

From Chateau Rouge, I paid my centime and boarded the 4, taking me past the Hotel Lutetia, and onto Raspail. For a half an hour, I was free of obligations. A discarded newspaper gave me a chance to brush up on my French but my envious attention was drawn to the legions of young bucks with long hair wearing the snappiest of trousers and American style jackets, each one trying to impress one of the many coquettes heading to work in the offices and the boutiques. Oh, to be fresh and young in Paris, I thought. I never was.

Outside the Metro station, I stopped for a pack of smokes and a casual glance around for anyone who may have paused to watch *me. No obvious tracker spotted, I continued into Montparnasse Cemetery; a place in which I'd gladly spend eternity, provided eternity began anon. I checked my wristwatch and saw that I still had a few minutes to kill before the agreed rendezvous. Enough time to catch up with a few old pals. Like Paul Bourget, for instance. A man swayed by his passions and his weaknesses. At least I was in good company with Paul. And fresh flowers at the headstone of the mighty Peruvian wordsmith Cesar Vallejo. Must have been placed there by his wife. Cesar may have been frail in body, but he had a mind that bewitched. I'd regrettably attempted a move on the enchanting Georgette during his illness but she gave me short shrift. The black heralds will be coming for me, dear Cesar and I can have no complaints. What's this? No! Leon-Paul Fargue. Damn! I did not know he was dead. I will raise a glass to you later, my witty, beautiful friend.*

It was time. I took the folded up newspaper from my pocket, placed it on the still dewey wooden bench situated opposite the resting place of Baudelaire and awaited the arrival of my connection. If I'd had the time, I'd have marveled at the inequity of the gravestone he was forced to share with a stepfather he hated but a familiar voice from over my shoulder meant that I didn't. I turned around, into the glare of the late morning sun and felt a chill. Grey skin, hollow cheeks, flat nose.

'You're looking well, Mr Miller.'

Considering you'd planned to let me bleed out before dumping me in the Mediterranean, I'd have to agree with you, is what I would've said, had I not remembered how brutally he'd despatched my fellow rail passengers en route to Marseille.

'Do you have it?' he asked, pleasantries over.

My mouth was dry, my lips locked. I nodded. He sat down.

'Show it to me,' he said.

I opened my jacket and undid the bottom buttons on my waistcoat.

'Slowly,' he said.

The sight of a man sitting close to another while he loosened his clothing was not something to turn a head in Montparnasse, especially in the shadow of Louÿs' resting place. Still, I did what I was instructed to.

From under my shirt, I took out the plate and offered it to the Englishman.

'Open it.'

I unfastened the binding and carefully peeled back the canvas to reveal a corner of the plate.

The Englishman lifted the other flaps and saw the ancient writing. He took it from me, tucking it inside his overcoat.

'So, we're good?' I asked.

'You know, Mr Miller. You caused me a lot of trouble after Marseille. You should've stayed dead.'

'What can I say? Sorry if I inconvenienced you?' I offered, snippily.

'You're coming with me,' he said.

'You don't need me. You've got what you wanted. The plate's yours.'

'There's enough dead men here. Let's not add to the number today,' he said, revealing the gun, holstered against his ribcage, and the tip of the blade he had tucked into the cuff of his shirt.

'First sign of any movement, I'll drop you. You got that?'

I nodded, acutely aware of how seriously he took his role. But what was that role, I thought. Was the Englishman actually The Crow or was he merely a helper-at-the-nest? Besides, I'd travelled here alone. Sonny's instincts were right. I should never have agreed to this. We walked, in very close proximity, to the corner of Edgar Quinet and into the back of a waiting taxi cab. As the Englishman didn't speak, I could only presume that the driver was part of the scheme. He took us on a circuitous trip around the Bois De Boulogne and up through Neuilly where we stopped, quickly changing cabs, with another driver, a musclebound hood with a red neckerchief and a *golden tooth which gave him the air of a pirate who at breakneck speed, continued the tour through the western districts and into Colombes. Looking back, I suspected - hoped - that this was a deliberate act so that I wouldn't be able to recall upon release where I was being taken. At the time though, the chances of surviving a second encounter with this vicious bastard were slim.*

Just before we pulled into a dilapidated courtyard, the Englishman opened the door and jumped out onto the quiet avenue. He lit a cigarette and stood by the tall green doors, checking to see if we'd been followed. After a few seconds, he gave driver number two the signal to open the cab door and drag me out, which he did with some relish.

'Is there any need for this?' I said, appealing to the devious limey fuck's native sense of fair play.

'You're starting to test my patience, Mr Miller. I'd kindly ask you to shut the fuck up otherwise my friend will see to it that those words are your final will and testament.' Unnecessary, I thought.

With the Englishman walking behind us, the driver took me down a flight of stairs to what appeared to be a large coal bunker. The Englishman passed him a long skeleton key and he unlocked the door.

'Get in,' he barked, giving me a shove. The room was dark, cold and, excuse my language dear Elie, smelled of the bad piss. Once I was inside, the door was closed behind me, the sound of the key turning in the barrel made my stomach turn. I put my ear up to the door, to listen for any clues as to what fate was about to befall me and I roundly cursed Benoit Castagne. How could he have been so foolish? Was I now just a loose end to tie up? My children. I'm not ashamed to admit but I burst into tears at the thought of them. Never again would I feel their uncritical arms tightly around my neck. Bereft, is the word. If I was to find some way to survive this and see their faces again, I'd need to cast them from my mind, banishing them from this awful place for their own good.

Unfortunately, the conversation between the driver and the Englishman was now imperceptible. As my eyes adjusted to the dim light that emanated from a small, but barred street level window, at least fifteen feet above the soggy ground on which I stood, I realised that those shafts were so faint that as soon as dusk hit we'd be in complete darkness. I needed to search the room for something, anything which I could use to help me reach that height or failing that, to use as a weapon of some sort. I'd never been much of a brawler but this time, if I was going down, I'd be swinging to the very last.

With my hands out, I shuffled around the room like I was Boris Karloff, feeling my way in the darkness. Just then, I heard movement. Something in this dungeon, other than me, is alive. Not mice. Too big for that. Rats. Jesus. That's all I needed, I thought. As I steeled myself for the skin crawl, the creature made itself known.

'Aidez moi, s'il vous plait?' it said, weakly and I nearly jumped out of my skin.

Maybe it was the jolt of surprise that did it but I remembered that I had a book of matches, from the hotel, in my jacket pocket. Quickly, I took them out and struck one. The weak flame was strong enough to cast enough light on the room and the figure slumped in the corner.

The matchstick burned onto my fingers so I lit another, and a cigarette with it. I had almost a full pack left which, I figured, would provide us with enough light and some small comfort during what might prove to be a very difficult few hours. I took another match and lit it so that I could see exactly where my 'cellmate' lay. On the wall was a metal fixing, the kind that looked as if it once held an old wooden torch. I'll get to the invalide in a second. I bound some kindling in a discarded sheet of newspaper and placed it in the fixing. I spent another match and woosh...we had light. For how long though, I couldn't tell. I approached the prone figure in the corner with an element of care. I didn't know what to expect. At worst, he might be able to give me an indication as to what I may be facing. I offered a greeting, in halting French, and he turned to me, a heavy, dark coat, obscuring all but the top of his head. In English, I said, let me help you, without thinking. I'd just placed my hand under his arm to help him up when I heard him say,

'Henry? Is that you?'

After a split second of shock, I lit another match. I could not believe what my eyes were telling me. The man under the coat was my old friend from the café's of Clichy, Joe Do Sappo!

I helped him to his feet and we embraced. It had been so long since I'd seen him but the years fell away as we hugged, two men thrown together by the fates, again!

'I don't understand, Joe,' I said, 'What are you doing here?'

'I have no idea. They want answers and I don't understand the questions.'

'How long have you been locked up?' I asked.

Joe shook his head, his eyes weary.

'Two, maybe three days. I don't readily know,' he said.

I looked around again, the need for an escape all the more urgent.

'They'll be back soon,' he said. 'Hurry.'

Though Joe was a good fifteen years younger than me, he was in no fit state to be scaling walls. Removing my jacket, I looked for grip spots in the cellar's decaying brickwork. On the first couple of attempts, I was unable to get a toe hold but by my third, I'd pulled myself high enough off the ground to get close to the narrow, wire lined window. Through the dirty pane, I could see the outlines of a couple of cars and the legs of two, possibly three people.

'Quick!' said Joe, 'Someone's coming!'

Getting up was much easier than coming down but as the brick started to crumble through my fingers, returning ten feet to the floor was as painful as it was fast. Joe came to my aid and lifted me back to my feet.

Winded, with skinned palms and bruised knees, the fall could've been much worse.

We sat in silence awaiting the return of our captors.

'You said they'd been asking you questions. Like what?' I asked.

'As I said, I have no idea about the things they're talking about.'

'Like what?'

'Holy relics and artefacts. You know me, Henry. I don't go in for that mumbo jumbo. They came to my flat and turned it over. They beat my old lady in front of me for Chrissakes, but they kept pushing. I told them that they'd made a mistake and that I couldn't help them. They dragged me into a car and brought me here,' he said, the emotion of the ordeal making this big man as vulnerable as a child. 'What are they going to do to me...to us?'

I levelled with Joe. It felt only fair. 'I'm sorry old friend but I think that I might have dragged you into this mess, inadvertently.'

'How so?'

I proceeded to tell him about the last time we spoke, just before I set out on my ill-fated journey to Marseille, the phone call I made to him from the Castagne's bistro and the parcel I was to deliver to New York.

'So you had the plate? The plate they've been busting me over?'

'I did but long story short, I didn't. And then, this morning, I did again,' I said. 'Does that make sense to you?'

I could tell from his expression that it didn't.

'This morning, Benoit Castagne gave me the plate to hand over to The Crow.'

'I thought The Crow was no more?'

'Seems like they're on the way out. But here's the thing. The plate they gave me was not the original.'

'What?'

'It's a fake. An identical replica of the original. It feels the same,

looks the same but it's a copy.'

'Where's the original?'

'You'd never believe it.'

'Try me.'

'It's in a fucking display case, at a café to the side of the Sacré-Coeur!'

'Not the Café Chappe?'

I nodded.

'Get out of here!'

'I'm serious. Priceless artefact, sitting on a shelf behind a bottle of Grand Marnier and a fucking soccer pennant. Thing is, no one this side of first century Jerusalem could possibly tell the difference. They'll check it out and they'll be convinced it's the real thing. And as soon as they 'verify' it, I'm sure they'll let us go.'

'What if they realise that it's a fake?'

'I've been assured that they won't.'

'But what if they do? They must have experts that can tell, surely?'

'Then in that case Joe, we're pretty much fucked.'

The big man laughed, and coughed.

'Help me to my feet, will you Henry?'

I obliged.

Joe stretched his large frame and walked over to the door.

'I can't believe you slipped them a fake,' he said with a chuckle.

'You know me, Joe,' I said.

Just then, he gave the door a heavy double rap with the side of his fist.

'Mr Hawthorne!' he shouted.

The door unlocked and the Englishman walked in. Joe removed his heavy coat and threw it towards me.

'Feel free to use this. I'd imagine that it gets very cold here at night.'

It took me a moment to comprehend what was happening. And then I became angry. I'd gotten to within ten feet of him when the Englishman drew his weapon. Joe put his hand over it and shook his head. It wasn't necessary. He knew that I wasn't armed and was physically no match for either of them.

'It really was good to see you again, Henry,' he said with a smile. 'And that information was invaluable.'

It was as though my guts had taken Sonny's best shot. A betrayal, the like of which I'd never felt. Of all the women I'd loved and lost, watched walking away, caught a furtive glance, intercepted illicit correspondence, found in flagrante, nothing had come close to this unexpected duplicity. I felt my legs reel beneath me.

'Why?'

'Money. And a number of other reasons, too lengthy to go into now,' he said, checking his wristwatch.

'Summarise,' I barked. 'I considered you my friend. You owe me that.'

'I owe you nothing,' he replied. 'If I was such a friend, why did you attempt to fuck every girlfriend of mine that you ever met? No, Henry. To me, you were furniture. You were there, I used you when I needed to and now you're broken. It would amuse me somewhat though to know that your last few hours as a wretched stain on this planet were spent contemplating the unwitting part you played in your own downfall. That is quite delicious.'

He paused for a moment, smiling.

'Maybe if you'd spent less time with Dostoyevsky and more with Dashiell Hammett, you might have seen this coming. So long, Henry,' he said, waving with a flourish.

I knew I didn't have long. Desperate, I tried to stall him.

'How much?' I said.

'I beg your pardon?'

'How much is The Crow paying you? My friends will double it.'

Joe and the Englishman looked at one another and laughed.

'How much is The Crow paying me?' he said. 'You think that I'm working for The Crow?'

'Well, aren't you?'

'Dear Henry, you still don't get it. I'm not working for The Crow,' he said.

'I am The Crow.'

Chapter 20 - From this day until forever

The distant sound of a door being slammed roused May from a long but rarely comfortable sleep. The painkillers offered to her earlier by Elvin's mother had quickly taken effect and she'd found herself giving in to the chemically induced rest that her battered body needed. She was oblivious to the sound of Elvin's parents, his mother, ironing, cooking and tidying while looking every inch the glamorous catalogue model she'd been before Elvin's father snapped her up. Neither did she hear the sound of Sixties Gold Radio, blasting out of the hefty transistor radio which sat by the kitchen window nor Mr Peterson himself, an old, wine coloured cardigan covering his smart shirt and tie, moving between the lounge, the dining area and his study, frustrated that much of his remaining mobility was courtesy of a modified electric chair. May knew that she was safe at the Petersons. And as she'd not eaten at all that day, she was famished. Squinting her eyes against the dimming light of the late afternoon, May searched for her spectacles, patting around the soft bedding, before realising, after a visit to the bathroom, that they were sitting on her head, tucked into her curls. Though the knowledge contained between the covers of Henry Miller's notes to Elie had spilled into her life, like oil on a pristine carpet, still she wanted to return to the book. Contained within those pages, she believed, was the key to whom she could, and more importantly, could not trust.

May washed her face then clipped her hair back. The red and still tender welt on her forehead was noticeable. She wasn't in the mood for too many questions beyond the standard, 'Do you have a special fellow you're seeing' kind of thing. Elvin said that his father once told him that he could tell when he was lying. He'd been around. Military, police, detective work. Even in his present condition, you'd have to get up early to get one over on him. Better not take the chance, she thought. May tousled her hair, covering up the mark and headed down the hall towards the smell of Mrs Peterson's cooking.

"There she is," said Elvin's mother. "How are you feeling, honey?"

"Tired but fine, Mrs Peterson, thank you."

"You must be hungry by now. Sit yourself down. Elvin isn't long home."

May looked around but couldn't see him.

"He's taking a shower. Tough day at the diner, from the sound of things."

May knew that wasn't the case. On a normal day, Elvin tended to go to the gym after his shift ended because what the doctors and specialists, with all of their testing and equipment, couldn't detect was that the fighting was a part of Elvin's make-up. His father, sitting under the angled lamp, reading a hard backed book, knew what was happening but said nothing. He'd give anything to be able to hit a heavy bag or to run a mile. Though he wouldn't say, he understood his son and figured that some risks were worth taking. His wife didn't need to know. But there was no gym today. There was no skipping and there was no sparring. Just Bob.

"Take a seat May and I'll fix you a plate," said Mrs Peterson, turning off the radio just as 'A Lovers Concerto' by The Toys reached its first key change. That song, May thought, so evocative. One recurring memory of childhood she had, was splashing around in the paddling pool on a hot summer's day while her mother, wearing a red floral dress, bursting with colour, and a wine glass at her bare, perfect feet, held a paperback open with one hand with a long cigarette between the fingers of the other. As the Petersons started their blessing, May sang to herself. 'Now I belong to you. From this day until forever…'

Elvin, his hair still wet from the shower, leant over to May and asked her how she was feeling. Before she could answer with more than an inconclusive nod, Mrs Peterson asked him how his day was.

"You know. Same as most. Busy breakfast, busy lunchtime, otherwise quiet."

"Busy lunchtime," repeated Mrs Peterson.

"Yep," replied Elvin, shovelling a generous forkful of meatloaf into his mouth.

"That's strange because I came by The Columbus. At lunchtime too and you were not there. Hadn't been in since breakfast, Miss Washington said."

Elvin's father stopped picking at the pre-cut meatloaf on his plate and looked at his son. The large chunk of food still in his mouth bought Elvin a bit of time to come up with a story which didn't involve the disposal of a body.

"Well, I'm waiting," said Mrs Peterson, impatiently. Elvin's raised finger, acting as a stop gap.

"Mmm...this has got to be one of your best meatloafs ever, Mom," he said, trying in vain to change the subject.

"Elvin Peterson, you have a bruise on your cheek and your knuckles are all scraped," she replied as he self-consciously slid his hands under the table. May spoke.

"Elvin's right, Mrs Peterson. This is a lovely meatloaf."

"Why, thank you honey," she replied, sweetly, before switching her focus back towards her son.

"So let's have it. The truth."

Elvin's father, still silent, put his cutlery down onto his plate.

"Just tell me that you weren't at that gym again," she said.

"Sheila, the boy wasn't at the gym," said Mr Peterson, his once full-bodied voice, cracked and broken.

"Oh really, Martin? So where was he?" asked Mrs Peterson.

"I was..." said Elvin, stuttering.

"Well, boy? Speak up!" replied his mother, becoming more agitated.

"He was running an errand for me," said Mr Peterson.

"He was what?" asked Mrs Peterson, disbelieving. "What kind of errand was he running for you, tell me? Was this something that I could have done?" There was silence at the table. Elvin's mother continued.

"What was so important that Elvin had to take time off, from a job that he is lucky to still have, to do it? This I gotta hear."

Elvin and May glanced at one another, expressionless. Mr Peterson had just gone to bat for them. Any motion now would destroy the structure of his cover up. Where was this leading?

"Damn it, Sheila," he said, as forcefully as he could manage. "I needed the boy to go to Portland for me."

"Can't I go to Portland for you?"

"Not for this," he said.

"Can I ask why?"

Mr Peterson looked straight at his wife. He reached over and took her hand.

"Sheila, I know things have been tough with my...you know. But it's our twenty-fifth anniversary in December and I just wanted to do something special, to thank you for everything. And our boy has played his part. Elvin has been taking the design ideas back and forth to this jeweller friend I have down in Portland. It's not much but..."

"Oh baby," she said, tenderly embracing her husband. A touching, private moment, May thought, the kind of interaction she had no recollection of from her own parents cold, truncated union. Beautifully crafted it may have been but it was built on a lie so impressively deceptive that Mrs Peterson, now seated on her husband's lap, had overlooked her son's noticeably bruised cheekbone and his grazed knuckles; the optic of a powerful falsehood.

After dinner, as May washed and Elvin dried, she subtly asked him how their employer was. Jerry was fine, tired but thanks to Miss Holloway's sharp intervention, he'd recover.

"Where is he and can I see him?" May asked.

The fable of the Portland jeweller seemed to bring Mr and Mrs Peterson closer than they had been in recent times. As Elvin made the call, May peered through the glass panelled door to the lounge where Sheila and Martin, the Petersons, watched their television programmes, huddled close. She'd always enjoyed visiting their home. Though Mr Peterson was strict, both he and his wife treated May with affection. They'd always been a tight family unit which made Elvin's economy with the truth and his father's augmentation of that deceit, an uncomfortable state of affairs. May knew why Elvin couldn't speak about what happened that morning, especially not to his mother. His father was different. Deep waters flowed beneath the stern demeanour of Martin Peterson.

"Mom, Pops?" said Elvin, zipping up his windbreaker. "May and I are heading out for a little while."

"Do you think that's a good idea?" asked Mrs Peterson, showing parental concern for the still weakened May.

"I really could do with taking a long walk down by the riverside. Fresh air and all that. Clear my head and help me sleep," said May.

"If you're sure now, honey," she replied.

"And Mom, can I borrow your car?"

"Make sure you don't be leaving French fries in the door pockets," she said. "Keys in the usual place, Elvin. And don't be too late."

Mr Peterson got to his feet. Although he spent most of his days in the chair, he occasionally had enough mobility to walk, albeit aided by sticks.

"I'll lock the front door. You kids can come in through the garage when you get back. Won't be a moment, Sheila," he said. When he wanted to walk, Mrs Peterson didn't fuss. The man she'd married didn't like to be ordered around.

The motion sensor in the garage detected their presence and the strip lights crackled into life. As Martin Peterson handed the car keys to his son, he held his hand.

"I've known your mother for a long time and I've made it my life's business keeping her happy. It hasn't always been easy but I can look in the mirror and know that I did my best for this family. And that means that I don't, won't and would never hurt her."

Elvin looked down at his brightly tagged sports shoes, ashamed that he'd forced his father into protecting him.

"We'll talk more tomorrow," he said. "But two things. You need to quit going to the gym. At least until this blows over."

"Understood," replied Elvin. "And second?"

"You'd better find me a Portland jeweller."

Chapter 21 - The Sacred Heart

'Why? I couldn't understand why Do Sappo would do that. Did I see it coming? No, I did fucking not. I had a vague feeling that he was a shadowy bastard but having been involved in... no, coerced into a number of convoluted, scarcely credible schemes that had gone south, 'shadowy bastard' was an accusation that could have easily been pinned on me. This was just the latest example in a worryingly long line of regrettable moves I'd made. Sitting in the dark, smoking the last of my cigarettes, searching for my bearings through the faint rattle and clang of a distant train, I had no way of letting my friends know, not only where I was but of the danger they faced from Do Sappo and his Limey fuck henchman, Hawthorne. With each passing minute, my resolve was being tested. Every scenario, I thought, ends badly. Sonny would come to my aid, surely? But Castagne ultimately calls the shots. Was I being sacrificed? Foolishly, I let my imagination take the lead. More scenarios, none of them pleasant, none resulting in me being tucked into the fresh Egyptian cotton sheets of the Hotel Lutetia by some considerate chambermaid.

No, I was going to have to bust out of here on my own. I foraged around, looking for a tool, a six inch nail, anything I could fashion into a makeshift shank. If this indeed was it, I was taking someone with me. The sticks, the branches and one single inch long, flat tipped screw I found scattered on the damp floor weren't going to

261

THE GIRL, THE CROW, THE WRITER AND THE FIGHTER

be of much use though. If I aimed one correctly, I could take an eye out and then...what was I thinking? Blinding a vicious killer with a twig. Ludicrous. Come on Henry, I thought. Brooklyn tough. Think. If you were fifteen years old, and old man Bauer had you trapped in his cellar in Brownsville for stealing a kiss from his least plump daughter, what would you do?

Fixtures. There's always fixtures. Especially in a place which had the grim feeling of a well-used slaughterhouse. I ran my hands around the perimeter wall, a film of greasy, moss infused water coated its surface. When I reached the corner, I tried the next. Halfway along, about waist height, I found it; a chain, about three foot long, doubled up on itself and bolted onto a ring, fixed to the wall. I dug into my pocket for the screw I'd found during my brief scavenger hunt and used it to pick away at the brickwork around the fitting. Once I'd penetrated the outer layer, the soft brick around it crumbled like chalk. I dug as deep as I could with the tiny screw. Now loose, I had to use as much brute force as I could muster to free the chain. And I did, losing my footing in the process.

I got back to my feet, dusted myself down and shivered at the filthy, wet patch on the side of my slacks. The chain may have been somewhat rusty but it was solid. With a good swing, the kind which Sonny would attempt, I'd say I had a one in ten chance of delivering a shot which might buy me enough time to break free. Provided there was only one of them. Right now, I had no option but to take those odds. I wrapped the chain tightly around my fist and waited for the return of my captor. It didn't take long. Within minutes, I heard footsteps from the courtyard and the muffled sound of voices. There was more than one. Damn. Oddly, my mind was drawn to Anaïs. What did she say? Life shrinks or expands in proportion to one's courage. That-a-girl. She always came through for me. Now if I could just get the first one...

The key went into the lock, the barrel turned and in walked driver number two. Quickly, I wound up my arm and swung the heavy ring towards his head. Thwack! Direct hit. He staggered to the side before dropping to his knees. I knew his accomplices were close at hand so I did a quick visual search for his weapon. Nothing found.

'Put the chain down, Mr Miller,' said the voice from the doorway. I looked up at the face from whence the voice came and saw it was that of Castagne's right hand man and behind him, the most welcome of sights.

'You okay, Henry?' asked Sonny rushing into the room. I would have hugged him but as I hadn't yet bought him flowers by this point, I thought against it. I did grip tight onto his shoulder, because that's what men did back then, Elie. Can you imagine your Clifford embracing another fella? While sober?

'You took your time,' I joked. 'A little tour of Clichy before you arrived?' my nervy attempt at gallows humour almost masking the deep angst I felt.

As glad as Sonny looked to see me, it was nothing compared to the relief I was experiencing. My impromptu act of violence had inadvertently created an issue; the hefty hood I'd poleaxed needed to be brought back upstairs. Even if Castagne himself was capable of lifting more than a bag of potatoes - at this stage, he certainly was not - men of his stature tend to be above this kind of thing. Me? I knock them down, I don't pick them up. Believe it or not, Sonny and Castagne's man, the youngest and fittest we had, struggled to lift my victim back up the dozen or so steps and into the courtyard where, what I could only presume was another of Do Sappo's adherents sat, tied to a chair and looking very pensive. He was not as muscular as the fellow I'd floored but had the air of a man you wouldn't trifle with. After checking on my well-being, Benoit Castagne removed his coat and gave it to his assistant. He took a pistol from the brown leather holster which rested on his much-reduced rib cage and cocked it. Until this moment, I hadn't realised just how frail this once mighty man had become. He spoke to the captive man in a local, heavily accented dialect that I only partly understood.

'You know who I am?'

Silence.

'You know what I need to know?'

Again, silence.

By this point, the 'hefty hood' was in a chair of his own and starting to return to the land of the living. Benoit asked his assistant if he knew the identity of the fellow that I'd cracked. No, he is not familiar and has no identifying belongings on his person, he replied, again in a strong Parisienne brogue. Benoit shrugged and placed his pistol to the captive's head. He ordered the other guy to take a look. Both Sonny and I assumed that it was a tactic, something to make him talk but as the first bullet exploded through the front of the hefty hood's skull, the power of which sent his body - and attached chair - careering backwards, the resolve of his bound colleague, gripping the arms of the chair he was tied to, wavered. The second shot, into the already dead hood's midriff was, I figured, for dramatic purposes.

This was not the first execution that Sonny and I had witnessed that week but the change of location, from a darkened St. Louis side street to an airless French suburb, didn't make it any less nauseating. We looked at each other, and didn't say a word. We didn't have to. We were in a world where rules and conventions didn't apply.

Castagne turned to the remaining captive and told him again. You know what I need to know. The captive remained silent. His face said that if he was to die, he would remain loyal to his paymasters.

Castagne's man placed his hand on his boss' shoulder and whispered something in his ear. Sonny and I remained outsiders in the matter and we were happy about that. Castagne spoke again. I have to apologise for the incomplete translation but their brief discussion went something as follows:

'I know your name. René Defour. The stall at Clignancourt is not doing too well, I hear? Pity. You should have come see me about that. Too late now, I guess. Cigarette?' said Castagne.

Defour nodded. Castagne's assistant took a cigarette out of his pack and lit it before placing it into the grateful lips of Defour. He took a deep drag and with his lips, rolled it to the side of his mouth.

'Regardless of whether or not you tell me what I want to hear, understand this. Your life ends here, today. Whether it is quick or protracted, that is entirely up to you,' said Castagne, with chilling clarity. Defour looked down at his chest, his heart pumping its last few beats and sighed heavily and repeatedly.

'Your choices so far have been bad ones. But this final one you make will determine whether the lovely Marianne and your sons will be removed from their beds tonight and taken by my men to the port of Marseille where they will be sold to the first Berber who offers me a thousand francs for each of their heads.'

Defour spat out the cigarette in a panic. As any good captured soldier would, he was prepared to lay down his life but this…

'Please no!' he yelled, helplessly. 'I beg of you. They have done no wrong,' his tough exterior cracking.

Sonny and I looked at one another. The horror in his eyes must have mirrored my own. It asked me, are we sure that we're on the right side?

Castange approached him and spoke quietly. 'Shhh. If you tell me what I need to know…'

'You won't hurt them?'

'No harm will befall them. On that you have my word.'

Defour's chest exhaled one last time and then came the sobs of relief. Benoit Castagne knelt down and, placing a hand on Defour's shoulder, leant in, close. Quietly, Defour related to Castagne the details of Do Sappo's move. Once he had finished, Castagne himself cut the rope which bound Defour. Merci, said the captive, rubbing his wrists. He could try to run but that would jeopardize his family and besides, he was heavily outnumbered. No, in his mind, he was already dead. He took one last deep breath and closed his eyes.

Castagne cocked his pistol and said something I didn't quite catch, before firing two shots from close range into his chest. Defour slumped to the ground. As Castagne summoned his lackeys over to remove the body, I asked his man what it was that he'd said, just before the shot.

'Personne n'est perdu qui aspire au salut,' he said.

No one is lost who yearns for salvation.

'So, what now?' asked Sonny.

'The Crow moves tonight. Now we wait,' said Castagne, handing the pistol back to his man.

As Benoit Castagne still had a few bullets left in the chamber, I reckoned that it was expedient not to inform him just yet that it was me who'd inadvertently told the actual fucking Crow where the real Sinner's Plate was located. Truth was, I just wanted to stay alive a little longer.

Sonny and I, along with Benoit and his man, piled into French Edward G's car and headed back into Paris, leaving Castagne's men to clear up a rather messy crime scene. It made sense. No point adding to the number of parties looking for us. From information gleaned from the late M.Defour, Do Sappo, the Englishman and their associates would make an initial strike on the café around midnight, just as it was preparing to close, with the intention of drawing out Castagne's men. At that time, the area around the Sacré-Coeur would be full of drinkers and carousers with the odd group of tourists. But as most of the police crews would already be done for the day, there would only be a small retinue of night time gendarmes in the area, handy if the situation developed into a full blown gun fight. With less police around, there would never be an easier opportunity to storm the café, overpower the staff and deliver a telling blow to the heart of Castagne's empire.

Thanks for that, I thought. As we didn't sign up for a 'gun fight', I presumed that we would remain, locked in our room at the Lutetia until the score was settled. I presumed wrong.

'*Gentlemen, you have a chance, which few men will ever receive, to write a chapter in the history of mankind. A chapter which must remain secret for now but in time will illuminate your names for millenia,*' *said Benoit with the conviction of a zealot.* '*Forget your writing, Henry. This is your moment.*'

Forget my writing? Benoit, you're making a compelling case, I thought.

'*And yours too, young man,*' *he said to Sonny.* '*The future of France, of Europe, indeed the world, is in our hands. We must not let down those who have fallen along the way, protecting us, helping us reach this critical point! Tonight, The Crow will come and The Crow will die. The Plate of Mar Saba will be one step closer to the Holy Land.*'

From my companion's expression, I could see that he was starting to buy Castagne's emotive cri de coeur. Maybe he wanted to impress a pretty waitress with an act of unspeakable courage. They say that impetuous youth is often the most doomed. You've got a lot to learn, young Charlie.

They dropped us off, not at the Lutetia but at an apartment on the Rue d'Orchampt, a few blocks from the café. There was food, wine, a couple of books and a phonograph for entertainment and though it wasn't fancy, it was comfortable enough. We were advised to rest and to not answer the door to anyone. So we didn't. The stresses of the day had caught up with me, hitting me like a keystone to the head, so I left Sonny to his own devices and napped on a soft, springy bed until around seven when the appealing smell of what my companion was preparing reached my nostrils. Some fresh meat and boiled potatoes, served with a beaker of red wine, cooked by a man who evidently ate out more often than he entertained. Not that it mattered. I appreciated the effort. Sonny's impromptu feast was thankfully not interspersed with talk of what we'd just witnessed. We knew what we'd seen and we had an idea what was to come. Going over it again was not helpful. Instead, we spoke of weightier matters, namely the gamine belle from the café. I'd seen how Sonny was looking at her and she at him so I decided that a gentle ribbing was called for.

'What do you think of the lovely Delphine?' I asked.

Sonny shrugged and continued to chew at his meal.

'She was quite something. Never seen eyes that shade of brown before. Quite something,' I said, casting the line a little further.

'Green,' he muttered.

'Excuse me?'

'Her eyes are green.'

'But with walnut flecks,' I countered.

'I wouldn't know about that,' he lied.

I stood up and checked my tie in the wall mounted mirror.

'While you were in the kitchen cooking up this fine concoction, did you happen to spot a press or a clothes iron?'

I could see Sonny looking up from his plate, his eyebrows arched. I didn't know how long I could maintain this without having a fit.

'Got to look my best tonight. Just in case Delphine is there. You know Sonny, I think that there was some chemistry there. The way she looked at me. You must have seen it,' I continued, 'Sonny, I think that I might be in love.'

Sonny stopped chewing and looked at me. The eyebrows were almost under his eyes by this stage. Just when I thought he was about to explode, he burst into laughter.

'You are one funny man, Henry.'

'I'm serious,' I replied. It was too good to let go just yet. 'If we make it out in one piece, I might ask her back tonight. What do you think?'

Sonny let out an exaggerated guffaw.

'You wouldn't mind staying out for a few hours while I show her how an experienced operator works, would you?'

'Old man, you are out of your mind.'

'So, you have no objections?'

'Why in the world would you think that a vision of perfection, like Delphine, would be interested in your saggy old ass?'

'You think she'd prefer you?'

'Of course she would. She said that I had a lovely smile.'

'When did she say that?'

'This afternoon, after you left. We talked a while and...'

'The poor child must be blind as well as deranged,' I sniffed. 'Look at you! Such a beauty wouldn't be seen dead with some bulked up Frankenstein's monster. She needs to be tempted, serenaded and seduced, not thrown around then tossed into a fucking pond.'

Sonny was laughing so hard, tears were running down his face. I threw him a napkin and poured the remainder of the wine into our glasses. As I went into the bathroom to freshen up, he was still chuckling.

I think he needed the release. Maybe we both did.

French Edward G returned to collect us at the stroke of nine and took us to a door at the foot of the steps where he'd dropped us that morning.

'Follow me,' he growled, turning the brass handle, his impersonation improving with each new attempt. As we had a couple of hours to spare, I hoped that given my inexperience in these matters, they may have planned a 'How to handle a firearm' course for us.

We followed the diminutive driver up a long spiral staircase, down a dark corridor and into a smallish room with a long, rectangular window.

'Gentlemen!' said Benoit Castagne, standing to acknowledge our arrival. He looked rested and dapper in a freshly tailored grey three-piece. 'Scotch,' he said, pouring healthy measures for Sonny and I. 'This will help keep your wits keen.'

We downed the shots and walked over with Castagne to the window. Through it, we could see the entire length of the café, the attractive

269

but bushed young Delphine reading a book behind the bar and the portly waiter with the shiny head, clearing the table of an amorous cadet and his broad who'd clearly decided that the café was cheaper than hiring a room for the evening. A few remaining stragglers nursed their drinks.

'But they can't see us?' asked Sonny.

Castagne shook his head. 'To them, this is just the mirror at the end of the room.'

As Sonny mooned over Delphine, I cast my eye to the artillery spread over two tables to the side of our host. I'd expected a couple of pistols, perhaps a machine gun or two but this was an arsenal which could've ended the siege of Stalingrad in a week.

'Gawp all you want, young man. She doesn't know that you're here,' said Benoit mischievously to Sonny.

'I'm not... I wasn't...' stammered Sonny as flustered as I'd ever seen him.

'Don't worry. I'm playing with you,' he replied. 'You've got to watch out for that one though. She might not look like it but she is as feisty as they come. Still waters run deep, I believe is the expression. Once this is over, I'll have Herve give her a couple of days off. Get her to show you the real Paris. But bring her tournesols.'

'Tournesols?'

'Sunflowers. Those are her favourite.'

From the table, I picked up a machine gun. It was much lighter than I'd anticipated. I gently pushed my finger against the trigger but stopped before the squeeze. As empowering as it was, and it was, I admit that I was more comfortable with the knowledge that I could cup life in my hands rather than wield death. But murderous men were coming and I'd seen enough Westerns to know that while running, living and seeing another sunrise was desirable, sometimes one had to take a stand.

As Benoit and Sonny discussed the finer aspects of Delphine's compatibility, I watched as the cadet placed a couple of banknotes inside the long black wallet and handed it to the waitress. His suitably warmed up dame looked down the room, straight at the mirror we stood behind, fixing her hair and straightening her skirt. She took her soldier boy's arm, and they left the café, bound together as tightly as they were when seated. Delphine pushed her hair back behind her ear as she placed the notes into the till. When she turned back to the counter, she saw something which made her call Herve over. Sonny and Benoit were now directly behind me, discussing tactics when Herve picked up a kitbag from under the table where the cadet and his girl sat, just moments earlier.

You know Elie, sometimes you look at a picture and while all the pieces might be in place, you instinctively know that it's not right. Like a jigsaw puzzle when someone inserts a piece from another box. You can't put your finger on the what or the why but your gut tells you that the sums don't add up. Castagne's man was alongside me, watching and from his expression, he thought as I did, just as an ear piercing fizz, a blinding flash of light and resonant thump to my chest blew the mirror, and most of the supporting wall, backward into the room.

I don't know how long I was out for. As I lay on the floor, buried under a hill of rubble and shards of glass, each breath an inhalation of heavy dust, I saw a silhouette of a man, walking through the smouldering hole where once stood the door of the café. He stepped over the twisted remains of a table and with his boot, brushed aside a collection of glass and crockery. He stood by the pillar, barely ten feet from me. Due to the force of the impact, I couldn't move if I'd wanted to. I had no idea if I was alive, dead or somewhere in between. I didn't have enough strength to look behind me to see who had made it and who hadn't. I didn't want to confront the possibility that...no. All I could do was look at the figure rummaging around between the isolated fires which were burning in the now demolished café.

A second man arrived. I was about to shout for help when, cutting *through the high-pitched tone, I heard the sound of their voices; one was English and one Quebecois.*

From where they stood, through the smoke and dust, they couldn't possibly have seen us. Had they been expecting us, they would've fine tooth combed the place and they'd have ended every one of us. But they did not know that we were there so I lay still, with two hundred pounds of glass and brick on my back and I watched. I watched them take what they were looking for, the only thing they wanted, and they left.

I wanted nothing more than to close my eyes and wake somewhere clean and warm, with the smell of salt in my nostrils and the taste of freshly fried fish hitting the back of my throat but this wasn't the Mediterranean. There was no Sevak, nor was there a lion headed dog. This was not going to be my calescent tomb. I couldn't afford not to fight to stay awake. As the dry hum started to subside, I could hear voices again, this time distant. I shook free my left arm and reached back to my neck. The relief I felt when I realised that the pressure bearing down on it was not trauma but a piece of a collapsed cross beam, was palpable. From there I was able to drag myself up onto my knees, my trousers shredded. I placed my hand on a bar and immediately recoiled from the heat.

Without my glasses, I had to move even more ponderously. To my right, sitting upright propped against the remainder of the far wall, was Castagne's man. He was out cold but his chest was moving. To my left, Castagne himself, face down, partially covered, not moving. I stepped between the dusty mountains of masonry and grabbed his arm, pulling him around with all the strength I could muster. Miraculously, he was still breathing but had taken a heavy blow to his forehead, the gash deep and bloody. That's when I saw Sonny. His body contorted around a demolished table.

My thoughts at this time were filled with deep remorse. Why did I drag him into this godforsaken mess? Who was I trying to save? Me or him? He'd suffered some lacerations, I could see that. His shirt sleeves were torn and embers still burned around his cuffs. I tried to call his name but I couldn't hear myself speak. I raised my voice, as much for my sake as his. I could feel that I was shouting. It hurt. Sonny lay there, unresponsive. I dropped to my knees. Let him be alive, I begged. Who? I didn't know and I didn't care. You can take me. If you need someone. Take me. I've lived enough. My children would one day understand. But he was just beginning. Just let Sonny live. I forced myself to look at his face. Peaceful, almost beatific. Beautiful, even coated with debris. Then, his head twitched and his mouth opened and groaned. I picked up the nearest receptacle that wasn't broken, a bottle of beer, and put it to his lips. He called my name. I'm here, Sonny. I'm here.

The first civilian on the scene arrived at that point and aside from repeating the words Mon Dieu over and over, I couldn't figure out exactly what he was saying. Aidez moi! I shouted and he ran through the dusty cloud and into the street. Within seconds, there were three or four people, helping us to our feet. Castagne's man was now up and despite the hit he'd taken, was co-ordinating the removal of his boss, through the kitchen. He asked if we were fine. I said that we were.

'We got lucky. A pipe bomb with a flash. The mirror took much of the blast,' he said. 'You must come with me. Right now.' I was about to follow when I realised that Sonny wasn't beside me.

'Quickly,' said Castagne's man, sharply. 'We have no time to lose.'

I wasn't going without Sonny who was now walking through the café, piecing together what had happened.

'There's nothing he could have done,' said Castagne's man.

Sonny stopped by the bar. His huge shoulders sagged. To quote Byron again, 'All farewells should be sudden' but really, that should come with a caveat.

Lying against the shattered frame of the refrigerator, was Delphine. Her arms resting on her lap, knees tucked in with her head, tilted slightly on her shoulders. The fine powder which coated her skin gave her the look of a goddess, captured in time, sculpted in marble by a master who has seen the heavens for himself. Amidst the grey, a singular canal of blood ran from the corner of one of those beautifully sad eyes. Sonny knelt down and gently brushed the dust from her cheeks. He took her hands to his lips and kissed them. In this moment, there was nothing to do but to stand alongside him as he cradled her lifeless body. If tenderness was a measurable commodity, Sonny would've had enough to walk up to St. Peter, strong arm him into making a deal to get her back and I'd have been right alongside him.

Maybe, had she survived, Sonny's path may have been different. Who knows? I get what you're thinking. It's too cornball, too hokey to suggest that something in him died that day but I do know that this moment was one for which Sonny was ill-prepared. Once his shock moves past grief and ferments into different emotions, more volatile and less controllable, the roles of protector and charge may have to be reversed. I was starting to rue the day that I ever encountered the Castagnes and that accursed plate.'

Chapter 22 - Your Move

Where are we going, thought May as Mrs Peterson's station wagon snaked down the circuitous route through town. The riverside stroll mentioned earlier was not on the cards. May knew that and so did Elvin's father. An unnatural blast of heat rose from the footwell and May stifled a yawn. She'd underestimated how much the day had taken from her so she cracked open the window an inch or so. The evening air was cool, and not too bracing. A brief downpour had drawn out the natural scents of the lush, well maintained suburb. As Elvin took a right onto the 202, May turned on the car's radio.

"D'ya mind?" she asked.

Elvin shook his head. "Just don't change any of her presets. I'd rather she found out that I was still fighting than she discovered WCGX Soul was gone," he said, only partly in jest.

Don't worry, thought May. WCGX was just what she needed right now. Harold Melvin. Dennis tended to look down his nose at Soul. May didn't. Dennis was a snob. And an idiot. He wasn't even particularly good looking. And he was a snob and he was an idiot. Aside from starting to question what she'd ever seen in him, May felt annoyed that she was still allowing him to invade her mental space. Since catching a glimpse of him in Portland on Saturday, she couldn't think of him without that woman. The one he was completely lost in. As the car sped out of Auburn, towards the Maine Turnpike, May turned to Elvin. Elvin was no snob.

And as much of a dingus as he was at times, Elvin was no idiot. Would Dennis defend her as Elvin did? Killed a man with a table leg to protect her? She knew the answer to that. Reaching over, she touched his bruised cheekbone causing him to flinch.

"Jesus, May!" he said, his concentration broken by her clumsy prod.

"Sorry Elvin. Does it hurt?" she said, lifting her finger towards the lump and poking at it again, with childish relish.

"Cut it out!" laughed Elvin. "Do you want me to crash the car?"

"Listen, this morning," said May, quietly, "I didn't get a chance to…"

"Ain't Nothing Like the Real Thing!" he said, butting in, turning the volume up. "I *know* you love this."

She did. May wound up her window, closed her eyes and allowed her thoughts to take her to North Carolina and her cousin, Ronald Jnr. Though she'd only spent a few childhood days with him, May held the belief that one could get to know a person intuitively between two short train stops while some folk, her own father included, had doors which could take lifetimes to unlock. Ronald Jnr was different. He never belittled or teased her, never snapped at her, nor did he blame anyone else for the frustrations and rough breaks that life handed him. She always dreamt of heading out to California to see if she could find a trace of him. Maybe when this blows over…

As the 202 became the southern stretch of the 95, the lights of Portland shone on the dark horizon. May was tired. And tired of questions. Wherever it was that they were heading, May hoped that this time, there would be answers.

A few miles to the north east of Portland, Elvin slowed the car down, turning off the immaculate streets, onto a secluded but far less comfortable road. The juddering from the pebble and bark chip driveway shook May from her slumber. From the window, all she could see in the formless black pitch was the swaying silhouette of tall, wind shook hedges.

"We're here," said Elvin. But where's *here*, she thought. May opened the car door and the brisk night air slapped at her face. At the end of a tree lined driveway, the shape of a dimly lit house formed. Elvin knocked at the door and stood back as the porch light came on. The door was opened by Rose Holloway.

"Come in, please," she said, looking over Elvin's shoulder. "How are you, May?"

May didn't answer. Until a few hours ago, this woman was someone she'd considered, if not an enemy, then someone who held her with a certain animus.

"Let me take your coat," she said. May held on tight.

"No, I'm good," she replied, tersely. "Where's Jerry?"

"He's resting," said Miss Holloway.

"Can I see him?" asked May, suspiciously.

"You'll see him soon. Please, come through."

May looked at Elvin who nodded. If Elvin reckons it's safe, she thought, she'd suspend her hostility, temporarily.

Miss Holloway bolted the door and led Elvin and May into the lounge. Seated on the couch were two people she wasn't familiar with; one slim, smiling elderly man with unusually dark facial hair and a nondescript younger man who looked like any middle manager at a savings and loan. Over by the log fire, sipping a drink and smoking a menthol cigarette was someone she did recognise.

"What are you doing here?" she said to Kenneth, instantly recalling their meeting at the bookstore.

"My dear. I'm afraid that it may have been my course of action, or should that be inaction, that has brought us to this unfortunate juncture," he said, in a conciliatory manner. "First of all, though, how are you?"

May needed to sit down. She took a seat by the fire and held her head in her hands.

"Can we get you something to drink?" Miss Holloway asked.

"Why are you here? And him?" she snapped back, pointing at Kenneth. "As for you two," she said to the men on the couch, "I have no idea who the fuck you're supposed to be."

Kenneth handed her a glass. "Here, drink this. It'll make you feel better."

"Do you know what will make me feel better? Seeing Jerry."

"Well, you can't," replied Rose Holloway.

"Why?" asked May.

"He's resting."

"I don't believe you."

"Look May, it's been a traumatic day."

"You think?"

"Maybe it's too early to tell her?" added the younger man on the couch.

"Tell me what? Why is everything a fucking riddle with you people?"

"We're only trying to protect you."

"Well, you're a bit late for that."

"Elvin, maybe it's best if you take her home."

"I'm not going until I know that Jerry's OK. Tell me where he is."

"For the last time, he's resting."

"What are you hiding?"

"She's hiding nothing, May."

Standing in the doorway was Jerry Hector. Bandaged and pale, weakened by the events of the morning.

"Can't a man rest in peace around here?"

May's eyes filled. She wanted to thank him. And embrace him. But given how frail he looked, she was worried that a hug might do more harm than good.

"We need to talk," she said.

Jerry nodded.

"There are things I need to ask you."

"All in good time, May. What I need you to do right now is to trust me. And everyone in this room."

"Everyone?" May asked.

"Everyone. I can vouch for them all."

May slumped down on the armchair by the fire. She was tired and sore. More than that, the presence of Miss Holloway, Kenneth from the Portland bookstore and the pair of strangers on the couch left her perplexed.

"Jerry, what is happening?"

"Something, that until today, we'd all hoped was left in the past."

Jerry placed both hands onto the back of May's armchair. May reached back and cupped his hands with hers. As baffled as she was, and as curious about his past, the trust May had for Jerry Hector came from her guts. Everyone in the room, with the exception of May, had their eyes on this bear of a man and every one of them was on their feet when it looked as though he may fall. Elvin was the first to him. May rose and quickly took his arm.

"I'm alright, dammit."

"You need to rest, Jerry," said Kenneth. "We can fill May in with the details."

"Thank you, Kenneth but there are things she needs to hear from me."

"You're not up to it. A few hours rest will do both of you the world of good," said Rose Holloway, as curt as she was if she was still patrolling the aisles of the Municipal Library.

Jerry shook his head.

"I'm fine, Rose. Honestly."

Elvin and May took Jerry's arm and led him back into the bedroom which doubled as his recuperation suite. From the look of things, the cuts and bruises he'd received during the struggle had been tended to by a medical professional, she thought, probably the same one who'd provided him with the surgical clothing that he was wearing. Jerry took the pillows he'd been resting on and stood them against the headboard. Gingerly, and with Elvin's assistance, he returned to the bed. May asked him if he needed a blanket. The shake of his head suggested not.

"I'll be outside if you need me, Mr Hector," said Elvin, closing the door.

"How's that noggin' of yours?" he asked.

"Pretty as ever," replied May, pointing to the side of her face which was now a melange of blues and yellows.

"The cabinet, over there..," said Jerry, pointing to the waist height mahogany piece behind the door. "There's a bottle of Lagavulin. And two glasses."

May brought the Scotch and the pair of tumblers over to Jerry's bedside table and poured a couple of measures.

"Won't this affect your medication?" she asked.

"This is my medication," he replied, knocking his drink back in one. May followed suit. "I'll give you this, May Morgenstern. You're tougher than you look."

"My dad used to say that," she said, "I never knew how to take it."

"Your father was a smart man," replied Jerry, pouring two more shots.

Not in May's eyes, he wasn't. He was a decent man but he too was a coaster whose life didn't amount to much.

"And honest too," added Jerry.

"That'll be why my mom left him then."

"Sometimes a straight line is not as true as it seems."

The revelations in Elie's book had shown that to be the case.

"Did my father know that you received your wounds not from Korea but on a St. Louis side street?"

Jerry tilted his head to the side, resting it on his fist.

"I wondered when you'd get to that."

Despite feigning ignorance back in the diner when she returned from Vegas, Jerry had previously known about the book. That was now evident.

"Had you read it before I opened the box?"

"I didn't need to."

"What else have you been keeping from me?"

"Elie didn't come to Auburn by accident, May."

Jerry handed the freshly filled glass to May and proceeded to level with her. What happened in St. Louis, was pretty much as was written by Henry. The Korean injury was a cover which very few people were in on. "But why?" asked May. "Who were you hiding from?"

"To make sense of that," Jerry said, "I'll need to explain who Rose Holloway, Kenneth Martin and the others are."

"Go on then."

"You know what a sleeper is?"

May squinted. "Wait a minute, Jerry. You're telling me that Miss Holloway from The Mooney is a CIA spy?" she said sarcastically. "Because that I could buy."

'Not exactly,' replied Jerry, unconvincingly. 'But she is an agent, of sorts. As are Kenneth and Herb and Bill."

"The two schlubs on the couch?"

Jerry chuckled.

"No, those 'two schlubs' are Mort Olsen and his son, Jeffrey. Appearances may be deceptive but they are two of the most precise operatives you could ask for. They conducted the clean up of your flat this afternoon. You'd never know that anything untoward happened. But if you'd like, Mort and Jeff can return it to the way we left it. Your call."

May shook her head, the thought of her lifeless lover's body on her floor made her recoil more than the taste of the aged Scotch.

"They're very good at their job."

"And that job is?"

Jerry grimaced. "It's a difficult one to explain, May."

"If you're not CIA and you're not KGB…" she asked, the latter more as a question than a statement.

Jerry shook his head. "We're none of those. In countries around the world, in towns like Auburn, we have people ready to answer the call."

May remembered Benoit Castagne's comment to Henry Miller.

"A State beneath the State?"

"Well, we don't have passes or uniforms and it doesn't provide a 401K but I guess that it's probably the most accurate description of who we are."

"Where does that leave me?"

"I made a promise to your father that I'd keep you from harm and today, I let him down."

"You got me out."

"But allowing Elie to get close to you was a mistake. I'm sorry May but you're involved now, whether you like it or not."

There was a reluctant but firm finality to what Jerry said. From reading it to living it. Vicariously, May could handle dipping her toes into this intriguing world. The reality of it had already proven to be quite different.

"Bob. He's definitely gone, right?"

"Yep."

"So, it's all over?" she asked, hoping again that Jerry would provide the kind of paternal reassurance he'd been dispensing since her own father passed. None was forthcoming.

"May, we have to accept the real possibility that if there was one Bob, there may be more."

Chapter 23 - Orange Missiles

By ten o'clock, Elvin called it. The effects of the day, and the whisky, had caught up with both Jerry and May. Rose Holloway promised to take care of him. As Elvin and May donned their jackets, wrapping up tight and warm against the now cold autumn night, the librarian took May's arm.

"I'd imagine that there are details you'd like cleared up," she said, quietly. "Stop by the library tomorrow. When you get up. There's no rush. I'll be there until six."

May removed her arm without a word. Her suspicion of Miss Holloway was long formed and wouldn't easily be surrendered. Once out of the suburb, Elvin took the fastest route back to Auburn. Even though the day had been almost as traumatic for him as it had for May, he kept his own counsel. With the sounds of WJSX Jazz from Boston coming through on the FM, May thought it best not to confuse matters further by trying to piece the puzzle together while this tired. She lay down in the back of the car. Elvin didn't attempt to persuade her otherwise.

Just before eleven, Elvin turned onto the street where his family had lived for the last fifteen years. May was awake but only just. The intermittent illumination from the well-lit streets of uptown Auburn penetrated the darkness, darting across the inner roof of the car like orange missiles. A second pulse of light, this time red in colour and more frequent. From her prone position, May couldn't see the squad cars and the ambulance parked outside of the Peterson residence but Elvin could.

"Oh Jesus," he said. May pulled herself up and repeated Elvin's panicked cry.

Elvin left the car, doors open and sprinted up the path to the front door. May followed as fast as she could. By the time she reached the hallway, all she could see was Elvin being held by two officers. Mr Peterson was in his chair, motionless with a third officer kneeling by his side. If anything has happened, she thought, I will never forgive myself. A nauseating concoction of confusion, guilt and fear filled May's pounding chest.

"It's okay son," said Mr Peterson, using the shoulder of the officer as leverage. His voice was hoarse. Elvin hugged his father as never before. May looked down the hallway, towards the extension. There was a pool of blood and a pair of legs, twisted and partially covered by a sheet of tarpaulin.

"Mom...where's Mom?" Elvin said through the panic.

"She's fine," said Mr Peterson, calmly reassuring his son. "The doctor's with her now. But she's fine, son. Just a little shaken."

"What...happened?" asked Elvin.

"Your father called us to report an attempted break in and robbery," said the police chief. "The suspect became agitated and attacked your father. In defending his home and his wife, the suspect was fatally wounded."

"You can't arrest him for that?" said Elvin, scared.

"No one is being arrested, Elvin," said Mr Peterson.

From the vicinity of his parent's bedroom, two medics appeared.

"How is she?" asked Mr Peterson.

"She's sleeping. We administered a shot, as you requested, so she'll be out until the morning," replied the young female medic. "Would you like some medication to help you sleep?"

"Thank you but I'm good," he replied.

"If you don't mind Martin," asked the police chief, "We'll be back in the morning to take your statement."

"Not a problem, Frank," replied Mr Peterson. "And say thanks to the boys out front for getting here so quickly."

"They'll be there as long as you need them."

"It's really not necessary…"

"Marty, you know that the PD can't begin to thank you enough for all you've done for us over the years so if you don't mind, finish your beer and go back to bed. We got this."

Mr Peterson bowed his head and raised a freshly opened bottle of beer in appreciation. With the burglar's body now bagged and on a dolly, Elvin saw out the officers, the medics, the officials from the coroner's department and double locked the door.

"So, what really happened, Dad?" asked Elvin on his return.

Mr Peterson sucked the last drop from his bottle and said, "Sit down."

"First of all, you're going to tell me what happened this morning," he said, straight. "And don't lie to me, boy."

Elvin relayed the events of the morning to his father as they happened. Mr Peterson's demeanour didn't change, even when Elvin revealed the grim finale to the story. Martin Peterson looked at May as though he was scanning her physical being for any sign of a potential deviation from Elvin's recounting. That's what he always did. Martin Peterson could spot the signs the length of a football field away.

"And tonight? Where were you?" he asked.

May spoke, telling Mr Peterson about the house in the Portland suburbs. She told him that Rose Holloway, from the library, was there. A couple of people she didn't know. An elderly father and son.

"The Olsens."

May and Elvin looked at each other again, confused.

"You know about the Olsens?" asked May. Martin Peterson didn't answer.

"May, you need to go back there. In the morning. And stay there until it's safe. I'll take Elvin and his mother to her sister in Vermont. She's been going on about us visiting…"

"I'm not leaving May," interrupted Elvin forcibly. "You go with mom to Aunt Carol's but I'm staying with May."

"You don't understand, Elvin," said Mr Peterson, his hoarse voice raised and resonating.

"No Dad, I don't. But she's had my back for years. I need to repay that so, with respect, if she needs me, I'm going where she's going."

May looked at Elvin in bewildered admiration. He'd always been nervous about standing up to his stern, autocratic father and felt that at times, he'd been a disappointment to him. The only time he felt his father's approval was in the ring. Martin Peterson looked at Elvin and through those thick lenses, he could see the same determination his son had when he was gloved up and 14-0.

"I need to show you something," he said. "Come with me."

May and Elvin followed Mr Peterson into his room, past the bed where Mrs Peterson was lost in a chemically induced sleep and into a small, windowless dressing room.

"Help me up," he said. May and Elvin each took an arm and steadied him. In an oak cupboard, hanging on a rail, was a line of Mrs Peterson's dresses and gowns. Mr Peterson pushed half to the left and half to the right, revealing a small, knee high, cast iron combination safe.

Before he opened it, Martin Peterson turned and said, "What I'm about to say, stays here and is for your ears only."

His fingers spun the dial right, then left and again, a couple of clockwise turns. There was a solid click and he depressed the handle, pulling the door open for the first time in years.

"Just after you were born, I was part of an operation which, if successful, could have ended U.S. involvement in Southeast Asia before it turned catastrophic. Following its failure, I became disillusioned with not only my superiors but our government's handling of such matters. However, the experience taught me one thing; that I was in possession of certain attributes which set me apart from my colleagues in uniform. On my return, I was approached by a group who asked me if I'd like to act as a consultant to their organisation. I agreed and I spent the next decade and change putting out fires on their behalf. And I was good at it."

May and Elvin stood in silence as Mr Peterson pulled a box from the safe. He removed the lid and carefully looked through the papers contained within.

"One specific job took up much of my time," he said, removing a large folder. "Without a doubt the most protracted, complicated assignment I took was overseeing the stewardship of an ancient relic."

"A plate?" asked May. Mr Peterson nodded.

"And I believe that's why you were attacked this morning."

"What about tonight's intruder?"

"It may appear so. The duty coroner asked why I shot him in the leg as well as the head. The official line was that as I'm incapacitated, I can't shoot straight. The truth is that I took his knee cap off so that he couldn't move without extreme pain. And I needed to know what he thought he was here for."

"Did he tell you?"

"He did not but I couldn't risk the chance that he might talk to someone else. They're professionals and as such, there's a strong possibility that they'll keep coming."

"That's what Jerry said," replied Elvin.

"Jerry knows what he's talking about."

Chapter 24 - Dust and Clay

'As rescuers entered the smouldering husk of the café, we survivors of the blast, followed Castagne's man slowly through a dark, labyrinthine passageway and out through a heavy door on the eastern side of the church.

There was no one waiting for us. We needed to get off of the streets and fast. As one of the best known faces in the city, getting Benoit Castagne away without being noticed was going to be difficult. We couldn't risk walking for a number of reasons, not least because Castagne was still suffering most from the recoil of the flash blast.

Anyway, where we needed to be, to be safe and for Benoit to receive the medical attention he required was too far to walk, covered in debris and dust. Even in the dead of night, that would be far too suspicious a course of action to take. As we were wondering how to get out of this latest jam, Castagne's man jumped in front of a car which had just turned onto the Rue d'Orsel. He went for his pocket but instead of a weapon, it was a badge that he flashed. The confused driver attempted to drive off but Sonny reached in and grabbed his lapels, growling at him with the demeanour of a ravenous bear. The driver lifted his hands off the wheel and slowly, as instructed by Castagne's man, opened the door. With one sharp tug, Sonny pulled him from the driver's seat and into it he stepped. I helped Castagne's bodyguard lift Benoit into the back of the car and on his instruction, Sonny floored it before we'd even had time to close the doors properly. As we took off, Benoit lay back and groaned heavily. His man told Sonny, still waiting for directions, to keep driving for the time being but not so fast as to draw attention. Taking the sharp bend at pace onto Boulevard de Rochechouart, Sonny clipped a wing mirror from a car parked too far out into the street. The impact drew me out of the temporary state of shock that I'd been in following the explosion.

'Was that a fake warrant card that you used?' I asked.

He didn't reply.

'Don't you think that a handful of men, stealing a car while covered head to toe in debris, right after an explosion under the Sacré-Coeur might raise the suspicions of the Gendermerie?'

'I think we'll be fine,' he said, very sure.

I looked at him, tenderly cradling the damaged frame of his boss. This was no master and servant relationship. Castagne's man looked up at the road ahead, quickly finding his bearing.

'After four blocks, on this side, you will see a café called Les Aperture. Take a right just beyond it. There is a telephone kiosk beside the Metro station. Stop there.'

'Understood,' replied Sonny.

Within the minute, Sonny had pulled up onto the sidewalk beside the station. Castagne's man placed his jacket under the head of his boss and told me to keep him upright. He leapt from the car and made his call.

Castagne's breathing was becoming more laboured. Though his lids were heavy, he was still lucid enough to answer some of the questions that had arisen following the attack on the café but weakened enough that he wouldn't want to wring my neck when I chose to clear my conscience.

Leaning close, out of Sonny's earshot, I informed him that in a momentary error of judgement, I'd let slip to Do Sappo in the cellar *about the fake plate and the whereabouts of the genuine one. His reaction was not what I'd expected.*

'We must live with the consequences of the choices we make,' he replied in a whisper, 'This is not your world, Henry.'

He was right. I didn't belong here, in the midst of actual, real chaos. Sure, I served a purpose. The noble stooge, a patsy. Subterfuge? Yes, but only of the fleshy kind. I've thought about those words many times since and one recurring conclusion I have is that the consequences he bore, the needless murder of Herve and Delphine, fashioned from our misguided sense of hubris, were much greater than mine.

'So, what now?' I asked.

Castagne leant back against the scuffed vinyl headrest and closed his eyes. Don't sleep, don't drift. Your man will be back soon. Stay with me. I engaged further. Did he think that there was a possibility that we were set up, perhaps by someone in his organisation? While he didn't dismiss the possibility, he was of the opinion that this time The Crow just had the drop on us.

'I'm sorry that I lost you the plate,' I said, genuinely contrite.

'It's fine, Henry,' he replied.

Everyone on the other side of the café's mirror was dead, so fine it wasn't but where we were, I appreciated his magnanimity.

I looked over to Castagne's man at the kiosk. I wanted to ask Benoit if he trusted him but as they appeared very close, I feared that even in his diminished capacity, that might tip him over the edge. But even at death's door, Castagne remained a canny bastard.

'You're not sure of him, are you?' he said, reading my mind.

I shrugged, stammering and stuttering over an incoherent answer.

'And you still don't recognise him?'

His question shot a bolt of realisation into my thick skull.

'The prison...'

Castagne's man returned to the back of the car and checked on his boss.

'It was you who gave me the glove, right?' I asked him.

'Oui,' replied the no longer fresh faced cadet, the one I almost pulled the trigger on after I was sprung from the holding cell. It was him alright. Incredible, I thought.

'That morning I escaped. Did you know it was me?'

Wryly he chuckled, before explaining that it was he who'd opened the cell door and he who'd left the coat with the gun, hanging on the nearest peg for me to take.

'And yes, I know you had it cocked and pointed at me.'

'What if I'd panicked and fired?'

'Then nothing. I gave you a gun. That in itself gave you the confidence to make a run for it. I wasn't going to complicate things by providing you with bullets too.'

As confused as I was earlier, this put me on a whole different level. I even caught Sonny, staring back at me, wondering what he had gotten himself into.

'Let's go!' shouted Castagne's man and Sonny dutifully obliged.

We sped west out of town to a chateau situated between the Bois De Boulogne and Longchamps. As we pulled into its courtyard, a small army of Castagne's people swooped in and took him away. He may have been conscious but his breathing had deteriorated from laboured to painfully shallow. His man, whose name we found out was François Cressy, went with him.

Standing there, covered in dust and grazes, Sonny and I took a moment. I reached into my coat pocket, rummaging through the dirt and debris for my smokes. Sonny was silent. The money he was due for looking after me was in no way commensurate with the devastation that he'd not only seen but felt. The plate was gone but to me it was poison, so good fucking riddance. That's what I was thinking as a coterie of Castagne loyalists led Sonny and I inside *for treatment. The superficial injuries, they tended to easily. Those deeper cuts might prove harder to treat. I didn't speak with Sonny again that night. Though exhausted, I lay sleepless in my cot, as the morning birdsong repeated the sweet lie, that everything was fine. Castagne was right. We must live with the consequences of the choices we make.'*

Chapter 25 - North of Paradise

The 'Fifteen', a growing interstate freeway, cut through the very centre of Las Vegas. Paradoxically, to get to the Westside, one had to travel north. Sonny drove his Fleetwood up the Fifteen and headed west into Jackson Avenue. Many of the Strip's established casinos didn't tolerate black patrons, never mind dealers and waiters so the 'Black Strip' was the alternate playground for many Nevadans of colour. By the time the former heavyweight champion of the world came to reside in Clark County, some of the barriers that penned in his predecessors had been forced down. But not all of them. As one of the most recognised faces in the country, wherever he went, Sonny Liston stood out. On a cloudless afternoon on Jackson Avenue though, he was just another porkpie wearing Joe.

After parking the Fleetwood, Sonny reached over into the glove box, taking out a book and a couple of compliment slips from The International Hotel. He headed into Weston's Oasis Multi Mart on the corner of Jackson and D Street. With an impressive array of hardware, books and records, as well as a sub-Post Office and an in-house tailor, the versatility of Weston's Oasis made it one of the most popular places on the Westside. Despite living across town, north of Paradise on Ottowa Drive, Sonny was no stranger here. They didn't make a fuss over him and he liked that. Sonny walked over to the fridge and took out a soda.

"Benny here?" he asked the old lady with the elaborately structured wig, seated behind the till. She looked up from her magazine and waved him through. Sonny cracked open the can, took a sip and pushed through the rainbow-coloured chainmail. Seated with his back to the door was Benny, the proprietor, a small, rotund man with smiling eyes.

"I'll be right with you," he said, soldering a tricky piece of wiring.

No rush, thought Sonny. He picked up a pen lying beside the racing section of that day's newspaper and took the compliment slips from his pocket.

"Got any envelopes?" he asked. Silly question.

When Sonny returned from the front of the store, Benny was ready for him.

"Put out your left hand," he said. Benny took his hand and turned it round. "Spread your fingers."

"Try this for size," he said, squeezing a gold signet ring onto the slimmest of Sonny's digits. "Now using your thumb, feel around the bottom of the band."

There was a small indentation. "Got it?"

Sonny nodded.

"Now push your thumb against it and look closely." From the small square of black onyx, two miniscule but sharp points appeared. "Quite ingenious," said an impressed Benny, "Now press it again."

Sonny pushed his thumb against the indentation and the points disappeared beneath the surface.

"Is it safe?"

Benny picked up an apple.

"Run the ring over the surface."

Sonny did as he was instructed and the skin of the apple remained intact.

"Now, again but this time, activate it."

Sonny did as he was asked and this time, there was a clear gouge.

"When activated, these two points make the incision. It doesn't have to be deep, you just have to break the skin and traces of the resin enter the bloodstream. You got it?"

"I got it."

"When you're done with this, I wouldn't mind borrowing it for a while."

"Sure thing," replied Sonny, removing the ring carefully and handing it back to Benny for cleaning. He took out a couple of crisp banknotes and left them on the table.

"Not necessary, Champ," replied Benny.

"For the Coke and the envelopes."

Benny placed his hands together in thanks and picked up the money.

"One more thing," asked Sonny, holding up one of the envelopes. "Could you mail this to Monterey?"

****

On the way back, the Fifteen was much busier. Workers heading towards the Strip and tourists by the busload, gearing up for the festivities. Sonny took his time. He'd locked on to some fine rhythm and blues on KRAS. He was in no rush.

On the street where Jackie Shilling lived, it seemed that every garden was being tended to. Trimming, pruning, everything perfect.

Sonny pulled his Fleetwood onto a pristine driveway and took the path to the front door. He rang the doorbell and its echoey, churchly chime caused the gardener, previously kneeling in the earth, to stop what he was doing and look around. A heavy-set Filipino maid answered the door.

"Can I help you?" she asked, nervously.

"Is Mr Shilling at home?"

"Mr Jackie is taking his afternoon nap right now," she replied.

Of course, Sonny thought.

"Who shall I say has called?"

"Can you give him this for me?"

Sonny handed over the keys to his Fleetwood and a brown envelope. The maid looked at the envelope. On the front was a name that was not that of her employer.

The name written on the envelope was Peterson.

"I'm sorry Sir. I don't understand."

"Tell him that his golfing partner said thanks."

As Sonny walked back down the path, he stopped by the gardener who looked up, shaded his eyes, and wondered where he'd seen this man before.

"You got tournesols?" asked Sonny. The gardener looked at him blankly.

"Sunflowers?"

"Not yet. Best waiting until March so there's no chance of a snap frost. These are violets, aster, geraniums," replied the gardener. "Say, aren't you.."

Sonny nodded and kept walking. He reached into his Fleetwood for the remainder of his belongings; his hat, shades and his kit bag. When Geraldine was away, he didn't want to be home. It felt too empty and anyway, he thought it would be better to be in company and in plain sight, especially at New Year. His suite at the nearby International had everything he needed.

Sonny strode into reception, through a crowd of revellers and day trippers eagerly awaiting their keys. Alonso, the long time duty house manager, greeted Sonny and ushered him away from the throng of tourists to a quieter part of the reception area.

"Good to see you Mr Liston. Your suite is ready," he said, handing over a key. Sonny pressed a note into the palm of his hand.

"What's new?" Sonny asked.

"Just getting ready for tonight, Mr Liston," he said. "There is one thing. Someone was asking about you."

"Who?"

"He didn't give a name," said Alonso. "He wanted to know if you were staying here. I told him that I wasn't at liberty to disclose that information. He then gave me a thousand dollars to pass on a message, if I should see you here. I said that I would. He's some high roller but he is not one of the International's guests."

Sonny stopped. All of the people who might still have a beef with him over the Wepner fight knew about his suite but none of them would dream of making a move here.

"Who is he?" asked Sonny.

"I have no idea but he's still in the bar."

"Show me."

From behind a glass bricked wall, Alonso showed Sonny the man who'd been making the enquiries. In a booth, away from the excited revellers, sat a large, grey haired man wearing a pristine blue silk suit, with a single place setting, nursing a Scotch on the rocks.

"That's him," said Alonso.

Despite his appearance, he was no mob Don. Sonny knew every one of those from Vegas to St. Louis. Nor was he an enforcer. Far too old for that job. Sonny was curious.

"Keep him here. I'll be back in ten."

****

Liston's suite on the fourteenth floor of the International was not as swank as others in the hotel but it was less expensive and had a better view of the Strip than the ones Tom Jones and Wayne Newton had ten stories further up. Originally, Sonny had planned to sleep until nine, go downstairs for a steak and a drink then see where the mood took him. He'd recently filmed a TV commercial for an airline and from that, he still had some cash to spend on nights like these. Sonny stepped out of the shower and wrapped the towel around his waist. He ran his hand across his face, his chin now sporting a light stubble. He opened the mirrored cupboard above the sink and removed an open razor. Sonny wielded the blade quickly and with precision.

Tap, tap, tap.

Using the towel around his waist, Sonny quickly dried off. He picked up the pale blue shirt that was on the bed and put it on. A couple of wet spots on his back spread through the shirt. It would dry, he thought. Sonny had just fastened the belt on his trousers when he heard a noise coming from the suite's lounge. It sounded like glass being smashed.

Sonny stepped barefoot into his patent leather slip on shoes and went to investigate.

"You don't mind, do you, Sonny?" said the blue suited high roller, standing by the drinks cabinet, unwrapping a towel filled with large shards of ice. "Can I call you Sonny?"

Sonny's eyes narrowed and his fists clenched.

"Who the fuck are you and how did you get in here?" he said in his most menacing baritone.

"I'm a fan. A big fan. Have been since the Eddie Machen fight, Seattle. Sixty, sixty-one?"

"Sixty," replied Sonny, instantly.

Of all his fights, that was the one contest where his opponent riled him up, and pressed his buttons. Sonny lost his calm that night and it almost cost him a shot. He wasn't planning on a repeat.

The high roller didn't give Sonny a direct answer. OK, he thought. You're here, in my suite and you want to play games? Sonny repeated the second part of the question, this time with an extra layer of threat.

The high roller dropped a piece of ice into a tumbler full of whisky and offered it to Sonny.

"This is the good stuff. Best Malt Scotch you'll find in Nevada, trust me…"

"You didn't answer my question. How did you get into my suite?"

"Five thousand bucks to the right employee would get me into the Oval Office," he said, savouring his drink. "In my experience, I've found that everyone has a price. You must appreciate that, Sonny."

Liston had heard this spiel many times and on each occasion, it irked him, triggering a reaction that required the utmost control. Not this time. Chest puffed and teeth bared, Sonny strode over to the high roller who stepped back, instinctively putting his hands up in defence. Sonny stared him down and cocked his right, violently plunging it straight through the mottled wallpaper and deep into the drywall.

"Will five thousand bucks pay for that?" bellowed Sonny. "What's the price of this?" he added, casually flipping the drinks trolley.

"I'm a businessman. I mean you no harm Sonny," he pleaded, concerned that he may be next. "Please. The briefcase."

The high roller pointed to a brown briefcase at the base of the bucket chair by the door.

"That's for you. Well, part of it is," he said, back tracking. "Open it. Please."

Sonny brushed off the chunks of plaster from his forearm, still glowering at the high roller.

"My name is Harry Levin and my company, Fener Corps, represents a group of likeminded business folk who would like to pay for the privilege of managing your fortunes," he said.

"I have a manager. And I already have a contract with some business folk that you don't wanna know," said Sonny, "They'd get a kick out of you breaking into my suite, that's for sure."

"I can take care of any outstanding agreements. Just open the case and say the word."

"You don't know them."

"They don't know Fener Corps."

Sonny's curiosity was stirred.

"Please," Levin urged Sonny towards the case.

Sonny picked it up and placed it on the counter. He depressed the lock and the case flicked open.

"There is $250,000 dollars in unmarked bills. Consider this your severance package. No one, least of all the IRS, needs to know about this."

This was the kind of purse Sonny was once used to. His recent fights however were bringing in a fraction of the amount on offer.

"What's the catch?" asked Liston.

"No catch," replied Levin. "Since Clay was stripped of the title, the division has lacked the drama and theatre needed to attract Joe Shmo in numbers the way it did when you fought him and Floyd Patterson. No one is watching Ellis against Williams. No one cares. Now that Clay's back, the public see him as a traitor, a draft dodger and an Islamic threat to our American way of life. He's no longer the good guy. This gives us an opportunity. "

"And that is?"

"The redemption of Sonny Liston. The return of the world's baddest man, reborn and fighting the good, Christian fight, live in technicolour."

Sonny snorted. "How in the name of hell are you going to manage that?"

"All in good time," replied Levin. He crouched down and picked up the still intact bottle of Malt Scotch from the upturned trolley. "Do you mind?" he asked.

Sonny nodded.

"1971 will be the year that sees America fall in love with Sonny Liston all over again."

America never loved me in the first place, thought Sonny. And it can kiss my ass now.

Levin poured a couple of large measures.

"What say we talk about it some more, right after we have a meal and see what those International hostess girls have to offer?"

"I'll be right back," said Sonny, without committing.

As he removed a fresh, pristinely pressed wine-coloured shirt from his closet, Sonny thought about Levin in the next room and his proposal; flattered that he was still considered box office but acutely aware that being extricated from the suffocating contract he had, was likely to be, at best, messy. In his experience, every manager promised Manna but delivered Maine. A briefcase full of dollars though would certainly help soften whatever blows he'd find himself repelling. After swapping over his wristwatch to something better suited to his change of attire, Sonny opened a drawer and picked out two pocket squares, a cream coloured one and another which complemented his new shirt.

Back in the room, Levin handed Sonny his drink and with it, a fistful of banknotes.

"Consider this your 'no obligation think about it fund' for the night," he said. Sonny gripped the money, around $10,000, and downed his Scotch in one.

"1971," he said as Levin closed and locked his briefcase.

"You've still got three, maybe four years left at the top," said Levin. "How old are you now? Thirty-seven, thirty-eight?"

He nodded. No need for further questions, he thought. As he reached for his jacket, Sonny felt his legs weaken as if his chin was caught by a perfect shot.

"Whoa, watch yourself Champ!" said Levin as Sonny staggered from left to right, his shin cracking against the sharp edge of the low table. He fell backwards, reaching out and clutching onto the arm of the red velvet chair in front of the TV screen.

"What's the matter, Sonny?" asked Levin, following him around the room.

Sonny was breathing heavily. He undid the top two buttons on his shirt, now marked with pools of sweat. Beads of perspiration dotted his forehead, running into his eyes.

"I don't feel too good," he said, rasping and wheezing, fighting for breath.

Levin leaned over and looked at Sonny's eyeballs, rolling.

He spoke, quietly.

"Where is it?" he said.

Sonny knew what he wanted. And now, he knew the true identity of the high roller. His name wasn't Levin.

"I can make this stop."

Sonny clutched at his chest and gasped for air.

"Just tell me where the plate is and I'll bring you back. Hell, I'll even let you keep the contents of the briefcase. After what that old fraud Miller dragged you into, it's the least you deserve."

Sonny's breathing was now weak and insubstantial. He muttered something.

"Where is it Sonny? You need to tell me now and you'll live. Quickly"

Sonny muttered again. His eyes were closing.

Do Sappo leant in.

"Tell me now!"

Sonny whispered something, almost inaudible. Joe Do Sappo, secure in the knowledge that what he'd added to the drink had depleted Sonny's reserves, moved closer. As he did, Sonny grabbed Do Sappo's lapel and threw a weak left jab across the cheek of his assassin. Do Sappo pulled away and put his hand to his face. Although the cut wasn't deep, droplets of blood seeped through the fingers of his right hand.

"Is that it?" laughed Do Sappo. "The final shot from the great Sonny Liston and all I got is a scratch? I'm sure your old pal will put up a harder fight than that."

Falling back, Sonny looked at Do Sappo and spoke his final word.

"Tournesol."

Joe Do Sappo took Sonny's deep red pocket square and held it to his grazed cheek. He reached into his coat and removed a small pouch containing a quarter full syringe, a tourniquet, a burnt spoon and a small packet of powder. Rolling up the left sleeve of Sonny's shirt, he tightly tied the tourniquet around his arm. The blood coursing around Sonny's veins had slowed to a stop but the rubber binding did its job. Do Sappo inserted the needle into the raised vein and emptied the contents of the syringe into Sonny's arm. Do Sappo flushed the remainder of the tainted Scotch down the toilet, rinsing out the bottle with cold water and the cash offered to Sonny, returned to the briefcase. The small packet of powder was left by Sonny's bedside table.

He didn't cover his tracks. He had no prints on record, no previous. Nothing. As far as the authorities were concerned, Joe Do Sappo didn't exist. He knew that many had considered Sonny a ticking time bomb and that an end such as this, was as predictable as it was inevitable. No official would look closely at the circumstances behind Sonny Liston's squalid demise. America's favourite boogieman was gone and despite his earlier words, Do Sappo knew that few would mourn his passing.

He took the elevator down to the first floor and the staircase to the Casino. The blood had stopped flowing from the gouge that Sonny had made but the mark was noticeable. He needed to get out without drawing attention to himself. As he passed through the slots towards the hotel lobby, he was joined by a tall man in a sober suit. They didn't speak. Outside, the tall man handed a ticket to a valet in a tight bright red dinner jacket which bore the hotel's crest. He picked up the receiver of the white phone in his booth and within a minute, a black Oldsmobile arrived.

"There you are Sir!" he said, handing the keys to the tall man who said thanks with a $20 bill.

As they drove down the Strip, the tall man turned to Do Sappo.

"Nothing?" he asked.

Do Sappo opened the top two buttons of his shirt and loosened his tie.

"No. Tear his place apart."

Sweat was now running from Do Sappo's brow.

"Turn on the air."

The tall man looked at the control panel. The air was on.

"I take it that he stonewalled?" asked the tall man but Do Sappo didn't answer. He looked in the rear-view mirror and saw Do Sappo shaking, violently, clutching his throat, eyes bulging in his bloated, sweat-sheened head.

"Motherfucker…"

At the edge of his mouth, blood foamed, escaping from his lips in jerky spurts.

Chapter 26 - The loop

With Martin Peterson watching over his inert wife, Elvin made it his business to keep guard over the rest of the house and May. Even with his father's assurance that the officers stationed outside would deal with any further perimeter breaches, he insisted. May had returned to the guest quarters but only after Elvin checked the room and locked the windows. Although she ribbed him for what she thought was an excessive level of protection, she understood. While her body clock remained out of sync with events, her mind was just about coming to terms with this visceral and dangerous new reality. May returned to Elie's book. The letters she'd read to this point had drawn a picture but without reaching the end, it was a sketch. Incomplete. At ten to two in the morning, May headed back to Paris, into a world of gangsters and lovers, of writers and fighters for anything that might resemble a clue, a pointer or perhaps, a warning as to what was coming next.

'I was in the deepest cycle of sleep when Sonny came to the room I'd been given and stirred me. It was just after seven. Unsurprisingly, he'd been awake most of the night.

We walked down the hall to the servant's kitchen. A handful of staff quietly went about their business. We were invisible to them. Over pastries and fresh coffee, Sonny told me that Cressy, Castagne's man, had received a tip off from a seemingly reliable source. The plate was heading out of the country. Today. Trustworthy or not, to stand this up, he still needed the where and the how.

'And we're required for what reason?' I sighed, my shoulders sagging. I was still weary from the attack on the café and I couldn't hide it. Sonny looked at me, his eyes alert, his jaw clenched tight. I knew. In the short time that we'd known each other, he'd already put his neck on the line for me.

'Alright,' I said. 'I'll be ready in ten.'

As we walked out into the Parisienne morning, François Cressy pulled up in a sleek, sporty looking car. He said it was a prototype. Citroen, I think. It was fast, he said and it needed to be if we were to get to Do Sappo, the Englishman and the plate before they left French shores.

'What about the source,' asked Sonny. 'Who is he?'

Cressy shook his head. Not he. She. And it was someone I thought I'd never see again.

We drove towards the Rive Gauche at an indecent speed. I crouched in the back, holding on for dear life, wondering how the last fifteen years had been to Xena. Ridiculous, I know but even though she'd set the metaphoric dogs on me, I'd always remained beguiled by the memory of the brief moment of closeness we'd shared. With Cressy focused, determined and Sonny demented with thoughts of exacting revenge, I felt a (very small) pang of guilt for giving less of a fuck for the pursuit of the damned relic than I did for the slim chance that I may once again be in close proximity to the enchanted kingdom between Xena's lithe legs. I'm sorry, Elie but that was how I felt at that precise moment. It's important that one remembers those bursts of vitality. I may have been in my sixties but I was not quite the weak fleshed, bone satchel that I am today. Anyway, we pulled up at an address on the Rue Des Grands Augustins. I can't recall the number but it had a red door. As Cressy rang the bell, Sonny helped get me out of the pitifully tight back seat.

'You know this broad?' he asked.

Broad? Xena Mortlock ain't no broad. Prepare to forget about Delphine, I wanted to say but thought better of it. Too soon.

We climbed three sets of stairs and each level stunk more than the last. The smell of yesterday's cooked cabbage and animal effluent invaded my nostrils. Cressy knocked, then pushed open the door. Along the dark hallway, leaning up against the walls, were partially completed paintings, in various sizes, shapes and styles but all of the same subject.

And there she was, backlit from the morning sun. The first impression of Xena in years made me feel quite giddy. She walked towards us slowly, a knobbled, petrified length of dark wood taking some of her weight.

'Is that her?' whispered Sonny.

It was. The last time I was in her company, she wore a similar chiffon robe. She looked at me, with those eyes. Still kohl black, defiant. We followed her into a room which appeared to be a studio, a bedroom and kitchenette all at once. She offered us a refreshment. Cressy and Sonny passed.

'Madame Mortlock, s'il vous plait ... what do you know?' asked Cressy.

Xena stared at me. Unnerving and spectral, slowly she stirred the contents of her glass. Her once elegant hands now angular and bony with the stained fingernails of someone whose mitts had become over familiar with scrubbing dirt than life's more tactile pleasures.

'We have enough time,' she said, pouring me a beaker's worth of her latest concoction.

I wanted to ask her about La Sainte, Militz, everything but she was right. We had enough time. Cressy however, thought otherwise.

'It is imperative that you tell us what you know, please.'

'Very well,' she said with the requisite amount of drama.

'The Crow has flown south.'

'Does he have the plate?'

'No.'

'Who has it?'

'His most trusted companion.'

'The Englishman...Hawthorne?'

'It is indeed with the Englishman.'

'And you know this for sure?'

'For sure.'

'Can you tell me how?'

Xena reached over to the window ledge and picked up a long-haired black cat who was deep in sleep. She cradled the cat in her arm, against her chest, as if it was a babe. The cat stirred briefly then clung on to her arm, closing its eyes and purring deeply as Xena stroked its belly.

'Have you ever watched a cat sleep? A fragile bag of bones, completely helpless. And all of a sudden, out of nowhere, it emits a howl so otherworldly that it chills your blood?'

'Madame Mortlock, please,' urged Cressy.

'Why does it do so?' she interrupted. 'Because instinct never rests.'

Cressy and Sonny looked at each other, lost, but I understood.

With each of Xena's cryptic answers, Cressy's patience was starting to wear thin.

'The Englishman is on his way home.'

It seemed that Xena and Hawthorne, the Englishman, were in regular receipt of certain medications from a loose-lipped Parisienne pharmacist. When pressed for a larger dose, the pharmacist advised that it would be dangerous to prescribe the amount asked for. The Englishman insisted that he needed the increased dosage as he was leaving the country. The pharmacist said that he had associates who could accommodate his needs, wherever he went. The Englishman told him that he was going to be in London on Thursday. The pharmacist said he would make the necessary arrangements.

'And you know this how?'

'The pharmacist and I have an understanding.'

Yep, she's still got it.

'When word about the explosion at the Café Chappe spread, I couldn't keep what I knew private. You know that Benoit, and Etienne, were good to me after the war.'

Cressy later revealed that her husband was in cahoots with Capitaine Bony and the Vichy government. Many of the revellers at those memorable pre-war soirèes were systematically rounded up by Bony, on Mortlock's say so, and dispatched East. Particularly if they were Jewish. Those considered 'deviants' fared little better. Most of those poor bastards just disappeared. After the liberation, some of the old scores were settled. Mortlock's factory in Alsace was handed over to the allies who stripped it bare then leveled it. He'd already moved his money into Switzerland, leaving Xena potless, susceptible and marked with a name as black as her negligee. As the allies moved across Europe, his body was found in a hotel bedroom, near Ardenne. Though it was ruled as self-inflicted, not too many suicides occur with two gunshot wounds to the head and no note. He did fare better than Bony, who was beaten, flailed and strung up on a lamppost near Pont Neuf. My guess was that if Cressy wasn't directly involved in the deaths of Mortlock and Bony, he knew someone who was.

'We need the address of the pharmacist,' said Cressy.

'And I need to take a piss,' I said.

As I took my tight bladder along the dark hallway towards the bathroom, I considered some of the women with whom I'd been closely entwined over the years and how only Anaïs hadn't been ravaged physically by the effects of Le Force Miller. I wasn't directly responsible for June's demise, much less Xena's but I had to reluctantly face the possibility that if I wasn't the agent of their travels, I did stamp their ticket. Their lives would've been a less traumatic adventure had I not appeared on their path. I'd tried to consider it a pointless emotion but the truth is Elie that guilt, like sin and obsession is merely fruit from another branch of the one tree.

I did what I had to do and headed back to the kitchen, stopping only to look at the vaguely familiar figure whose image dominated the artwork, stacked against the walls.

The subject was male, gaunt but handsome...and not as immaculate as he once was.

'You!' roared a voice. I jumped in fright as the door slammed shut. Standing in front of me was the man who had once chased me straight into the arms, and the truck, of the Castagne Brothers. He gripped me by the lapel of my jacket and pushed me up against the wall. As he muttered some incomprehensible abuse towards me, I noticed a few things. Firstly, his breath stank of tobacco, wine and chronic halitosis, probably caused by the remaining few teeth in a head, that was once a magnificent temple, now a pale, haunted ruin. In an attempt to prevent him beating me, I grabbed hold of his arms. As physically diminished as I was then, I found that I was able to hold him quite easily. Even through the thick sleeves of his coat, I was able to fully wrap my hands around the contours of his weak wrists. Seeing Xena's light dimmed was nothing compared with the hollow, dead eyes of this once Immaculate Boy. I was about to release my grip when Sonny's fist careered beyond my peripheral vision and into the side of Immaculate Boy's jaw, loosening fixtures he could barely afford to lose.

'Leave him alone!' yelled Xena, feebly pushing past Sonny and I. He was still counting planets when we helped him to his feet and into the darkened boudoir where Xena administered his 'prescription'. After she'd given us the address of the pharmacist, Xena would return to her blocks and her canvases, mixing dark blues and browns on her old palette, her grip tight as she searched deep in her memory for a glimpse of something which would make her boy immaculate again.

As soon as he saw Cressy walk through the doors of his apothicaire, *the pharmacist folded like a deck chair. He willingly gave up not only where and when the Englishman was going to make his next medicinal pick up but added that he'd asked for some tablets for sea sickness. Now we knew how he'd be getting to England. If we left immediately, I said, getting into the spirit of things, we could catch up with him. It was about five hours to the coast. Slice half an hour off of that in Cressy's car, said Sonny, as keen as I to get moving.*

Castagne had people in Boulogne-Sur-Mer and in Calais itself, said Cressy. Problem was, as Sonny rightly pointed out, not many in Castagne's organisation would be able to pick him out of a line up.

That's why they'd dragged me away from my Californian idyll. What about delaying the departure of the ferry? That could work, replied Cressy, provided that the Englishman was foolish enough to take a commercial sailing. If he was in any way mindful, he'd sail from any number of the fishing villages along that stretch. Cressy was right. Stopping him in France was already a long shot. He had a head start on us. What we had though, was an address in Queensway where we knew the Englishman was going to be a few hours hence and one terrified pharmacist whose home and business addresses would suffer concurrent gas explosions should anyone learn of our intentions.

Once we'd left the confines of the city, Cressy and Sonny shared the drive, through the trunk roads and villages not yet scarred beyond recognition by the Autoroutes. While they tried to impress each other with their car handling skills, I succumbed to age and tiredness on the narrow and uncomfortable back seat, napping almost all of the way. We had a brief refuelling session, just south of Lens and Cressy made a couple of calls. Castagne hadn't given up and neither must we. Slight change of plan though said Cressy, urging us to trust him. What else could we do?

We bypassed Boulogne and Calais, instead heading to Saint-Inglevert, a small village about five miles from the coast. Cressy parked the car behind the service station and we walked for about fifteen minutes before finding ourselves in what looked like a private airfield. The feeling of dread that was taking hold of my gut was one shared by Sonny.

Outside of the large corrugated iron hangar, sat two small white airplanes, neither of which instilled in me any sort of confidence. My trust in M.Cressy's plan, whatever that may be, was eroding the closer we got. A short, wiry man, who resembled a three-quarter sized David Niven, climbed out of the cockpit and asked, in French, what business we had at the Flight Club. Cressy pulled out his warrant card and demanded to search the two planes. Out of the question, said demi-David. He and Cressy became animated and their voices got louder. Again, I wouldn't attempt to accurately translate their dialogue with any degree of certainty but it sounded as though Cressy said something about customs. From the gist of it, he wanted Sonny and I, his lackeys, to carry out a spot check of both planes as there had been reports of smuggling in the area. The pilot, simmering with rage, was sent to fetch the flight records for the last year. Once he was out of sight, we climbed into the plane, Cressy strapped himself in and urged us to do the same. Problem was that there was only one passenger seat. You can either sit on Sonny's lap or he can sit on yours. Either way, hold on tight. With the keys left in the ignition, Cressy fired up the propellers and we started towards a short strip of gravel that presumably doubled as the runway.

The words 'we will only have one attempt at take off' were not what Sonny and I needed to hear at this point. I don't know about my companion but for the next hour and a half, I felt as if I was in a waterless washing machine while having the life hugged out of me by a terrified bear. Cressy could've reassured us but he didn't. His job was to get us to England as quickly as he knew how, and that he did. Thanks to Cressy's skills and the help of his RAF pals, we landed safely in a place called Biggin Hill, in the pouring rain. On the lush English verges, the grass as green as our gills, Sonny and I each left a little piece of Paris.

By Cressy's reckoning, we were now ahead of the Englishman but rather than run the risk of an accidental encounter en route to London, we decided that the sensible move was to forgo public transport. Instead, we hitched a lift on a military truck headed towards Hyde Park on manoeuvres. Fifteen miles of bumpy road was as soothing as a fucking day spa after the flight so we weren't complaining. As anonymity was key at this stage, three men fitting our description checking into a single hotel felt like an unnecessary gamble. Thankfully, the Castagne reach went further than the European mainland. We hunkered down in a spartan safe house in Sussex Gardens, a short walk from Fitzallans Pharmacy and began to formulate our plan to intercept the Englishman and retrieve the plate. We had two hours.

The set up was simple. We'd stake out the drug store and wait for the Englishman to enter. Give him a minute to get his fix or whatever then we'd swoop. Cressy first then Sonny and I to back him up. A pretty straightforward plan, right? We took to Queensway early, figuring that the distraction would ease the nerves. A couple of hundred yards down the street, we found Fitzallans. Its green and white livery, clear and bold, standing out among the newsagents, shoe stores and milliners. On the corner directly across from it, stood a pub. The Prince something or other. A stiff drink would certainly go some way to easing the tension, we thought. Outside the doors to the Prince Something, a group of men waited, patiently. Men in suits and trilbys stood alongside cap-wearing truck drivers and bakers, checking their watches, smoking themselves into their own little London fog. Inexplicably, in a town as renowned as this, sinking a day time drink was subject to some ridiculously arcane licensing laws. One cap wearing fellow, sensing that we weren't locals, explained that the pub opened in five minutes, at 5.30pm. Why? I still don't know.

Anyway, I needed some smokes so I bummed a couple of oddly shaped coins from Cressy and headed over to the little tobacco kiosk to see if they had anything better than burnt wood chippings. The diminutive fellow behind the counter asked what my preference was. I'm not sure, I said. American? He replied, You're in luck! We've got Camel, Lucky Strike and Marlboro. Yeech. Got anything French, I asked. We do indeed, he said. Gauloises and Gitanes, Sir. I was about to go for the former when I spied a brand that dear Tony Grier used to smoke on Corfu, especially when drunk. Capstan Full Strength, please. I said, slapping down the coins on the counter. And a pack of gum for Sonny. The tobacconist took about half and I scooped up the remainder, chucking it into the pocket of my coat. I lit the first Full Strength cigarette I'd had in days and savoured the moment.

From where I stood, I could hear the slam of the bolt from the pub door being pulled down, clear as a bell. As the men, Sonny and Cressy included, shuffled inside, I stepped from the sidewalk and into the road. The loud warning blast of a taxi horn made me jump into the air and back to the safety of the sidewalk. I'd forgotten that the limeys drove on the wrong side. Yeah, yeah, sorry, I shouted back at the cab driver who pulled up and continued to bark at me as if he were a puce faced dog. And that's when I saw him. The Englishman. In the cab. Getting out of the cab. Paying the driver. Walking into Fitzallans, satchel in hand.

I pulled up my collar, tilted my cap down over my brow and ran over to the pub. I pulled Cressy and Sonny away from the bar and told them what I'd seen.

'Are you sure it was him?'

'He's only tried to kill me two, no three times so, yeah, I'm sure,' I replied.

'What can I get for you gentlemen?' asked the barkeep.

'Malt Scotch. Three,' said Cressy, pulling a large white note from his wallet.

'Make them doubles,' I added.

We took our drinks over to a high table beside the large window which looked out onto Queensway and Fitzallans drug store. In all of my experiences with Castagne, his associates and this damned plate, I'd never felt as keenly apprehensive as I did at this moment. While the bar chimed with the release of the day's stresses, our corner of the pub crackled in silent tension. Cressy finished first. You know what to do, he said. Sonny checked his wristwatch against the clock in the bar. Two minutes, then we follow you. Cressy nodded and walked out. Sonny threw back his drink and took two sticks of gum from the pack I'd brought him. He offered one to me but I'd already lit another cigarette.

'It's time,' said Sonny.

We skipped between the slow-moving traffic and found ourselves at the door of the drug store. Sonny peered through the curved windows which bookended the door. Can't see Cressy. What about the Englishman? Here, he said. You look. Nothing but a mother and child at the counter, behind which stood a petite middle-aged woman and a tall bookish man, both dressed in long white coats.

'I'll go first, you follow in thirty seconds,' said Sonny.

He held the door for the mother who nodded in brusque appreciation. The child looked up at Sonny with a sugar stick in his hand and his mouth wide open. From our brief spell in London, it was clear that there weren't too many fellows of Sonny's stature, and hue, to the pound, so to speak.

I counted to twenty then pushed open the door, the little bell on the brass bow above signalling my arrival. To our left, Sonny looked at a display of sunglasses. The definition of the word optimism is trying to make a living selling those in this town, I thought. The bookish man left the counter and approached Sonny while I drew the attention of the lady. Naturally.

'Can I help you, Sir?' she asked.

Under her demi wave, behind her brown horn-rimmed glasses, I could tell that this one was an unextinguished firecracker.

'Sir?' she repeated. I blanked. My eyes were drawn away from her deep laughter lines and her fiery sensuality and onto a shelf which featured a selection of felt rings and band aids.

'Insoles,' I blurted out.

'Certainly Sir.'

As she bent down to open a drawer, I caught a tantalising glimpse of a shapely ankle. I was just about to imagine something illicit yet vulgar when I heard the bookish man state with a quantum of surprise, 'Oh my goodness.'

I turned to see the Englishman gripping tightly onto Cressy with a revolver pointed at his head.

The sound of the weapon cocking stopped Sonny from moving another step closer.

'Keep your hands where I can see them,' he said. 'Up!'

Both Sonny and I held our hands out, slowly. 'You too,' he said to the staff. The bookish man obliged but my girl collapsed to the floor, out like a light. My natural inclination was to assist but the Englishman pointed his gun straight at me and slowly shook his head. I got the message.

Sonny scowled at the Englishman, goading him to put down his firearm and take him on. As tempted as he might have been, the Englishman knew he still had the whip hand in this encounter.

I had little idea how the standoff was going to end, much less how he intended to make his escape without this becoming the kind of bloodbath I'd witnessed on the train to Marseille. Until, out of the corner of my eye, I caught a glimpse of two English Bobbies walking on the street opposite. I felt that I had to take this chance. On the counter beside me, was a glass jar, filled with the same sugar sticks the little boy had. I slowly moved my left hand behind it before scooping it towards, then through the glass door, instantly drawing the attention of everyone in the vicinity. In a moment of panic, the bookish man made a brave but foolhardy lunge towards Hawthorne, which triggered his destructive instinct.

The Englishman put his first shot straight through his would-be attacker's forehead but before he managed to get away his second, Cressy drove a thick blade back and straight through his left shoulder. His second shot, fired in the direction of a window display, was discharged so close to Cressy's head that its spark caused his hair to ignite. By this point Sonny's huge frame had almost enveloped mine as he sought to protect me from the havoc. As Cressy clutched his head, deafened and writhing on the glass and blood splattered floor, the Englishman grabbed his bag and pushed his way towards the back of the store, desperate to escape before the law arrived. Once again, Sonny and I found ourselves on a floor, covered in debris as this bastard made another undeserved getaway. As the curious faces started to tiptoe into the drug store, Sonny pulled me to my feet and, on the wounded Cressy's orders, we set off after Hawthorne and the plate. We didn't stop to give a statement.

A couple of quick turns and we found ourselves in the alley behind the store. Left and right we looked but all we could see was trash cans and empty boxes. Sonny was on his toes, darting a few feet here and there. I'd see much more clearly if I gave my glasses a quick clean. I took a handkerchief from my pocket and rubbed the lenses. Sure enough, it did the trick.

'Sonny!' I shouted.

On the ground were small but thick globules of blood. We followed the trail up the alleyway to the street. Back on Queensway, we could see that a large throng of people had now gathered outside the drug store. A police car sped past us, pulling up as close as they could to the incident. Hawthorne must have headed in the other direction, said Sonny and I agreed. Like fish swimming against the stream, we split and slowly walked towards the tube station, looking in windows, checking the ground for signs of blood.

'Over here,' Sonny called.

I darted across the road and on the map outside the station was a bloody mark. Had Hawthorne leant here, composing himself, perhaps removing the blade Cressy had forced into his shoulder? At the entrance to the station, a member of staff was mopping something. We stopped to have a look. What happened, I asked nonchalantly, lighting a cigarette?

'No idea guv,' he replied, 'maybe a dog with a cut paw.'

What makes you think that, asked Sonny. He replied, there are little dabs of blood from here to the lift. He asked us what was going on down the road but we didn't stop. Hawthorne was here. Inside the station. If he makes it to the platforms, we've lost him and the plate.

'Tickets!' yelled another tube worker, sitting in a small box beside the elevator. Sonny kept running. 'Ere you! Get back.'

I stopped and dipped into my pockets, pulling out all the coins I had left from the tobacconist.

'Is this enough?' I asked. He gave me a nod and scraped the money into his drawer like a Coney Island fortune telling machine.

I got to the elevator just before the doors closed. A grumpy looking operator on a high stool barked at her other passengers to move up and away from the gate. A quick plunge, a sudden stop and the doors opened again. As we flooded out onto the low level passageway, caution was the watchword. The Englishman was wounded but remained a danger. He could be behind any number of pillars or corners. I tried to stay as hidden in the pack as I could. Small dabs of claret on the dirty tiling indicated that he had passed this way. I was looking for Sonny and found him on his tiptoes, searching for Hawthorne from behind one of the platform's many dimly lit alcoves.

'Anything?'

'He's definitely on this side,' replied Sonny.

And there's nowhere for him to go, other than down the track. The rattle of the rails and the movement of the passengers told us that a train was approaching. While the more impatient commuters looked up the tunnel, checking their wristwatches, we continued to scour the tiled brickwork for signs. The train arrived and the platform cleared. We were just about to step out of the shadows when we spotted him, boarding a quieter carriage near the train guard at the back. Once he was onboard, Sonny and I made a dash *for it and pushed our way into a much busier middle car. At every stop, from Notting Hill to Victoria and St. James's Park, we waited and watched for him to disembark but he never did.*

We walked through the train's adjoining doors and settled for the car next to his. Given his propensity for spontaneous acts of murderous violence, we were happy to keep a safe distance until we felt it was right to make a move. He made his at Embankment. Where was he going? If he was meeting his connection at say, Whitehall, he'd have gotten off at Westminster. We didn't know but we had to find out. Instead of heading for the exit though, Hawthorne took the twisted staircase towards the Northern Line. Maybe he knew a medic at one of those big hospitals overlooking the Thames that he could call on to help with Cressy's puncture mark, a wound which would require more than a needle and a boat trip to mend. Hawthorne turned on to the southbound platform and took up a familiar position; near the back, tucking into the alcove as best he could.

'What's the plan?' I asked Sonny.

His brow furrowed, suggesting to me that the position to which he was appointed was that of the brawn and not the brain. Alright, here comes the train. Let him make his move first and we'll figure out what to do as we go, I said, winging it. Again, he took the carriage at the back, near the guard. Just before the doors closed we made it onto a carriage two cars from where he sat. We passed under the river to Waterloo. If he was going to seek medical help, this was where he'd get out, I said to Sonny. The tube pulled into Waterloo and most of our car disembarked, heading towards the train station upstairs, I presumed. Pulling my cap down, I looked out. He must still be onboard. Next stop, Kennington, as far south as I'd ever been in London and again, we went through the same charade. We were only a couple of hundred yards into the tunnel when the tube juddered to a halt. Signalling, most likely. Sonny stood in his half-hidden vantage point by the connecting doors.

'Something's happened,' he said, opening the door and walking through. I followed him. By the time we got to Hawthorne's carriage,

there was a crowd of people hovering over the flat out train guard.

'I'm a doctor,' I lied. 'What's going on?'

'There was a fella bleeding all over the carriage. He had a knife sticking out of him. The guard went to ask him if he needed help and he sparked him out. That's when I pulled the emergency cord.'

'Where is he now?'

'He took the guard's keys, opened the back of the train and jumped onto the fucking track,' spat the toothless cockney. 'Never mind the electricity, the stupid twat. Place is full of rats. Wouldn't catch me going down there.'

So, we two stupid twats went straight after him. Sonny jumped onto the track and helped me down. Apart from the light emanating from the tube, there was nothing for the eye to fix upon. Where do we walk? I'd forgotten that Sonny was a rube. We need to stay in the middle of the running rails, I said. Where the stones and wooden sleepers are. The electric rails should be to the side, I think. We need some light, said Sonny so I lit a match.

'This might help', said another helpful passenger passing us down a heavy, box shaped, metal lamp. Though the lamp wasn't particularly powerful, its effect was instantaneous. I led the way, walking carefully on the ballast, every footstep crunching and echoing down the soot encrusted tunnel. Sonny put his hand on my shoulder and whispered for me to stop.

'Listen,' he said.

In the airless, unending passage, there was nothing but our pending extinction. Hawthorne, the Englishman was here. Somewhere. Waiting. Tread carefully now. Just then, there was a distant rumble. Behind us, our train whinnied like a mechanical equine, chuntering slowly away, towards its next stop. We kept on. A further twenty yards on, there was a slight curvature to the left. As we approached it, Sonny and I slowed to a crawl, the dread of the expectation almost tangible.

I shone the light round and there stood Hawthorne, leant against the track wall, bag held tightly to his midriff and more importantly, his gun at waist height, pointed at us.

'Did you ever imagine, Mr Miller, that your final moments would be spent in a rat shit covered tomb like this?'

'I hadn't, no.'

'And to think, you could've gone in the cool blue Mediteranean. Or in Montparnasse. You'd have liked that, wouldn't you?'

'Got to go somewhere.'

'We're all going now,' he said. 'I would've liked to have taken a crack at your young accomplice. He looks game.'

'Put the weapon down and you'll get your chance,' said Sonny.

Hawthorne tapped the barrel of his gun against the handle of the embedded blade, wincing ever so slightly.

'With this hanging out of me? Not likely,' he cackled, spitting a mouthful of blood onto the track. 'I like this one. I see a lot of me in him.'

'I am nothing like you,' replied Sonny vehemently.

'You're exactly like me!' shouted Hawthorne. 'A soldier boy, hired by rich men to scrape the shit from their path. Your naivety is blinding you to that fact.'

'I don't kill innocent old men and…young women.'

'You will,' he said. 'Above us, right now you could go into any alehouse, bookbinders or office building, lay down ten pounds and someone will bring me the body of my enemy. No questions asked. You'd be surprised what a man will do for the right reward. The threat of the rope? Casualties of war, my friend.'

'I am not you friend,' replied Sonny.

'That you are not. Enough of this charade. Get on your fucking knees,' he said. 'You too old man.'

We did as we were told.

'Hear that?' he asked. 'That's the trains running again. And where *you are is right where you need to be. Are you ready to see the promised land, Mr Miller?'*

'You first, Mr Hawthorne,' I said.

Above ground, he may have been a street-smart soldier but down here, he was out of his element. The signs were there. Maybe it was the effects of that deep knife wound which meant he wasn't aware that he was leaning up against a switch box, situated perilously close to the live rail. He'd even allowed the distant train movement to distract him from the swishing of the track by his feet. I suppose that it must have been his diminished state otherwise he'd have felt the tightening of his trouser leg caught between the shifting blades of the points which had just been thrown. As the train came down the track towards us, Sonny's unease became manifest. I gripped his arm tightly and asked him to trust me. Have you ever played chicken, I asked?

When I was a youngster, my friends and I would ride the Rapid transport system back in Brooklyn. The Nassau Electric and the Union Elevated, from Sunset Park all the way over to Rockaway Beach. I knew those lines more intimately than I did most of my wives. Sometimes we'd get chased into the depots, like the one at Canarsie. If you were caught, you'd be beaten or worse, hauled up in front of the Transit Authority before getting a bigger whupping from your folks. We got to know every inch of not only the line but the track. Chicken? London rules are the same as New York rules. Last one to move wins.

The train came to within ten feet of us then banked swiftly to our left. The driver spotted Hawthorne but it was far too late for his braking mechanism to engage. Even at a reduced speed, the train snapped the Englishman like a bone-dry twig.

Chicken. You lose.

Sonny and I got to our feet and went to the front of the now static carriage. The driver was already on the radio to his controller. The shock on his face overrode the need to ask why the two of us were standing there, carrying a tube lamp, looking up at him.

The plate. The plate was now under the train. We had no idea if it was still in one piece or, like Hawthorne, a splintered mess. Suddenly, the lights along the tunnel walls came on. From my rudimentary understanding of rail operations, I deduced that, because of the drivers call, the electrical feed to the tracks had been cut. Sonny swiftly dropped to the ground and I followed suit, shining the lamp along the undercarriage, looking not for signs of Hawthorne but of his bag.

'Can you see it?' I asked.

'Jesus,' replied Sonny, surveying the track for long dead hide but finding only a fresher variety. He crawled further through the ballast, squeezing between the track plates and points.

'I think I got it,' he said. 'Shine more to my left.'

Even in death, Hawthorne didn't release his grip on the plate easily. It took a couple of forceful tugs but suddenly, it was free. Sonny handed the bag back to me and shuffled backwards and out, just in time for the cavalry to arrive.

'What you doin' down there?' came the voice.

'They're the blokes who chased after him, officer,' said the toothless cockney passenger to the tall policeman.

'See? He's got your lamp.'

The guard who'd been socked on the jaw took his lamp back and checked it. 'It's mine alright.'

'Where's the suspect?' asked the policeman.

Sonny pointed under the train. Soon, more officials arrived along with a crew of emergency workers. As they scooped Hawthorne into bags and spread sand over what remained of him, we were told to wait by the mouth of the tunnel. Fine, I said, failing to disclose that we had no intention of hanging around for the inquiry. We stood, in silence, for a couple of minutes before making our move, slowly and backward, away from the scene. Just as we were about to vanish from the eyeline of the officers, I noticed one of them pointing our way. Shit, whispered Sonny through his teeth.

We were approached by a fellow who identified himself as a detective, or an inspector detective, I can't recall but he seemed to outrank the uniformed men.

'We'll need you two gents to accompany us to the station,' he said. 'To answer a few questions.'

He called over a couple of uniformed officers who he ordered to take us to the van. Sonny was no stranger to police interaction so he put out his hands, expecting to be cuffed.

'That won't be necessary Sir,' said the detective. 'We just want to talk. Unless there's something you want to tell us?'

My mind was racing but I needed to remain calm. The officers walked us down the track to the Kennington platform.

'Is it true,' Sonny asked, 'that you guys don't carry guns?'

'That is correct,' said a middle-aged officer with a neat moustache. I looked at Sonny. I knew what he was thinking. I shook my head quickly and he sighed. We'd be wanted all over town if we started anything here. They'd probably try to finger us for the murder of the pharmacist earlier. My feeling of dread returned and I started to think of reasons why I shouldn't let Sonny get us out of this mess, here and now.

Outside of the station sat a black, unmarked and windowless van. The moustachioed officer opened the back doors and directed us in. Sonny and I took seats opposite each other and the door closed on us. We waited until we were sure that the officers had departed before exploding.

'You should've let me take care of things.'

'And done what?'

'We wouldn't be sitting in the back of no police truck, that's for sure.'

'If we reacted, they'd presume we're guilty and then it becomes a hell

of a lot harder to contain this. They still hang people for murder here, you know.'

Sonny slumped back. He had no fondness for being caged, even if it was for questioning, much less for miscarriages of justice.

'So, what now?' he asked.

'Check the bag.'

Sonny leaned in as I undid the clasp and pulled back the now dirty leather flap. Cautiously, I reached in. First time. Out it came. I ran my hand around the cloth binding. Thankfully, it seemed intact. I handed it over to Sonny to check but as I was about to delve back into the Englishman's blood marked bag, we heard the sound of a door slamming shut and the ignition of an engine.

London's a big city and given that they've got their bobbies on almost every corner, I presumed that we'd be taken to a nearby station house for the interview. After half an hour on the road however, I realised that this was not the case. Figuratively and literally, it seemed as if we were being taken for a ride.

Soon, we'd turned away from the noisy, well lit streets. Our road now was as dark as it was rocky. Realising that we might have to fight our way out of this after all, we scoured Hawthorne's bag for weapons. Surely he'd have a spare gun, or at worst, a knife? Instead, we found a single silk stocking, a long, battered tin, a ticket for passage - Gothenburg to New York City on the Nina Cin - and an old, unmarked photograph of a woman and child; a motley collection of components, all useless to us at this stage. As I looked at the subjects in the photograph, calm yet stilted and awkward, Sonny opened the tin. With a shudder, he handed it directly back to me. Inside were two needles, a syringe and a length of ligature. Had he forgotten the reason why Hawthorne had to visit a pharmacy?

'I don't like needles,' he said to me, convincingly. Even back in State, as many of his fellow inmates tried to get through a long sentence by immersing themselves in a narcoleptic fog, Sonny's trypanophobia kept his corporeal state sharp. But here and now, it

was all we had. I fixed the bayonet of the needle to the body of the syringe, and Sonny? He's got those fists. The van stopped and there was the sound of metal scraping along concrete. A gate perhaps? We made a left turn then another and drove for a minute before coming to a complete stop. Jabbing and stabbing, that was the plan. Sonny stopped me.

'Wait,' he said. 'We're not cuffed. Let's look around. A move now will end with us being killed. For certain. Let me scope the situation out.' As we were down to the last page of the playbook, it was about the only move we had left.

'Gentlemen,' said the officer who opened the door. 'Follow me.'

We stepped out of the van. The sun was down. There were no other officers, no guns and seemingly no threat. He led us along a pebbled path to a nondescript compound building with closed wooden shutters over the windows. As soon as he opened the door, he told us to help ourselves. I was way ahead of him. The smell of freshly cooked food hit me like one of Sonny's pile drivers. Too many missed meals recently. I'd lost so much weight that I'd had to make a fresh hole in my belt. Sonny made it to the counter before me and bombarded the poor grandma behind the pots with culinary questions. What's this? And that? Stews, soup, roast beef slices, fresh boiled potatoes, carrots and cabbage. Pile it high. Times two. We didn't say another word until grandma brought us each a mug of strong, sweet tea to wash down her simple but delicious fare.

'So what now?' I asked, wiping gravy from my chin with a coarse serviette.

'Dessert?' replied Sonny.

I'd have laughed but I was too weary. I took my tea over to the stove in the corner. I wanted to take a look at the photograph from Hawthorne's bag again. The light was better there. I studied it for some time. The mother holding the child. Too much movement from the latter, nothing but concentration from the former. The picture could be anyone. Suspending disbelief for a moment, I imagined my own mother and I as the subjects. An ache filled my heart. If a malevolent miscreation such as Hawthorne could carry this picture then perhaps, I thought, he was not irredeemable. A host of brutal slayings might suggest otherwise but was there a corner of his own soul, small and hitherto untended, which wasn't corrupt and murderous? I carried no physical reminiscences of my mother nor of my own children so Hawthorne had points over me on that score. Maybe he was the child in the photograph. Not quite the path his mother would've wanted him to take. Was it this disappointment that drove him into the barbed embrace, the punctured arms of pharmaceutical respite? Some, like the once Immaculate Boy, might need a fix to ease the pain of a broken bone or two and a life ill spent but the Englishman? Perhaps his torment was deeper and more profound. Or maybe, as Sonny opined, he was just a cunt.

The moustachioed police officer returned before I could deliberate.

'You should be clear for take off within the hour,' he said.

I beg your pardon?

A flight? We are going home! New York. I wouldn't mind if we flew into St. Louis at this stage. Our stock of medicinal sleeping aids was sadly depleted but the thought of leaving this lethal continent left me giddy with excitement. My experiences of Europe had become increasingly painful. I wished that wasn't the case but it was. As I was beginning to plan my long haul, inflight drink regimen, in walked our old friend Cressy, dashing my hopes of a swift return home. Aside from a packing to the scorched side of his head, he seemed physically unaffected by our latest travails. Sonny spoke first.

'We have the plate.'

He assumed, correctly, that Cressy knew about the Englishman's fate at the hands - or wheels? - of the 144 to Archway.

'We need to depart soon. I'm led to believe that there's a storm due,' he said. 'We have no time to waste.'

His instruction suggested that we were leaving England by the same means as we arrived. Couldn't we wait until daybreak?

'Out of the question,' replied the mustachioed officer. 'As a favour to M. Cressy, my captain has managed to put a temporary block on the investigation. You have been presented with a very small window of opportunity which you need to take otherwise we'll all be questioned about what happened in Queensway.'

Cressy nodded and shook the officer's hands in appreciation. As Sonny took the opportunity to visit the rest room, I waited with Cressy as he pored over his flight charts.

'Are you sure you're up for this?'

He did not answer. Maybe his ears were still suffering the effects of a gunshot fired in close proximity. Perhaps he was angry for letting Hawthorne get the drop on him again but I'll admit that was more my fault. 'At least we got what we came for?'

'You think?' he replied. Sonny returned and joined us. 'Yes,' I said. 'Hawthorne is tomato soup and we have the plate.'

I took it from the bag and handed it to him. He unwrapped it.

'This,' he said, cracking it off the edge of the table, 'is a fake.'

'What?! You're telling me that I... we, went through all of this for another fucking fake?'

My anger was nothing compared with Sonny's. As swiftly as a sprinter off the blocks, Sonny grabbed him by the lapels, lifting him back and up off of his feet. Only the hard block wall stopped him from driving Cressy into the Channel.

'You gotta lot of explaining to do, bub.' he growled menacingly.

'Put me down,' replied Cressy, the click of his pistol's hammer reminding Sonny's rib cage of the maxim that a bullet to the guts tends to trump brute force. Calmly, he repeated, 'Sonny, put me down.'

The big man reluctantly released his grip.

Cressy motioned for us to join him at the table. 'I wasn't entirely honest with you,' he said. 'This trip was about stopping the

Englishman. Nothing else. Why? It would have been much harder to convince you to accompany me on what was a mission fuelled by the need for revenge. Let me explain. When I was a child, with my mother long dead, my father, unable to cope with the pain, drank himself into a pauper's grave. That left me, ten years old, starving on the streets of Clichy. In the winter months, I'd make my home in a hollowed out wall behind the posters at the Gare Du Nord. Like other street rodents, I'd scrounge for food, fighting with everything I had for a stale croissant or a pastry. During the summer, I'd spend my days stealing pennies from the pockets of the tourists who congregated on Montmartre's narrow avenues, watching artists create images of a city that was alien to people such as I. And there were many of us.

One kid who shared my struggle, Henri, was not as fast nor as strong as I. The bread roll he stole from the table outside the Chez Rambeau came at a terrible cost. The patron took exception to this improvised theft and came at Henri with his cane. I ran but when I saw how hard he was being hit, I went back to help. Henri just gave up. Infuriated, I snatched the cane from the cruel swine and gave him some of his own. I was small but from my time on the streets, I knew how to hurt. Fortunately for me, just before the Genderme arrived, an unlikely savior intervened. Etienne Castagne was walking by when he saw the commotion. I did not know who he was but understood his importance from the way the patron deferred to him. He picked up the prone body of little Henri and carried him down into the Café Chappè. Seeing his life ebb away, I wept for the first time in my life. Every emotion that had built up during my ten pitiful years, flooded from me. Was he my brother, Etienne asked. He was. Nothing more important than the fraternal bond, he said. Be proud that you defended his honour. He didn't ask me about my family or my situation. He could see that I was from the streets. You will stay here, he said. There's a bunk out in the back, that's yours. Sweep the floors, clean the dishes. Anything M. Herve asks you to do, you understand? I nodded. Herve brought me some fresh milk, bread and cheese. I will be back to look in on you, he said. And he did.

Etienne Castagne saw something in me that day that no one else did, before or since. From that moment, I was indebted to him, and his brother. When they asked me to become a police cadet, I did. They taught me the importance of language, of culture and of brotherhood. There is a proverb that is found in the Talmud and the Koran. Save one life, save the world. That is not something I say lightly. I was not there for him in February when the Englishman ran a knife through his ribs, on the same streets where I was saved and I must live with that burden. On The Crow's orders, that man was responsible for the deaths of not only Etienne but of many we cared about.'

'Delphine,' said Sonny, quietly.

'Indeed. The Englishman needed to be stopped.'

'So we stopped him,' said Sonny. "What now?"

'The Crow will come again. When? I don't know but a weakened Benoit means a vulnerable Paris. We may still need your help.'

Just before midnight, the flight marshall at Biggin Hill finally cleared us for take off. The full tank that they kindly provided would see us all the way to a private airfield near Longchamp, weather permitting. As turbulent as the return flight was, we were all too drained to care. Cressy, focussed as ever, held the controls firm and straight. After consulting his charts, he'd decided to take a riskier but more direct route meaning that we'd be back in Paris sooner though we'd have to spend more time over the Channel. Given what the ailing Castagne brother meant to him, I wasn't going to argue the point. As with our outward flight, I sat on Sonny's lap for the entirety of the journey. It was not as awkward the second time around. I remained awake but Sonny slept from Sussex until the lights of Amiens inexplicably made me pine for Corfu and the friends I'd left behind.

We arrived back at the chateau just before daybreak to the news that Benoit Castagne had succumbed to his injuries during the night. Cressy remained remarkably composed as he directed his boss' grieving staff. As we had no practical support to offer other than sympathetic but weak platitudes, we slunk off towards our quarters. Both Sonny and I felt like intruders.

'I don't know about you,' I said, 'but I could do with a stiff drink.'

'Me too,' replied Sonny.

We couldn't find any hard liquor but we rustled up a few bottles of beer from the staff mess, sat out on the balcony between our rooms and watched a trickle of people turn into a stream, arriving to pay their respects to the big man.

'Today's Sunday, right?'

'I think it's Friday,' replied Sonny. It was actually Saturday but we were all a bit out of kilter. The beer went down so quickly and smoothly that Sonny went for two more. Saluting the dawn. At the end of the balcony sat a pigeon. A big, plump one, its head ticked like the second hand of a clock, looking for an elusive crumb or crust. Sonny arrived back and the bird flew off which was unfortunate as along with the beer, he brought a carafe of wine and a couple of fresh croissants. Beer number two went down as easy as the first as did the pastries. The bird returned. It was no longer intimidated by Sonny but if it possessed the brain of an eagle or a vulture, even a crow, it would've been. The crumbs that had fallen onto his shirt, he picked off and placed in his palm. Sonny made a surprisingly authentic sounding call to the bird and sure enough, it came towards him, slowly at first, then with more confidence.

'Sonny's not gonna hurt y'all,' he said turning to me. He pursed his lips, asking me to keep quiet.

'You ever tried pigeon?' I whispered, recalling the succulent bird that Benoit Castagne provided for me, prior to my trip to Marseille.

He nodded then whispered in return, 'Back on the farm, this bird would already be in the pot.'

'Can I ask you something, Sonny?'

'Sure.'

'Down in St. Louis, that night...you know.'

'Yeah?'

'Why didn't you just rob me and get gone?'

He snorted. 'Man, I've been asking myself the same thing since I fucking met you.'

I laughed then caught myself. This was a house in mourning, for Christ sakes. Keep it together, I thought. Decorum.

'He's a hungry little son of a bitch, ain't he?' I said. The bird finished the crumbs and flew off. Sonny wiped his hands.

'Did you know that a bird eats more than ninety times its own body weight, every year?' asked Sonny

'I did not,' I replied.

'I got that from Father Alois.'

'Your priest?'

'In the joint,' he replied, 'you know, reading books wasn't for me but he'd get a few of the younger boys together, and encourage us to think beyond the life, you know? I liked when he talked about the things you wouldn't normally care about, like how much a bird ate or when they say that blood is thicker than water. He would explain to us about the different densities of the two. That kind of thing.'

'Sounds like a good man.'

'He was. He's the reason that I started boxing seriously. Five years is a long time in State if you ain't focussed. He knew that if I didn't learn my trade...'

'I understand. Did he help with your release?'

'No, that was Johnny Vitelli. Word got round about my capabilities and suddenly five years became one.'

'With that kind of pull, it's safe to say that Mr Vitelli isn't an employee of the St. Louis Social Work Department.'

'That would be correct,' laughed Sonny. The pigeon returned, with *another, eager for fragments of pastry. Sonny tore another piece and held it out.*

'Look at the chest on this one,' he said. 'We didn't see birds this large on the farm. They tended to be carrion, scavengers, that kind of thing. On the rare occasion that we did, Momma would pluck it and cook it. Once Pop took what he wanted, we'd fight over the rest.'

Sonny's eyes fell to the floor, the memory of those hard times as fresh as if they'd just occurred.

'One time,' he said, 'my brother Roy trapped a bird. Wasn't much, a scrawny thing about half the size of this fellow but he snared it good. Part of him wanted to run to Pop to show him his catch, to make Pop proud. But he didn't. He decided to keep the bird, fix its leg and with a few seeds he could find, build its strength. He might eat it later he told himself but at that moment, all he wanted was to look after it. A few days later, Pop noticed that Roy wasn't in the field so he went looking for him. He found him, with the bird, in a clearing by the stream. For leaving his field and for keeping the bird, Roy got a double whipping that night. Pop made Momma strip and cook the bird and as Roy lay whimpering and bloodied on the floor, like a broken dog, Pop sucked the bones of the bird dry. He could be a cruel man,' said Sonny, staring out over a field, abundant and colourful, far removed from Arkansas.

I didn't know what to say to him.

He finished his beer and shooed away the birds as he stood.

'You asked me why I didn't rob you.'

I didn't speak.

'The greatest lesson I ever took from Pop was not how to work a field, not fix a truck or shoe a mule. It was that cruelty had no place in my life. A man could be big and strong without looking to denigrate another. I will never whip a man who offers me no threat. And you, standing in that alley, fearful, offered me no threat. Father Alois taught me more about the man I want to be

in one year than Pop did in twenty. I know who I am and I know what most people think when they look at me. But they're wrong. I am more than the whipping of a man. Get some rest, Val,' he said, patting me on the shoulder.

Had I been guilty of underestimating him too? I guess I had. For the rest of his life, I'd never make that mistake again.

A few hours later, there was a knock on my door. I woke with a start from my deep slumber. Disorientated, I got up and answered. It was Cressy. I rubbed my eyes and ushered him in.

Before I could offer my condolences again, he spoke.

'Tomorrow, you will go to the UBS bank where you will find all of your previously withheld residuals, unlocked and waiting for you, as promised, under the name of Mr Valentine.'

He passed me a card with numbers on it. 'They will be expecting you.'

Benoit had come through for me. I toasted his memory, and my windfall, with the remainder of my now flat beer.

'So that's it. We're done?' I asked, wiping the drip from my lips.

'You are no longer obliged to help us,' replied Cressy, staring out over the gardens. 'Unless you want to.'

I shook my head. No thank you, I thought.

'What about The Crow?'

'The Crow will come again. There is no doubt about that.'

That afternoon Sonny and I left the chateau to the mourners and took to Paris. As my money was tied up in a Swiss bank, the now cash-rich Sonny gladly fronted me a couple of francs. We cut through the arrondissements as if we were demobbed GI's. Before we went in search of my favoured whorehouses, we spoke of life and of love, of film and art, and the speed of a Sugar Ray Robinson combination. Sonny told me that he loved Paris because no one feared him there. He was free in all the ways a black man couldn't be back home. Maybe we should get an apartment here, a bar perhaps. We could call it 'Val and Charlie's', he said, the wine starting to take effect. We talked of everything but the Castagnes, the Englishman and the plate. But it was always there, like an unresolved couplet or a cocked arm. I'd guessed that Cressy had spoken to Sonny earlier at the Chateau. Paid him what was owed and then some. That would be the smart move. Then make an appeal to his sense of injustice.

I didn't know which was greater, the feeling of dread I had when Cressy was around or my admiration for him. While the 'state beneath the state' mourned the passing of their capo, around the bars, news circulated of the sudden death of the city's most beloved gypsy guitarist. As Sonny and I raised glasses to both men and shed some drunken tears for all we'd lost, I couldn't avoid the inalienable truth that I wasn't willing to allow Sonny to serve as bait alone.

Chapter 27 - Stulti Morietur

The smell of freshly fried bacon woke May from her rest. Throwing on her robe and slippers, she picked up Elie's book and followed the enticing scent towards the Peterson kitchen where Elvin stood at the stove. His father was awake, had already eaten and was poring over the old papers, looking for clues with fresh eyes.

"What we know is that when Henry and Sonny returned from Paris in 1953, they had the plate with them. So dangerous was the knowledge of its whereabouts that neither man knew where the other had placed it. It was only later that I found out that Henry had taken it first and hidden it under the floorboards of a gallery in Northern California. And there it stayed for years until the owner sold up. Once Henry's health started to fail, Sonny took it and one brief scare aside, we know that he kept it safe for the last ten years of his life."

"Scare?"

"If the status of the plate was under threat, the holder would place a coded call to the other. In May of '65, on the eve of his second fight with Ali, Sonny made that call. I know that he took it to Vegas soon afterwards."

"So where is it now?" asked May.

Martin Peterson took his glasses off and rubbed his eyes. He hadn't slept much that night. The frisson of excitement had given way to weariness. But while his body was struggling, his mind remained sharp.

"That's a question we've been pondering for years, May."

"May I?" she asked.

"By all means, Miss Morgenstern," he replied, passing over the folder. "Henry received a similar envelope a few days after Sonny's death. Enclosed was a book, a pulp novel called…"

Martin reached into the box and took out a well-worn paperback.

"…'Fools Die On Friday'. We checked it through but it contains nothing of significance. However, the note Sonny tucked inside it did. Henry kept the original but there's a Xerox of it in the folder. Numbers of bank accounts he'd set up and the aliases he used. There was one numeric code that we thought were coordinates but we got nothing from that either, unfortunately."

May looked at the lurid cover of the dime store book. A gaudily inked half-dressed woman stood behind an unimpressed, bow-tie wearing man. I'll save this for later, she thought flicking through the tattered, coffee-stained pages. She emptied the contents of the second envelope onto the table.

"That was given to me by Sonny's neighbour. The money clip, jewellery, and cufflinks were what he had on his person when we found him."

"What's this?" asked May, picking up a discoloured pocket square. Upon it, there was writing. "Verencor. Is that Spanish? Sounds like it."

"I initially thought that it was Latin."

"And you don't know what it means?" asked May.

"We have no idea. It was in Sonny's trouser pocket when he died. It's his handwriting, see?"

Martin held up the envelope and a compliment slip. It clearly matched that on the pocket square. "It might mean something or it might not. We've been poring over these pieces for years and are no closer to working out what they mean or finding that plate." He looked across the table at the book under May's hand.

"Is that what I think it is?"

"It is."

"May I?" he asked.

"By all means, Mr Peterson," she replied, smiling back at him. May had never seen him as engaged as this. Just then, Elvin handed her a warm and equally desirable plate; sourdough bread with four slices of bacon, the rind crispy. Just the way she liked it.

"Is that fresh coffee I smell?" she asked.

"Heavy on the cream, heavy on the sugar," said Elvin. "Coming up."

At that moment, in the Peterson kitchen, it could've been any normal morning, with a happy family having breakfast.

Until May opened the folder to see photographs of a bloated male body, days dead with a hypodermic needle protruding from his arm.

"Sonny?" she asked.

Martin nodded. "It was the day after New Year's. I was at a hotel in Pismo with Elvin's mother at the time. We drove out to California for Christmas and left Elvin with my brother's family. It was the first vacation we'd had alone in a couple of years but something, a gut feeling, told me that I should check in. That's when I heard that Sonny was found dead at the International. I made the call and the House Manager confirmed it. He'd keep a lid on things until I got there. I told my wife that I needed to go back to Vegas immediately. She had a few books she wanted to finish so she stayed by the pool. I said I'd be back before nightfall. When I got to the hotel, thankfully many of the holiday makers had already checked out because the smell hit you before the elevator door opened. I called a few people and we managed to get his body back to his house and onto his own bed without too much fuss before Geraldine returned. Mort Olsen made a call and had some of his Vegas associates take care of the clean up."

"Why did you move him into his house?"

"We had to make it look like he'd overdosed or certain elements in the Nevada PD would've started sniffing around and that could have jeopardized everything. We cleared the hotel suite and his house of materials relating to his involvement with us."

"Maybe Sonny hid the plate somewhere in his house," suggested May.

"That would've been too risky," replied Martin. "But by the time we moved from the hotel to his house, it was clear that we weren't the only party that had considered that possibility. His place had already been turned over. They, and we, found nothing. So we put Sonny in his bed, got out and tipped off the department. If anyone was going to take the blame for this, better the Mob than us. I didn't know his wife but I knew people who did. They broke the news to her and brought her back to officially find his body."

Jesus, thought May. She'd no idea how deep this went.

"I took Elvin and his mother East before heading back to Vegas on the Saturday for his funeral. Over the week, the papers were full of speculation, the manner of his death, was he murdered, that kind of thing. But before anyone got close to piecing together the fragments of this puzzle, I would make sure that another story, featuring a junkie mistress or Sonny selling cocaine for Red Rodney, pushed it off the front pages. Ignominious, I know but strangely, I reckon he'd have appreciated it. There were hundreds there, many more than the chapel could hold. Joe Louis turned up late as he was shooting craps somewhere. Sonny would have laughed at that. Poor Geraldine didn't make it out of the limo. Even though it was expected, I heard that Henry took his loss very hard. I couldn't say that I was more than just an acquaintance of his but from the brief time we did spend together, I could see how fond they were of each other."

Martin flicked through the pages of Elie's book.

"Given what you now know, is there anything in these letters that you think might help?"

Where to begin, May thought.

"I'd very much like to take a closer look at it," he said, "once you've finished with it, of course."

May would've given it to him now if she hadn't still had a handful of pages to read. 'Fools Die on Friday' would have to wait.

"Sure thing. By the way, how is Mrs Peterson?"

"Still dead to the world," he replied, caring not for his turn of phrase.

"She'll be fine until lunchtime. The officers outside change their rotation at twelve. Her sister will be here by then. In the meantime, finish your sandwich and get dressed. We pick Rose Holloway up in half an hour."

****

Elvin reversed the family car away from the garage door, turning it around on the oval shaped driveway. By the doorway, Martin Peterson sat in his wheelchair, giving instructions to the officer who'd just arrived. May watched, still smarting over the fact that she'd have to spend more time with Rose Holloway than she would've liked. Elvin's father wheeled down the metal ramp which zig-zagged in front of the Peterson's doorway, stopping in front of the car.

"Take your bags out of the trunk," he said, "we're not taking that car."

There was a clunk. The mechanised garage door slowly opened.

"Move the bikes away, son," Elvin did as he was asked. Martin Peterson drove his chair into the garage.

"This..." he said, tugging at the heavy linen covering, "was Sonny Liston's car."

A cloud of dust blew past, settling around the trees which lined the Peterson's driveway.

"A 1970 Fleetwood. Quite something."

Indeed, it was, May exhaled, impressed. She'd never seen such an elegant looking vehicle.

"How did you manage to get hold of this?" she asked.

"It was the strangest thing," replied Martin. "A couple of years back, I received a booklet for an auction in Las Vegas. Lincolns, Thunderbirds, a whole host of muscle cars and this; a 1970 Fleetwood, seven point seven. I knew instantly that it was Sonny's car. Seems it had been sitting in the garage of his Vegas neighbour for years. I made a few calls and here it's been, ever since."

"Did you know him well?"

"I'm not sure anyone did."

Aside from Henry, thought May.

Martin threw the keys to Elvin. "Take it out nice and slow." Elvin climbed into the car and turned on the ignition. He couldn't help but make the engine roar, eliciting a roll of the eyes from his father.

"Sorry!" shouted Elvin. He wasn't though.

The Fleetwood rolled down the incline and pulled up beside Martin and May.

When Elvin got out to help his father, Martin stopped him.

"Help me in, Elvin."

"Into the driver's seat? Are you crazy?"

"Rose lives over on Williams. That's about two blocks from here."

"Two? Closer to twenty. Dad, you've not driven in years. With your condition...it's not safe."

"I'll decide what's safe. And anyway, it's not stick."

"There are police officers literally outside our house," said Elvin. "And what about Mom? She'll go nuts."

"The last time your mother was this wasted, Sly Stone was in town. Elvin, give me the keys."

Elvin turned to May for support but she stared at the ground, nervously patting her hair over her ear, reluctant to get involved.

"Son...please," asked Martin Peterson, his eyes pleading with his boy.

Let me do this.

A short drive. Half a mile to Rose's house. For the first time in years, Martin felt alive and vital. Elvin handed the keys over.

"If you swerve a foot over the line, I'm pulling the brake and taking over."

That sounded like a fair trade, thought Martin. Elvin helped his father into the seat. May sat behind Elvin but watched Martin as he delved back into muscle memory to start the car, release the brake and depress the gas.

"Not too heavy," warned Elvin. Martin nodded and lifted his foot. That's better. Though the Fleetwood was only crawling, Martin Peterson's withered body and soul soared.

By the time they'd reached Rose Holloway's house, Elvin's father had barely the strength to deploy the handbrake. As Elvin pulled it into position, Martin sat back in his seat with his eyes closed. He wanted this moment to last but knew that it couldn't.

"I'm afraid you've failed your audition to be our getaway driver Mr P," said May, placing her hand on his shoulder. "But keep practising." Silently, he put his hand over hers, grateful that her show of support didn't come with the kind of patronising sentimentality that he hated.

Elvin helped his father out of the car and around to the passenger seat.

"Mind your legs, May," said Elvin as the seat slid back, giving his father room to stretch out. May positioned her legs over the back central reservation in the footwell. If Rose Holloway was joining them, then she'd better scrunch up, May thought.

Elvin held the door open for Miss Holloway. Once again, she was immaculately turned out, wearing a blush pink top with a pencil skirt which complimented the starched, pale grey mackintosh over her shoulders. This attention to spotless detail was another of the many reasons May disliked Rose Holloway.

"Good morning everyone," she chirped. "How are you, Martin? It is good to see you again."

"And you Rose," he replied. "You got enough room in the back?" he asked. May's legs were still stretched beyond the middle. Miss Holloway looked at her, smiled and said, "Perfectly fine here."

The road towards Portland wasn't especially busy now that the morning traffic was almost gone. As Elvin drove, Rose and Martin engaged in the kind of small talk which May felt was not only tedious but inappropriate given their proximity to danger. A few days ago, she'd have put her headphones on, dug out a mixtape from her satchel and drowned out the unwanted outbreak of inanity. Dennis and his ninety minute sonic tokens of affection seemed so far removed from the world she currently inhabited. As no obvious clues could be gleaned from the Vegas envelope and its contents, May reached again for Elie's book. Perhaps the final few pages might elicit the crucial, tantalising piece of the puzzle.

"I'm sorry May, but is that…"

"Yeah," she grunted.

"Would it be possible for me…"

"I'm not finished with it." Like a twenty-four-year-old infant, May pulled her legs back over to her own side, squeezing them into the cramped space behind Martin's seat. It was uncomfortable but she wasn't going to give Rose Holloway anything.

"As you've got longer legs, if you'd like, we could swap seats…" offered the librarian.

Unimpressed by Miss Holloway's olive branch, May continued with her display of petulance, pushing her knees deep into the back of Martin's passenger seat and into his back.

"Sorry Mr P," she said.

"Sorry for what?"

"For kneeing your back."

"Don't worry, May. I never felt a thing."

That's odd. She had felt her bony knee cap come into contact with what she presumed was Mr Peterson's back. He must have lost some feeling. Maybe it was a spring, she thought. It was an old car. Clutching Elie's book tightly, she again pressed her knee into the back of Martin Peterson's seat. May again felt resistance and it wasn't a spring. She sat up and put down the book, shooting Rose Holloway a 'I dare you to touch it' look before pressing gently into the plush upholstery.

"You don't feel that?" she asked Elvin's father.

"I don't feel anything, May."

"What is it?" enquired Rose.

"I'm not sure," she replied, tracing her fingers around the leather, feeling for a shape.

Portland was approaching.

"It's the next turn off, Elvin," said Rose.

May ran her fingers over the area again, then reached over into Miss Holloway's space and tried the same with the back of the driver's seat. There was a clear difference. Behind Elvin, she could feel the springs holding together the structure of the seat. She slid back to her side and again felt for the shape.

There's something in the seat.

Once they'd left the freeway, Elvin pulled over and helped his father out of the car. May asked Rose to step outside so that she could stretch out and look underneath the seat for a zip or a catch to open it. With Martin, Elvin and Rose looking on, May lay down across the footwell.

"Maybe this will help," said Martin, removing a pocket-sized flashlight from the side of his belt.

"Elvin, check under the front," said May.

"What am I looking for?"

"A zipper, a fastener or a catch. Anything that'll open up the cover."

"Can't we just cut it open?" asked Rose.

All three of her fellow passengers glared at her.

"Rose, this is a 1970 Fleetwood. How would you feel if I took a knife to...say... a hand printed, precious diary?"

Miss Holloway shuddered.

"Exactly."

"Nothing obvious," said Elvin, "What about...?"

"Shhh..." said May, demanding silence. Martin understood. A detective would step back and look again.

May studied both seats visually and with tactility. They were identical except for a barely visible join in the piping at the back of Martin's seat. Delicately, May pulled at the quarter inch, faded white trim. It came away from its sister piece directly above it. Slowly she continued to separate the thin vinyl column from its seam; six inches, nine, a foot, two...

Once the piping was removed, May could see a gap in the binding. Carefully, she forced her fingers in, loosening the strong interlaced thread until she could feel another level of vinyl, a panel pulled flat but taut. This piece was held in place by a series of stud fasteners. May slid her fingers under the gap between the first two and open it popped. She did the same with the others until the panel resembled a flap. Deliberately, she reached in behind and could feel something hard beneath the folded plastic sheeting.

"What is it?" asked Elvin.

As May gently removed the item and placed it on the back seat, Rose leaned in, her eyes now as wide as her mouth. For once, she was lost for words. Martin Peterson too.

May could hear his deep exhalations but she didn't look up. She slowly peeled back the thick, protective layer.

"Hello, gorgeous."

Chapter 28 - Herb's Ford

"If they leave within the hour, they'll be there by this time tomorrow. I just think that it'll be safer for us to avoid using public transport. If they take the 95, 495, the 81 and the 70, it should be straight forward. Yes, they'll travel in convoy. I'll make them aware of the protocols. Thank you. We'll speak tomorrow."

Jerry Hector placed the phone back on the receiver and returned to the kitchen. As Rose and Martin sat in the living room inspecting the now recovered plate, over the large oak dining table, stood the Olsens. Sipping on his third coffee of the day, Mort marked out the route on the map while Jeffrey, his son, spelled out the next course of action.

"We take the lead, you follow. Two cars only. On the freeway, we stick to seventy. No need to go faster and draw attention to ourselves. You stay within one hundred yards of us at all times. If you fall behind, we will call you, using the call sign Delta One. You are Delta Two."

Jeffrey pointed to a town on the map.

"This will be the first stop. Pike County, Milford, PA. There's a gas station with a diner called The Wilkes just past the Montague turn off. We can fill up, get some chow and be back on the road, on schedule."

Jeffrey passed the baton to his father who continued with the pre-briefing session. "After that first stop, three hour turnarounds, to change drivers. No need to get tired. Three hours driving, three hours rest. We'll take my pick up and you can take Herb's Ford. Both have a full tank of gas and no known issues that may slow us down. I'll make sure there's a couple of weapons in the back should anything arise. The two of you can drive, I take it?"

Both Elvin and May nodded but it was the previous comment which made them think.

Jerry spoke. "Mort, to be safe, I think that one of you should accompany the kids. This is all new to them and I don't want them to trip up on something simple."

Mort stroked his dark beard and pondered the request.

"Well, neither you nor Martin are in any condition to undertake this particular journey."

"If I may," said Kenneth, "I would love to play a small part in the mission. I've never been on 'active duty' as they say."

"There is a reason for that, Kenneth," said Jerry.

"What better than an extra pair of hands?"

"Two?" said Rose.

"Herb and Bill won't be here until nightfall," said Mort Olsen, considering her offer. "Rose, can you drive stick?"

"It's been a while but…"

Elvin interjected. "That's settled. Kenneth can go with you guys and Miss Holloway can come with us. May and I can handle most of the drive, can't we?"

May said nothing but arched an eyebrow in disapproval.

As the Olsens and Kenneth pulled out of the leafy driveway, Martin shouted over to his son in the car behind.

"Stay focussed. Nothing stupid, you hear. Back in one piece. Both of you."

Elvin nodded and released the handbrake, easing Herb's Ford down and onto the street.

On the driveway, Jerry wrapped against the elements, took the handles of Martin's chair. Two scarred, diminished men, hopeful yet fearful and as anxious as any guardian watching a loved one leave for destinations unknown. This was now out of their control.

As Elvin drove away, May took a long look at Jerry. He did seem better today but a nagging worry remained that like M.Cressy, she might never see her mentor ever again.

Chapter 29 - Spinning Wheel

For most of the first leg, May had pretended to sleep. Up front, Rose Holloway gleaned every nugget of information she could from Elvin about the attack and what he knew about Henry Miller, Sonny Liston and the Plate of Mar Saba. While Miss Holloway listened intently to Elvin's straight and sober recounting of the incident, his lack of context frustrated her. She exhorted loudly at certain points in Elvin's testimony in an attempt to 'wake' May. No dice, thought May. Even though Jerry vouched for her, May's instincts told her that there was something Rose Holloway was holding in reserve.

The Milford turn off was reached almost to the minute of the Olsen schedule. Slowing down on the approach to The Wilkes Diner, Elvin yawned, stretching his arms out over the steering wheel and back again. The near five hours that he'd spent driving - and being interrogated by Rose Holloway - had taken its toll. Now it was May's turn. Three hours beside Maine's most inquisitive public servant. This was going to be tough, she thought as she stretched her stiff legs on the woodchip and bark.

"Ah, the country. How fresh is that air? Breathe it in!" said Kenneth lighting a menthol cigarette. He offered May one. She shook her head. Over bacon, pancakes with syrup and some of Elvin's wings, she'd come up with a suitable strategy for handling Rose Holloway.

"I hope you don't mind but I've taken the liberty of ordering for you," said May, taking the vacant seat at the counter closest to Elvin. "I've gone for Duck A 'l'Orange and Lemon confit." He looked back at her, stone-faced.

"For two," she added.

Not that The Wilkes served the finest French cuisine but if the fare placed in front of him wasn't wings, a burger and a large soda, his part in this operation would be over and May knew it.

"Half a slice of pecan pie and a black coffee, please," said Rose Holloway, climbing onto the seat next to May.

May'd been hoping that Rose would've taken the hint and joined the Olsens at a booth out back.

"Best to remain in our groups. Don't want to be drawing attention."

"We're at a backwater diner and besides us and the staff, there are precisely four people here," replied May snarkily. "I think we'll be fine."

Elvin, uncomfortable with the air of hostility, made light of the situation.

"Four people and a dog, actually." Rose smiled as he continued, whispering. "Have you done anything like this before, Miss Holloway?"

"You mean, 'Visit St. Louis'?"

They both understood what she meant.

The waitress brought her order. "Could I trouble you for some cream? Fresh, please."

"Sure thing."

Rose Holloway looked at herself in the mirror behind the counter. She sipped her black coffee and pushed back a stray strand that had escaped from her tightly tied hair. "I've never been to St. Louis," she said.

The remainder of their scheduled thirty minute pit stop was spent in awkward silence, punctuated by the oddly reassuring sounds of Johnny Mathis and Perry Como on auto play from the jukebox. Songs that reminded May of childhood. Simpler times? Maybe. Maybe not. Instinctively, she tugged the hair at the side of her head, flattening it over her ear.

As always, Mort took care of the bill. Jeffrey incurred a withering glare from his father for leaving a less than generous tip. Mort instantly doubled it with a tut and a resigned shake of his head.

Outside the diner, Elvin, just back from checking in on his mother, safe and well at his aunt's house, threw the keys of the Ford to May but in the dusky twilight, she missed them.

"Where's Kenneth?" asked Jeffrey, checking his watch against the vintage clock which hung outside the diner.

"We need to get on the road."

"I thought he was already in the car," said Elvin.

"Maybe he's gone back to the john. Can you tell him to hurry up?" asked Jeffrey, passing the keys of the pick up to his elderly father.

Elvin nodded and jogged back towards the diner to check.

As May scrambled around for the keys on the dimly lit ground, Rose said, "Maybe you should put your glasses on."

"Maybe you should mind your business," she responded. "And while we're on the road, don't be giving me the twenty questions you gave to Elvin on the way here."

"So I was right, you weren't sleeping?"

As May grimaced, Rose smirked and Elvin searched for Kenneth, Mort Olsen switched on the ignition of his trusty pick up truck for the last time.

The blast which ripped the body clean off the chassis, rained chunks of fiery metal down in the direction of May and Rose, who lay singed and shocked, on the bark-chipped ground, thirty feet away.

"May!" roared Elvin, sprinting out of the diner. He slid onto the ground and dragged her away from the blaze. He sat her up against the back of the Ford then returned to do the same for Rose.

"It's not over," she repeated, catatonically. "It's not over."

"Kenneth...where's Kenneth?" asked Rose Holloway, dirt covered and breathing heavily but trying to remain composed.

"He wasn't in the restroom."

"Where was he?"

"I thought he was already in the pick up."

"I'm not ...I don't know," Elvin replied, confused.

By this point, the four people and a dog who had been in the diner were standing in the parking lot. The manager and the waitress used their extinguishers on the Olsen's pick up but it was a futile exercise.

"We need to go," said Rose, quietly.

"We can't," said Elvin. "What about the Olsens and Kenneth?"

"There's nothing we can do for them now," said May. "Rose is right. We need to go."

"Surely we have to wait for the police?"

Rose Holloway dropped to the ground and looked under the body of Herb's Ford. May checked the doors. They were still locked. She put the key in the lock and slowly turned. The mechanism activated and for a second, the three remaining travellers held their breath. Rejecting Elvin's offer to drive, she opened the door and climbed in.

"Maybe it's best that you wait over there, just in case," she said, passing to Rose the bag which contained the plate.

Elvin pleaded again to let him start the car.

She ignored him. May Morgenstern might have been scared witless herself but she was determined not to show it.

Key slotted in. Foot on brake.

Here goes.

Straight ahead, directly above the smouldering wreck of the Olsen's pick up, the leaves of the overhanging sycamore crisped and crackled with the heat. There was an odd yet compelling beauty in the scarred tree. If this was it, she thought, that would be a fitting final ponderance.

She held her breath, turned the key and the car started.

May climbed back out of the car. "Are you able to drive a little longer?" she asked Elvin.

He nodded and took her place. "Pop the trunk," she said.

As the final vestiges of daylight left the skies above rural Pennsylvania, Elvin drove. Tired though he was, the latest sobering installment had sharpened his focus. Rose Holloway sat beside him, in silence.

In the back seat, May spread out. Though her Walkman batteries had long since run flat, she continued to wear the headphones. It helped her detach from the incessant, ever present threat and to concentrate. The seemingly random manner of the explosion was shocking but no more so than 'Bob' finding then almost killing her in her own apartment. May stared back down the road they'd travelled. If they can get to the Olsens, she thought before stopping, unwilling to consider further permutations. And Rose Holloway. What was the librarian's part in this? Back in Portland, she seemed very keen to join them. But Jerry trusted her. May didn't. Keep watching. In the long footwell, lay the Olsen's final bequest. Just in case.

They made the town of Snow Shoe, PA just around midnight. A long day of driving, and that second soda downed at The Wilkes diner, had caught up with Elvin. The showery spells they'd experienced driving across Monroe County and through the town of Jim Thorpe hadn't helped. They'd pull in when they could, but not at a diner or a truck stop this time. Too risky.

On the State route 4002, Elvin pulled into the gravelled space in front of a car wash that was closed for the night, turning the car and its lights off. There was no traffic on the road, nor in the sparsely populated town was there a house for a couple of hundred yards in either direction. This was as good a place as any for a quick stop. As his need was greater, Elvin went first. May stepped out and stretched. The orthopedic insole in her boot tended to hurt if she wore it for lengthy periods. She should've taken it off earlier. Elvin returned, relieved and showed May where to go. Not ideal but needs must, she thought, finding a safe spot in the rough ground behind the building.

"As you're driving, I'll take over in the back," said Rose Holloway through the darkness, cutting May off midstream.

"Jesus, you frightened the life out of me!" said May, hurriedly composing herself.

"You may want to use these."

Rose passed her a small pack of tissues.

"Thanks, I guess."

"I never travel anywhere without them. Not that I'm accustomed to relieving myself outdoors but if you can handle the next three hours..."

"I think the three hour rule went up with the Olsens, don't you?" said May, trampling through the thick undergrowth back to the front of the building.

Rose Holloway shrugged and straightened up her skirt.

Despite Elvin's protestations, May took the wheel. By the time they were back on the I-80, the exhausted Elvin had succumbed to sleep. May kept one eye on the road and the other firmly on her rear-view mirror and Rose Holloway. The reassuringly constant highway lights faded as they drove beyond the county lines. To keep her mind from straying back to more morbid thoughts, May turned on the radio and searched for something not too taxing. None of the presets were tuned. The late Mort Olsen clearly was no music fan. She settled on the first FM station she could find. Bread, Three Dog Night and Blood Sweat and Tears, none of whom she was particularly fond of. The familiar sounds of Boz Scaggs with 'Lowdown' though was as welcome as a warm blanket on a cold night. Connie Barzagli had this album. It actually belonged to one of her siblings. Michael or Carlo...might've been Terry. May couldn't recall which one but she did remember Connie commandeering it because that's what Connie did. May wondered what she was up to. She wouldn't have believed any of this.

"Speed up. Just a little," said Rose, pulling May out of her reminiscence.

"What's up?"

"Probably nothing but I'd rather make sure."

May checked her rear-view. In the distance, two bright spots on an otherwise quiet stretch of road, about a hundred, maybe a hundred and fifty yards behind their car.

Probably nothing.

May put her foot down, gradually picking up speed. Seventy-five... eighty... eighty-five miles per hour.

The lights remained at the same distance

"OK, now slow down. If they're not following us, they'll pass."

May eased off the gas. Seventy-five... seventy... sixty-five...

"A little slower still," urged Rose.

May took it down to fifty five. Still, the vehicle behind stayed a hundred yards behind.

"Right... hold on," said May. The instant burst of acceleration woke Elvin.

"What's going on?" he asked. As May sped down the I-80, pushing Herb's Ford out of cruise and into the high eighties, Rose spoke.

"I think we're being followed."

For the next ten miles, May drove as fast as the car could handle. They were miles from the safety of a town but a road sign indicated that there was a turn off for DuBois airport coming up. Rose told May to take the exit.

She reckoned that if the vehicle behind was going to the airport they'd turn off too but if they followed Herb's Ford back out onto the I-80, their suspicions would be confirmed.

"Then what?" asked Elvin.

Then what indeed, thought May as she slowed to take the exit. The vehicle behind followed suit.

Within a mile, they'd come to a four-way roundabout. Fourth exit, Airport. Straight on for the road back to the interstate. It would be one or the other. May entered the roundabout, slowly. Rose and Elvin checked for the following vehicle. First exit, not taken. Second, the westbound route to the I-80, not taken either. Third, east on the I-80. This is it, May thought. Last exit to Dubois. She indicated to turn off and the vehicle behind followed. At the last second, May cancelled the signal and sped up. Thirty... forty... the car clinging to the road as she took the westbound turn back towards the I-80. May looked in her rear-view mirror. The anxiety she'd been fighting, now had a reason to exist.

As Rose sat in silence, Elvin checked the limited arsenal that May had taken from the trunk after the last pit stop. Standing between them and their pursuers, was one semi-automatic pistol with a couple of clips and a pump action shotgun. They had no idea what they'd be facing beyond the intimidating glare of two bright headlights. May looked in the rear-view mirror again. The lights appeared to be getting closer. Rose confirmed May's suspicions. This was it. May held the speed to a firm seventy and tightly gripped the wheel. Elvin climbed into the back alongside Rose and rolled down the window. He had never fired a shotgun in his life. The vehicle closed in on them, sitting almost on the tail of Herb's Ford.

"I'm going to try something," said May. "Hold on."

On the empty interstate, May began to weave in front of the pursuing vehicle, causing it to slow down. She touched the brakes gently forcing the van in pursuit to weave to avoid collision. If it was the plate they were after, they'd be foolish to risk a crash, May thought. Still, she was intent on goading them into making a move.

On the stretch of open highway, just after the turn off to a town named Corsica, the pursuers made their move. Pulling alongside Herb's Ford, they shone an industrial light into May's face, causing her to turn away.

"I can't see," she yelled.

So strong was the beam that neither Rose nor Elvin could look in the direction of it. Elvin pointed the shotgun towards the light and discharged the weapon. The light exploded in a blistering flash which caused the pursuer's van to swerve and clip the front left fin of their car. Fighting against the spin and struggling to see clearly, May was powerless to prevent Herb's Ford catching the start of a metal roadside barrier which, at pace, flipped the car up and over. May closed her eyes as the interior lit up to a deafening round of gunfire. Then silence.

****

A spinning wheel was the first thing May remembered seeing when she came to. She watched it until its context seeped through, like the wet grass on which she lay. The first thing she felt was the pain from her arms and shoulders where her captors had cut her from a safety belt before dragging her through the dirt. Though her eyesight flitted between very blurred and slightly less so, her hearing still hadn't adjusted enough to pick up the sounds of Elvin's low moans of pain. The first words she heard were, 'Leave the old broad. She's dead.'

What followed came from a more familiar tongue.

"Isn't it incredible how the wheel turns? I suppose I must be grateful to Rose for sending you my way. Poor Rose. She had no idea, she really didn't. Too tightly wound. I tried, I honestly did but she didn't bite. Too loyal to that hick shithole and its one redeeming building. When one spends a lifetime around books, the tendency is to study them, not the people who read them. That's where we differed. She guarded them as if they were Holy Writ itself. Me? Much as I adore the thrill and the adventure of the printed word, weekends spent on Fifth Avenue I'll cherish even more."

"Kenneth?" asked May, baffled. "The Olsens..."

"Unfortunate but necessary."

"Are you...The Crow?"

"I don't know whether to be flattered or offended, my dear. Would you like me to be?"

"I... don't know," said May, clutching her head.

"Like the Olsen's and dear, dear Rose, it's always wise to have a respectable front. Keep stacking 'em high and selling them fast, Kenneth. Sure thing. Like you, after a fashion, beavering away in Jerry's ghastly little café, only I'm not stacking pancakes for fat ingrates for twenty bucks a day."

"Plus tips," said May, spitting blood and gravel onto the ground. "You know nothing about me."

"That's where you're wrong. I've given this some thought actually. We're much the same, you and I. Willing participants in a scene which shouldn't concern us. And why? Because we both understand that life should be more than managing a bookstore or pouring endless coffee refills. That's why it was so delicious when you hitched your skirt at Johnny, or should I say, Bob? I really didn't expect his rough charm and dreadful acting to work on you as easily as it did."

"What's your point?"

"My point is that you have little bargaining power at this juncture in our little human comedy. But, from the moment we met, over Henry Miller of all people, I thought you had something, May. I believe that we can write a mutually beneficial finale to this story."

"Where's Elvin?" she asked.

The bookseller nodded to his associates. It was obvious to May that Elvin's injuries were of little concern to Kenneth's accomplices. Both were tall, strong and heavily armed. And not much older than she.

As May cradled her injured friend in her arms, Kenneth lit a menthol cigarette and took a long drag.

"Where is it, May?"

"Where's what?"

Kenneth tilted his head back and blew a plume of smoke skywards. "Take the boy," he said.

"No!" howled May grabbing onto Elvin who was in no condition to fight back.

Forcibly, they stood him up and slammed him against the side of the van. Elvin shouted in agony. His entire weight was taken by his right leg. His left was unnaturally twisted.

As the blows rained down, May intervened.

"OK, stop! I'll tell you where it is."

Kenneth motioned to his accomplices to stop, but not quick enough to prevent another unnecessary punch into Elvin's midriff.

"Please!"

"That's enough!" commanded Kenneth.

"It's in the trunk," she said.

Kenneth looked towards the men holding Elvin. They looked back at him, confused.

"Do I really have to spell it out?" said Kenneth, sarcastically.

As it was clear that Elvin, beaten and broken, was going to offer little threat, he was again thrown to the ground, landing heavily.

While Kenneth's men circled the upturned Ford, looking to access the trunk, May scurried over to comfort her friend.

"Boss, we can't get to it."

"What do you mean, you can't get to it?"

Kenneth looked over at the car, fifteen feet away. His men were right. To get to the trunk, they'd have to turn the car over.

"I shouldn't need to say this but if you move, I'll have one of the boys kill your friend."

"Not able to pull the trigger yourself?" asked May defiantly.

"Good heavens, no. I positively hate firearms."

"Shall we pull the old broad out first?" asked the first accomplice.

"Nah, leave her in. From the looks of her, it'll be her proper first tumble in years."

"Gentlemen," said Kenneth, "Seriously. A modicum of respect, please. That 'old broad' you're referring to was a friend of mine."

Kenneth's men stopped laughing. Upset the boss, don't get paid, tended to be the rule. They started to rock the car, back and forth, hoping to roll it into place.

May put her arm behind Elvin's head. "You ok?"

"I think my leg is broken," grimaced Elvin.

May's eyes darted around for something she could use as a makeshift weapon. If she'd learned anything from the writings of Henry Miller, it was that it was never over until the fat man was buried. By the dipped headlights of the van, all she could see were some broken branches and a couple of stones.

"Where are the guns?" she whispered.

"I don't know, May. Probably still in the car."

Damn. Kenneth and his cohorts had built up a steady rhythm and in another couple of pushes, the car would flip round. They might be distracted enough for her to grab one of the branches, she thought. There must be something...

"And over it goes!" called Kenneth, proud of his part in the realignment.

The roof of Herb's car had taken the brunt of the impact, with the struts, attaching the roof to the door, collapsing under the pressure. The front passenger door, closest to May and Elvin, fell open as the car bounced to a stop and from it, dropped Mort Olsen's handgun.

May thought about making a leap towards it but in doing so, she'd leave Elvin open to attack and this time, she reckoned, they wouldn't be so friendly.

"Can't get it open, boss."

The second of Kenneth's accomplices tried and also failed. As he returned to the van for a tool to help them crack open the trunk, May slowly moved closer to the gun.

"What are you up to?" asked Kenneth, mock suspiciously.

"He needs his glasses," replied May, inching back towards Elvin. Kenneth took a long drag on his cigarette as his associate returned from the van with a long crowbar. While his men tried in vain to open the trunk, Kenneth stared at May and Elvin.

"It's no good boss," said accomplice number one. "It's shut tight."

"Maybe we can go in through the back seat?"

Kenneth sighed again, impatiently.

"Do what you must," he said.

"What about the broad?"

"Get the door open first and we'll see."

With Kenneth's attention diverted momentarily, May again edged slowly towards the gun. Elvin watched on.

The twisted structure of the frame made the door difficult to open.

"Maybe, if I may be so bold as to suggest, that you use the goddamn crowbar on it?" said Kenneth, becoming more frustrated with his charges.

The taller of Kenneth's hired help did as he was instructed. He inserted the crowbar into a gap in the frame and pulled. His colleague grabbed the door and with a forced twist, off it came. Face down, on the back seat of the car, lay the still body of Rose Holloway. As the smaller accomplice pulled her from the car, the sight of the torn stockings on the ankle of the woman she'd unfairly considered her nemesis boiled May's blood. She hadn't liked Rose Holloway. So what? The librarian didn't deserve to go like this. May stretched for Olsen's handgun and gripped it tightly. She flicked the safety and pulled herself up.

"Take your fucking hands off of her," she shouted, moving the gun between Kenneth and his accomplices. For a moment, everyone froze. Kenneth and his men, one holding Rose Holloway's ankles, the other the door of Herb's blue Ford, all stood perfectly still, surprised and fearful. Kenneth himself had never looked down the barrel of a loaded weapon and it showed. May knew that as much as she held the advantage, this standoff couldn't last. She needed to choose which one of Kenneth's associates to shoot first.

Two bursts in quick succession and down went the first accomplice. Kenneth shrieked, drawing his hands wide in surrender. Still gripping the door, the second accomplice looked at the car, then at May then towards the car again where a second blast of noise and light tore through the silent Pennsylvanian night, sending him, and the door, hurtling backwards.

May, looked down at her weapon, still cocked and cold, then at Elvin whose confusion mirrored her own.

"Tightly wound I may be but what you said about Auburn, well, I cannot let that one slide," said Rose Holloway, sitting on the torn edge of Herb's back seat, uncharacteristically dishevelled and shoeless. She held a pistol in her right hand. "But thank you for defending my honour. Tell me. What were you offered? Let me guess. A stipend and a suite at the…"

"The Langham," replied Kenneth.

"You know, I might've been tempted by that myself," she said with a rueful chuckle.

"We could always share," replied Kenneth. "We did have some fun, didn't we, Rose? Do you remember that time we took the funicular to…"

"Shhh," she said, finger to lips, as if she was patrolling a section of her beloved library. Rose's firm but curt tone ended any possibility of a reprieve. With the pistol trained on Kenneth, she leant back into the car and grabbed May's bag, handing it to her.

"Check it's still in one piece."

May delved into her bag and felt around the edges of the plate.

"Is that the…" asked Kenneth.

"It might be," said May, "but then again…"

"I'm sure even you would appreciate the irony. All war is deception. Maybe one day when you will have your own suite at The Langham, you'll look back on my folly and…" Kenneth stopped, his mask down, deflated. "Life… is just so disappointing, don't you think?"

There was no reaction from either Rose or May as Kenneth flicked away the stub of his menthol cigarette.

"Don't think of me too harshly, dear Rose."

Rose Holloway smiled at Kenneth before firing two shots into his chest.

"I won't think of you at all."

Rose lowered her gun, as heat rose from the exit wounds on Kenneth's back like a duplicitous spirit leaving his body.

"We need to get Elvin to a hospital."

Rose and May helped Elvin into the back of Kenneth's van and returned to the clearing. They took what they needed from Herb's blue Ford then pushed it as far into the dense undergrowth as they could manage. Between them, they dragged the bodies of their pursuers away from the sight lines of passing traffic and those few early morning ramblers who might take in this unremarkable stretch of highway. A downpour of rain would help dilute the thick pools of blood situated where the three men had fallen but in the meantime, autumnal leaves would have to do. Rose explained to May that before they'd left, Martin Peterson, as precise as ever, had made sure that tracking devices were fitted into the trunks of both vehicles. As the Olsen's were no longer around, a local chapter, sympathetic to the cause would soon be charged with the clear up of the incident site.

As they continued down the I-80 in search of a truckstop with a payphone, May started asking questions of a woman she didn't know. This Rose Holloway, a cold-blooded assassin bore no resemblance to the other Rose Holloway, repressed librarian. OK, scratch that. Little resemblance, she thought.

"So, Kenneth is not The Crow?"

"Hardly. He wouldn't have the funds to finance a pursuit such as this. And as we just witnessed, neither the expertise nor the panache to see it through."

"When did you suspect that it was him?"

"When you did. We had suspicions but no proof."

"Is that why you sent me to Portland on a book hunt?" asked May angrily.

"We didn't want you involved at all."

"So why was I?"

"You were insistent and as I said, we weren't sure."

"Were you sure about the man who attacked me yesterday? Who just happened to be the security guard at Kenneth's shop?"

"I did not know that."

May was starting to think that she was being used, like Castagne did with Sonny and Henry. As bait.

But if May thought that Rose was about to provide either comfort or an explanation, she was mistaken.

"You'd better snap out of this, May Morgenstern. Feeling sorry for oneself at this stage is counter productive. You're scared and confused. I understand that but this is what we've chosen to do. I spent hours last night arguing against involving you two. The most sensitive operation we've ever undertaken is no place for those who aren't professional. A school classroom this is not. When Jerry told you of the risks, did you think he was exaggerating for effect? At the next stop, you can stay with Elvin and I'll continue on to St. Louis alone."

May didn't speak. She looked back at Elvin. They needed to find a medic and soon. He had to make it. Though her head hurt, years of secrecy, betrayal and violence had taken its toll on everyone. But nothing was going to stop her from going to St. Louis with the plate. Rose Holloway knew the young waitress wouldn't be dissuaded. May was going to see this through to the end, however bitter it might become.

A roadside sign said Vettersfeld's Truckstop, 2 miles.

"That'll do us," said Rose.

Established in the late twenties, the gas station just past the Lime Ridge turn had a roadhouse no bigger than a double garage. A neon sign, almost as big as the truckstop itself, told anyone within a three mile radius that it was open twenty-four hours a day.

Rose drove the commandeered van into the empty lot and parked up.

"Stay here and make sure Elvin is comfortable. I'll make a call. Sit tight."

"Wait," said May, stopping Rose from leaving. She removed a handful of napkins from the pocket of her long coat and dabbed water from her bottle onto it.

"Can't be drawing attention to yourself," said May. Gently, she flattened Miss Holloway's hair and wiped away the traces of mud and blood from her face.

"Better."

"Where's your firearm?"

"It's here," said May reaching into her other pocket. Rose Holloway took it from her and checked it.

"Keep the catch off. Just in case."

Rose took Kenneth's long coat and wrapped herself in it. May climbed over the front seats and into the back of the van.

"My Dad's gonna be pissed," said Elvin.

"Not as much as Herb when he finds out that his Ford is going to be a gopher motel," replied May. Elvin laughed then groaned in pain.

May checked the rudimentary splint that Miss Holloway had fashioned around Elvin's leg.

"How does it look?" he asked.

It didn't look good.

"Fine to me," she lied. Elvin knew it. They'd known each other for years but reassurance from a friend was what he needed right now, even if it was fabricated.

"Once this heals, I'm going back in the ring. Officially. I've decided. That's what I want to do."

"What about your folks?"

"Good or bad, I can make my own decisions. I'm not a child."

May nodded.

"I never did thank you for ... you know ... that scene in the flat."

"To tell the truth May, I didn't know I had that in me. That I might be capable of..." said Elvin quietly. "But I'd do it again, a hundred times over and not lose one minute's sleep."

May held Elvin's hand, squeezing it tightly against her chest.

"You're going on to St. Louis, aren't you?"

May didn't respond.

"Just make sure you get back for my return bout. And I want it to be in Lewiston, at the Center where Sonny fought Ali. That would be something, don't you think? And I want you in the front row, right where all the blood and gore lands." Elvin was struggling to keep his spirits up.

May knew that there would be no more fights.

"Now, go get me a soda."

May cradled Elvin's head and kissed him.

"I'll make it a light one. You need to get back to one thirty-five," she said, patting his stomach and winking.

Outside the roadhouse, beside a rickety wooden booth which housed Vettersfeld's solitary payphone, stood Rose Holloway. The long woollen coat that Kenneth no longer needed wrapped around her tiny frame, almost smothering her. Leaves swirled around her feet like dancers in the wind, vying for the attention of a teacher whose mind was elsewhere. In Kenneth's pockets, she'd found an unopened pack of menthol cigarettes and a book of matches that bore the legend, Langham Hotel. She took out a long white cheroot and opened the book. Written inside was a number, under a name. Fener Corps.

"They'll kill you," said May.

"So I hear," replied Rose, changing the subject. "How is he?"

"Not great. We need to get him to a hospital or..."

"I know. I'm just waiting for Jerry to call back to tell us where to go." said Rose, inhaling deeply. "Care to join me?"

"Why not?" replied May, sheltering under the corrugated lip of the diner's roof. "I didn't know that you were a smoker."

"My dear Miss Morgenstern," mocked Rose Holloway, "there are volumes upon volumes of information on me about which you have not the foggiest."

"Like you and Jerry?"

Rose laughed.

"I knew it," said May.

"You are so far from the truth, it's actually frightening."

"What?" laughed May. "I can totally see you and Jerry getting cosy in a cabin somewhere. You'd compose love poetry while he stoked the fire, if you know what I mean?"

"I'll say this for you. You've certainly retained your over-active imagination."

"So, you're saying that nothing has ever... you know?"

"Jerry is a dear friend. Loyal and true but..."

"But?"

"I'm afraid neither of us has the capacity to..." Rose paused, "... make a connection in anything more than a spiritual and platonic manner."

"Like Elvin and I?"

"Not quite. Both Jerry and I are..."

"Oh!" said May, the penny dropping. "Oh. Jerry? No, I don't believe it. He's so...masculine."

"One's identity is not defined by one's public image."

"My father used to go on fishing trips with him. Wait a minute..."

"Your father was also a dear friend to Jerry, nothing more salacious than that."

"Did he know that Jerry was...?"

"Of course."

"He never said."

"Why would he? It was nobody's business but Jerry's. Do you feel any less fond of him now?"

May thought before answering.

"I guess not."

"Well, that's that."

The phone in the box started ringing.

"You'd best not keep Elvin waiting," said Rose, lifting the receiver. She waited until May was out of earshot before she spoke.

"We've got something."

In the van, May sat Elvin up and opened his can of soda. It wasn't diet nor was it light but Elvin didn't care. Rose Holloway took the wheel and headed towards the town of Williamsport, where a recently roused and sympathetic pair of medics would be waiting at the Regional Medical Center to check in a party of three, under the name of Herman, and administer emergency care to Elvin's leg. While he was in surgery, Rose Holloway and May Morgenstern rested on adjoining beds originally intended for post-op patients. According to the sign outside of the room, it was closed for sterilisation and was not to be entered. Rose and May drifted off, with pistols under their pillows, just to be safe.

Chapter 30 - Bait

'As sharply as I fell asleep, I awoke with a pitiful inelegance. A hundred cigarettes and perfume of the previous night's excesses burned a hole in the back of my parched throat from which demonic forces were attempting to escape. I needed a curer or this 'nightmare' might just settle in for the day. Blindly, I patted around the perimeter for my glasses not thinking for a second that I was wearing them. That's how drunk I was. Absurd but alive. Though I felt every second of my years, I proudly wore them as if Auriol himself had pinned the Lègion d'honneur to my pants. No carpet slippers for me just yet. I just had to take a piss then find and extricate my young ward from the boudoir of some exhausted tart and we'd be off, doused in dirt but sated.

So, it was with some surprise that I found him, sitting on the balcony, sipping a soda, watching the world go by.

'Good morning Val,' he said, 'I ordered up some room service, should be here shortly. Eggs Florentine fine with you?'

I purred with satisfaction.

'Where are we?' I asked.

Sonny picked up the menu and read, 'The Peninsula. My treat.'

'If it's good enough for Gershwin, it's good enough for me,' I said, 'though unless you want to spend all of your money in a day, we should probably go back to the chateau later.'

'Guess so,' he said, draining his bottle.

'Did you have a good night?' he asked.

'I can't remember but I think so. You?'

'It wasn't St. Louis in the summer time but it'll do,' he laughed.

'So what next?' I asked him.

'Have some fine French food for breakfast, then a long soak.'

'No, after Paris,' I said.

Seems Sonny had bid adieu to our guests very early in the morning and, with a far clearer head than mine, had been thinking of that poser and little else since.

'I can see why folks love this town. It gets under your skin.'

'You should stay,' I said.

'That's what Cressy thinks.'

'So?'

'I want to fight. And that's not for Cressy or anyone. That's for me.'

'If you stay, and work for Cressy, isn't it better than cracking heads for John Vitelli or waiting for a call from Frankie or Blinky?'

'Whether it's here, St. Louis or going back to Arkansas to work Mose's farm, it's time for me to set my own course. If I fall, so be it. From now on, it'll be my call.'

I couldn't argue with his logic and I had no intention of spoiling the moment. The youthful Sonny had neither sophistication nor sophistry but he had a clarity and singularity of vision that I greatly admired. I always did. I've long said that a man is like a picture. It can tell you everything and it can tell you nothing; a thousand different things to a thousand different people. Whatever you've heard about Sonny Liston, the tawdry tittle tattle of the gossip columns and the dark insinuations about his associations, disregard it. All of it. They knew nothing of this fellow's character. Forged under a wicked yoke, tested and twisted by the Blinkys and Frankies of this world; Sonny remained the indomitable master of his own vessel.

We set sail later that week. Monsieur Cressy made sure that we remained well fed and properly recompensed. If anything, he was even more persuasive than his lamented mentors. As they say, one catches more flies with honey than with vinegar. After three weeks at sea, drinking, talking and carousing, with a little writing thrown in, we were back in the land of the free. Ha! Returning from a more liberal and enlightened country with a person of colour, it was depressingly apparent how backward our homeland still was. Less than ten years after young men like Sonny took on legions of other young brainwashed men, they'd return home to find their own places of worship ablaze, while not being able to eat, drink or even take a leak beside the men they risked their lives with. Freedom? Don't make me laugh.

As Sonny needed to catch a train to St. Louis, we bade farewell at Pennsylvania Station. I said I'd follow his nascent career with interest and Sonny promised to read some of my works. To the best of my knowledge, he never did even though I sent him some of my more 'adult' offerings. But I couldn't hold that against him. We spoke on the phone occasionally, usually after one of his big fights and always under the protective cloak of our Parisienne codenames. Meeting in person? Well, that was only twice. First time, he was preparing for a fight in Cleveland, against Zora Folley, I think. I was about to return to France for an extended period and asked him to accompany me, only partly in jest. He remarked that his fee had gone up somewhat. Name your price, I said. I'll pay it!

Being in his company again made me want to embark on another adventure and for a moment, we tossed around the mechanics of that remote possibility. But I was approaching seventy years old and Sonny...well, the world, and all that it entailed, was about to become his. He asked me if the trip was related to Cressy and his interests but I assured him that it was purely literary. He did however ask a final favour of me which I felt honor bound to accept. Only if it's not too much trouble, he asked. It was the least I could do.

Since his passing, I have continued his wish, and with the help of

M. Cressy, we've made sure that on May fourteenth, the day they met, fresh sunflowers should be placed on the modest but well-tended mound in Montmartre, where Delphine Delauney rests.

So, in accordance with our earlier agreement, I passed him the plate and again, he became 'the bait'. I told him that I hoped his stewardship of it would be as uneventful as mine had been. Given the loss he sustained in Paris, far greater than any he ever encountered in the ring, it would've been fitting had he'd been the one to receive the call to return the relic to its rightful place. In the meantime, it would take a fearless specimen to dare attempt to take something this precious from the meanest man on God's earth. I was not home when he called for the last time. And comment on his passing will remain for my thoughts alone, suffice to say that while one might rent his form, they could never put as much as a cent of a down payment on his soul. Give me a thousand righteous men, put them in a line and I'll still take my friend, Charlie. He was in the truest sense, a man.'

Chapter 31 - No More Tears

"Don't concern yourself with the Ford. It's the least of our worries," said Herb, picking up his disposable coffee cup by its cardboard handles. He'd driven the near five hundred miles from Portland to Williamsport very carefully but still, in less than eight hours. He took a gulp, looked over the top of his red framed spectacles and said, "And anyway, it wasn't even mine to begin with."

The medical center's caféteria was perhaps the smallest of the eateries May had visited in the last 24 hours but it was certainly the brightest and most clean. She cared little for the café's choice of piped-in music but, over fresh, maple syrup covered pancakes, she thought that letting it slide might be wise. As Rose had taken the opportunity to shower and change into fresh clothing, Herb finally acceded to the nurses repeated warnings to only smoke in the designated blocks. This left May alone with the one man who could provide the answers to the questions that had been piling up like lunchtime order slips during Two for Tuesday's back at The Columbus.

"How are the pancakes?" asked Jerry, pale but focussed.

May held up a finger. Once she'd savoured this mouthful, something that only a few hours ago seemed unlikely, she'd give her verdict.

"Pretty good actually," she said, wiping the syrup from her lips.

"Better than Elvin's?"

Of course they were, she thought but loyalty mattered.

May scrunched her nose and shook her head. Just as May knew when

Elvin was lying and vice versa, Jerry shared that intuition.

"Does Mr Peterson know? About Elvin and…"

Jerry leant forward and spoke quietly. "He does."

"Is he upset?"

"Wouldn't you be if your kid was almost killed? We should never have let you two get involved. That's my fault. We'll be safe in Williamsport for now but as soon as Elvin is well enough, we'll get you both back home."

"What about the plate?" asked May.

"What about it?"

"It needs to be returned."

"And it will be."

"By whom?"

"Rose will deliver it. She's more than capable."

May couldn't argue with that point. But she did anyway.

"And who's going with her?"

"She's going alone."

"Like hell she is, Jerry," said May. "Something's not quite right. Bob and Kenneth…they might be gone but this is not over."

"What makes you think that?"

"Call it a gut feeling."

"All that needs done now is for it to be returned to St. Louis and we can finally draw a line under this mess. We've lost too many good people already."

"Don't you want to see this through? After all this time and what Henry, Sonny and you have had to endure with this damned plate?"

"Rose will take care of it."

"I'm going with her."

"Goddammit May!" roared Jerry, slamming his fist down hard on the formica, their cutlery chiming as it scattered across the surface of the table. The cafe's few patrons turned towards the pair.

"You're not," he said, his voice returning to a whisper.

"You're not my father, Jerry. And I'm not some stupid kid."

"Before you set off for St. Louis, do you know what Elvin asked of me?" said Jerry, seriously.

May shook her head.

"You know he's had a hard time with things recently. Watching his father waste away while having his own dreams ripped from his hands can't have been easy for him. So, I asked him how he felt about what happened. Behind the goofiness, he's quite a sensitive boy so I expected him to be full of remorse and concern but what he said chilled me. He told me that he liked the feeling."

Jerry's words made May feel uncomfortable.

"That might be bravado or just the nerves talking but I know that he feels wasted as a short order chef in a diner and I don't blame him. So he's asked me to teach him about this life, with everything that it entails. Do you understand what I'm saying?"

May listened silently.

"What happened at your place was one thing, but choosing to take this path comes at a tremendous cost, and it's one you'll spend a lifetime trying to repay. Everything and everyone you care about, will eventually be used against you. I couldn't forgive myself if I allowed him, or you for that matter, to develop a taste for what I'd been involved in."

"What was it you said to me when I first started working at The Columbus? Don't settle for this, you said. There's a big world out there. Write your own story. Well maybe this is Elvin's."

"Come on, May. This is very different," said Jerry. "And you know that." She did.

May cut a chunk of pancake and dabbed it into the puddle of syrup that had congealed on her plate. She stuffed it into her mouth and said, "Well, I'm going and that's that."

"Your father was exactly the same. Stubborn to the last. He was a good man. A good friend," said Jerry, turning his face away from May. "I promised him that I'd look out for you."

"And you have."

May placed her hands over Jerry's. "You have."

"May, there's a few things I'd like to share with you…"

"It's OK. Mr Peterson explained about what you guys do. The state beneath…?"

"Not just that. Although I'm not your father, you're about the only family I have."

"And I feel the same way, Jerry."

"Life has been quite complicated…for me. Your father, God rest him, understood. But I'm afraid I haven't been entirely honest with you."

May held Jerry's hands tight. "A straight line is not always as straight as you first think. You told me that. It's OK, I understand too. I've got you, Jerry Hector," said May before pausing.

"That is your real name, right?"

"Yes May, it is."

"One thing, though," May leant over to Jerry and whispered menacingly, "Don't even dare to ask if you can borrow my Streisand video."

Just then, a refreshed Rose Holloway strode into the cafeteria as if she was starting her morning rounds at the Auburn Municipal Library. May found it hard to believe exactly how this tiny woman, with her hair pulled tight above her penciled eyebrows, had so skillfully yet brutally extricated Elvin and her from certain disaster.

"How's the boy?" she asked.

"The surgery went smoothly but he's still heavily sedated," replied May.

"His leg?"

"Saved but he'll be joining Jerry and I in the Auburn gammy singles dance club. Wanna join? Long waiting list. Long…."

Not keen on frippery, Rose moved straight onto business.

"Have you spoken about St. Louis yet?"

"Herb and May will stay here with Elvin and we can either…"

"Forget it, Jerry," said May. "I wasn't joking. I'm taking that plate to St. Louis, end of story. You're in no state to be making this trip. You're staying with Elvin until he's fit to travel. In the meantime, Herb can drive us to Baltimore or Pittsburgh, whichever is closer. We can fly Eastern or United to St. Louis from there."

Jerry's look urged Rose to see sense and back him.

"Sounds like a plan," she said. "Let's get going."

Chapter 32 - You Never Can Tell

The well-maintained buildings of Lafayette Square and its associated green spaces were exactly how May Morgenstern had pictured them. Tall townhouses, painted in deep reds and pastels. Well-tended lawns and trees, positioned in perfect symmetry. Picturesque. On the last leg of the twenty mile drive from Lambert Airport, May was impressed with what she saw of this corner of Missouri. Very different from Portland. Very different from Auburn.

Rose Holloway hadn't spoken much since they picked up their rental car and May didn't want to push it. The journey of The Sinner's Plate of Mar Saba had been as perilous as it had been protracted. Knowledge of the relic came with a price. From Casper Militz and the Castagnes to Delphine, Sonny Liston and the Olsens. Bob. Even if it didn't kill you, as Jerry and Elvin found, it still cost you. They were close now and May could feel it. Travelling by air, they couldn't risk taking weapons with them and as much as that frustrated her, May would feel a lot safer at this point if at least one of them was armed.

"Whatever happens in there," said Rose, "regardless of what is said and done, just stay with me. OK?"

Clear as mud, thought May, flattening the hair over her ear.

"Let's go."

As May opened the wrought iron gate, tiny flakes of black paint came away in her hand. She shook it clear and walked up the steps to the door of number 14. From a distance, the property looked impressive. Up close, one could see the cracks. Rose straightened out her clothes and rang the bell. Above the door, the white casing of a camera pointed down at an angle, its red light blinking.

The door opened.

"Welcome back to Clarion, Miss Holloway. I trust you had a pleasant trip?" said an attractive middle-aged lady in a colourful headdress.

Firstly, thought May, you said you'd never been to St. Louis before. And secondly, you gotta be kidding.

"Yes, thank you," replied Rose curtly, her tight, painted lips curling briefly upwards before settling back into the position of tightly sealed.

She handed over her coat and bag.

"May I take yours, Miss?" asked the lady.

"No, I'm good," said May, tightly clutching her bag.

"As you wish. Please, follow me."

They were escorted into a large room which reeked of smoke and faded grandeur. May recognised it from Miller's writing.

"Mr Moreau will be with you shortly. Can I get you something to drink?"

"Maybe later," said Rose. "May?"

A Pepsi and a handgun would be nice, thought May.

"Not for me, thanks."

The assistant left the room.

Just as May was about to launch into a diatribe over the lack of available sodas, Rose looked at her and shook her head, ever so slightly. May stopped. Rose slowly scratched her earlobe and from that, May deduced that they were being listened to. They stood in front of a painting showing an 18th century battle.

"Last time I was here, there was a Rothko on that wall."

"That's quite a memory you have. We had a Sill on this side but we kept the Paalen in the upper quarters as it frightened off our clients. Dear Miss

Holloway, how are you?"

"Mr Moreau, let me introduce you to..."

"The redoubtable Miss Morgenstern. Yes, it is an honour to meet you."

"Charmed," said May, blushing.

"I cannot thank you enough for all you've done for the organisation. This is truly a momentous day."

Moreau pressed a button on the intercom.

"Sufiah, some jasmine tea please," he said, "And for you?"

Both May and Rose shook their heads.

"That'll be all, thank you."

"I did like that Rothko."

"Me too. But our clients seem to prefer a patriotic romanticism to the surreal and abstract so we had to let it go."

"Well, that must have been painful," said Rose, brusque with a familiar hint of sarcasm. Moreau's eyes narrowed as he looked to bring the subject back to familiar territory.

"Anyway, to business."

Just then, there was a knock on the door and Sufiah entered. She poured Moreau's tea.

He took a sip of his infusion and continued. "Where were we?"

"You were talking about replacing Rothko with these hideous Leutze knock offs," said Rose. May, remembering what was asked of her in the car, didn't react.

"I'm sorry that they're not to your taste but, I can assure you that..."

"I didn't realise until now Moreau," said Rose, "just how hopelessly vain you are."

"I beg your pardon?"

"I mean, the suits, the assistant, the upkeep on this place. Can't be cheap."

"Though times are tight for many publishers, I can assure you that we're doing just fine. Where are you going with this Miss Holloway?"

"I suppose if you sold the Sill and the Paalen, that would keep the lights on for a year, maybe two. But the Rothko? Sell that and you can easily afford...a suite at The Langham, for instance. Couldn't you?"

"I don't quite follow."

"How many companies are you a director of?"

"Three. Maybe four?"

"Seven would be the correct answer," replied Rose.

"Many businessmen have diversified interests. I am no different. What is your point?"

"What does Fener Corps mean to you?"

Moreau didn't move but his eyes darted upwards.

"Fener? Oh yes, Fener. It's a dormant company of which I was once a partner. I believe that I inherited it when an old associate passed. Damn shame. I've been meaning to wind it down for years but with one thing or another, I've never gotten around to doing so."

"Your late associate. His name?"

"Miss Holloway, I fail to see the importance of ..."

"Was it Harry Levin?"

Moreau took a long sip from his tea cup then nodded his head.

"You see," said Rose, "that's where we'd been going wrong all these years. We were looking for Joe Do Sappo when we should have been looking for Harry Levin. Isn't that right?"

"How did you find out?"

"By a series of chances as it turned out. Had May not been attacked by the detective at Kenneth's store, she wouldn't have needed to seek refuge at the Peterson residence where your back up assailant was waiting for his opportunity to strike. It was a grievous misfortune that he found Martin Peterson slightly less incapacitated than you all presumed he was."

"Good old Marty."

"And if losing your most accomplished assassin to a half-blind beanpole, an aged, arthritic restaurateur and a waitress with a surgical boot was bad luck, losing your second best to a terminally ill cripple would have to be considered a mortal blow."

"And the plate?"

"That was all Miss Morgenstern. She's much smarter than her unkempt appearance may suggest."

"Thanks," said May, adopting Rose's sarcastic tone.

"Once Kenneth volunteered to accompany the plate to St. Louis, our suspicions were confirmed."

Moreau snorted.

"I'll grant you, the Olsens were dispatched with a modicum of professionalism but that's the only part of your scheme for which you deserve credit," said Rose. "If you wanted us dead, you should've done it in the car park at the Wilkes Diner, there and then. Kenneth could have taken the plate, blown the whole place sky high and made it look like an accident. No-one would have been any the wiser. But like you, vanity was his downfall."

"Kenneth's dead?" asked Moreau, disguising his shock.

"You hadn't heard? Oh, I'm sorry," she replied, her sarcasm now tinged with anger. "If you want to pay your respects, you can find what's left of him, and his friends, in a container park just outside of Pittsburgh. I can provide you with the address if you'd like."

"Was that really necessary?"

"With a gun pointed at my friends, what option did he leave me? Even then, we were still in the dark as to who was backing his rather bold move. Until, in the coat pocket of a dead man, there was a book of matches with a 314 area code number and a name, remarkably similar to one left by the late Mr Liston and found by Martin Peterson. Between him, Jerry Hector and a few well-placed sources, years of mystery were cleared up in hours."

"Tell me, when did you figure out that Do Sappo was Levin?"

"When Mr Miller revealed to Benoit Castagne that Do Sappo and The Crow were one and the same, our associates here and in Europe started to search. Our initial understanding that he was Canadian military quickly turned cold. That's fine, we thought. The files of certain operatives remain inaccessible, even to us, so we went back further. School, medical, insurance. Every search turned up blank. There was nothing to show that Joe Do Sappo actually existed in Canada. We widened our search but still nothing. Mr Do Sappo was proving to be incredibly elusive. But once we had Fener Corps, and the name Harry Levin, the game changed. Little bursts of information appeared. Like a boarding house in Buffalo once owned by a couple who left the Greek enclave in Istanbul in 1920 with their young son for a better life in the US. Their names, Charis and Levinia Saffo, known to their neighbours, one of whom was kind enough to talk to us in great detail this morning about his old friends, Harry and Levin. And can you guess the name of the quarter they emigrated from?"

Moreau gestured for Rose to continue.

"That's right. Fener, in the Fatih district and that's where their son Iosif, or Joe, was born. What we don't know exactly was what happened to Levin, Do Sappo or whatever name he chose to go by and for how long you were involved but those details will no doubt come out in the wash."

He smiled. "Brava, Miss Holloway. Brava. What can I say?"

Moreau reached into his desk and removed a pistol. As May recoiled in her chair, Rose put her hand on May's arm.

"Where is it?" he said coldly.

"We have it here," said Rose. "May?"

May removed the covered relic from her satchel.

"Bring it over," he ordered.

She placed it on his desk.

"Open it."

May peeled back the protective layers then returned to her seat beside Rose.

Moreau looked closely at the relic. He took a deep breath and exhaled slowly. Tears formed in his eyes. "You have no idea how long I have waited for this moment. It's beautiful. Exquisite."

Moreau pressed the intercom.

"Sufiah, have my car ready," he said, delicately touching the plate's contours.

"Now that you have what you want, can you at least explain why?"

"I was first approached by Mr Levin in 1964. I had no idea who he was at the time but he was aware of our interest in the plate. I gave nothing away at that stage, but like a predator, his pursuit was relentless. I'm afraid that he wore me down, with sweet promises and unerring accuracy. I was flattered but I was loyal. Eventually, I succumbed to temptation."

"Hadn't you been well looked after?"

"Certainly. But once Do Sappo met his unfortunate but ironic fate at the hands of your Mr Liston, my share became complete. And I'm sure you'll agree, Miss Holloway, that twenty-two million dollars will bend even the strongest will. A fabricated name on a dead man's deeds, a holding company with an arcane moniker."

"So, what now? You're going to kill us?"

With his weapon now pointing at Rose and May, Moreau sat on the edge of his desk.

"It wouldn't have been my first course of action, no. But I'm afraid, like you with poor Kenneth, you've left me with little choice."

As May gripped onto the arm of her chair, Rose spoke.

"And do you know what? If it wasn't for Kenneth, I'd have gladly handed the plate over to you and returned to Maine, blissfully unaware that you had no intention of returning it to its rightful place."

"Its rightful place is... oh, my. I almost gave it away. Tut tut. How careless of me."

Moreau pulled back the hammer on his pistol.

"By the time Messers Peterson and Hector learn of your demise, The Plate of Mar Saba will be in the hands of one very grateful collector and we can finally draw a line under the awful mess we seem to be in."

"And you?"

"I'll be somewhere, far from St. Louis, raising a glass to both of you fine ladies tonight."

At that moment, there was a knock at the door and before Moreau could answer, in walked Sufiah.

"Your car is ready, Sir," she said.

"Good," he replied without turning away.

"And Sir, I also took the liberty of removing the shells from your pistol."

"What?" yelled Moreau, pulling the trigger. Nothing. Again. Nothing. Enraged, he swung out and caught Sufiah on the cheek with the back of his hand, knocking her to the floor. As May sprung to her feet, looking for a weapon to strike him with, Rose Holloway stayed calm and delivered a glancing blow to the side of his head. On the other side of his desk, May picked up a floor-standing ashtray and pitched it towards the legs of the advancing Moreau, catching him just below the knees. He dropped to the floor in agony. Rose helped Sufiah to her feet and over to her chair.

"Twenty-two million dollars, you say?" asked Rose, picking up the ancient artefact.

Moreau looked up to see the principal employee of the Auburn Municipal Library, casting The Sacred Plate of Mar Saba across the room, like a frisbee into the fireplace, splintering the plate into pieces.

"No!" screamed Moreau in panic as the fragments of the plate came to rest all over the slate gray hearth.

"Jesus," said May, falling back into her seat.

Moreau scrambled around the floor, picking up shards of the now destroyed relic. "What have you done?" he sobbed.

"I'd save my energy, if I was you," said Rose.

"I can't breathe," he said, loosening his collar.

"Quite a remarkable thing this is," said Rose, removing a ring from her finger. "Used to belong to Sonny Liston. It was developed by our French friends back in the sixties. We didn't know for sure if it actually worked so thank you for clearing that up."

"Save me," said Moreau, gasping for air. "I can give you anything you want. Name your price."

"I have everything I want right here," replied Rose.

As Moreau breathed his last, May put her hand over her eyes and sighed deeply, relieved.

"Is it over?" asked Sufiah.

"Yes, my love. It is now."

****

"According to this," said May, reading from a folded map, "The McAdam would have been right there."

In the place where once was an elegant hotel, stood a modern, multiplex cinema. A large neon sign proclaimed the news that on screen one, 'Back to the Future' was showing for the twelfth straight week. As May consulted the map, Rose Holloway looked at the film's outsized billboard.

"Loud, vulgar nonsense. Looks just like your kind of thing, May," she teased.

"I'd almost forgotten but you're quite the snob, aren't you?"

Rose Holloway smiled and shrugged her shoulders.

"For your information, it's actually a wonderful piece of cinema, it combines comedy with science..."

May could see that Rose had gotten the reaction she'd hoped for.

"We really should start heading back to the hotel. I hear St. Louis can get a little dangerous at night," said the librarian, without a trace of irony.

"Can I ask you something about this afternoon?" asked May.

"Certainly."

"When did you know that Levin was Do Sappo?"

Rose smiled again.

"When Moreau pulled the pistol on me."

"Hang on. So, you had no idea? Surely all that stuff about Do Sappo's parents in Buffalo and the quarter in Istanbul…"

"That? Oh, I made it up."

"What?!" said May, stopping in the street.

"Think about it. To collate that kind of information from scratch, with testimony from old neighbours?" Rose laughed. "Come on. Even with a full complement of staff working on it, that would take days if not weeks. No, all we had was the name Fener Corps from the matchbook. From that we were able to tie Harry Levin to Moreau. Nothing more than a hunch. He'd been very careful about covering his tracks. So much so that Sufiah was completely in the dark for years."

"You trust her?"

"As much as I do Jerry. Or you. All I did was drop the line. If Moreau didn't take the bait, what had we lost?"

"A priceless relic?" replied May.

"I was never going to play catch with the real Plate of Mar Saba. You know as well as I that the Castagne's provided a number of replicas."

"So, you did read Elie's book!"

"I may have snuck a peek here and there while you slept."

"You really are devious," said May, impressed at the depth of Rose Holloway's subterfuge.

"What now?"

"The clean up operation should be close to complete. Everything that linked us to that property will have been destroyed."

"And the plate?"

"It'll be returned to Mar Saba presently. Sufiah and I will ensure its safe arrival."

"You're not heading back to Auburn?"

"I've not taken any leave of note for nearly ten years. I think that the 'Mooney' will survive without my presence for the next month or so. And you?"

May pointed at her map.

"I was going to take a trip over to Chuck Berry's house first thing in the morning. It's only around twenty, twenty-five blocks from here."

"No, what are your plans after you've satisfied your baser cultural urges."

"I'll probably head back to Auburn, as soon as I can get a flight. I want to make sure Jerry and Elvin are ok."

"They'll be fine, May. Trust me. And The Columbus Diner, and everyone who sails in her, will still be there, brewing gritty coffee and inedible pie, for years to come."

"You don't like the pie? You should've said."

"And hurt Jerry's feelings? Never."

As they turned onto Market Street, Rose stopped.

"Can I speak candidly?"

"Sure," said May.

"Perhaps it's time, May, for you to look out for yourself. And taste life. Not just an infrequent sip from the neck of the bottle either. Drink it up, all of it. Let it spill from your lips, fill your belly and allow chance to carry you wherever it may. Only then can you say that you've truly lived. The experience of the last few days has been more than most could reasonably bear but you're still here, skittishly pulling hair over that beautiful ear of yours. I've watched you do that very same thing since you were an awkward, difficult little girl, lost in worlds of tall tales and great adventures. But in this world, the real world, as you now know, one's life can be altered or snatched away, in any number of random ways. So, consider yourself liberated, May Morgenstern. The real world needs more difficult girls, don't you think? Take flight and live your life. Not someone else's," said Rose Holloway before hastily re-erecting her shield. "Listen to me sounding like a Hallmark motivational card. Do it. Don't do it. It's your choice. Either way, I couldn't care less."

May didn't sleep much that night. Maybe it was the howling Missouri wind and rain against her window or the intermittent sound of an engine's valves opening up as red turned to green on the street below. Maybe Rose Holloway's impassioned plea was not only aimed at May but at herself?

Whatever it was, her mind was not still. Auburn roots ran deep and they were pulling her, for sure. Wings and ball games at McGees with Elvin, getting chewed out by Jerry for joshing instead of serving. The comfort of certainty. All of the hotel's television channels were showing static except for one which had infomercials about vacuum cleaners and knives on rotation. Who'd want to buy a cleaver at night, May pondered. On second thoughts…

Tomorrow, she'll say goodbye to Rose and Sufiah and after visiting Chuck, head home to Maine and her small, but perfectly adequate apartment above Mrs Krupa's and start to put all of this madness behind her. That makes sense. A very 'May' course of action.

May switched the television off. Underneath it, her recently full mini bar was running low on stock. She took another small bottle of beer, her fourth so far, and the last remaining candy bar from the top shelf of the fridge. Climbing back into bed, May reached into her satchel for her glasses, her Walkman and Elie's book. The words of Boz Scaggs resonated. One more for the road. Rose Holloway might not approve, she thought, cracking open another beer. But Henry Miller would.

Chapter 33 - Elie

'And that is about all I have to say. Perhaps I let myself ramble a bit too much but I felt that you deserved to know what happened. Casper Militz was not killed by me but by an Englishman, on the behest of a Quebecois, in an attempt to frame me. They're long gone now and the name of your father is as much dust now as his bones. I hope that my account of events can provide you with an element of closure. Closure. Scratch that. Closure's one of those words best left for realtors not real people. Elie, please don't let the thinnest of genetic strands keep you bound to pieces of the past which you had no control over. Let them go. Like you, I understand the crushing loneliness you've been feeling since your husband's passing. Regardless of what anyone might say, the chasm it leaves is almost impossible to fill. And it'll come at you, like breakers. You just need to hold on. Hold on and ride it out. That may appear cold and harsh but that's the only truth I've got. Your wellbeing is of paramount importance and the measures that Clifford and I put in place for this eventuality are bonafide, trust me. It may not be as temperate as Nevada but the town of Auburn is pretty and functional but primarily, it's safe. A good place for you to see out the remainder of your years.

If I was able, I'd consider joining you. We could sit in the town square, a half-blind libertine and his showgirl, turning heads as we feed the birds. Ha! A little anarchy is good for the soul. There are a number of people, some I've already mentioned, who will be expecting your arrival. They will make sure that anything you need will be taken care of. I cannot tell you any more about the location of the plate but some day, one of those smart fellas will put their coffee down and figure it out.

I will not write again. It pains me too much. Anyway, my children are here and the wrestling's about to start. Ride that wave, Elie.

Love, as ever

'H'

Chapter 34 - Edmond Dantes

"So, your dad is fine with it?"

May waited for the response.

"He understands that it'll be good for me. Even with the stairs. It's time, you know? He's just happy to still have me nearby. Mom's coming over tomorrow with some of my things."

"What about Jerry?"

Again, May waited. The connection wasn't the clearest and there was an echoey delay on the line.

"He's cool. He drove me back to Auburn then went straight over to The Columbus."

"Does he ever rest?"

May removed the wide-brimmed hat she'd bought that morning and fanned herself while she waited on Elvin's response.

"No. Haha! So tell me about Chuck Berry's house. Did you get to meet him?"

"Yeah, he invited me in for a pastrami sandwich."

May knew what was coming.

"Really?"

"No, you dingus. Of course not."

She waited.

"It was tuna."

May smiled at the thought of Elvin eventually getting her joke.

"Hahaha!"

Elvin roared down the phone. It felt good to hear his laugh once again. That, she was going to miss most of all. From the foyer of the hotel, May could see Rose Holloway by the entrance, her lilac skirt flowing in the cool breeze, the scent of Mitsouko caressing each passer by. As the inscription read, 'This bud awaits the touch of the sun, ready to bloom.' In this light, all loose and free, May swore that Rose looked twenty years younger. The bloom had burst into life. Maybe she'd started following her own advice? Borderline attractive, even. Sufiah, taking the librarian's hand, clearly agreed.

"Listen Elvin, I've got to go. I'll call you when I can. And make sure that, if you ever get around to washing that stinky body of yours, don't let the bathtub overflow."

As May waited, her lip trembled.

"Sure thing. You take care of yourself May. And get home in one piece."

"Elvin?"

"Yes, May?"

"I just wanted to say…"

"Yes?"

"You're a dingus."

May waited to hear Elvin's throaty laugh again before hanging up.

As the late autumn sun scorched the Marseille cobbles, Sufiah, Rose and May took the more shaded route through the winding back streets of St. Victor, down to the harbour. As they reached Quai de Rive Neuve, May was taken aback by the number of vessels bobbing in the water.

"This is like Portland...times a hundred."

"Incredible, isn't it?" replied Rose. "Come over here a moment, May."

May followed Rose out onto a long jetty.

"Do you see that little island? Just over there?"

May shielded her eyes from the bright afternoon glare but she could make out a small rock formation, about a mile from the harbour.

"That is the Château d'If. The setting of Dumas' Count of Monte Cristo."

"Wow. I borrowed that from the Mooney."

"You did. Two weeks, July of 1973."

"Really? How can you remember that?"

Rose looked at May and shook her head.

"You've got to stop doing that," laughed May.

Past the catboats and cutters, the small sloops and bulky speedboats, at the very end of Jetée D12 sat a small, unremarkable fishing boat.

"This is ours?" said May. "We'll be lucky to get out of the harbour in this, never mind make our first port of call."

"Looks can be deceptive," replied Sufiah, mischievously. "You should know that by now, May."

At the back of the boat, a small man with wiry grey hair was tying knots in a length of rope.

"Good afternoon ladies," he said, his accent as thick as the tobacco in his pipe. Sufiah and Rose handed over their cases to him and he helped them climb on board. The man saw May's apprehension.

"Do not worry, young lady. It's perfectly safe. The Durango has sailed a million miles and a million more yet to come."

May took the man's calloused hand and slowly stepped on board.

"This route may not be as treacherous as it once was but it does remain a challenge for the faint-hearted," he said.

No. It can't be. This makes no logical sense.

"You up for this, May? If not, you can wait for us back at the hotel with your trashy novels and your MTV."

"Stop teasing her Rose," chided Sufiah. But May's thoughts were elsewhere.

"Sevak reckons we should make Sanremo by nightfall," said Rose.